HEROES OF THE MISTY ISLE

The EMERALD SEA

The Quest of Brendan the Navigator

SANDY DENGLER

MOODY PRESS
CHICAGO

ISBN: 0-8024-2295-0

1 3 5 7 9 10 8 6 4 2

Printed in the United States of America

Contents

NOTE:

Place names used here are, for the most part, the present names. Take, for instance, "England." The land we know as England was not yet called England in A.D. 550. Rather, a number of small kingdoms struggled in turmoil as invaders and defenders parried.

The use of modern terminology is especially anachronous in reference to the heavens. Many of our present and familiar star names are Arabic (e.g., Deneb, Altair). As best we know, the Celts had no congress with the Arabic. They used their own names for the stars, and, except in a few cases, we no longer know what those were. The names I shall mention, then, are not the names the Gaels employed. In fact, because of several phenomena, such as the stars' proper motion and the earth's nutation, many stars have altered position since Brendan's day. The North Star was not then close to true north, for instance.

As much as possible, people's names follow closely those of the churchmen of whom we have record, Brendan, Enda, and their ilk foremost.

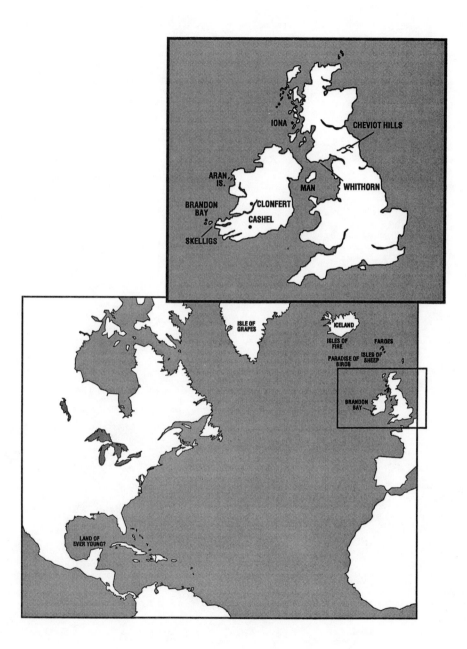

IONA

CHEVIOT HILLS

ARAN IS.

MAN

WHITHORN

BRANDON BAY

CLONFERT

CASHEL

SKELLIGS

ISLE OF GRAPES

ICELAND

ISLES OF FIRE

FAROES

PARADISE OF BIRDS

ISLES OF SHEEP

BRANDON BAY

LAND OF EVER YOUNG?

1

Angelica

This was not just foolish. It was fatal. He'd kill her for spurning him, and no one would call him to account.

He would wait until dawn to come after her. No need for him to hurry. With his tracking dogs and fast ponies, he would cover four miles in the time it took her to travel one, and the dogs would bring him straight to her.

Slashed with gray streaks of clouds, the eastern sky glowed pink-purple. As she waded out into the brook, she imagined his huntsmen gathering the hounds. Just about now they'd be leaving, the hounds pouring out the ringwall gate and the huntsmen hard on their heels. Here would come Larkin on his favorite stallion, his brown tartan flying, with his clan behind him.

Or would he? She was promised to his son. Perhaps he'd simply send his son. No. Larkin loved nothing better than victories, whether they be over armies or a single young woman. He was coming.

She sloshed downstream through liquid ice, slipping and sliding on the submerged rocks. Her toes ached. So did her heart. This would not fool the dogs, but it was the only chance she had.

A quarter mile farther, she scrambled across bare rocks into a dark and gloomy tanglewood. She must stay in dense growth that makes riding a pony difficult or impossible. Her feet ached.

She smelled smoke. A slight breeze drifted up from the south. Probably some hunting party was camped against the sheltered north side of the wall. Angles or Picts, they would be no friends of hers.

Did she hear dogs behind her? Something crashed through the brush very near. What foolishness, what foolishness! Her heart dragged through the thicket behind her, overburdened with stupidity. Then fear squeezed it. Dogs or wolves, something was at her heels.

She burst out of the wildwood into a little glade heavy with morning mist. She stopped cold, sucking in damp air. A man was kneeling in the grass.

He looked to be an average sort of man, not too young to be callow or too old to be of interest, not slight and not burly, not lank and not stubby, not blond and not swarthy. Mild, and yet handsome. Not given to war. That was reassuring—and utterly alien.

A graceful man he was as well. He flowed to his feet as he crossed himself. A Christian! Few enough there were of those.

He smiled pleasantly as he drew a blue cloak close around himself and nodded. "The top of the morning to you, lass." Irish. Extremely Irish.

She had a great deal of difficulty understanding the thick Irish version of Celtic. "Good day. God bless—"

Two great hounds exploded into the glade. They gave voice, a thundering cacophony, as four others joined them. Swift as a snake, the stranger grabbed her arm and pulled her behind him as he backed up against a tree.

He began purring in dulcet tenor, talking to the dogs. They circled close around and continued barking, but they did not feint or encroach. She began to feel a small measure of safety. If these dogs belonged to that hunting camp and not to the Larkin, she might escape yet.

"Ah hah!" Mac Larkin himself, clawing and struggling, stumbled into the glade, a dead fern frond wrapped around his ankle. Sweaty, he gulped air.

She was doomed.

He yelled at his dogs. They ignored him. Not until his huntsmen came straggling into the open and called them away did they cease that wild barking.

Mac Larkin's beetle brows, as thick as his father's, arched as he studied Angelica's protector, then flattened out. She had known him less than two months, and already she could read his thoughts in those black caterpillars. Again like his father, he let his brows tell the world what he was thinking—not that he ever thought long or deep. Now, she could see, he was regarding this brave fellow with disdain.

One by one, the rest of the Larkin popped into the glade on foot, until the little opening was crowded with panting, churning dogs and smirking warriors. They watched Mac Larkin for direction.

Mac Larkin drew his sword with a flourish and held it before him two-handed. "Your morning walks never carried you so far astray before, Angelica."

She stayed behind the stranger and said nothing. So long as the Irishman was willing to shield her, she was willing to let him. Cautiously, she peeked around him.

"Stand aside." Mac Larkin gave a little wave of his sword tip, a casual gesture for so lethal a weapon.

The Irishman stood motionless. "She's your wife?"

"Yes."

"Not yet!" Angelica tried to sound strong. "I'm promised, according to his father and mine. But I've not agreed yet."

"Indeed." The stranger nodded. "In Erin, brave friend, our women are the equal of our men, as well it should be. If she's not acquiesced, the deal's not done. A forced marriage is no marriage."

"You're not in Erin, and you enter my affairs at your peril. Stand aside."

The Irishman smiled. Even from behind his back, Angelica could see his cheek bunch. "Woman, you were in the midst of asking God's blessing upon me when these people intruded. What is your faith?"

"Christian, sir."

"Good! Wonderful." He seemed to be addressing Mac Larkin. "Ronan of Skellig Michael, your servant. And you?"

"The son of Larkin of the Picts. And I never give orders a third time."

"Pict. Interesting. Just before dawn, I departed from a hunting party of Angles. I trust they're not associated with you."

"Angles?"

"To the south, hard beside the wall. Successful too. They've three roebucks hanging from an oak."

Mac Larkin leered. "An unpleasant prospect. I'll see to them after I've retrieved my bride." He looked not at the stranger's face but at Angelica's behind the man's elbow. "I'm still trying to decide whether to kill you here or drag you back and kill you in front of the silly girls who helped you."

Angelica was about to retort, "No one helped me!" but all she cried was *"Aaah!"*

For Mac Larkin lashed out swiftly, suddenly, with both arms and his sword. The stranger was literally lifted away from Angelica. He flew several feet and slammed into the wet, brown grass.

One mighty stride brought Mac Larkin to her. He seized her arm in a grip strong enough to hold his stallion. His warm breath stank. "He's lucky I decided to kill you later. Had I struck with the blade of my sword instead of its butt, I would have sliced you both in half. You know that, don't you?"

A moment before, fear had paralyzed her. Now fury welled up in its stead.

He grinned. "Ah! The fire is back. I don't like you as much when you're frightened." Gripping her wrist in that death grip, he sheathed his sword.

"What about him?" A huntsman gestured down at the prostrate Irishman.

"It's neither sporting nor noble to kill a fool. Leave him. Shane, Hurley. Take her back. When you reach the horses, tell the hostler to bring them to us at Whin Cross. Dickett, the rest of you, come with me. We'll teach the Angles not to trespass—" he chuckled, as if he knew anything of humor, let alone nobility or sport "—and dine on venison tomorrow."

The man Shane took over the death grip. His chief's son had spoken. She understood.

Mac Larkin summoned the dogs, and the huntsmen crashed their way into the woodland southward toward the wall. Hurley, so young he didn't yet shave, carefully picked his way into the forest. Shane followed, pulling Angelica roughly along behind him.

Just before the forest swallowed them, she twisted to look over her shoulder.

The Irishman, that fellow who knew nobility full well, did not stir.

14

2

Boyd

On the small island of Innishfrack off emerald Erin's coast lived six dogs and a rooster. Not long ago, horses and cattle had lived there too, grazing the open leas from the top of the gently domed hill down to the rocky shore. Invaders from Connemara, though, came off the mainland half a mile to the east, herded them into the sea, and drove them away—an arduous, very wet cattle raid. Now the leas were overgrown, and the rank grass was studded with weeds.

Many more chickens had once lived there, but the dogs had caught them all—all but this one wily rooster who spent his days on the thatched roof of the farmhouse and ventured down to eat only when the dogs napped at midday. There had once been a prosperous farmer and his family, but they had all died of the plague. The cattle raiders had paused to cremate them and bury their ashes in clay jugs.

Rooks from the mainland, great black birds with bare, evil-looking countenances, found the neglected grainfields almost right away and set up nestkeeping in the abandoned outbuildings. Clearly, rooks and chickens and dogs do not sin so grievously as to bring down plague upon themselves.

* * *

"I don't like the appearance of this." Boyd Blond Hair looked out across to the neglected leas of Innishfrack as their curragh bobbed uneasily in a rising surf. "Too many rooks." Boyd swung his brawny arm to point to the birds, and two companions hastily stepped back.

"Another one, aye? Eh, Boyd, I weep for Erin." Brendan moved in again beside him and sighed. The wiry little monk sighed often and well for one so slight of build. A bit scraggly after a week and some at sea, his graying hair riffled in the wind. The front of his tonsure, shaved from ear to ear, was growing in as fuzzy stubble. The breeze picked up the long stray ends at the back of his head and tangled them within each other.

The largest of curraghs, this vessel bore a sturdy mast and thirty crewmen. In boats of this size, one could sail forever. But then, some monks set forth in tiny curraghs with no sails at all and drifted asea wherever God would send them.

The size of a ship bears little relationship to its importance. The same with men; Boyd towered above the puny Brendan, but he counted Brendan his better. Brendan showed no fear, ever, in any situation. Boyd could read the land well, but Brendan could read the sea better than anyone else in Erin.

From birth, signs and miracles had ordained Brendan's life.

Boyd was an ordinary man, albeit unusually large.

"Do you see the dogs?" He nervously scanned the shoreline. Abandoned dogs always haunted ruined farms.

"Were it winter, I'd expect them down on this lee shore. But summer? They could be anywhere." Brendan's eyes did not leave the island as he called, "Mochta! Pray thee, bring me a lance too when you come."

Boyd grimaced. "I hate killing dogs."

"What would you propose we do with them?"

"I don't know. Take them ashore?"

"Enough feral dog packs raid the raths already. Let us not add to the problem."

They furled the sail and plied the oars to bring the curragh up against a sloping shore of loose, pebbly shingle. Boyd, being the largest man of the crew, leaped out into the surf and steadied the boat as his compatriots cautiously or wildly or casually leaped out.

Boyd and Mochta pulled the heavy vessel farther up the shingle and tied its painter to a sturdy shrub. They had to use ropes to drag her—her stitched leathern hull was much too slippery to grip when wet, because it was permeated with mutton grease to keep water and barnacles at bay and because wet leather is always slimy. Dry, though, it leaked. Her ash ribs had a tendency to break at the wrong time, her oaken gunwales creaked ominously in storms, her heavy linen sail required three men to lift when it was rainsoaked—which was usually. All in all she was a beautiful little vessel.

16

Ashore, the unwieldy curragh wallowed clumsily, partly awash. At sea, she plowed water with steadfast purpose. She was born for the sea.

Boyd was not. He hated the queasy feeling any kind of heavy sea induced. He hated days upon days of bobbing with nary a landfall near. Right now he stood upon solid, immobile land, and he relished it. Mochta handed him his lance, and he fell in behind the rest of the crew as they started up the grass-tangled slope.

How many raths such as this one had they visited in the last year as Brendan sailed up, down, and around Erin's coast? Dozens. Not one had escaped at least a few deaths from the plague. Some of them lost every person in the family.

All these unattended raths called to Boyd. They were fine farms—not a thing wrong with them save that tragedy had struck. Few families had extra sons remaining alive whom they might send out to repopulate the abandoned lands. This property here, like so many others, was just waiting for an enterprising colonizer to come in, take over, rebuild, and prosper.

Boyd ought to do that—destroy the dogs that would destroy him and then tell Brendan good-bye. Mend the thatch, rebuild the dug-out portions of the wall ringing the main farm buildings, bring in new stock. Look at this grass! Look at the grainfield beyond! This island would support a family with no trouble at all.

The lead crewmen laughed and pointed to the conical thatched roof sticking up from behind the ringwall. A rooster perched on its very peak, crowing lustily.

Boyd did a jogging double-step to catch up to Brendan. "Any word in the records as to who lived here?"

Brendan shook his head. His wild-man hair rippled in the dank breeze. "Out here in Connaught, monastery records are sketchy under the best of circumstances. And these are not the best of circumstances. I suppose somebody on the mainland could tell you if you had to know."

"Not have to. Want to. I'm thinking of settling."

Brendan stopped and studied him. Brendan was not an old man—in fact he was still on the early side of his prime. But his eyes seemed ancient and wise. "Build a monastery?"

"There's none here."

"Apparently there are no people here. Not anymore."

But there were indeed dogs.

From the protection of an empty rock-and-thatch bier outside the ringwall, three haggard curs eyed the approaching party warily. Two tails wagged tentatively. The third reserved judgment. How Boyd hated this! And Brendan was such a gentle man, intent upon doing God's will. Brendan must hate it worse.

With a quiet, purring voice, Brendan directed operations. Surround the bier. Encourage the dogs back into it, where they will be trapped. Strike, even if they are reaching to lick your hand. They are starving. There is no hope for them elsewhere. Already too many dogs roam Erin, abandoned by too many plague victims. To release them from their torment is a blessing. Do not hang back. Courage, men!

Boyd knew the litany by heart as did every other man here.

Brendan and two others stepped into the stinking darkness of the windowless cattle shed. Boyd waited by the door. Dogs yelped. Brendan cried out startled. Here came a scrawny, ragged bitch out the door at a staggering run, dragging the lance that had pierced her flank.

With a muttered curse, Boyd stabbed at her only moments too late. He took off after her, running his best. Compared to the many here who were fleeter of foot, his best could not be called good. He galumphed down the slope, trying not to let the tangle of rank grass seize an ankle and throw him down.

She disappeared, gone to ground somewhere. Weeds higher than Boyd's knees hid her. Still muttering, Boyd walked back to where he had last seen her and began tracking. He found the bloodied lance, and tooth marks in its shaft.

The blood spoor trailed down toward the shore. Apparently she was hiding very near to where they had beached the curragh. That seemed logical. Here in the lee of the island, she would find shelter from wind and weather, even if pursuers took over the abandoned buildings.

"Hey!" Boyd bolted forward. Three other dogs were ripping at the greased leather hull of the curragh! Boyd waved his arms and his lance. "Get! Go! Back, you curs! Get back!" He called to Brendan with a ululating howl.

Already they had torn apart one of the lower hides. A gaping hole exposed the boat's ribs and framework. Snarling, they tugged at the loose leather. It would take days to repair the damage done already, and the dogs didn't seem ready yet to cease damaging.

"Get away! Scat! Go!" Boyd jabbed with his lance at the first mutt he came to, a big male. Showing teeth like marlinespikes, the dog wheeled, cowered, and snapped at him. One of the other two ripped the calf of Boyd's left leg. He spun to meet the threat, his lance slashing, and the big male sank his teeth into the back of his other leg.

Boyd abandoned attack in favor of retreat. He tossed his lance up into the curragh and grabbed the gunwale. He hauled himself aboard even as another set of jaws seized his sandal, engaging his big toe as well. He kicked and squirmed and dropped to the deck. Bleeding worse than the injured bitch, he leaned over the side and stabbed downward with his lance.

He got one of the nasty curs, when the dog darted in for another try at the boat hides. The big male made off with an arm's-length chunk of leather. The third dog, still uninjured, worried a loose flap of hide out under the prow, where Boyd's lance could not reach.

Here came Mochta with five others down the hill. They broke into a run, roaring. A fine thing, what? Why could they not come to the rescue when first he called out? The remaining two dogs fled. Boyd tried to keep track of where they were going, but they disappeared around the western shore, still running too fast to be approaching a lair.

Boyd's mates derived a great deal of merriment from his lack of success, and speculated at length about what he must have looked like as he humped up over the boat's gunwale, the curs literally on his heels. A jolly picture!

They posted a guard, but of course the dogs did not return.

The next morning, Boyd and two other crewmen—"Boyd's protectors," they insisted upon being called—ranged out in search of the injured bitch. They lost her trace, but that afternoon while out digging clams, their navigator, Leeson, came upon her mangled remains. She had been savaged by her own companions.

The two surviving dogs escaped cleanly.

3

Ronan

Silent as a night breeze, Ronan of Skellig Michael worked his way along the base of the ringwall. He paused, listening. Either he would die tonight, or bards would sing of his heroism forever. His breastbone fluttered a bit, for he feared he knew which it would be. He ought to pray more before undertaking this last daring move.

From the oilskin bag at his belt he pulled a chunk of raw venison. With a mighty fling he tossed it over the protective palisade of wooden pales topping the earthen ringwall. Dogs instantly snarled and snapped on the other side. A man's voice called out sharply.

Ronan moved six feet farther and tossed another chunk over the top. He hastened forward now, not toward the gate but along the wall to the opposite side of the compound, as distant from Larkin's sentries as possible. A thief or rapist would want to stay as far from the dogs as he could. Ronan wanted those dogs with him, and quiet. On the other side of the wall they would be tracking the scent of his raw meat, following along as he hurried around the outside. He couldn't afford to waste either a moment or a piece of meat.

He stopped and judged his position. This would do. He tossed another chunk over the top and followed it with a noose on a braided leather rope. He tugged the rope. The noose caught and held, gripping pikes somewhere in the top of the palisade.

He hand-over-handed up the rope with his feet braced against the pales, wall-walking. Then he froze, listening. But the only sound was of dogs snuffling and jostling. He reached the top, the points of the vertical poles, and gripped the horizontal brace bar in both hands. With a mighty heave, he pulled himself up, locked elbows, and threw a leg over the top to perch on the bar.

A dog began barking below. Others joined it in a happy cacophony. Quickly Ronan tossed out another chunk to silence the pack. He was down to six now—he must ration his bribes carefully.

Yanking his dirk, he paused only long enough to cut through as many lashings on the brace bar as he could reach. He flipped the noose free, looped its rope over his arm, swung his leg over, and dropped inside, skidding down the flank of the grassy ringwall. The dogs swarmed about him, and he threw them another slab of meat. He hacked through the lashings at the bottom.

He had just insinuated himself into the deepest sanctum of Larkin's lair. This was a tomfool stunt. A good servant of God gave his life in the name of Jesus. Not for a woman he didn't even know.

He wasn't even certain of her name. Angelica, was it?

He patted the oilskin-wrapped lump inside his tunic. Still there. He threw the last of the meat to Larkin's dogs and tossed them the bloody oilskin pouch as well. The dogs fell to squabbling and fighting among themselves.

Ronan recognized by smell the midden beside him. This then was the kitchen shed. He stood a moment, eyes closed, picturing again the diagram a farmer had drawn in the mud. The ringwall, the gate, the kitchen. Thus oriented, he hurried along the inside wall. When the dogs finished fighting over their gifts, they might come investigating, but that wasn't likely.

Carefully he worked his way to the front of the little round, thatched cott. Lamplight flowed out from under the hung cowhide and across the beaten mud at the door. He was about to move forward when he heard footsteps. He froze. Slowly he raised his blue cloak far enough to partially cover his face. The fellow might not see him.

He recognized the smell of the fellow—Larkin's huntmaster. The man must have found the oilskin pouch and deduced that someone was invading. But could he? During Ronan's one brief encounter with him, the man seemed as quick as dirt and half as bright.

The huntmaster stepped up to the doorway and rattled the hide. "Lady?" The gravelly voice confirmed his identity.

From inside, a woman's voice asked, "What?" She sounded exactly like the frightened young woman who had taken refuge behind Ronan's back.

"Lady, is your cat with you?"

"Yes. Why?"

"The dogs fell upon something, and I can't get it away from them. I was afraid it might be your cat."

"No. She's right here."

"Good. Good. Must have been a hare or stoat. Good night." The huntmaster turned away and headed across the compound, a black figure dissolving instantly into blackness.

Ronan waited. After what seemed an eternity, the lamplight from under the hide went out. The remaining dull red glow dimmed as she banked her fire.

Now.

He rattled the hide and whispered, "I'm a friend. Please, woman, make no sound to betray me." Quickly, he slipped inside, from near darkness into utter darkness.

She gasped and whispered, "The Irishman!"

"Ronan."

"Of the Skelligs. How did . . .why . . ."

He addressed perfect darkness, for the fire was fully banked. "I wish I knew why. I've never done anything so utterly stupid before. Tell me the truth, woman. Are you married?"

"No. Larkin thinks I'm holding out at my father's behest, so that he can negotiate a better price. But I don't want to be married at any price."

"Why not?"

"To an honorable man, certainly. To a powerful man, perhaps. But Mac Larkin is a miserable lout. And Larkin hardly better. I don't want my children to be the next generation of the Larkin."

Ronan nodded unseen in the blackness. Good. Her resolve seemed firm and logical. "If you leave, you're abandoning your clan. You can never return. Never see your kin again. Don't you think the price is too high?"

"I thought of that. I also thought of how my poor father will suffer if I refuse. He's not nearly as powerful as Larkin."

So far, Ronan's recollections of that painful encounter with

Mac Larkin seemed to be correct. "The farmer who showed me what lies where in here also told me of a prized stallion Larkin keeps tied beside his door. Is it there, do you know?"

"It should be. He ties it there every night." Her sweet voice unexpectedly moved him. "Larkin will kill you. You know that, don't you?"

"He has to catch me first." Ronan kept his own voice down to a light whisper. "Forgive my brave words. They're no reflection of my skill at derring-do. I've never attempted this sort of thing before."

"Why now?"

"When I figure it out, I'll explain it to you. Do you want to make one more attempt at escape?"

A long, long silence later, she whispered, "Yes."

"Lead me to his stallion."

"You're mad!"

"I'm beginning to suspect so. Where is your cloak?"

"On my pallet. But . . ."

Ronan waited.

She rustled in the darkness. Moments later, crackling blue flashes of light told him she was throwing the woolen garment over her shoulders. She rustled again as if moving about. "I'm ready."

He reached out, bumped into what proved to be an arm, and took one of her soft, delicate hands as he moved toward the doorway. He felt the slightest bit of reluctance as he drew her behind him out the door into the dangerous night.

They moved silently across the compound. This was the tricky spot, right here. Should anyone see them in the near darkness and demand identification, he was doomed.

Surely more by reckoning than by seeing, she worked their way to a large hut. He could hear a horse on its picket line, sidling, churning in place, twisting and turning. Even though he could see nothing, he could picture sharp little ears thrust forward toward him, the delicate nose held high.

He let go of the soft hand and groped to find the hard, cold tether line. With a practiced touch he plucked the bowline loose, untying the stallion. He snatched up the little stud horse's lead

23

line and led both it and Angelica toward the back of the compound.

"This is foolhardy!" Angelica suddenly dug in her heels. "You can't possibly ride that horse out of here with me on it as well."

The stallion waltzed around them in a tight circle. Ronan had his hands full. "I don't intend to. I agree it's foolhardy, but we'll make it." He tried not to think about so many enemies lurking so near, as they and the pony made their way to those loosened pales beside the kitchen midden.

The dogs still milled about. They recognized Angelica—Ronan could make out a few tails wagging—and crowded closely, eagerly around them. A couple of them yapped experimentally, but they didn't seem to think that people on the inside of the compound were folk to be seriously barked at.

Ronan gripped the pony lead in his left hand as he threw the leather noose with his right. It clunked in the darkness above and did not return to him. He tugged. It felt solid. Clumsily, struggling, he looped the bight of the rope over the pony's head. And now he pulled that wrapped lump out of his tunic.

"What are you doing? What is that?" she whispered.

"A chunk of venison with a teasel head bound to it."

He had it unwrapped. Instantly the dogs snatched away the meat-tainted oilskin, snarling. He reached far back to slap the chunk against the base of the stud pony's tail. The teasel bur snagged instantly into the tail hair with its hundred tiny hooks. The dogs went wild, pressing in, snapping at it, yowling and growling.

The stallion squealed in terror and kicked wildly at his tormentors. The pack hard on his heels, he lunged and bolted.

Ronan could hear the top binder-bar creak. He dragged Angelica aside. The chaos of dogs and pony and cracking timbers filled the compound and reverberated off the darkness all around them.

And here it all came. With more noise than a battle, a major section of the palisade crashed down through the blackness.

Ronan dragged Angelica to the ringwall. "Up we go. Be careful. The dew has made the grass slippery." He clawed his way up the earthen wall, using the fallen pales to pull himself. He pulled the woman behind him. She didn't seem to be trying very hard. But then a yowl told him she was holding onto a cat.

Men were yelling all over the place. Either the pony had broken the rope or the noose had come free, for dogs and pony were thundering off across the compound beyond the banqueting hall.

Ronan and the woman stood poised on the top of the wall for the fleetest of moments.

"Wait!" She gripped his arm. "Do you realize what this means? Do you really, truly understand what we're doing? There's a price on my head now. And in a few more moments, you'll be worth a small fortune."

"I'm willing. Are you?"

She hesitated. Then, "Yes."

For a moment only, he listened to the confusion at the far end of the compound, of shouting men and barking dogs. Then, taking her wrist firmly, he wrapped a steadying arm around her waist and leaped with her off the wall into the outer darkness.

4

Desmond

"Hi-*yaah!*" Willis leaped out into the road, brandishing his oaken club.

His victims, a half-grown lad and a mild-looking friar, stopped in their tracks. The lad was scared white. The friar, a mid-sized man with plain features, stared a long moment. The friar's face melted from a startled gape to a pleasant smile. "Oh. Of course. A robber. Blessings on you, lad."

Irish accent! Frustrated almost beyond words, Willis tossed his club over his shoulder. "Why me? Why can you Irishmen not stay home where you belong? I've not met an Irishman yet who had anything worth taking. Why do you come abroad to clutter up our roads? Off with you. Go!"

Trembling, the half-grown lad cowered behind the monk.

"Well, now, just a moment. I may have a little something." The friar loosed the leather pouch at his waist and opened it. "Mm. I've a bit of copper, I think. And . . . yes. I thought there was a silver piece in here. Some gentleman's donation for the poor. You're as poor as any, I assume, or you'd not be reduced to robbery. Here you go." He extended his hand, offering four small coins.

Willis raised both hands, palms out, lest this misbegotten monk place the money in them. "No! Who do you take me for? I'm a far prouder man than would accept money for the poor. The very thought of it! Here!" Willis dug into his own purse. "Here, here! I'll show you how proud I be. Here's my own donation to the poor, right here. Take it."

The monk kept the same bland smile on his face. "I never refuse alms to distribute to the poor. But are you sure you don't need this?"

"Take it! Take it and be gone." Willis thrust three coins into the monk's hand. How he despised robberies gone awry! These

Irish monks were a curse on the decent English citizenry such as Willis, people making a modest living by their chosen trade.

"Thank you, thank you." With a generous flourish, the monk signed the cross in Willis's face. "Your gift be multiplied to the work of God among the poor! Thank you!" He mumbled a string of Latin words—or perhaps they were Greek—and smiled more broadly.

Willis had just been blessed. He hated that.

The monk continued on his way down the road, cheerful as a rooster in a henhouse, and the callow lad followed closely and nervously at his heels.

Dejected, Willis kicked the bushes by the roadside. It took him almost five minutes to find his club. Of all the luck. An Irish monk. Why could they not stay in Ireland, all of them?

He settled himself behind the great oak tree, the same position he'd been sitting in since early morning, and listened again for approaching footfalls. Did Irish monks not know how difficult a robber's life is? You wait all day, getting cramps in your legs and ants in your garments, chasing annoying flies, on the off chance that someone might come by.

And as often as not, that someone is traveling in the company of a retinue so large that you'd have to have ten men with you to force them to stand and deliver. Willis was a slight man, a man not as strong as many. That in itself limited him in his choice of victims. No, it was not an easy life, the life of a highwayman.

Of course, if Willis could afford to buy a sword, perhaps his luck would improve. A club did not command the attention a flashing bronze sword would. Or iron. That was it. An iron sword—the damascened iron that the nobles and some of their retainers carried.

Fat chance he'd ever lay hands on an iron sword if he kept giving his money to the poor.

His stomach growled, and why not? He hadn't eaten since last evening, and that was no feast—some stolen rye bread. He thought about the Irish monk and the lad behind him. They appeared well fed and rosy-cheeked. He hadn't noticed any packs or sacks that would indicate they were carrying victuals with them. He knew, though, that the wandering Irish monks depended primarily upon the largess of the local people among whom they traveled. Generous largess, it would appear.

Mostly on impulse, Willis climbed stiffly to his feet, shouldered his club, and headed down the road after the monk and the boy. What would he say when he caught up to them? What would he do if they didn't let him join them? He'd think of something.

When he saw no one ahead as the road straightened, he broke into a jog. Irish monks were fast.

Romans built this road, legend claimed, though no Roman *caliga* had trod this path for centuries. They built the abandoned stone wall too that snaked up and over the hills several hundred feet off to Willis's left.

The wall towered three-men high, wandering through forest and moor, hill and dale. Along this particular stretch, it followed a rough scarp jutting above the ragged moors. Abandoned mile castles—guardhouses the old ones used to call *castelli*—studded its length, spaced at every mile. Between the mile castles stood smaller turrets, all unpeopled—ghostly garrisons from days long past, when there was order in the land.

Willis could almost feel the specters of Picts and Romans, condemned to walk the wall forever. This whole moody region got on his nerves. He'd leave this land and travel somewhere brighter perhaps, if he hadn't been born near here. Somehow it didn't seem right to leave.

The monk had stopped ahead in the glade by the cooper's brook. He and his young companion had left the road and settled themselves into a nest in the grass hard against the stone wall. They sat leaning against the stonework, their legs stretched out in casual repose.

"Ah! There you are!" The monk waved cheerily. "Our robber friend. Join us, pray thee."

Willis winced. Why did he bother to associate with a man holding such low regard for Willis's trade? Why enter the company of a fellow whose pudding lacked a few currants? Willis was hungry. That was why. And that was always and sufficient why.

He flopped into the grass beside the friar. "I did not ask you where you're from or where you be headed or what your name might be."

"Desmond, from Munster. My associate, Ibar. We're bound to wherever God sends us. Yourself?"

Wherever God sends us. Now Willis absolutely knew the man's cakes had baked too long. "Willis Gray Mantle. So where do you ken God's sending you?"

"Ibar here opines we've gone too far already." The monk Desmond sniggered, but he didn't seem to be mocking his young companion. "I hope to establish a center of learning somewhere in the area. A monastery."

"A whole company of monks, eh?" *One monk is monks aplenty.* "'Twould support a great company here, for 'tis a rich region. There've been farms here since the beginning of time. Plenty to eat." Willis eyed his new acquaintance. "I trust you've plans for your next meal, eh?"

Desmond Friar shrugged amiably. "Something will turn up."

Willis pondered this a moment. Obviously, these two had no idea where their next meal might come from. But equally obviously, they weren't in any direr straits than Willis. He had no idea either. He could do worse than hang about with them, and he might just do better, if their luck held.

His certainly wasn't holding.

An instant later his luck dried up completely, for a pack of hunting dogs, huge animals and burly, came roaring up the track from the east. He knew the dogs. Larkin's.

The baying ceased as they burst into the glade. They swarmed around the monk and his lad and bared their teeth at Willis. The friar remained at repose.

Willis snatched up his club. He pressed back against the stone wall as his heart pounded its fists upon his breast.

The dogs milled in confusion all around the monk Desmond.

Now pony feet came clattering along the road from the east. Many pony feet. Willis had barely readied his club when the riders burst out of the birch copse to the southeast. Immediately, their leader left the road and brought his troop thundering up to the defenseless party at the wall.

Defenseless? Willis owned the only weapon, and that was but a club. A club was poor defense indeed against eight armed riders. No, nine. Ten! Not to mention that horde of ravening curs. Ten, and Larkin at their head. Willis was doomed.

Larkin, burly and boisterous, looked bigger than his sweaty

little pony. In fact, Larkin was sweating too. His brown and black tartan cloak fluttered dramatically. The silver brooch holding it at his shoulder shone in the filtered sun of the light overcast. Larkin's black beard and generous eyebrows moved about his face whenever he laughed or frowned or roared. He did a lot of all three.

Behind the burly chieftain sat his burly son on a pony just as burdened. Larkin's lad shaved; otherwise he looked much like his father. He had the same beetling brows. Willis did not trust either of them any farther than he could throw their ponies.

"Well, well! Willis East Bogg! You dare show your face around here! And you've a monk for protection, I see." Larkin chuckled.

Willis cowered inside. Outside, he put on a show to fool a wise man. "The club for protection, the monk for company."

Larkin combined a laugh with a roar. "And neither of much use to you."

His son seemed in even darker spirits. "This is not the monk. 'Twas a different man. I wouldn't doubt he knows where his cohort is, though."

"No question of it." Larkin glowered at the monk and at the callow lad beside him. "Rowan of Someplace Michael. Where is he?"

"Someplace Michael." The Irishman pondered the question but a moment. "Skellig Michael? There is a brother in this area from Skellig Michael?"

"You know him?"

"Ah, no, but Skellig Michael—now there's a gleaming light in the world! A band of brothers have built a splendid retreat at the top of a peaked island just off Erin's coast. So now they're sending their people abroad. Wonderful! No better scholars. I look forward to meeting him. Wait! Rowan? Or Ronan?"

"You do know him?"

"Some years ago. He's a monk of Clonfert—was once. I was at that time outside the immediate order, and he was just beginning study within it. A rather quiet young man, articulate and comely but distant. Hard to know."

Willis smiled broadly, hoping that a cheerful demeanor might defuse the situation. "Should we come upon this monk, we'll be certain to tell you right off. Indeed we will."

His cheerful demeanor did nothing for the situation.

Larkin's son glowered. "He's not a monk, the villain. When I find him, he dies slowly."

Willis shook his head. "I'm sorry. I haven't seen him."

"Surely you have. You see everyone on the road eventually." Larkin slid off his lathered pony and started forward. "Whatever he paid you, it wasn't nearly enough, Willis East Bogg. Speak." Almost instantly Larkin stopped. He stared, not at Willis but at the friar.

From his casual seat against the wall, the monk had raised his right arm. He held his hand, palm out and fingers stretched straight, in a strange way. "Belay your hostility. Join us in friendship."

Larkin didn't move. He scowled. His beetle brows crowded together into a thick blob like a woolly caterpillar curled with its head tucked in. "Who are you?"

"Desmond, a man of God from the court of Cashel in Munster, most recently from Clonfert, bringing God's blessings upon you."

"From the court. A prince then?"

"In fact, I am. A grandson in the direct line of Oengus, the greatest of the kings of Cashel. Oengus was the first of the high kings to embrace the Christian faith. Converted by Patrick himself. I am also an heir of heaven together with Jesus Christ, the Prince of Peace. You can be a fellow heir as well, if you so choose, a prince in your own right."

"Prince of Peace?" He swore. "I already am a prince." Why could he not stir from that spot? He stood as if rooted, halfway between his pony and Willis. "Larkin Round Face, Prince of Picts."

Desmond's extended arm never wavered. "There is immense virtue in peace, because God values it, if for no other reason. Larkin, Prince of Picts, you have just blasphemed against the living God by assuming for yourself a prerogative that is God's alone—to damn or to save. You greatly need His forgiveness, and His aegis. Will you receive them?"

The mighty Larkin stared at the amiable friar.

Willis realized then that the warrior's gaze was directed not at Desmond but at Desmond's outstretched hand. Behind Larkin, his

31

son and his cronies watched him for his next move, his next direction, and found none. Even the dogs churned in pointless confusion. "Desmond . . ."

"Kinship with the Prince of Peace provides many blessings, not the least of them being great power. Do you ken?"

"I ken." Larkin's voice, uncharacteristically plaintive, murmured, "Desmond. Release me."

Desmond altered the shape of his outstretched hand enough to sketch the cross in front of Larkin's face, then laid his arm in his lap.

Instantly the burly Larkin did a double-step backward an arm's length.

What have I stumbled into here? Willis didn't know whether to run or to hide behind the friar. His palms sweated as he gripped his sorry, ineffectual club.

A bit of defiance returned to Larkin's voice. "I have formidable power already. I don't need forgiveness or aegis from anyone."

"You speak truly when you call yourself a Prince of Picts," Desmond purred. "You are indeed, but not 'Prince of all Picts' or even 'Prince of Many Picts.' Is that true?"

"My extended clan numbers nearly a hundred."

"Only half of whom are loyal to you. Occasionally, I hear, you even suspect the loyalty of your son here."

Never had Willis ever seen Larkin so enervated. In fact, Willis generally didn't see Larkin at all—Willis avoided this giant as much as possible, considering how Larkin loved to torment him and any other robber in the region. Except that this time the burly warlord was seeking to torment a Ronan. Whoever Ronan might be.

The Prince of Picts studied Desmond. "What would you have me do?"

"First there is the matter of the remission of your sins through the blood of Jesus Christ. That is primary. Pray God's forgiveness for this latest blasphemy and all others you've committed. Accept His sovereignty over your life, for it is surely there, as I have demonstrated. Ask Him to implant His Holy Spirit within you. He will do it, and you will become His child."

Larkin scowled so hard that his brows nearly came down to meet his beard.

Willis didn't understand what the monk meant, but he rejoiced to see Larkin's discomfiture. Perhaps Irish monks were good for something after all.

Larkin wheeled away and swung back aboard his pony. He barked something terse at his confederates. His huntmaster called the hounds onto the track toward the west. They obeyed reluctantly, still intently sniffing about the wall. The fellow called sharply, and they trotted off after his pony.

Larkin's son groped about in a sack across his pony's withers and brought out a barley loaf. He tossed it to the monk. Another fellow loosed two gutted hares from his saddle and threw them in a furry arc to the monk's feet. The band returned to the road without a backward glance and continued west, following their dogs.

Willis stared at the hares. "Ye did not so much as say a word about food."

"No need. For all their roughshod ways, the Picts are an honorable people. He knew when a gift was appropriate, and what other gift would there be?"

Somehow it seemed that was not the explanation. Willis ought to ponder the point, but those hares were calling to be roasted. He would consider this surprising run of events later. He did, however, make three decisions that night:

The loaf was large enough that he could steal an extra chunk for later.

He would not be taken in by the monk's God talk.

He would, though, stay very, very close to this strange and lucky Irishman.

5
Enda

"Manannan Mac Lir himself it was, and riding a great white horse on the crest of an ocean wave. At full gallop they came, the horse running amain to stay on the crest—not behind the crest, not ahead of the crest. And its great nostrils roared."

By the half-light of the fire in the center of a tiny, cramped room, Brendan actually looked a bit like Manannan. His eyes glittered with the memory of his vision. The faltering firelight danced in them.

Great, burly Boyd watched Brendan's face closely. Boyd had dutifully memorized the story of the Lord's walking on the water, and of Peter's brazen attempt to duplicate the feat. But this was something new and different. This was a tale rooted in the times when the old gods roamed free, before ever mankind arrived in Erin. Was Brendan sincere with his story, or was he spinning another of his yarns? Was a moral lesson to come?

Brendan continued. "I watched the wave surge across the shallows and break up on the shingle, leaving its foamy white line. As the wave broke, that horse leaped—still galloping, thundering, it mounted up into the sky. Manannan and his horse were coming, of course, from Tir na n'Og."

Tir na n'Og. The Land of Ever Young. Boyd would not have guessed that the vision would take that particular twist.

Brendan's voice softened. "And then the clouds parted—lifted off the surface of the sea. Bright light broke through on the far horizon, and I saw it ever so briefly. The Promised Land. The clouds closed quickly, but that swift glimpse was sufficient. Ah, I wanted it! That was years ago, my first visit to the Arans here. I still want it, even more."

The fire turned smokier, pouring its pungent gray vapor upward. The smoke lay flat across the room halfway between floor and roof, as if this domed clochan were a vessel upside down and the smoke, the most delicate of beverages, were filling it. The stuff assailed Boyd's nose and made his eyes water. Brendan's eyes watered as well.

Boyd glanced across the fire to their host, the venerable Enda, and frowned. Enda's eyes were watering, but the problem didn't seem to be smoke. The smoke was drifting away from him.

Enda, lean and white and hoary with the grace of years, was so old he had probably helped lay the tiered white bedrock of these Aran isles. He certainly did not act old, though. When he spoke, he spoke with constant animation, arms flying, hands performing intricate dances among themselves to illustrate some point.

Enda's voice lay just as soft and wispy on the gentle night. "Tir na n'Og. The Other World. Ever since people have lived here—both humankind and the Fir Bolg before them—wise men have claimed that you can see it sometimes from the western edge of this island." He looked at Brendan. "You know Erc was once a druid, don't you?"

"Do I know? Could I ever forget? He reared me, Enda. He was as good a Christian as any on earth and taught me all the faith, but he had a strong streak of the old ways about him to the end. Aye, and he taught me of the Promised Land!"

Erc? Who was Erc? A couple of heads bobbed. Everyone seemed to know of Erc except Boyd. Boyd was losing interest in this evening's conversation. Besides, he didn't do well in close quarters. Just he himself took up the space of two men, and beside him and Enda and Brendan, four of Enda's monks sat pressed close about. Enda took up extra room with his flailing gestures. No one sat too close to him. The clochan was becoming uncomfortably warm with so many bodies in it, plus the fire.

They fell to talking then about heaven and worlds other than earth. They argued about whether Jesus Christ descended to the nethermost of hell or merely to a nearby Other World in the three days between His crucifixion and resurrection.

Boyd, being a practical sort, rarely listened well to discussions such as these and hardly ever took part. On impulse he excused himself and worked his way out the door of the beehive hut into the night. Sure and the monks must have noted his departure—he left considerable open space behind—but no one said anything.

He realized as he stretched mightily how tight and close that clochan felt when seven people clustered around its fire. To loosen up, he walked out the gate of Enda's monastery and up the slope westward.

Boyd had never visited the Aran Islands before, though he'd heard about them his whole life. Enda, the ancient and wizened brother-in-law of a high king now dead, had virtually started the monastic movement in Erin single-handed. Even yet, with monasteries scattered across the land and perched on many an island, his settlement of Killeany here on Innishmore still boasted the best and brightest of Erin's saintly scholars.

Well, Columcille's Iona rivaled this, and so did Ciaran's Clonmacnois and Brendan's own Clonfert. And Skellig Michael. Still it was understandable that Enda and Brendan, being of a philosophical bent (and more than a little stubborn, the both of them!), would rattle on ad infinitum about death and heaven and the worlds beyond. That didn't mean Boyd cared a whit.

From the Killeany settlement at the island's eastern shore, the land sloped upward sharply toward the west. In black outline, a domed hill rose between Killeany and the dying sky. Night took forever to arrive in summertime. Then, just about the time one got used to the long, long days, they shortened to next to nothing, and by the time you got used to that . . .

Boyd had to put all his attention into walking now, watching his step, choosing his route. The moon wouldn't be up for another half hour, and darkness had nearly completed its overhead march. He left behind the last of the trees, a few scrubby yews huddling in sheltered spots with their shoulders humped against the constant sea wind. Low stone walls crisscrossed the open pasturage.

As Boyd climbed higher, he noticed places where the grass was gone, roots and all. There the wind had stripped away the soil down to bedrock. Deep fissures cut the bald rock surface into squares—miles and miles of terraced squares, it appeared.

With its unique cry, a curlew rose off the meadow to his left. Its mighty wings whispering with every beat, it lifted into the rosy air, headed directly over him. Abruptly it veered away and, in a long swooping arc, sailed beyond a craggy staircase of rock.

Boyd stopped. The way that curlew suddenly altered direction, you'd think someone was coming up behind him. He looked downhill at the scrub and walls and emptiness and saw no one. But it was curious. He continued on upslope.

Half an hour later he quit walking, for he had come to the very end of Erin. The land stopped at a blocky white cliff, knife-edged, dropping precipitously to the roaring sea below. He stood on the brink with naught but sea and sky before him and let the night wind cool his sweaty face.

"Sea and sky." Brendan's voice behind him told him why the curlew had reacted strangely. The monk stepped up beside him. Brendan's head came to Boyd's armpit level, barely. "How I love them, Boyd."

"I gathered as much by the rapt look on your face whenever we're sailing down the wind. What was all this about Tir Na n'Og and a high brazzle?"

"Hi Brasil. Tir Na n'Og, the Other World, the Promised Land, the Land of Ever Young. All of them are the same thing."

"And who is Erc?"

"The man who made me what I am. I consider Enda my spiritual mentor. Bishop Erc ought be considered my spiritual father." Brendan paused awhile to watch the sky changing from one vivid mantle to the next—orange, red, purple, the colors of evening. "He was a druid converted to the faith late in life. He taught me both worlds, that of Jesus and that of eld. You see, my mother dried up when I was but a few months old. Now the story is starting to spread that a hind would appear daily from the forest of Slieve Luacra to nurse me. And that the abbess of the monastery school at the foot of the slieve, a rather strange little lady named Ita, shape-shifted into the hind."

Here came another story Boyd could make neither heads nor tails of. "Shape-shifting. Didn't Patrick say—"

"I'm just mentioning the story going around. When I was but a year old, Erc carried me away from my parents and put me in Ita's school near Kileedy. As soon as he decided I'd received what I needed there, he took me out of Ita's school into his school for monks. He put me under Jarlath of Tuam. Jarlath was ordained by Bishop Erc, you know."

No, Boyd didn't know. Nor did Boyd care. He couldn't stand abbots and bishops who thought they knew everything and what was best for everybody. He held back what he would prefer to say and limited his remarks to "A bit high-handed, I'd say."

"Perhaps. He claimed I was dedicated to God before birth. At conception, in fact. He said he knew the hour when I was born because he saw the woods afire and yet nothing was consumed there." Brendan smiled. "And he taught me seafaring."

"Also about the old gods, I'd guess. Manannan Mac Lir."

"Ah, yes. The king of both the sea and the Land of Promise as well. But you knew that."

Boyd watched the sky spread its fiery colors across the water, watched the water pick them up and fling them about. "I do. But I don't know if the vision you described concerning him was lesson or jest."

"Neither. It is my dream. The sea. Promise. I believe they are closely intertwined, Boyd. Manannan is perceived as the god of both for a reason. The promise is out there, across the sea. Or perhaps the promise is the sea."

"The promise is our Lord and Savior Jesus Christ. I would never accuse or suspect you of blasphemy however mild, Brendan, but . . ." He gave the but a bit of extra emphasis and let it hang free on the night wind.

"Well-spoken. He is the promise, of course, but He also makes promises. 'In my Father's house are many mansions.' Where, exactly, beloved Boyd? Where is His Father's house? Identify that location, and I believe we will be talking about the same place."

"Tir na n'Og."

"The ancients knew a thing or two. They identified the Other World to the west. Out there." Brendan's face and eyes, his whole being, slipped off a thousand miles away. "The Promised Land. Did you ever hear of a bard named Oisin?"

"They claim he lived at Tir Na n'Og three hundred years. He returned, and when he touched earth again on Erin, all those three hundred years fell upon him at once."

38

Brendan nodded. "He barely had time to describe the land before he expired. He said he saw gentle men and handsome women. Sweet love, sweet bird songs, sweet honey. No sin, no dying."

Boyd was not a clever man, but he could tell which way the wind blew without having to wet a finger. He studied Brendan closely. "And no plague to ravage the gentle men and handsome women."

Brendan's face took on the weight of a thousand dyings. "And no plague."

They stood awhile in the liquid night, with the wind hushing past their ears. Who would want to go to the trouble of finding Hi Brasil, with Erin so close to being paradise? Boyd twisted to look eastward. The moon was just now squeezing itself up out of the black mainland silhouette. It washed the sky gray as it came.

Presently Brendan said, "Boyd. Join us tomorrow, please, Enda and I, as I tell him about Barrind."

Barrind. Boyd knew that name. "He's the old man who visited you at Clonfert last month."

"The very same." Brendan cast longing eyes westward a few moments more, turned, and started back down the slope toward Killeany and their night's repose.

Boyd followed, partly to let his abbot go first and partly to ponder Brendan's dream. The elder monk talked long and eloquently but never to no point. Whether or not the vision of Manannan Mac Lir hid a joke or a sermon, it meant something.

By the time they reached the island's eastern shore, the moon rode high behind a veil of light haze, her halo showing plainly, and Boyd thought he had figured out where Brendan was leading with all this. His primary interest now was whether he had guessed correctly.

The next morning they met with the ancient Enda immediately after matins. Boyd thanked God privately and fervently that they were not gathering today in another of those cramped clochans. The beehive huts were constrictive enough for one person, the usual occupancy, much less Enda and his violent gesticulations.

With none but Boyd and Brendan at his heels, the abbot of Aran wandered down to a sheltered sand beach, talking non-stop, arms and hands flapping about like linens on a clothesline. He stopped so suddenly that Boyd almost barreled into him. "Brendan," he boomed in a voice much stronger than an old man's ought be, "tell me about Barrind's son."

Boyd kept an ear to this conversation because his abbot asked him to. But his mind wandered despite his best intentions to listen well.

Right here on Innishmore, sturdy people scratched a comfortable life out of the shelved white rock. Others did well by rafting firewood and house timbers from the mainland to the island. Here, as elsewhere, women outnumbered men. Boyd could become a part of this. He could attach himself to a clan either here on the island or ashore, build a small monastery (with rules amenable to marriage and family), and enjoy a complete life. Right here. Surrounded by the sea and yet in spirit with the land. Yes.

Brendan was staring off across the inlet. "He came to the monastery much agitated. After the amenities, I asked him some questions—nothing probing or difficult; we were simply talking—and he broke down. This is a very, very heavy emotional experience for him."

"What is?" Enda captured Boyd's full attention by skipping a stone out across the water. He got three skips out of it despite the shallow ripples.

"He's been there, Enda. His son took him to Tir na n'Og and brought him back. They even spent a few weeks exploring the land. The Land of Ever Young. He described it to me."

Enda had picked up another flat stone. He stopped in mid-fling to stare. "What corroboration do you have?"

"The others in his son's monastery. His son established a brotherhood."

"Mernoc. Yes."

"He told how his son and he embarked on a westward journey through fog. Many details, Enda—he'd not have made them up. And they came to a land he described as the place God will give to His saints later. Not we who hold the faith now, but generations in our future."

Boyd mused that unless more monastic societies embraced the marriage of their brethren, those who held the faith were

40

bound to diminish. He espied a smooth flat stone in the shingle beneath his feet and picked it up.

Enda kited another stone across the water. It skipped once and disappeared. "They sailed deliberately? They didn't just go wherever God took them?"

"Deliberately."

"And how long gone?"

"There and back, forty days in all."

Boyd offered the aged monk his flat stone.

The fellow studied it a moment, nodded, and handed it back. "You try it."

The very thing Boyd had hoped the man would say! With a childish eagerness he had not felt in years, he flung it sharply, underhand with a twist. It soared out across the water spinning, hit and skipped, altered course slightly as it hit and skipped again. Again. Again. Four.

Old Enda smiled, bobbing his head. "Once upon a time, this withered old arm was strong enough to send a stone out like that."

Boyd was smiling too. "I had forgotten about skipping stones until you reminded me this morning. Many's the lake I filled with flat stones in my youth."

Suddenly, unpredictably, Enda wheeled and locked eyes with Brendan. The old man pointed to the shingle at his feet.

Boyd stared in amazement. Brendan considered old Enda his mentor, but how did these two communicate so clearly without words?

Without hesitating, Brendan knelt in the loose cobble in front of Enda and bowed his head.

Enda laid a hand on Brendan's tousled head as he slipped into a fluid, lilting Latin. Enda was blessing his protégé, putting the seal of God upon Brendan's yearning to sail afar.

Boyd crossed himself at the close of the blessing. The final bit of the gesture as he touched his breastbone came nowhere near touching his heart. His heart lay on the cobbled stones at his feet. Brendan was just now receiving the clearest of invitations to go a-voyaging. Momentarily, he would sail up to Mernoc's island, thence to the Land of Ever Young, the paradise reserved for the saints.

It sounded dramatic and inviting in a way. But settling on some abandoned farm and finding a wife sounded far more inviting.

Brendan rose to his feet with tears of joy in his eyes. He glowed.

Enda did not bless Boyd. Enda didn't even look at Boyd. The two men were embracing, oblivious to Boyd beside them. God's hand through Enda did not rest on Boyd. Let Brendan fulfill his destiny. Boyd would remain at home to fulfill his.

6

Thief

Here it was, a year later, and Ronan, late of Skellig Michael, could still remember clearly his last day of happiness. He could recall every detail, for he rehearsed those final happy moments daily.

In a situation somewhat unusual for the southwest coast of Ireland, a bright sun and clear skies made that particular afternoon sparkle. Vivid black choughs with their blood-red beaks swept and darted along the rocks and ledges of Ronan's island home. Gulls mewed out over the churning waters. There on the small, pointy island of Skellig Michael, from the front door of the oratory in the monastery compound eight-hundred steps up the flank of the peaked isle, one could gaze out upon the distant mainland across the reach, peer down into the roiling waters at the base of the rocks, see forever across the blue-gray line of the sea's far horizon. The view dazzled mind, eye, and heart.

Ronan and his companions were applying the final touches to the new clochan just downhill of the oratory. Like an inverted boat, the rounded hut of dry-stacked stone huddled on a ledge behind a low stone wall. But for the wall, it seemed more exposed than the rest of the clochans that crowded together on the steep slope. Other low walls laced among them, separating each from its mates and affording each monk in the bustling commune a privacy as complete as he cared to make it.

Ronan remembered stepping up onto the wall to survey their monastery. He recalled the pure, driving happiness of listening to the rushing sea so far below, of simply watching unfettered sunlight pour down upon the dozen oval domes. The oratory apart, each clochan marked a focused point of piety. Each one sheltered monks devoting themselves to prayer and study, a single-minded testimony to the glory of God. *Gloria in excelsis deo!*

43

And then Garron had collapsed. Ah, Garron! Garron, from the land of the Franks, claimed to be a direct descendant of Vercinge-torix. He spoke execrable Gaelic and splendid Latin and Greek. His bubbling good cheer and unbridled piety brightened any day. He died at sundown. Still fresh in mourning, two others sickened the next day and died. Then others. Ronan watched his best friend cross into the shade, as well as two fellows he did not particularly like.

Victuals ran out when their supply boat from ashore was two weeks late in coming. Because of sickness on the mainland, said their fisherman friend, normal life activities had all but ground to a halt. Some ri tuathe could not muster enough civil servants to keep up with the burying. The monks of Skellig Michael sent a delegation of men to the mainland to help with last rites, burials, and cremations. Ronan rowed ashore as one of them.

For four months, he worked in that capacity for the ri ruirech at Currane. When the ri himself died, Ronan personally carried the gentle, harried king out to the periphery of his rath, buried him, and then simply continued walking eastward. Now he could not say why he so abandoned his calling and duties to wander aimlessly.

He sat cross-legged before his fire and watched low, bluish flames slither across the dying coals. Angelica. He still could not grasp how demons could have driven him to so foolish an undertaking. Demons? Surely not. Ronan shared a lot in common with the apostle Peter.

Peter foolishly ventured out upon the water and his Lord bore him up when he sank. At the Lord's behest, Peter cast his nets when he knew the gesture was useless—and reaped bounty. He threw an unbaited hook into the water and came up with a coin-laden fish—just enough coin, in fact. That illustration was lost on the Irish, for they did not bother with currency. Value was measured in cattle and slaves, useful commodities, and not in good-for-nothing metal.

But did Ronan's determination to help a frantic woman come from God or from his desire to invite death and be done with this life? Either way, the farmer who found him injured came from God. As did the friend of the farmer who provided Ronan with the layout of Larkin's compound and where the woman would be sequestered. As did also their success as they made good their escape. As did also the fishing curragh conveniently beached and waiting for them to buy passage to Erin, far and safely away from the Picts.

She was gone now. So quickly she entered his life and so quickly left. She would do well at Kildare, once she mastered the local brogue. Her Pictish accent grated on the nerves of sensible people. He missed her churring Pictish more than he would have guessed.

Tomorrow he would continue on. He had eaten enough. No longer hungry, he tossed the last of his second roasted wood pigeon over his shoulder. Absently he licked his fingers.

He thought yet again of Garron and the others. The brothers of Skellig Michael. What a time it was while it lasted! They had built an aerie halfway to heaven, a haven lodged in the steep flank of a remote isle beyond the edge of the earth. Apart for God. Apart with God.

Ronan had been blessed to take part in a grand experiment, a movement that could have lasted a hundred years had the plague not struck. Were any brothers at all left out there? Time had warped and shriveled his concern into mere curiosity. And the curiosity no longer tugged at him strongly enough to draw him back.

The grass rustled behind him. He twisted quickly to glimpse a small, gray-brown animal diving into the bracken at the glade's edge. It was not hedgehog-colored or cat-hued. It was not dark enough or brown enough to be a pine marten. It had to be a dog. But he'd not seen or heard dogs in this wood before. He got up and searched for the remains of that wood pigeon. Gone. Yes, definitely a dog.

He restoked his fire just before he curled up in his cloak beneath his brush shelter. He ought not let it go out yet. If he caught another wood pigeon in his snares, he'd want to cook it tomorrow morning before he left. Besides, the nights were not so warm that a fire didn't feel good. That night he dreamed of a cold blob the color of that scurrying animal, but he could not specifically recall the dream next morning.

Half an hour before sunrise he walked down to the oak grove by the creek to check his snares. Remembering the dog—he still thought it had been a dog—he wedged his last chunk of barley cake in the crotch of a rowan, up high where a dog couldn't reach. On the way out, he picked and ate some low-growing berries that were almost ripe. You don't wait until they're ripe, or the squirrels and the birds will have got them. Their sharp aftertaste felt like skin on his teeth.

One of his snares had worked. Trapped in a tangle of light cord on an oak limb, another wood pigeon struggled. He wrung its neck and returned to his fire. The wood pigeon and that remaining chunk of barley cake would make a nice meal with which to start the day.

He dry-plucked the pigeon, gutted it, and skewered it on a roasting stick. He propped the stick close over the fire and crossed the glade to get his barley cake.

It was gone.

Impossible! A dog couldn't reach up there. A jay or something must have pecked at it enough to dislodge it, and some ground-dweller ran off with it. He looked closely, but he found no crumbs.

The loss of the barley cake greatly saddened him, and that was ridiculous. It had been a gift of God, freely given him by a lonely farmwife whose husband was out working with a burial detail. Probably he need only go back to her, and she would give him more.

But it weighed him down, all the same. So many things weighed him down. He turned back toward his fire.

"Stop!" He bolted forward.

A brindled dog, gangly, huge of foot, and probably not yet full-grown, was reaching over the fire, snapping at the wood pigeon. The dog wheeled and scooted, its tail between its legs. It scampered away into the undergrowth of ferns. Ronan heard it rustle and crash about.

Then, along with a loud crunch, the dog yelped.

Ronan took his time working his way through the brush. He peered down into the pit he had dug and artfully covered with loose fern fronds. The sun had not risen far enough to light the bottom of the two-foot-deep hole. "You down there, puppy dog. I lay my snares and traps in other than just trees, you know."

Now what?

He should pierce the dog with a fire-hardened sharp stick. After all, dog meat tasted as good as any other, except otter. Dogs were a curse on the land, especially when they ranged in packs. This fellow would do the world no good, and he would provide a satisfying meal (particularly if Ronan could beg more barley cake). On the other hand, there wasn't much more meat on this scrawny pup than on the wood pigeon.

Emboldened, the dog tried to jump out. His legs were too short. And he couldn't claw up the sides of the hole, though he certainly tried—when Ronan dug the trap he made the bottom wider than the top. The little brindle dog sat down on the uneven floor of the hole, his tail giving a tentative and occasional wag, and watched Ronan. The puppy's eyes were huge. Huge feet too—great splaying paws on thin, thin legs.

Ronan noticed all that before he noticed the festering gashes on the dog's shoulder, the result of an apparent encounter with something big and ugly.

"I also observe your great, round, distended belly, puppy dog. It surely holds worms. It probably also holds my barley cake, aye?"

Wag, wag, wag.

"Ugly as a troll you are and not half the thief."

A discouraging thought seized Ronan suddenly. He leaped up and hastened back to his fire. It was not likely that this pup roamed the forest alone. While he was diverting himself with a useless dog, it would be nothing for the rest of the pack to depart with his wood pigeon.

But no. The bird sizzled on its stick, a few inches too close to the heat, probably, but otherwise cooking nicely. Ronan stooped and turned the bird to brown the other side. Then he sat down and leaned back against the log that was his chair and backrest.

What should he do with the dog? If he killed it now, it would probably putrefy before he ate it. This was summer, after all, and, the heavy gray overcast not withstanding, meat spoils quickly. On the other hand, if he kept the cur alive and available for butchering in the future, the little dog might escape, and he would have nothing.

Good thing the dog entered his life now and not a week ago. A week ago, he and Angelica were still on their way to Kildare. Angelica and her little yellow cat. Ronan didn't particularly like cats, but hers was tolerable, except in the presence of dogs. Then it tunneled into your clothing, and if your skin happened to be in the way, too bad. Traveling with a dog would be misery.

Angelica.

He wondered how the cat liked the women's quarters at Kildare.

A great, inexplicable sadness seized him. Again.

He watched the wood pigeon darken. On Skellig Michael, the brothers ate no meat except on certain feast celebrations. They served meat to guests but not to themselves. Here in the woodland, Ronan ate meat nearly every day, for that was usually the food he found. He felt guilty.

He let his wood pigeon cool a bit before he ate it. He left the skin on the back and tail intact and threw the remains into the puppy pit.

He broke camp then, carefully dousing and scattering the fire, rolling and tying the sheepskin that was his bed, bringing in all the snares, and dropping all the deadfalls, lest they catch something to no purpose.

But what about the brindled dog?

Slowly he shoved hand-scoop after hand-scoop of dirt back into the hole, hesitating long enough to give the pup time to maneuver. By the time he filled the hole half in, the loose dirt floor was high enough that the dog could scramble out with a little help. It scooted away beneath the brackens.

That solution to the dog problem satisfied him as much as any solution would. He would not take more off the land than he needed at any moment. To this point, that had been his rule of existence. No need to break it now.

He'd broken enough rules already.

7

Fanchea

A sullen and murky sky spit rain at Ronan as he emerged from the forest. A harsh north wind raced past him, tossing the rain in his face. He paused on the brink of an open meadow and looked northward across the bay beyond, across waters as sullen and murky as the sky. His bread was gone, his dried mutton exhausted. His only possible meal, the brindled dog, stayed a rod or two away from him, beyond grasp. Not that Ronan felt like grasping it.

He picked his way down the hill through close-cropped, waterlogged grass. It never ceased to amaze him how standing water could remain as if suspended on a slope this steep. Cow tracks cut up the grass and carved numerous horizontal trails across the hillside. Nearly every muddy cow track contained its own little puddle.

The bay hooked around into a sheltered cove at the base of the hill. And in that cove a band of monks was building a curragh. A huge boat it was, much too large for the usual complement of four or six men.

Curiosity overcame lethargy. Ronan walked down to them. Troll the dog ranged out aside, bounding and rollicking down the soggy lea.

Ronan counted fifteen men as he approached. Sixteen. Here came a fellow with a ragged little pony. No, not a sixteenth man. A woman. She looked as sullen and murky as the sea and sky. Her pony dragged an extremely rickety cart through the muddy ruts. Its solid wooden wheels wobbled and clunked.

Upon closer inspection, Ronan decided this woman was not so much sullen and murky as tired and sad. Her appearance intrigued him. Locks of amazingly dark hair had slipped down out of her turban. Her skin appeared somewhat the color of a roasting chicken. She was probably quite pretty when her face didn't droop with sorrow. Light of frame and short of stature, she moved gracefully even in her sadness. There was no plodding, shuffling manner about her as one saw so often in broken women.

As he approached, the woman joined the work detail by the huge curragh. The pony lurched to a halt, and the woman dug into the back of her cart. Her voice droned, listless. "Bread and cheese. I boiled up a pot of stirabout for you. It's probably cold by now. When you're steaming ribs, set it by your fire. 'Twill warm up soon enough."

A slight, spry little monk thanked her profusely. "And honey!" he exclaimed. "You brought honey for our bread. How thoughtful." The fellow's wild-man hair whipped in the wind. It was long enough to blow into his eyes if his face turned just so. He hadn't shaved the front of his head recently—even from a distance, Ronan could see the fuzz. His tonsure was growing in.

He knew the man. Brendan of Clonfert. Once upon a time, when he still had happy days, Ronan had studied at Clonfert, though not under Brendan himself. Clonfert was up the river a far way. What was Brendan doing here? And then, vaguely, Ronan recalled that Brendan was born somewhere to the south of his monastery, in this area.

The sad woman shrugged. "The skeps are full this year. Might I have a hand with late wheat harvest?"

"We'll send you Boyd and Crosan," the monk named Brendan promised. "Rest now, pray thee, and join us for our evening meal. We shall regale you with further tales of our Lord's mercies toward His people in Israel."

She looked at him evenly. "I'd do with less of tales about His people in Israel and more of a little practical mercy toward His people in Erin." She led off her pony toward the lee of an abandoned stone wall.

A woman after Ronan's own heart!

"Why, who's this?" The little monk wheeled as the brindled dog bounced directly to him. The monk dropped to a squat, and the puppy, with only a moment's hesitation, approached the man's outstretched hand. A few brief sniffs, and the dog rolled over to get its stomach scratched.

Ronan gaped. In all the weeks that Troll tagged close behind him, eating his scraps and bread heels, never once did it come within touching distance of him. And there it lay squirming beneath the hand of a total stranger who hadn't fed it a single thing.

Now here came a giant of a monk toward Ronan. Burly of build and voice, the fellow lumbered like the fattest of oxen. His tonsure shone, or perhaps he was balding naturally in front. His fair hair was neatly trimmed behind, and Ronan could tell that were the wind not toying with it so fiercely it would be neatly brushed as well. Ronan knew this fellow too, though he could not recall the name.

The cheerful monster smiled broadly. "Boyd Blond Hair from Clonfert of Brendan." His voice rumbled, deep as a well.

"Of course. I remember now. And I recognize as Brendan the man with the natural affinity for dogs. Ronan, formerly of Skellig Michael. I began orders at Clonfert some years ago."

The giant's voice softened. "We're honored. What a twinkling star in God's bosom, the brethren on the Skelligs!" He wagged his considerable head. "I'm sorry I don't remember you, Brother Ronan, but I'm no good at names and faces. Join us. I'll introduce you to the others then."

Ronan smiled bitterly as they headed for the great curragh. "Look at that. The cur's not that friendly toward me, and I've been feeding it."

"You think yourself has no touch with dogs? At me, it will growl. Let me present you to Brendan."

Brendan stood up and smiled. The dog flipped instantly from back to feet and slunk around behind the little monk, its tail tucked tightly. It snarled as Ronan and Boyd approached.

With a foolish grin, Boyd spread his hands. "My point just made."

Ronan remembered the abbot well now, even after all these years. He remembered Brendan's crackling, happy eyes and vibrant smile. He remembered the exuberance even more than the slight, wispy build. Brendan must have shrunk—he had seemed a giant when Ronan first entered orders. He remembered too a fellow named Erc, older than rocks, who visited on one occasion. Why should he remember that?

Boyd Blond Hair rumbled through the presentation, and Ronan performed the appropriate obeisance due the abbot of a community no longer one's own, but his attention was already on the boat.

They had completed the oaken frame. Now one crew was steaming ash ribs as another applied them. This process always fascinated Ronan. To make something as hard as wood into something as flexible and whippy as these ribs; to bend them so and lash them down against the frame into unnatural shapes and curves; to see them return so quickly to their original rigidity— was amazing. Ash is hard enough but oak is worse, and the monks had similarly bent the oak frame into the long, graceful curves of the great curragh.

The boat skeleton amidships was doubly reinforced with secondary oak strips lashed against the primary framing. So they were going to step a fairly large mast and sail.

No coastal vessel, this. Deep-water sailing.

"Yes, I remember you. So you're on the Skellig now! Wonderful! Join us at our evening meal," Brendan was saying. "Your worn sandals tell me you've traveled long. Rest and abide with us awhile."

"I'll lend a hand, if 'tis a hand you need."

"And if we need one, we'll call upon you. By all means. What have you committed to memory?"

"Hosea, Joel, Amos, and part of Obadiah, so far."

"Excellent! Excellent! Boyd knows the whole of Job, and Malo recites Jonah, but I don't believe we have Joel at all, do we, Boyd?" And with a few further brief pleasantries, the monk returned to his boat building.

Boyd introduced Ronan to the others as the brother from the Skelligs, and Ronan knew he wasn't going to be able to remember all their names. Since neither the steamers nor the benders were falling behind, no helpful tasks presented themselves to him. He wandered off and settled himself against the wall, six feet from the strange, dark woman.

She had melted back against the uneven stones, her spine bowed, her eyes closed. She did not look at him as he sat down, although she surely heard him.

He contrasted the lively energy of Angelica with that of this drained and wearied woman. In fact, he found himself comparing her dark hair with Angelica's honey-colored tresses.

Lately he caught himself comparing everyone to Angelica. How silly. That brief episode in his life had passed.

The puppy made a pest of itself as it rollicked near Brendan and assiduously avoided the hulking Boyd. But the dog was not Ronan's. Let these stalwart brothers handle the problem, if a problem it was.

Ronan turned his attention to the woman and wondered at her ancestry, that her hair would be so dark, her skin so tanned. He watched her breathing. She was not asleep. He ventured, "Ronan, Skellig Michael."

She opened her eyes and languidly turned her head toward him. Nothing else about her moved. "Yes. I heard. Fanchea."

"Fanchea. Certainly not Enda's sister. She died."

"Don't be too sure I've not died. Who is Enda?"

"Brother-in-law of Oengus, high king of Cashel. Fanchea was the king's sister. She was a devout woman who thoroughly tamed the wild, warring Enda, they say. He now heads a highly respected monastery out in the Aran Isles. On Innishmore."

"No," she said quietly, "I'm not that one. My brother is a warrior, but, believe me, hell has conquered him. Strong ale and strange women."

"My sympathy."

She looked at him again with large, dark brown eyes. "Thank you. He's not ventured near our rath in a year. Three times I sent messengers begging his assistance. Apparently he's too busy."

"I'm not attached to a community at the moment. You mentioned needing help with your wheat harvest. I would like to."

She studied him for a long moment. "A blessing on you." The head returned to its position nestled, to use the term loosely, among two protruding rocks. The dark eyes closed.

"This Brendan failed to mention why he would build so sturdy a boat. He plans to travel afar?"

"To the Land of Promise."

"We're all going there eventually, Lord willing."

"But I believe he intends to come back."

Ronan grunted, marring the near silence. How does one respond to a notion so nonsensical?

Nonsensical but profoundly appealing. A land without aging or sorrow. Ronan could respond to that. In fact, he would jump at a chance to undertake such a journey. If you succeeded, you walked the Promised Land. If you failed, you died at sea and walked the Promised Land. A traveler on such a voyage couldn't lose.

Wearied, the dog settled beside the brother feeding the steamer's fire (what was the man's name? Crosan, as Ronan recalled, surnamed The Laughing Monk). The cur licked its paws a few minutes and subsided into a deep sleep.

"Ho! Brendan!" A baritone voice from up the track jarred Ronan back to wakefulness. Had that fellow not roared, he would not have realized he was drifting off.

"There he is! Conn!" Grinning, Brendan left off boat building to join the man. They met nearly in front of Ronan and the woman Fanchea. "What brings you down here?"

"The brethren. I have with me forty oak-tanned oxhides. The donkeys are half a mile behind me, and coming."

This Conn was, without equal, the most handsome young man Ronan had ever seen. His strong, masculine features—really quite an open, honest face—seemed chiseled as from wood. He carried himself like a prince. Quite possibly he was one.

"Good. Good! We're nearly ready for them." Brendan paused and frowned. "I was hoping your word would be that you have changed your mind. Better, that God changed it for you."

"Hardly." Conn smiled warmly. A most winsome smile it was. "I'm a farmer, Brendan, not a sailor. You know that. So does God, for all that. But I want to help build."

Over at the boat, one of the monks, a strong tenor, began the evening prayer office. A baritone picked up the counterpoint. In perfect rhythm, the rest joined the litany.

Grinning, Conn and Brendan rejoined the builders, singing a harmony to the litany. Together, the brethren sang it end to end in Greek, and never for a moment did the work of ribbing the boat slow down. With the final "thanks be to God," they completed the office by commencing a hymn in Latin.

The woman's voice beside him purred, "You are staring, Ronan of Skellig Michael."

He realized his mouth was still gaping open. His tongue felt dry. He twisted toward her. "I've never quite heard vespers done that way before. They were supposed to be gathered in an oratory, reverentially rendering worship."

"Work is as much worship as it is play. They're trying to make the most of the daylight."

"So they do this every day—this singing the offices as they work?"

"All but Sundays. On Sundays they do it as they walk the tracks from rath to rath, rendering assistance. They were by my rath two weeks ago and helped in the slaughter of two hogs."

Ronan's heart ached. Now and then a rath failed to summon hands enough to harvest grain, particularly if the yield was heavy. But there was only one reason that the people on her farm would need help with something as simple and basic as butchering hogs. "How many died in your rath?"

"Half the women, all but one of the men." A pause. "My children."

What could he say? There was not a rath in Erin that had not felt the sting of wave after wave of disease and other calamities these last few years. Her children. Her voice sounded so flat, so lifeless, as she said, simply, "My children."

"I heard you say your skeps are full. When were your bee-hives last attended?"

"The middle of last summer." She grimaced. "You should hear the old crones complain. Not that so many have died, or that we lack laborers for the harvest, but that no one's bringing in the honey."

"Ah. Of course." Ronan resettled himself back against the wall. "No mead for the long winter evenings."

"Or the short summer ones, for a' that." Her attitude, some-how, had softened. She turned her head to regard him again. "Isn't it strange? By and large, the strong died, and the weak ones still live. We've six left who are too feeble with age to work in the fields and but two able-bodied adults—myself and Alain, my hus-band's brother."

55

"And no one to bring the rest of the honey in."

She almost smiled. Almost.

He closed his eyes. "It's been many a year since I last waved a smudge pot or stole a honeycomb from the noble bee." He didn't ask her permission to help. He simply said, "And I look forward to it."

8
Brendan

Scudding up the wave and down the wind, they mounted toward the lowering sky. The wind shrieking like banshees. Waves as high as mountains. The water towering before and behind in massive piles. The curragh, which had seemed so mighty as they were building her ashore, now appeared the size of a flea on a horse. It had about as much control of destiny as did a flea on a horse too.

From the bow Brendan screamed, "Don't let us breach! Don't let us breach!" As if Boyd and Mochta back here on the tiller would deliberately let their boat swing sideways. What? Did Brendan think Boyd might idly try it out of curiosity to see what would happen? Boyd already knew what would happen. Should this curragh be tossed sidewise to the waves, the sea would flip them and dump them and roll the boat over and over. They would all be lost, this far from land.

Boyd braced himself against the framing to port and shoved one extended leg against the framing to starboard. He wrapped both arms around the oaken tiller, pressing it against his belly with his elbows, to keep their nose pointed upslope.

On the other side of the tiller, Mochta locked his hands and forearms against the bar and braced against a crate he had jammed hard into the stern gunwales. He looked very, very weary. And terrified.

Frigid seawater had soaked Boyd's woolen cassock. His cowl was so heavy with water that it half choked him as it hung down his back. He couldn't feel his fingers. The howling wind skimming in behind them whipped up the lacy spindrift on the sea surface and flung it into the curragh. The salt burned his cheeks.

They sailed to the crest of another mountainous wave. The curragh's bow thrust up out of the water completely, pointed skyward, as the sea fell away before them. Her ribs creaked. With a loud crack, a stick snapped somewhere. The curragh's leather skin groaned mightily as it stretched and rubbed. The boat was literally bending, supported aft by water, suspended afore in air. Balanced amidships on the knife-edged top of the wave, now she plunged nose downward, dropping like a stone onto the steep downslope. The tiller popped out of the sea as the stern swung upward.

Boyd yelled, "Stroke! Stroke!" The tiller's sudden release nearly dumped him on the deck.

Mochta cried out and lurched forward.

Twelve fearstruck men dipped their oars deep and hauled away. Only the oars could keep their course true now. Then they were sliding wildly down the wave slope, the tiller bit into the water, and Boyd could right their course again. The minuscule, mere dot of a craft raced down the wave before the wind, skidded out across the long, long trough, and began her climb up the next mountain.

A death-defying ride over a tumultuous wave is one thing. Doing it over and over and over for seven hours straight is quite another. Boyd's only rest came in the troughs, when he could hold the tiller true simply by collapsing across it and letting his weight do the work. Worst of all, he could not be replaced. If they would keep from breaching, the massive, bull-strong Boyd had to remain one of the two brothers on the helm.

Seven hours? No, a considerable portion of a lifetime! Scripture told how God made the sun stand still that Joshua might complete a battle. But why was He making the sun stand still now, to no purpose whatever save Boyd's abject misery?

Curiously, though, cresting the next wave seemed a bit less terrifying. Had the wind slacked somewhat? It no longer slung spindrift into Boyd's face quite so viciously. By slow, casual degrees, the storm was abating, though the waves piled up as high as ever.

Forward in the prow, Brendan shipped his twelve-foot-long oar. He came staggering aft, for the deck still heaved despite the slackening wind. He stepped in behind Boyd and gripped the tiller firmly. "Rest, brother."

No second invitation was necessary. Boyd abandoned the tiller for the first time in two watches and lurched forward. The oarsmen sat on sea chests along either gunwale. Brendan had carefully balanced them, that man in that position, this man in this place, to maintain trim. Brendan thought of everything. Down the center line, but for a narrow walkway, they stowed their cooking and sleeping gear.

Boyd did not bother to seek out the roll of sheepskins on which he usually slept. He flopped down upon the first sheepskins he came to and didn't care whose they were. Gentle hands—Griann's?—covered him with a spare wool cloak and a few more sheepskins. It took more than one sheep to protect a man the size of Boyd. He closed his eyes.

Sometime later he opened them. What time was it? Through a thin mist, the first quarter moon rode high. He crept out from under his pile of covers, carefully stepped over the mounds of sheepskin that were other sleeping brothers, and worked a tortuous path to the rail.

The sea had calmed down greatly. The waves they rode now swelled to no more than six or eight feet, trough to crest, and they mounded over, round-topped. It was a sea you could live with. The wind cut more or less at right angles to their course, the linen sail twisted hard aslant.

Boyd listened for night birds. But for the slosh of breaking waves on the bow, and the constant creaking of their vessel, nothing stirred.

He followed the gunwale to the stern, trying to step over sea chests without kicking them and causing too much noise. The constant clunks and rattles reminded him that a graceful man he was not. He settled in against the stern by the tiller opposite Brendan.

The happy seafarer smiled at him in the sallow filtered moonlight. "Riding out that storm put us well to sea. We're headed back now."

"How do you know? The darkness looks all alike to me."

"The position of the moon. And three major stars poked their noses through the mist an hour ago. Regulus rising, Capella and Aldebaran setting. Home is that way." He pointed forward.

"I shall take your word for it." Boyd leaned back against the gunwale framing and stretched mightily. He felt much refreshed, and that surprised him, as utterly wearied as he had been when he lay down. "Any sign of ripping?"

"None. Every stitch of our linen cord has been holding secure. No major rubbing, no tears, no structural defects. This shakedown voyage must be considered an unqualified success."

Boyd nodded happily. He thought briefly about the hundreds of hours he and the others had spent sewing oxhides together and stretching them across the ash ribbing. It had taken three brothers working together to pull the skins taut, hold their top edges against the whipping, and stitch them securely in place. Indeed, it required two strong men just to sew the hides together—one to force an awl puncture and the other, on the opposite side, to quickly press a bronze needle through the new hole before it closed up. To suffer through all those months for naught would have been discouraging to the extreme.

On the other hand, he utterly detested riding out a storm. He wished the boat could have been tried out in some less violent way.

He pondered for a few minutes the wind direction and the time of year and the direction Brendan had pointed not long ago. "We're not going directly home. Right?"

"Very good. I was thinking of calling at Iona. Ask Columcille's blessing on us, since we're so close."

"So Enda's blessing was not sufficient?"

Brendan grinned sheepishly. "You can't be too rich or too blessed."

"Pick up more men for the journey? Fourteen backs, however strong, may not be enough if you run into many storms like this last one. You need a few more souls."

Not we. You. Did Brendan catch the significance?

Apparently not. He shrugged. "Eighteen to twenty would be better, I agree. The fact that Crosan declined at the last moment to come along doesn't bother me. The Lord will work with what we have. I'm not worried."

You ought to worry. You'll not have me to help you on your next voyage. One day soon Boyd would have to voice that thought aloud. Now did not seem the time or place. He snorted. "Easy for you to say. You didn't haul on the tiller for eight hours straight."

Down inside, Boyd was glad Crosan had elected to remain ashore. Raths all around that area were short-handed, Fanchea's in particular, and, frankly, Boyd didn't trust that Ronan. The man may have been one of the brothers from Skellig Michael, but he was *from* Skellig Michael. The question nagged at Boyd—why did the man not remain on the Skellig? And besides, the somber monk seemed furtive, or depressed, or both. Crosan could keep an eye on things.

Brendan chuckled. There was a glow about his face. He was of the sea in the same way that seals and gannets and puffins are of the sea—comfortable anywhere upon the waters at any time. He was made for this.

Boyd did not get seasick the way several of the brethren did (in fact, three brothers were hanging over the bow gunwale this very minute). Still, he did not feel the same easy comfort that Brendan obviously did. A constant queasiness plagued him whenever he left solid land. But that was the least of it, really. In fact, the taxing drudgery of manning the tiller so long did not loom as a major factor either. He could not tell why he determined to turn his back on this life. But he did.

"Brendan, brother? Do you think your journey in search of Hi Brasil will take a long time?"

"If Barrind's remarks be accurate, and the Delightful Isle as close to the Promised Land as it would seem, far less than a season."

"Good. Good." Boyd would, Lord willing, remain ashore, but he did not relish a lengthy voyage studded with storms for anyone. Not even for Brendan the Happy Seafarer. He straightened and frowned. "Now what have we out there?"

Brendan stood erect and squinted in the darkness. "A blue martyr, I'd essay."

Boyd had heard of such often, but never had he seen one. These were the men of the faith who turned themselves loose upon the sea to be carried where'er God willed. No tiller, no intent. Foolish, foolish monks, to waste themselves on this hostile sea when they could be doing such glorious things on land!

Brendan halloed. Three piles of sheepskin on the deck stirred. But there was silence, except for the gurgling, slapping conversation between wave and boat hull and the constant creak of hundreds of lashed joints.

Brendan and Boyd drew against the tiller together, a matched set of like mind. That kind of unity always pleased Boyd. Their curragh dipped against the leading sea and heeled sharply.

The night was not black—nights rarely are. Sullen grays spread from horizon to horizon, deep grays and dark. The overarching gray, mildly pearlescent, now hid the moon and stars. The other gray, virtually featureless, heaved sinuously. It alternately hid a black blob, then revealed it.

Their new course carried them in beside that black blob within the quarter hour. As they closed on it, Boyd attempted in vain to make out a sail.

"To oars," Brendan called. He staggered forward to the bow as the men on watch took up oars. Boyd resumed his old, familiar place at the tiller.

Sleekly, gracefully (Boyd prided himself in his ability to exactly place a curragh's bow just about anywhere he wished), they moved in alongside the black blob, so closely that the port oarsmen shipped their oars. Mochta tossed over a hook to engage the blob's forward brace. Boyd secured the blob's tiller aft with a light line. The blob took form in the gray as a dainty fishing boat.

Brendan's craft dwarfed the tiny curragh. It couldn't be more than ten feet long. Not only did it sport no mast and sail, it possessed no oars. Wrapped in sheepskins, a man in a Roman tonsure sat cross-legged amidships. He scowled at Brendan's curragh and at Brendan himself.

By now all of Brendan's thirteen monks stood about wide awake. Apparently, finding a fellow voyager out here in nowhere was powerful incentive for giving up a night's repose. They lined the near rail and shooed their companions to the far rail to trim the lolling craft.

Brendan greeted the fellow cheerily in Latin.

The fellow glared. Lowering, he snarled, "You're interfering with God's purposes in my life. Sail on."

"What are His purposes, pray thee?"

"They are His to know, not yours. He will deliver me on a foreign shore or consign me to the deeps, but whatever His intent, it certainly is not to board your vessel."

"You were not invited to board, friend of God. Mochta? I perceive he has no capacity for cooking aboard. Dig out that boiled lamb and barley meal, pray thee, and wrap it in an oilskin. Cooked food shall be our portion to him."

"I'll not accept," the fellow blustered. "God's will may well be that I starve. No."

"Indeed, it may well be, my dear saint—"

"Beautiful are the deaths of His saints. Sail on."

"But on the other hand, He may be intending you to dine upon lamb and barley meal. I seriously doubt that we would cross paths with you on the endless expanse of these wild seas if God did not ordain it. With whose monastery are you attached?"

"No one's."

Boyd's mind boggled. He could not imagine a monk's taking off on a commitment of this magnitude without the prayer cover of a monastery—preferably a large one. You entered a brotherhood and, on occasion, you departed from a brotherhood, but always you sought the brotherhood's common will and blessing. It was your security. No one went forth alone, any more than one would try to live outside the protection of a clan. Even Brendan, himself an abbot and a leader of the church, sought the blessing of others. Indeed, they were on their way to Iona for that very thing.

"That has ended, beautiful friend," Brendan called. He could put the ring of heavenly authority in his voice when he had to. He helped Mochta lower the oilskin into the fellow's curragh. "You are now under the aegis of Brendan of Clonfert. Go in peace." The moment his hands were free he signed the cross, blessing the man in both Latin and Greek.

Perplexed, the voyaging brother stared at the oilskin bundle before him.

"Friend?" Boyd called. "With no sail and no oars, however did you survive the storm in that little curragh?"

The monk looked up. His Roman tonsure looked ridiculous. A ring of shaggy hair encircled his head. After cutting his hair around the sides to resemble a little thatched roof, he had shaved it bald on top. "It was the will of God and nothing else," he replied. "I prostrated myself in prayer, and He delivered me."

His tone of voice suggested he didn't really need Brendan's help or blessing in this adventure. This was interesting. The man suffered no struggle against the elements and yet had not capsized. Just let the boat bob. The hand of God be praised.

The wandering monk cast off Mochta's line and the landing hook. The vessels drifted apart. As soon as they cleared, Brendan ordered his oars into the water to pull away. They reset the sail. The curragh ceased lolling and moved forward with sturdy purpose.

Brendan took over the tiller.

Boyd watched the gray skies a few moments. "Brendan, friend, how do you know which way we're going with the moon and stars now obscured?"

Brendan grinned wickedly. "God's purposes, Boyd friend. God's purposes."

God's purposes. Brendan was not a man who mocked. He was, however, a man who knew the sea and winds and currents and clouds and birds and . . .

Boyd dismissed the puzzle as a problem for the morrow. He curled up in his sheepskins and went back to sleep.

9

Crosan

The smoke boiled up around Ronan and made his eyes burn so badly he could not see. He coughed. He choked. His nose dripped. Once upon a time, he had been good at this skill of manipulating fire and bees. Today he was botching it. He gave up. Hacking and gagging, he set down his smoke pot and staggered backward from the hive.

"Allow me, brother," offered a familiar voice beside him.

Ronan still could not see. "Crosan? You keep bees?"

"I keep many things," came the rich and lilting voice.

Crosan the Clown, Crosan the Laughing Monk, interested Ronan in the same way cockfighting interested him—with morbid fascination. Never still a moment, Crosan rollicked through life with the same élan and artlessness as the brindled pup. At one time a jester in the court at Meath, Crosan had accompanied his deceased king to burial at Clonmacnois and simply remained there as a monk when the rest of the entourage went home. From the monastic settlement, he somehow moved to Clonfert (details about this were sketchy, as Ronan recalled), and now Crosan worked at the building of a great curragh—that is, when he was not helping the widow Fanchea harvest late wheat.

A simple story and not unusual—so why did Ronan feel on edge whenever this wise fool ventured near? Why did Crosan's boundless good cheer grate so on his nerves? Why should Ronan detect the hint of a sinister core beneath the jester's veneer of gaiety? And Ronan seemed to be the only person to do so.

Though his nose still ran like the Shannon, Ronan's eyes had cleared enough now that he could watch Crosan as the Laughing Monk took over.

"I keep the faith," warbled the irritating lark. "I keep the peace. I keep trying. I keep my own counsel. I keep the feasts,

Christmas and Easter foremost. I keep out of trouble. And at Clonmacnois I kept bees." In the stone bowl of the smudge pot, Crosan stirred a wad of damp grass about in the burning fat, rejuvenating the smoke. He held the pot high aloft in his left hand as with his right he gently tipped one of half a dozen skeps sitting along the margin of the meadow.

Skeps always seemed so illogical to Ronan. Why would bees want to live in a conical basket two feet high and turned upside down? And yet, each skep housed a whole colony. No. Not so. Leaves and autumn debris had blown up against the bases of two of the six skeps here. Bees are very tidy housekeepers. They never allow debris to accumulate around the base of an active hive. Therefore these two skeps were abandoned—and safe to enter.

Crosan waved his smudge pot beneath the upturned lip of his skep, filling it with smoke. With a happy chuckle he lifted the basket and began cutting away the laden honeycomb inside. One comb for men, one for the bees. One comb for men, one for the bees. Take a little, leave a little, that the colony might have food enough to survive the drab and flowerless winter.

Ronan lifted one of the two abandoned skeps. He found four small combs. He punched into a cell of one and tasted its dark amber sweetness. Still good. He took all four.

He mused aloud, "Few of God's creatures are busier and more active than bees. I wonder why smoke is so effective in rendering them quiescent."

Crosan cackled. "It worked on you well enough."

Ronan fought a quick battle with anger and immediately lost. "I've never heard a bee cough, but then I've never listened closely." Embarrassed and provoked, he raided the second abandoned skep of its three small combs and stood about uselessly as Crosan completed his conquest of the job at hand.

They combined the harvest—Crosan's bounty and Ronan's seven small bits of comb—into two large oilskin-lined baskets. They ran their carrying pole through the baskets' corded slings. Crosan probably would have left the smudge pot behind had Ronan not scooped it up. Crosan took the front end of the pole and Ronan the nether end, and away they went, headed back the track toward Fanchea's rath.

The baskets were not well centered on the pole, so that Crosan carried far less of the weight than did Ronan. Between keeping the pole from cutting his shoulder in two, and keeping the smudge pot from igniting his cloak tails, Ronan was dearly wishing he had stayed with the wheat reaping.

A sort of symbolism seemed to be involved here as well, and Ronan didn't like it. Crosan led. Ronan followed. Crosan would be first to greet whomever met them at the gate. Ronan the tagalong could but wave from the rear. No, he couldn't even do that, with the pole in one hand and the smudge pot in the other.

By the noisy rill that clambered down a steep crease in the slope, Conn joined them. Conn, the handsome one. Conn, fresh from Clonfert. Conn who claimed to be a farmer and was therefore sent out into the countryside while the others tried out the new curragh. Although he had been sickling grain all day, he didn't appear the least weary. Ronan envied him.

Conn might be a farmer but more so he fancied himself a poet. Why he became a monk instead of a fileh, Ronan did not know, for Conn's poetry was actually rather good. It made Ronan uncomfortable whenever Conn started quoting stanzas in front of Fanchea.

Fanchea's rath, like most farms, perched like a small round crown on the brow of the hill. Grainfields and meadows lay like blankets on the hillside around the farm's ringwall. Brush fences and barricades, some woven of thin withes, some simply piles of branches, kept cattle and sheep out of the grain. The three men left the level track along the base of the hill and commenced their climb up toward the wall.

Conn shook his well-groomed head. "Most people would have had their late wheat in two months ago. Longer. These poor people were so late getting the seed into the ground, they've scant harvest. The grain heads didn't fill well at all."

"Will they get anything?" Ronan thought about the dark-eyed Fanchea putting in an entire wheatfield virtually unaided. The miracle was that they managed to plant the seed at all.

Did Angelica ever work the fields? They had conversed at great length on the sea voyage from Pictland to Erin, she and Ronan, and she talked about her father's penchant for hiring lazy workers, but she never mentioned working herself. She was probably the daughter of a boaire of high status. She had that elegance about her.

"Enough for stirabout, like as not," Conn said. "Not much seed-quality grain. I finished shocking it. Tomorrow we can bring it in." He studied the overcast, no doubt gauging the position of the sun behind it. "About time for vespers." He launched into the litany of evening prayer in Latin. A magnificent voice, the lad had—a rich tenor, reaching high and yet ringing strongly in mid range. He enunciated every syllable clearly, as befits a poet.

Crosan chimed in behind him, and Ronan picked up the litany rather listlessly. This was supposed to be worship, sung to God from the very heart. He was fortunate to remember the words. He did far better with Greek. He found himself depending upon Conn's smooth Latin to get him through it. Were Conn to blunder, Ronan's contribution would collapse.

But Conn did not blunder. No surprise that. They were finishing the kyrie as they entered the ringwall gate.

Ronan glanced about, wondering if Fanchea were close at hand. He didn't see her. She was probably inside the small, cone-roofed house, although she did little other than heavy fieldwork. An aged crone had just milked a black cow by the gate. The old woman abandoned the oaken milk pail—left it sitting in the dirt—and hastened over to the great baskets of honey.

"Set it down right here. Right here." She peered eagerly into the baskets at the stacks of honeycomb, and her eyes crackled as brightly as her voice. "Good. Good. I just happened to crush some apples this afternoon, and you know how quickly apple-must goes bad."

Ronan left off singing the office to smile. "When you heard we would tend the hives today, aye?"

"By chance. By chance. And I dug out the mead pots from under the wall, as it happens. I shall fetch the comb knife." Crippled and bent, she scurried away. Her pail of milk sat forlorn and forgotten. The black cow, its part in the day's routine completed, wandered out the gate.

More symbolism: Here came Fanchea bringing in fuel. Just as she entered the gate, the setting sun broke through a crack between the cloud cover and the far sea horizon. It washed her in a rich peach glow that gave her skin the vivid beauty of an earth goddess. She let her huge bundle of brushwood slide to the ground from her shoulders.

Ronan's voice faltered, and that was stupid. He was nearly into his forties now and certainly not subject to the kind of idle mooning that a young swain might suffer. He wasn't taken by her in the least. Ah, but sure and she was beautiful in this light, with her black hair and dark eyes.

He wondered what Angelica's honey hair would look like thus illumined.

Crosan abandoned the evening prayer litany. "Behold! Fair Etain!" He bounded over to her in exactly the same manner as would the brindled pup. "Lady," he crowed, "the bounty of the bees has come to you. Oh, but look! One of the bees, enthralled with your beauty, has accompanied its bounty to your door." He reached out to her and from a fold in her cloak plucked a living bee. In a dramatic flourish, he opened his hand. Drowsy with autumn lethargy, the bee crept out across his flat palm, paused, and lifted off.

Fanchea gazed after the departing insect, rapt. The first smile Ronan had ever seen from her spread softly across her face.

Ronan wanted to scream, *Don't be swayed by a simple sleight of hand, Fanchea! This man was for years a court jester! An entertainer. A clown!*

The office of evening prayer ended abruptly, halfway through. Conn fell silent, frowning. "How did you do that? There are no bees abroad in this weather!"

But Crosan was already into his next illusion, pouring a handful of damp wheat out of her sleeve. She stared at the sleeve, at the Laughing Monk. Her whole face brightened as that first feeble smile took hold and grew stronger and crinkled her eyes. In one long moment she lost ten years off her appearance.

It's a trick, lady. It's not magic—it's mere amusement.

Even as Ronan was shouting his warnings in his mind, another part of his mind pulled his thoughts up short. *This is the first time you have ever seen anyone break her pall of sorrow. Look at her! The smile. The peace. Do you have that effect on her? She lost her husband and three children in the space of two years. What a heavy burden for any person to bear! If simple sleight of hand can bring a ray of pleasure, who are you to begrudge her?*

Here came the doddering oldwife with a butcher knife and a clay pot. "A fine lot of honey, Fanchea, do you see?" She settled herself on the damp ground beside the baskets and began the messy, arduous task of removing the honey from the comb. The prospect of well-fermented mead, obviously, provides powerful incentive indeed.

Now Crosan was explaining to Fanchea how hard he and Conn worked this day, cutting and shocking wheat, and how he afterward helped with the skeps. He described how much they had accomplished. He promised that on the morrow they would take out the pony cart and begin the fetching in of her grain. His narrative failed to include Ronan. As he babbled on, he scooped up her bundle of brushwood and dumped it over by the door. He turned back this way and froze, open-mouthed.

Ronan twisted to look toward the gate. He tried to speak, to say something casual, and he could not.

It was Angelica.

She looked ragged as a beggar and twice as woebegone. Her lovely hair drooped. Her face drooped. She pulled a battered cloak close around her, her arms buried in wool, as if she were eternally cold.

In nowise stunned, Troll the brindled pup bounded over to her eagerly. He went readily to anyone except Ronan—or Boyd.

Fanchea gathered up her skirts and crossed the yard promptly. With a pleasant smile she welcomed the honey-haired sojourner as if it were the most natural thing in the world for a foreign woman to show up at her gate.

And then Ronan realized that Angelica was just as dumbstruck as he.

She found her tongue before he did. "Ronan!"

Fanchea looked at her, at him. "Oh. You two know each other?"

Crosan leaped into action before Ronan could get his mouth or his legs to move. The Laughing Monk strode smartly over and scooped up Angelica's hand in his. "Crosan of Clonfert, ready at your service, fair lady." His kissed her lovely knuckles.

70

Ronan had never before seen that gesture. It fascinated and appalled him. Such familiarity.

"Angelica." Her voice faltered, poised teetering on a ridge between propriety and terror. Her blue eyes flicked to Ronan.

He finally got himself in motion and crossed to her. "Why aren't you at Kildare?"

"He's here, Ronan, on Irish soil. Mac Larkin. He traced me to Kildare. I barely escaped." Her voice tumbled off the brink into terror and nearly dissolved as the words rushed forth, crowding each other. "He'll find me, Ronan, and kill me! Kill us! He deduced it was you—I think he knows it was you—and he wants to kill you too. That's what a farmer said outside Kildare. Mac Larkin put the word out that the King of the Picts is here to reclaim his bride and there's a reward for me . . . for your head . . . oh, Ronan!"

She collapsed against him and commenced sobbing. He wrapped his arms around her because he didn't know what else to do.

Fanchea stared. "Kildare? She traveled all the way from Kildare?"

"Which is why her skirt hem is snagged and torn and her shoes wore out a hundred miles ago." Ronan arched back to see her better. "And I'm sorry you lost your cat."

She giggled through her tears and stepped back. "You were never very happy with my kitty. This may not be good news for you." She withdrew her arm from her shawl. Her cat, that miserable cat, looking just as frail and trailworn as she, curled in the crook of her arm.

"What a lovely thing!" Fanchea reached out to scoop up the cat. "We just happen to have fresh milk. May I?"

"Of course." Angelica instantly released her pet into arms as loving as hers, it would appear.

Ronan smiled briefly in spite of himself. "Angelica, you've crossed the breadth of Erin, from coast to coast. He surely won't be expecting that. Do you have any reason to suspect he knows you're out here?"

"I don't know." Her face immediately melted into that look of sorrowful terror. "How did he find me before? I'm not safe anywhere in the world."

"You're safe here, lovely lady." Crosan could afford an easy bit of bravado. It wasn't he who took the blow from the butt of Mac Larkin's sword, or who ripped out a palisade, or fled a foreign country. From the folds of her cloak, from nowhere, Crosan plucked a late-season aster.

Her mouth dropped open. For the moment her fear disappeared. If the man weren't a monk, Ronan would swear he was flirting with the women.

Ronan had seen no wives in the neighborhood of the boat-building project, but that didn't mean there were none. Some monasteries made full provision for spouses, others tolerated them, and a growing number refused to recognize marriage as being acceptable for men and women devoted fully to God.

Ronan had never occasioned to ask about the rules of marriage at Brendan's Clonfert. He must do so at the first opportunity. If Brendan allowed wives, Crosan's bravado and his little magic tricks represented much, much more than idle entertainment.

10

Troll

She walked in glory. Her touch healed and gladdened. When she spoke, beauty sang new songs.

Angelica.

He curled up against her legs now, lying on one of her delicate and lovely bare feet, and licked between his hind toes. Her knees drawn up, she sat under the wych elm hard beside Fanchea's east gate as she carded wool.

Troll never did like the smells of sheep and wool, not since they beat him with a club for chasing lambs. But when she reached down idly and scratched him behind the ears, Troll quickly and immediately forgave the vague lanolin smell on her graceful hand. He would forgive anything about her, anything at all, even the lingering odor of that hideous cat. His tail thumped in the damp dirt.

Here came the Laughing Monk up from the track. Troll eagerly accepted the frequent goodies Crosan proffered, though apparently no tidbits would be forthcoming today.

Crosan chuckled and commented that the brindled dog seemed to have found a friend.

Her lilting voice cooed a word of praise about Troll. That perfumed hand scratched him again behind the ears. His tail thumped harder.

On the far side of Angelica, Crosan dropped to a tight squat, balanced on the balls of his feet. Crosan possessed much better coordination than did most human males. He chuckled again and averred how much he enjoyed working on Fanchea's rath. The false note hidden deep at the back of his voice made Troll listen with greater caution. Troll knew when truth was being spoken and when falsehood. Dogs always do. Humans did not seem to possess that particular discernment.

When Angelica averred how much she valued her refuge here, no hint of falsity or overstatement showed through.

Crosan the coordinated one started to tilt off balance. He steadied himself by reaching out and bracing with a hand on Angelica's knee.

Instantly she pushed him away. He tipped back and sat down heavily, laughing. The abruptness of her move startled Troll. He rolled up onto his belly. She had tensed, and that put him on edge also. He moved off a few feet—a precautionary measure even though he could not imagine her raising a hand against him. Still, his prior master had demonstrated a marked inclination to kick the nearest thing whenever he became upset, and too many times Troll the puppy had happened to be the nearest thing.

Angelica and the Laughing Monk exchanged words—hers guarded, his carrying that dual ring of gaiety and falsity. She rose smoothly to her feet. Crosan clambered to his. Troll edged back a bit farther. He intended to stay well out of kicking distance. Neither of them seemed to notice him.

Angelica started to move away. Crosan blocked her path, crooning false words in low, dulcet tones. There was an urgency to his manner that disturbed Troll. Apparently it disturbed Angelica as well, for her voice rose.

With one finger, Crosan traced a line across the neck of her garment, from shoulder to shoulder. She swatted his hand away, speaking sharply. Very sharply.

Should Troll growl, reflecting Angelica's disturbed attitude, or should he slink off? It's not wise for dogs, even very worldly-wise dogs, to meddle too closely in the affairs of men.

Angelica pushed past Crosan, roughly shoving him aside, and marched away down the trail toward the wheat-stubble field. Troll dismissed the tension in the air and bounded cheerily ahead. He loved going down to the wheat-stubble field. So many intriguing smells lingered in the disturbed soil there. Hares, red squirrels, and badgers crisscrossed the field seeking out fallen grain. Foxes and stoats moved through there as well, no doubt seeking out hares, squirrels, and possibly even badgers.

Crosan, skipping nimbly, caught up to Angelica and fell into step beside her. He talked about winter solstice, and druids pouring out the sacrificial blood of children. Troll paid scant attention to the people-talk. Red deer had moved through here recently, leaving tantalizing spoor.

Angelica talked about the tragedy of child sacrifice, for Jesus had already paid all forever.

Crosan replied about this sacrifice having something to do with the turn of the season rather than souls, but Troll was thrusting his head into a particularly aromatic clump of gorse and didn't bother to discern the speech. Troll sat down then and curled around until with his hind leg he could scratch his itching ear. He shook his head, listening to his own ears flap wildly, and continued on down the track ahead of his queen.

His nose told him Ronan had passed this way recently. That was all right. Troll knew Ronan would just as soon eat him as not, but he admired the man anyway. Ronan could be depended upon to share what he had. The man treated Troll like a dog. Troll related comfortably to that. He liked Ronan for that reason. On the other hand, he didn't have any reason to dislike the giant Boyd. He just did.

Here was fresh squirrel scent! Troll bounded forward. He spied a quick small form in the duff ahead, heard it rustling. A squirrel bolted and flowed up a low oak.

Troll gathered himself, lunged mightily, and hit the tree trunk four feet off the ground. With teeth and claw he scrambled to the first limb, hooked his legs over it, and hauled himself up. He stood on his hind legs on the first limb reaching for the second, but already the squirrel had danced out on a rattling branch and leaped to another tree.

"Troll!" Angelica stood on the track, laughing brightly.

Troll sensed her delight, and it pleased him. He hung his nose over the side with all four feet close together, hesitated until he could wait no longer, and dropped to the ground. He didn't mind climbing trees. He dreaded leaving them. He ran to her side and bounded off ahead of them again.

The trail divided, one way going to the wheat-stubble field and the other toward the copse. Troll heard an ax chucking, beyond in the copse. Crosan and Angelica probably did not—human ears are worth little when it comes to really finding out what goes on. He smelled that Ronan had walked out in this direction. No doubt he was cutting wood in the copse. That activity delighted Troll also. As woodcutters brought down trees and brush, clearing the woodland floor, interesting birds and animals flushed out. Every now and then, by hanging in close to woodcutters, Troll could lunch on hare.

With a double bend, the track descended into a little dell thick with oak and hazel. Marvelous! Coppiced hazel almost always offers ample opportunity to put up a hare.

Troll glanced over his shoulder. He didn't want to range too far from Angelica, especially on this winding trail.

Crosan was describing how the gentry—the spirits of the past who live within the hills—slip out of their deep-earth lairs over the winter solstice to walk among men and perchance to play a trick or two. Troll paid no attention. As humans have very little sense of hearing and next to no sense of smell at all, so do they enjoy very little ability to discern spirits.

Troll knew when spirits roamed abroad, and they made him exceedingly nervous. Angelica and Fanchea's Holy Spirit, in contrast, gave him a good feeling. He discerned it in the two women and in some others—Brendan and Ronan in particular. It resided in Boyd as well, but Boyd irritated Troll nonetheless.

Angelica discussed the protection of the Holy Spirit. Troll knew all that. Ah! A boar had passed this way, probably yesterday. Here is where it dug about, churning up the loose dirt by the trackside. The low scrubby bushes were nearly rooted out of the ground.

Troll stopped. He stood at attention, his ears up, watching Angelica. Crosan had gripped her arm. He was speaking rapidly and earnestly in low tones. She shook her head and tried to pull free. He held her closer, talking, talking.

With the back of his mind, Troll listened to the ax in the copse beyond. He was certain from their attitudes that neither Angelica nor Crosan detected it.

Crosan pressed his muzzle against Angelica's.

Angelica squirmed away. She shouted, "No!"

Troll both heard and smelled the fear in his beloved queen. What Crosan was doing or why did not concern him. Her reaction to it did.

The dog bolted forward, snarling. Never before had he threatened a human being. Wise little dogs avoid that sort of angry confrontation. Troll threw wisdom to the wind. With a furious growl, he leaped at Crosan's face. Troll had not thought out what to do once he reached the man's face, but his leap failed to carry him that high, so it didn't really matter.

Screaming, Angelica fell back, lost her footing, and sprawled on the track. In the same instant, Crosan yelled and flung up his arms to shield his head.

As he dropped, Troll felt his teeth rake Crosan's thigh. The dog didn't leap again. He stood, braced solidly, his throat growling and his teeth bared, between Angelica and the furious, frightened monk. The nape of his neck tingled and prickled. The dog felt a certain heady exhilaration as Crosan took a stumbling step backward.

The monk shouted at Troll to go away. The puppy in Troll—and Troll still had a great deal of puppy inside—wanted to break and run immediately, obeying the voice of someone who would as soon kick him as look at him. The grown male dog in Troll held his ground and barked fiercely.

Troll no longer smelled fear in his Angelica behind him. The crisis must be past. She shouted loudly at Crosan to go away, just as Crosan had yelled at Troll. Angry, Crosan feinted toward Troll. Puppy won out over dog. Troll tucked his tail and ducked aside.

Then he heard footfalls off toward the copse. Ronan was running in this direction, but neither Angelica nor Crosan appeared to hear him coming. Crosan approached Angelica, and the smell of fear returned to her.

Troll didn't know what to do. As much as he wanted to protect his queen, he felt uncertain about tackling the quick and clever monk. The man shouted much too loudly to be harmless.

Crosan pulled Troll's queen up against him and shoved his muzzle against her neck. Then Ronan arrived, all sweaty and panting, ax in hand, and roaring.

Crosan let go of Angelica and twisted around. His demeanor changed instantly from anger to caution. Troll's changed from fear and confusion to wariness and confusion. He did not trust Ronan, but Angelica seemed to. She scrambled to her feet, begging Ronan not to chop up the Laughing Monk.

Crosan spread his hands. He assured them both that they had misread his intentions. He urged them to destroy this unpredictable dog who attacked without provocation. Then he promised to destroy the dog himself.

Angelica and Ronan together threatened Crosan with bodily harm should he try to hurt Troll. Troll was much too excited to make absolute sense out of the heated verbal exchange. But he could pick up the good feelings of those two and the ill feeling in Crosan.

Shrugging, protesting, pleading, Crosan backed away and, at Angelica's insistence, turned back up the track toward the rath.

Angelica dropped to her knees and called to Troll. Basking in her recognition, he tumbled in against her. Her touch! Ah, her touch! Those elegant hands rubbed him behind his ears and scratched his neck where it tended to itch a lot, as her perfumed voice spoke his praises over and over.

Angelica rose to her feet then, and she and Ronan began walking uphill toward the rath. They talked together in soft voices for a few moments, and Troll detected greater and greater tension in his queen. She stopped. She buried her face in her hands and began to sob. Troll stood helplessly by, unable to decide how to comfort her.

Ronan seemed to suffer the same dilemma. He flapped his arms about inanely. Then, very cautiously, as if she were a cracked egg that threatened any moment to break completely, he drew his arms around her. She sank against him.

Troll would have paid the matter better thought, but just then a hare squirted straight out of a brush pile beside the track. Away it bounded up the hill.

Overjoyed at the prospect of the chase, Troll took off after it. There is no pleasure in life greater than to catch a hare.

And he was certain his wonderful queen would surely be the first to agree.

11
Willis

Willis Gray Mantle despised manual labor, and he was buried up to his armpits in it. He abhorred idle philosophy, and his ears ached from being endlessly assaulted by it. He detested religion, and he was constantly assailed by ideas that crazy monk Desmond insisted were nothing less than the very words of God Himself.

In short, Willis's whole life tumbled about him, out of control, as if he were a leaf being swept down a dashing mountain freshet. Willis would quit this region in a heartbeat, to ply his preferred trade of economic redistribution in some other clan's district, if it weren't for the food and Larkin Round Face.

Willis feared the blustering warlord as much as he hated him, and he hated Larkin as much as he feared him. Larkin the despot, the martinet, the ogre. Larkin—and Willis could not stand having to admit this—was currently experiencing a most distasteful spate of unrelenting prosperity. Everything the beetle-browed cur touched, it seemed, turned to gold.

"Ever since I tossed those hares into Desmond's lap," the oaf claimed, "my fortunes have done nothing but multiply. See how the God of Rome and the Irish blesses me! What less can I do but build His monastery? It will be the finest center of learning in the world!"

How unpleasant. Because Larkin, that misbegotten hatchling from beneath some toadstool, was using the sweat of Willis and nearly threescore others to build Desmond's book shed. Oh, the misery of it!

Willis would probably have slunk away in the dark of night already but for the food. Not only did Desmond and his callow assistant, Ibar, eat sumptuously, they cheerfully opened their overburdened table to anyone who cared to sit at meat with them.

Deer, hare, boar, pigs and cattle, fish (though Willis did not care for fish particularly), sheep and chickens all made their sacrifices to the monastery board.

Meat aplenty. Barley cake, wheaten bread, oat bread, gruel, flavored stirabout, buttercakes, currant cakes, porridge, and hearty fried bread—who could walk away from that? And that was not to mention the variety of leaves and beans and other vegetables that the monk kept serving.

The only disadvantage to these daily repasts was that Larkin made him work for them. He kept quoting a nonsense line Desmond insisted was the word of God, "He who does not work, let him not eat." What a shame and a pity that Larkin had ever heard that.

Willis glanced at the sky. They'd be singing nones in another hour or so. Desmond paid an inordinate amount of attention to saying offices. If it wasn't matins, it was primes. And if not noon-song, vespers. Every three hours from cockcrowing to bedtime. Larkin claimed to like it. "Good way to know the time!" he'd cackle, but then that was Larkin.

Bedtime was inviting, notwithstanding the horde of fleas that lurked in Willis's sleeping pallet. But bedtime was a long time coming yet.

Willis stood now to rest a brief moment on the crest of the ridge. Before him to the north, Hadrian's old wall snaked from east to west. Since long before Willis's clan settled in this area, that gap in the wall called Knag Burn Gateway served as a link and a barrier between the wild forests of the north and the wild forests of the south. The old customhouse still stood in use, but it obviously had seen far better times.

The Romans, so tradition decreed, abandoned the wall and the land a hundred years after the customhouse was established—and a hundred years before Willis. In the middle of history, they were, those Romans. Now the like of Larkin infested the land. Bah!

Nestled in a draw not far from the gap, Desmond's monastery was rising rapidly. And well it should, with all the labor Larkin was pressing into service. Every manner of men, from warriors to plowboys. Women. Any children strong enough to carry stones. Ponies. Willis. Bah!

80

A huge, ring-shaped wall of earth encircled the large wooden building they called an oratory, the refectory wherein those ample meals were served, and a cluster of huts for the more dedicated monks. Less dedicated monks lived outside the wall and came in for lessons and meals. Mud huts, stone huts, wooden huts—each monk built his own, and a more motley assortment of hovels he'd never seen.

The oratory was half built, Desmond's scriptorium (whatever that was) roofed but still open. Only the refectory could be called complete. Much work remained, and Willis knew who would be stuck with much of it. He himself—while Larkin, that blustering child of a jackdaw, "supervised."

Life is not fair. With a hearty, well-deserved sigh, Willis shouldered his bundle of withes and started down off the ridge. The waning light of late afternoon washed across the abandoned Roman defensive wall (the past) and over Desmond's brand new ringwall (the future).

Willis dropped his bundle by the ringwall gate and wandered on inside. Sometimes, if he treated the cooks with sufficient deference, he managed to wangle a bit of a snack. Supper would not be served until an hour after dark, that the workmen might take full advantage of every bit of the diminishing daylight. A wee snack would go very nicely now.

The aroma of roasting venison swirled through the compound, and it smelled as if the cooks were baking wheaten bread today. Willis paused a moment and closed his eyes, inhaling deeply.

He crossed to the fire pit behind the refectory and greeted the burly head cook. "Def, my fine friend, and good evening. You be feeling stout, I trust."

"Stout indeed, Willis. I've no samples that need tasting this afternoon. You'll just have to wait for supper. I suggest you continue working until then, like all the other souls here." Def loomed nearly as large as Larkin himself. Where Larkin abounded in hair, however, Def was bald—a clean chin, thin, pallid brows, receding hairline. But that was all in the front of the man. Viewed from the rear, Def looked quite like Larkin, broad and forbidding.

"What? No bread that baked a tad too long? No bit of venison that dropped into the fire and is spoilt?"

"None such."

"Yourself be far too efficient a cook for my own taste, Def. Good morrow."

"Good morrow, saucy fox." Chuckling, Def wandered off toward the sharpening block with a butcher knife in his hand.

From nowhere a javelin whistled past Willis's ear and sank into Def's back. The *thuck!* as it struck and the cook's brief, startled grunt were the only sounds to mark the sudden death of Def of Whin. He dropped, jerked violently, and lay still.

Willis spun on his heel to glimpse Picts wearing green tartans pour almost silently in through the gate. He dived behind the nearest cover, an oaken tanning vat, and squirmed like a lizard across the bare dirt beyond the refectory.

Willis did not bask in anyone's good graces save perhaps Desmond's—certainly no man wearing a tartan was kindly disposed toward him. His one salvation in this raid lay with the Irish monk.

It was green tartan. He knew that pattern well enough. Ugly customers they were, from the hills up behind Willis's native East Bogg. He scrambled to his feet and ran for the cluster of monks' huts.

Desmond's little mud-and-coppiced-hazel hut looked exactly like all the others—no bigger, no grander, no sturdier. Its interior permitted a man to lie down stretched out, so long as he lay along a diameter. Even Willis had to duck to enter the hide-covered doorway, and Willis was not a large man.

He abandoned all politeness and ripped in, literally—in his haste he yanked the dry steerhide down off the door opening. "Master, I beg you, save us! Larkin's enemies have entered the gate!"

Desmond remained as he was, kneeling on his sheepskin pallet, sitting back on his heels. One of those book things lay open before him, but he couldn't have been reading. Until Willis accidentally tore off the door cover, it would have been too dark in here to read.

"I am more a servant than a master, Willis."

"Very well then—servant. But save us from those wily ruffians! You know! Put out your hand or something, like you did that other time." Willis extended his own arm, palm outward, to demonstrate in case Desmond had forgotten. Desmond was a wonder at recalling spiritual matters (that business about "he who does not work, let him not eat" notwithstanding), but he did tend to neglect remembering practical things.

"Peace, friend. Sit here and explain to me who the—"

The little room went dark as a deep and unfamiliar voice roared, "Aha! Irish accent!"

A terrifying madman crouched in the doorway, blocking the light. His green kilt swished as he swept himself inside. The stubby iron sword in his hand glinted, once the light returned.

"Your hand!" His heart in his throat, Willis darted behind Desmond. "Put out your hand!"

"You are Desmond, Larkin's talisman!" cried the Pict.

"I am Desmond. As for the talisman aspect—"

The ogre reached forth and seized Desmond's arm. Willis was doomed! For some reason the monk's magical power was not working. In truth, he wasn't even trying to make it work.

Laughing wickedly, the cutthroat hauled the feckless monk out the door.

Outside in the muted sun, the fellow roared something to a green-kilted companion about bringing the assistant as well. Another cutthroat, equally terrifying, plunged through the door. Willis shrank back and tried to make himself disappear in the gloom, to no avail. The man seized his arm and practically broke it off dragging him out into the light.

Willis was about to protest, "But I'm not his assistant! I don't even know the fellow!" But then he noticed the number of lifeless bodies strewed about, some of them in monk's garb. Blood pooled here and there. Desmond, as yet unharmed, was being boosted aboard a shaggy dun pony. Willis changed his mind about speaking out.

They shoved Willis up onto a pony also. Willis hated riding choppy-gaited ponies. In his early youth, he had cleaned stables. Ponies were the curse of the working class, and now here he went, riding toward the gate *chopchopchopchopchopchop* and bouncing around like a huckleberry on a flat rock. He gripped the mane as best he could, and still he nearly slid off.

A score of raiders now swarmed about in the cramped compound within the ringwall. Over by the kitchen, two hoisted a beer keg into the lap of a mounted third man. The fellow's overloaded pony, not too stout to begin with, took a faltering step forward and dropped down on its haunches. The two companions roared. Laughing like jackdaws, men carried off pilfered food, stolen garments, squawking chickens, and screaming women. Dogs barked. Hogs squealed. Acrid, stinking smoke boiled out from the refectory door.

Willis's mount was one of a herd of ponies that clattered in staccato out the ringwall gate. In fact, it trotted along rather in the middle of the mob, a most dangerous place to be. Should he lose his grip and slide off now, the scores of hard little hooves right behind him would beat him into the mud. The scores of hard little hooves directly ahead kicked chips and boluses of mud up into his face. And the ponies to either side, neither of them with a rider, decided to crowd through the narrow ringwall gate just as Willis's pony passed through. They very nearly dislodged his legs and scraped him off.

Who was issuing the orders here? Willis recognized him—or thought he did. Travis, the king's name was. No, Tavish. That was it. He headed up a ragtag clan from the north, a motley assortment of raiders tucked back into the Cheviot hills. Insufferably proud, they called themselves a ruling clan. As far as Willis could recollect, they could count on one hand the number of reasons to be proud and still have fingers left over.

Yes, that was he. Tavish. As Larkin was big and dark and burly, Tavish was short and square and burly and fair-complexioned. The silver strands sprinkled through his orange hair turned his sideburns white. Tavish had shaved his chin and let his mustache grow. That mustache (Willis remembered now—a legend it was, and Tavish's mark), a great orange blob of hair, covered everything below his nose and swept in huge, long wings down the sides of his mouth. Willis couldn't see his upper lip or the smile corners at all. His eyes, mere slits, crinkled deep in his head, protected by amazingly bushy, graying orange brows.

Willis glanced back. Smoke boiled out of the oratory now, and the refectory was well on its way to becoming an empty black spot in the middle of the ringwalled yard.

And that infuriated Willis! He had put up with weeks of constant manual labor and periodic preaching to erect those buildings. They were excellent buildings. And these brigands torched them. It was unthinkable.

Desmond did not seem to take seriously enough the work that had gone into those buildings or the danger and disrespect in these cutthroats. Obviously Desmond was not about to curse their wicked souls, so Willis would.

He pondered the phrasing of his curse for a long time, but then he had a long time. The raiding party, stolen cattle and ponies and slaves in tow, rode north, back into the hills. It was a slow, lengthy track to take.

Desmond blessed in the name of Jesus; therefore cursing probably would follow the same route, since it was the reverse. Or would it? Did one invoke the devil for curses, or did God take care of everything? Perhaps he should have paid more attention to the monk's theological spoutings, for the information would be useful to him now.

As the night closed in and weariness replaced fury, Willis's thoughts grew a bit muddled. Thirst entered the picture as well. And still the mounted party thundered on. His pony doggedly kept to the trail, every ragged *trip, trap* threatening to shake him off its back. How he hated riding!

12
Ibar

Ibar wanted to be home in Cashel and the fosterage where he grew up. If not there, he wanted to be in his birthplace, the small rath on the Blackwater near Erin's pleasant south coast. If not there, he wanted to be back at Clonfert, fishing in the Shannon and watching lapwings forage across the river bottomlands. If not there, he wanted to be almost anywhere except here.

He struggled out from beneath a stinking stack of dried hides. The refectory was burning lustily, flames and smoke fighting each other for the chance to reach heaven first. The oratory would go next—it had quite a good start already. The kitchen shelter would no doubt go too, so close was it to the blazing refectory. Already its thatch smoldered.

His eyes burning, Ibar crept along the base of the ringwall to the gate and gained his feet to run out. He paused. Wailing women were dragging the dead and dying out the gate. Were Desmond, poor Desmond, here, he would be reminding Ibar to do his Christian duty. With great reluctance, Ibar jogged back into the compound, grabbed a prostrate monk by the heels, and began pulling.

In all, they dragged seven men and two women out of the burning compound. Both women were found beside their bloody battle-axes, defenders to the end. Three of the men still clung to life, but they would die in a day or two, when the infection took over. For all his fifteen years, and ten of them in schools, Ibar had never come upon the like of this.

The sights and sounds and the hideous smells engulfed him. Keening women. Moaning injured. Smoke. Heat. Crackling flame and the stench of hissing, smoldering thatch. And Desmond—carried away by those murderous brigands.

Desmond, gone.

Numbly, Ibar stumbled up the track to the old customhouse, not by deliberate design but simply because it lay both upwind and fairly distant of the burning compound. If anyone manned the house today, he was hiding. And no wonder, with those green-kilted ruffians about. A dozen peddlers and merchants had set up tables and shade frames under the trees here. But they had fled as well. Their goods and foods for sale sat abandoned, vulnerable to any passing thief.

Ibar wanted so much to run west and just keep running until he came to the sea. He even entertained briefly the foolish notion of swimming home to Ireland. Accompanying Desmond across the sea to evangelize the Picts had seemed an attractive adventure when his mentor first proposed it.

He stopped long enough to wipe his face and nose on his tunic sleeve. He was too old, too educated to weep. Weeping embarrassed him. He wiped his eyes one more time with the heels of his hands and continued on.

He followed idly the base of the great wall, still westbound, for no other reason than that Hadrian's work of so long ago prevented his walking northward. A mile from the burning monastery, the wall lay breached, not by clamoring warriors but by lazy farmers. Boaires building their ringwalls and sometimes even the farmhouses within them had, over the years, pilfered much of the wall's dressed stone.

On impulse, Ibar climbed up into the ruin. He slipped and slid, trying to claw his way up the interior fill dirt. Finally he topped out onto undamaged stonework and began walking back eastward in the direction of Knag Burn. Erin retreated farther behind him with every step.

Then he froze in midstride. Up ahead, a person wrapped in a brown cloak sat on the broad walltop gazing north. If this was a lookout for the raiders, Ibar was done for. Should he turn back and run and draw attention to himself? Jump down over the side and possibly break every bone?

The distant head turned toward him, regarded him a few moments, and gazed off again. He approached cautiously until he was certain of his identification.

She lived somewhere close, he knew, because she came to

the monastery frequently. She had put in many days of work, hauling rock and wood shoulder-to-shoulder with the men. And that had always amused Ibar, for she was only a slip of a girl. The top of her head came perhaps to his ear, and he outweighed her by a stone or more, and he didn't have his growth yet. Her freckles, though, intrigued him most. A vivid orange-brown, close to the color of her glowing red hair, they spattered her face and forearms. Today her hands were bloody, not yet washed from tending the wounded and dying.

Without looking at him, she asked, "What do you think will happen now?" Her voice droned, flat and colorless.

He sat down without further preliminary. These were not normal times calling for customary greetings and salutations. The end of the world was happening. "I don't know. Where do you think they took him?" He looked past her at the inverted cone of smoke pouring into the sky. His hands were blood-smeared too.

"Cheviots, those hills up north. That's where Tavish and his clan live."

"You know him?"

"I know the tartan." She looked at him with eyes blurred by sorrow. "Why didn't he resist? He didn't lift a hand."

Ibar shrugged. "He came to preach to the Picts. One Pict is much like another, I suppose. Larkin, Tavish. It wouldn't matter to him."

"But why that horrible little Willis?"

"I don't know." Anger flooded him suddenly, as though a fire magically flared up before his face. "Yes, I do. That Willis East Bogg is a betrayer. A spy. Tavish sent him to us to spy out the monastery and probably even let them through the gate. Tavish first rode down upon us moments after the little thief rejoined us. That has to be it."

"Of course." She nodded. "And Tavish kidnapped Desmond to obtain the good fortune Larkin's been having."

That was ridiculous. "Desmond's hardly a good-luck charm! Larkin obeyed the will of God and prospered. That's not—"

"Looking at it from afar, it is. Tavish doesn't understand about doing God's will."

"True." Ibar stared at the hills to the north, wondering if

somehow he could see a party of riders and among them a saint of God. He knew what he ought do. He ought take to the track and follow the party. Now, before the next rain, with all those ponies' feet cutting up the ground as they passed, a blind man could follow. He ought rejoin Desmond and minister not to Larkin's Picts but to Tavish's.

Or what he really ought do was oversee the rebuilding of the Larkin's monastery and Larkin's faith. Continue the work Desmond started here. That's what he ought do. It was the job he had pledged his life to.

He was fifteen years old. He had never in his life ever told another person what to do. Back home, even his dog had been reluctant at times to obey. Sorrow placed a pony and a quern on his shoulders and then sat on top of the burden. Sorrow is heavier by far than ponies and grinding stones.

He looked at her. "You worked long at building, and it's gone. What are you going to do now?"

She studied the emptiness beyond the rock wall. "Go somewhere is what I'd like to do. Somewhere different. My mum died the winter before this, and since then my father's been hollow. He doesn't even talk to people anymore. Our clan is decimated, and they were never warm toward our family to start with. My father— no one liked him. I don't want to stay home." She looked at him.

He took that as an invitation to speak. "I want to go someplace where it's warm. Where you can wade a stream and your toes don't ache, or you can even swim across without getting bitter cold. Where you don't have to wear wool."

That was obviously not her dream. She seemed to dismiss his yearnings as nonsense. Her voice took on that softness again. "I'd like to go far and see wonderful things. I want to see such wonderful things that I'd forget all this."

Such wonderful things that you forget all this. How that siren called to Ibar! "Have you ever been to Erin?"

She shook her head. "Is it wonderful?"

"And more. I've seen emeralds. Have you ever seen emeralds?"

She shook her head again.

"Desmond is a prince, you know. There are several in the court at Cashel who wear jewels." Ibar's thoughts skipped about, like butterflies tasting flowers. He could scarcely control them. "An emerald is a deep green jewel, translucent like glass so that the light plays through it. All Erin is an emerald, with light playing upon a dozen shades of green. The whole face of the land, and the sea as well. Emerald land, emerald sea."

"Lovely, aye?"

"Aye. Do you wish to see it?"

"You're going home?"

"I believe so."

"And your home is among kings?"

Desmond's home, not Ibar's, was among kings. Ibar's home was the rath of a ri tuatha south of Cashel. But scant difference, actually, when you're so many leagues distant from either place. He held his peace.

She drew her knees up and crossed her arms upon them to rest her chin there. He noticed her face was tear-streaked. Soot from the fires emphasized the clean little lines. She studied the distance a long time, her face blank and her mind, no doubt, off and lost somewhere in those undulant hills.

If Ibar were half a man, he would journey forth into those hills, track down Desmond, and reattach himself to his master. Then he would ferret out the perfidious Willis East Bogg and slay the traitor. With that Willis in Tavish's employ, would the evil Pict then kill Ibar in retaliation? Probably not, since this was an affair of honor. And if Tavish killed Ibar, so what? Ibar had earned his crowns. At fifteen he already had sacrificed his love of the native soil to journey abroad in the name of Christ, just as did Columba, and—

Her voice jarred him back to that ancient rock wall. "There's a combed mantle and a nicely crafted spindle that I don't care to leave behind. I'll go get them. We'll depart at sunrise."

The suddenness shook him. Of course. This was certainly God Himself calling him to return home. Study more, perhaps. Grow the rest of the way. You don't hitch a goat to pull a plow, and you don't send an untried boy to labor among the spiritually dark and corrupt Picts.

* * *

90

Exactly twenty-four hours later, as the westering sun hung low near the line where misty forest meets misty sky, Ibar began to wonder whether that had actually been God calling. Doubts assailed him.

What would happen when he returned to Cashel alone? How would the prince's relatives respond when Ibar explained to the greatest warlord in Erin that he didn't care to follow after his master? He shuddered.

He might return instead to Clonfert. He and Desmond had spent several years in study there. Brendan rarely stayed in his own monastery. He was always out sailing to other places, to other brethren. Brendan probably would not even know Ibar was back.

Perhaps Ibar could just slip quietly back to his ancestral home on the River Blackwater.

Hardly.

At age fifteen Ibar was a man without clan or country or brotherhood, thanks to that greedy ogre Tavish, and he saw no prospect in his future of remedying that.

With the red-haired girl straggling behind him, Ibar followed the trail out of the forest into an open meadow. The meadow gave this round hill a bald pate surrounded by a ring of tangled forest, like a Roman tonsure. From a ringwalled farm off to the right, dogs barked, but they didn't come running. Evening is when dogs are fed—no wise cur goes galloping away with dinner in the offing.

To the north, Ibar could just make out the harsh, straight line of the old Roman wall. Someone had been pilfering building rock from it along here as they had back by Knag Burn—the Romans certainly didn't leave those erose notches along its profile.

The smell of cattle hung in the damp air, a happy smell evoking childhood memories. In the trees below the brow of the hill, a flock of fieldfares and redwings chirped good-bye to the day and probably to each other.

For the first time in two hours, Ibar could see more of the sky than just the crease directly overhead among the treetops. The gray overcast ended in a flat line a short space above the flat horizon. The sun dropped down now into that space, flaring brilliant evening yellow. Its brightness half blinded Ibar and made him squint to see the path. The sun paused on the rim of the world, shrank back a moment from taking the plunge, then began the slow, majestic process of squeezing itself below the horizon into night.

What would men do without the night? How else does one hide sleep and love and skulduggery but with the curtain of night?

From fifty feet behind him, the red-haired girl asked, "Shouldn't we be calling at that farm for a meal and lodging? 'Twill be dark in minutes."

"Desmond and I came this way recently, remember? There's a tanner's rath at the bottom of the hill by a stream. The smell's not too wonderful, but his stirabout is excellent. He flavors it with lamb."

The track pushed into the forest below the hillcrest as an awl pushes through leather. Few things are darker than a forest after the sun goes down. Perhaps they should have stopped at that rath. Then he heard trickling off to the right. Good. They would parallel the stream for another quarter mile. Then the track would cross it, and they would come to the tanner's rath a few hundred feet beyond.

"We're almost there," he called.

He had to raise his voice, because she now lagged almost a hundred feet behind him. Ibar had warned the girl against carrying too much away with her. A stone at home becomes a hundred-weight on the trail. He carried naught but his comb and an extra cloak. She struggled beneath the burden of a copper pot, her drop spindle, two knives, and two cloaks.

At least he had been able to talk her out of bringing along her grinding stone as well. Imagine hauling a quern across the world to Erin. She would find querns aplenty in Erin, he told her. They're even carried aboard some of the larger boats.

Larger boats. And then revelation burst upon him like sunrise on the sea. Of course! He would not go home at all. He would cross Erin and sail out to the island of Iona. Because of Ibar's ten years of schooling, Columcille's monastic colony there would surely greet him with open arms. He would not stop at Clonfert.

That was it! Perfect. He would journey to Iona.

He really ought to hold back and let the red-haired girl catch up. He waited as she came staggering along, then fell in beside her.

In fact, he ought to find out a few of the details about her that he had not yet learned.

"What is your name?"

13

Tavish

If Willis Gray Mantle ever came into fortune and respect as a clan leader, he certainly wouldn't disport himself the way Larkin and Tavish did. Oafs, both of them. It was bad enough that they frowned upon Willis's chosen trade and even used their considerable military might to discourage it. But look at Tavish now! He behaved as if Desmond had hung the moon, just as Larkin used to. Certainly, Desmond was a good man, but he wasn't God.

At least a hundred people, counting in the numerous children, greeted Tavish and his band as they clattered into the biggest ringwalled compound Willis had ever seen. Green kilts were everywhere. Women as well-armed as the men laughed and hooted and waved. The sun rode low, giving the dozens of warriors gathered here longer shadows than they deserved.

Willis slid off his pony's back, deeply relieved to be on foot again. His legs ached. What a trip! What a long, miserable trip.

The triumphant returnees paraded Desmond and Willis across the compound to a huge wooden building. Every face grinned broadly. Every hand lifted in happy greeting. The joyous din they raised pierced through one's ears to rattle one's brains.

It seemed curious to Willis that the raiding party who stole Desmond numbered very few compared to the full count of warriors here. Why would the magnificently mustached Tavish take only a small band of fighting men with him, if kidnapping Larkin's good-luck talisman were so important an undertaking? Why not attack with full force of arms? Why leave the most of his might behind?

Willis could see only one possible answer. These retainers remained behind to defend something, and whatever it was, it was more valuable even than a talisman. Somewhere in this compound, perhaps back a souterrain, perhaps beneath a stone, perhaps behind a wall, fortunes lay buried.

At a great oaken door, Desmond and Willis were greeted with obeisance—Desmond was probably accustomed to it, but this was a first for Willis—and conducted into a banqueting hall.

And what a hall! Wonderful aromas of bread and meat mixed with a strong, healthy smoke smell, the scent of greatness. People crowded in, settling themselves upon cushions along the low tables. Willis had attended a banquet only once before, his mother's sister's wedding feast, and that not nearly so large as this. He knew the way seating was ranked, though he'd never seen the full practice of it. His mother's little sister didn't know anyone truly prominent.

Here was Tavish's place of honor, and his woman's beside him. Tavish took it, settling himself with a haughty, dignified air. There sat his chief druid in white finery. The fellow who handled the logistics of the raid, Tavish's right-hand man, would no doubt take the other seat of honor there, his earned place.

But as Willis gaped, the warrior led Desmond to the honored seat, the highest of the high seats, and Willis right beside him! It took Willis a minute, but not more than a minute, to adjust himself to this unaccustomed deference. He would enjoy it to the full as long as he could, until they discovered their mistake.

The flagon passed by. The ale tasted bitter and strong, not to his liking. But ale is ale. He quaffed his share and sent the flagon on down the row.

Here was where he could settle another point of curiosity. How did the mighty Tavish manage to eat and drink with that mustache, never mind trying to kiss women? Willis leaned forward a bit for a better look. Apparently Tavish was willing to pay the price for his magnificent mustache, and apparently the price was to sift through hair everything that came near his mouth. He drank deeply, and as he passed the flagon on, his mustache dripped. No one seemed to notice, his wife least of all. She laughed and cackled and exchanged raucous, ribald jokes with revelers nearby.

Boisterous toasts and congratulatory statements rolled on and on. Willis was ravenously hungry, but he could wait. They were, after all, toasting Tavish and Desmond and Willis himself.

Somewhere in this compound, he was convinced, riches lay hidden. So long as Tavish continued pampering Desmond, Willis would have the run of the place. He could sniff and search, examining all the nooks and crannies, mayhap to uncover secrets, without being called to account or suspected of spying. He'd explore the souterrains first, under the guise of admiring Tavish's handsome provision for his people.

The flagon passed through again.

Souterrains—long low tunnels—threaded back into the ringwall. The ringwall was nothing less than the bosom of their mother, Earth, drawn up protectively around the rath. The souterrains both hid and gave, trusting Earth with the produce of the upperworld and offering it back to her for blessing. Riches hidden in a souterrain would be particularly blessed then, having been enfolded so in the mother. Yes, that's where he'd look first.

Following a lengthy and altogether unnecessary oration about the greatness of that rival clan leader Larkin, Tavish's field commander toasted Larkin as the first fallen in the raid. A worthy foe, Larkin, claimed the warrior, and his defenders male and female all put up such a rousing fight.

Everyone stomped and cheered for the fallen Larkin.

The flagon passed.

Desmond frowned and leaned toward Willis. "Who fell first in the compound, do you know?"

Willis wiped the ale off his mouth. "Def, the cook."

"You're certain?"

"A javelin. *Thwunk!* I'm sure."

Desmond wagged his head. "Larkin told me that morning that he was going out hunting. So I suppose they must have fallen upon him in the field before they reached the monastery."

Willis picked up the reasoning. "And Def then became the second slain."

Desmond nodded sadly. "What a cruel end. The man Larkin was a glorious convert. Glorious. God rest his soul."

Willis would not have called the black-bearded old bull glorious by any means.

Now the assemblage loudly prevailed upon Desmond for a word or two.

He stood up, the better that his soft voice be heard. In Pictish strongly tinged by that irritating Irish accent, he spoke. "Five hundred years ago in a little town in Judah, a baby boy was born. Wonderful miracles attended His birth, but the Romans paid no attention to them. He was the Son of God and the Prince of Peace, but the Romans didn't heed or bother to understand. They feared and despised Him just as they feared and despised you, the Picts. They tried to wall you in, and they tried to murder Him.

"The Romans are gone now. Vanquished. A force no more." The soft voice hardened and rose. "But the Son of God still lives, and you still live! And it is my great joy to be able to introduce Him to you. Praises to the Picts, the lords of this land, and all praise and glory to Jesus, Son of God, Lord of heaven and earth!"

General libations followed the enthusiastic cheering. Obviously these fellows especially liked the "praise to the Picts" part. Finally, to Willis's great relief, the actual feasting commenced.

A nubile lass with a shy smile served him a loaf of wheaten bread and a slab of mutton. The meat dripped rich juice onto the table before him. Quickly he ripped off a chunk of bread and blotted up the sweet fatness.

So Larkin was gone. In a strange way, that saddened Willis, and he could not figure out why. Roaring, laughing, howling, threatening Larkin, Prince of Picts. Prince of a few Picts. Two- or threescore in all. Not these Picts. When he thought about it, there had been a certain nobility to the man, a commanding presence. And he surely couldn't fault the fellow's enthusiasm for building a community of monks.

Everyone engaged Desmond in conversation. No one bothered talking to Willis. No matter. He busied himself with the flagon that passed from hand to hand along the table, as each banqueter took a sip or two. The ale wasn't nearly as bad as he had first opined. He let his happy palate dwell upon the mutton and beef and luscious joints of pork. And he thought about how best to explore the souterrains certain to be tunneled into the walls of this great rath.

He would begin by cajoling the cook. He was very good at cajoling cooks. Ah, big, sad, burly Def. Then he would talk about stores and about provisioning for so many warriors over the long winter. He would entice the cook to boast of the wealth of grain and roots held in mother Earth. And then . . .

The flagon passed. Many greasy fingers had made it awkwardly slippery to hold. He had judged too hastily. The ale was actually rather good. He sipped and sent it on to Desmond.

Desmond handed it on without drinking and leaned toward Willis. "You haven't been hearing any more details of the raid, have you? Who besides Larkin and Def died—and who escaped?"

"No more than what I told you on that hideous ride from there to here, about my own observations. I've heard nothing here tonight, no."

"Big Larkin and Big Def." Desmond pondered a few moments, then grunted. "Peter's second letter claims that sudden calamity befalls false prophets. And several times in the psalms, as I recall, evildoers experience sudden destruction. I'm worried. Do you suppose my efforts have not been God's intent? Do you suppose this sudden calamity came because of my error? Perhaps I wasn't supposed to stop where I did. What if God intended me to come up here to start with?"

Willis stared. This revered saint, this man of God who so freely spouted the words of eternal life, was expressing doubts? Desmond, he thought, held all the answers in the palm of his hand. Desmond knew God, and in return God could not restrain His almighty Self from blessing anyone who came near the man. What was this? And what would happen to them both, should Tavish learn that Desmond, the so-called man of God, harbored uncertainty?

If Willis's head weren't floating from all that delicious ale, he could probably work out this latest puzzle, the way he had worked out the presence of the hidden treasure. Now though, when he needed it most, his mind buzzed from thought to thought like a fickle honeybee and lit solidly on none of them.

He was seriously considering taking a nap when Tavish finally declared the feasting done for the day. Warriors and ladies and artisans drifted out the great doors at either end. Someone wakened the druid. He spoke a few kind words to Desmond that Willis did not quite catch and gracefully absented himself. The din of merriment in the echoing hall subsided to a happy rumble.

Tavish and his wife personally escorted Desmond and Willis out into the clammy night. A gaggle of inebriated well-wishers followed behind and to the sides, and laughing they were. By ones and twos the group evaporated, the way steam rising from a cauldron dissipates on a cold day. The hour was late indeed—the third-quarter moon rode high, in and out of broken clouds. Dogs barked outside the wall.

Either Desmond had refrained from drinking heavily from the common cup, or ale did not affect him. His voice sounded as strong and determined as ever. "Tavish, friend, I'm worried."

Willis wanted desperately to tell his mentor, "For the love of life and all holy, quiet!" but he didn't know how to do it.

"How so?" Tavish sounded elated with the evening. He glowed like the sallow moon.

"I fear for you, friend. You're seeking to benefit from the blessings God bestows through me, aye?"

"Aye!"

"And that raid on Larkin's people—you committed mayhem for naught but personal gain."

Tavish looked at him oddly, his jumbly orange brows knitted. "Why else would one commit mayhem?" His face softened in the dim moonlight. "Oh, of course. There's also honor."

"There's also honor. Not yours. Larkin's. I fear for you. I fear retaliation."

"Larkin's dead. 'Twas the first order of business we attended to, and for a reason. He was too dangerous alive. The eulogies tonight about Larkin—there was nothing dishonest in them or overblown. He was a champion of his clan and a worthy opponent for any warlord." Tavish paused, his broad face spreading even broader with happiness. "Now his luck has ended. Mine has begun. I have welcomed you into our clan thrice over. Behold what we built for you." He waved a powerful arm.

Before them stood a larger, much roomier hut than the ill-made mud-and-wattle hovel Desmond had erected for himself by Knag Burn. It even boasted a proper door. Flickering yellow lamplight leaked out through the crack at the bottom.

"It's quite spacious." Desmond nodded. "Palatial."

"Thank you. We didn't know exactly how to furnish it. A pallet, of course, with a tow mattress, spread thickly with sheepskins for good rest. A water jar, a plank, a cushion, a lamp. Whatever more you need we will provide. Rest now. We'll talk tomorrow. How does your litany go?"

"You mean the compline? 'Grant us, O Lord, a restful night and sweet repose.'"

Willis noticed a black shadow move across the light leaking out from beneath the door. Days old at most, and already this hut had mice.

"Aye, that's it. The very thing!" Tavish grasped the looped-rope door handle and yanked. He yanked again, promised to shave a bit off the door first thing tomorrow, and jerked it open on the third try.

From the lamplit hut, a giant black bear of a man leaped out at Tavish, roaring!

"Larkin, friend! Praise God! Praise God!" Desmond squealed with delight.

Willis squealed with terror.

Tavish reared back in fear and anger and snatched for the sword on his belt to defend against Larkin's great, waving broadsword. "How did . . . be you Larkin or his ghost? Speak!" He swung his own iron sword up, flailing in the moonlight.

"Nae his ghost." It was Larkin himself, all right. That voice rumbled too deep, too powerful, for a sprite. "I would not ken you be so foolish, Tavish, as to steal my abbot without killing me. Sure and you know better!"

In one amazing moment, Tavish the shocked and startled host became Tavish the fearless warlord. Rock steady, the strong man's hands gripped his sword before him. The fellow's transformation intrigued Willis, but, much more, it horrified him. Blood was about to be shed, and some of it might be Willis's.

Larkin stared directly at Willis and snarled. "Traitor! Open the gates to the enemy and then feast with him, is it?"

Willis quailed. Not a doubt lingered that some of the blood spilled would be his—not with Larkin of that mind. A traitor? With accusations like that flying, he was doomed. He shrank back, letting Desmond come between them. Why didn't Desmond raise his hand and stop everything, the way he did that first time he met Larkin?

Tavish didn't seem to care any more about Willis than Desmond did. He seemed to be trying to spot his troops and confirm his position without letting his eyes leave Larkin. He achieved his purpose remarkably well, considering that it was impossible. "I can assume the men guarding my perimeters are gone."

"You have good people. They didn't embarrass you. They were hopelessly outnumbered. In a stroke, Tavish, you accomplished what I yearned to do for years. With your insult, you united all the branches of my clan behind me." Larkin stepped in closer to Tavish, his broadsword at ready.

Willis recognized three of the men moving in behind Tavish and his wife. They weren't Tavish's.

Desmond took a stride forward, closing the distance between himself and Tavish's wife. The move obscured Willis from Larkin's immediate view. All three men were speaking now in elevated tones.

Willis hunched slowly, carefully, smoothly, and stepped aside, directly behind Desmond. He took another sidestep and another. He stood erect beside one of Larkin's henchmen and pretended to concentrate his attention on the two warlords.

The fellow glanced at him and returned to the drama before them. Willis sidestepped again. Again. Luck! By taking another few steps backward he could slip behind some sort of little outbuilding.

Assuming the banqueting hall was oriented east-and-west, the east gate of the ringwall ought to lie in that direction. Willis skirted a woodpile, stumbled over a log, fell flat on his face, regained his feet, staggered sideways into a low shed that smelled strongly of pigs, groped his way along a split-rail fence against the ringwall, bumped into a standing quern, almost fell, tripped again, fell to his knees, then gave up trying to be a proper man and crawled along the wall base simply because it was easier in this utter blackness than was trying to stand up. The coy moon had now disappeared completely. Willis found himself not far from the east gate.

Half a dozen more crouching, silent warriors glided in through the gate, swords in one hand, javelins in the other. If Larkin's clan had indeed united behind him, one was looking at a hundred fifty fighters, and a hundred at least on Tavish's side. The world was about to burst asunder, and Willis didn't want to be anywhere near it. He crawled out the gate through dank and beaten mud, from blackness into blackness.

Still on hands and knees, he felt his way down the road westward, holding to the track by senses beyond ear and eye, as does a blind mare. When the moon finally deigned to show itself again, he regained his feet and hurried forward, without cloak or club. His head still buzzed, but one thought forced itself upon him, abundantly clear: he must never show his face in this country again—in either the lands of the Tavish or the lands of the Larkin.

Where would he go? Larkin, Tavish, and their loosely related clans held the territory round about. Except for the little Pictish pocket, Angles roamed nearly everywhere to the east. A pox on mankind, those haughty Angles. Willis would not travel east.

West was as good a direction as any. In his forays against the wealthy, he had bumped into Britons now and then, and he suffered no loss to speak of by their hand. Britons claimed most of the land to the west and south. He would travel to the west coast and north.

Besides, in ever-increasing numbers, Willis had heard, the Irish were pouring over into the lands of the Picts to the northwest. Already the Ulstermen had seized most of Argyll and the islands in that area. And now, rumor had it, they were forging alliances with the Cruithne of the north.

Despite himself, Willis had begun to feel a certain degree of comfort around these inscrutable Irish men of God. Not the least point, they were unfailingly generous with their bed and board. They knew nothing of garnering wealth or handling coin—according to that feckless Ibar, no coin at all circulated in the land of Erin—but one could live quite comfortably among them. That would suffice nicely.

Besides, what they didn't know might well work to Willis's favor, for if there was one thing he knew, it was coinage. Since Willis could no longer safely remain in his homeland, perhaps he would venture among them, these strange Ulster Irish to the north and west, to the very coast and beyond.

Desmond rarely mentioned Ninian, the monk of eld who traveled this land for years preaching God to the Picts and Britons.

But he spoke highly and frequently of a wayfaring monk named Brendan at Clonfert and a religious leader named Columcille—Columba, the Dove of the Church. Apparently the Dove led a monastic colony on one of the islands—Iona, as Willis remembered.

He would certainly find safety out there.

And he couldn't find his way through an unknown land to a place called Clonfert, especially if memory did not serve him correctly and he were somehow getting the name wrong.

So, for lack of anywhere better to go, Willis would travel to Iona.

14

Whithorn

"See? I should have brought my grinding stone, like I wanted to." The red-haired, freckle-faced Anne Green Head waved her Roman silver piece in Ibar's face. She was using that tone of voice again, the inflection that said so plainly, "I should never have listened to your advice."

Ibar watched the River Cree ferry push away from shore and, lurching, begin its brief, ponderous trip to the other side. The Cree was a ridiculously small stream to require a ferry, but it was a ridiculous ferry—a simple leather coracle poled back and forth. You couldn't carry sheep or pigs in it, let alone cattle. Any animals one took along would have to swim alongside. But over that short distance, you'd lose not even a calf.

Ibar imagined a river like the Cree with water so warm one would not suffer. And when you reached the other side, the heat of the sun, warmth like a fire on a hearth, would dry you out quickly and comfortably.

The coracle bumped into the far shore, and its passengers— a farmer and his daughter—scrambled out. They slipped and slid up the muddy bank and disappeared into the covering forest. Ibar would have to admit that Anne's cloak fit the daughter perfectly.

Anne pressed her point home. "I could have sold the quern as well, just like I did the copper pot and the extra knife, and now my extra cloak."

He wrinkled his nose as they continued their way down the muddy trail, headed not west now but south. "You didn't get nearly enough for it. That was a perfectly good combed-wool cloak, worth much more than an old Roman ducat."

She strolled casually beside him. She kept up much easier now that her load had been reduced piece by piece to a few coins. "Silver ducat. A denarius, see? And it's one silver piece more than yourself has come up with on the journey. It takes money to sail to Erin, I'd trust."

"Indeed it does, though Desmond purchased our way over here with naught more than a blessing. He's a wise brother, and I'm a neophyte. I doubt my blessings are considered that valuable by your average boatman."

"We must be prepared to pay. I long ago learned never to depend upon the largess of others."

Now what did she mean by that? Every once in a while, she'd come forth with an enigmatic statement, some casual reference to a life Ibar could not begin to guess at.

Nor did he try. Her life was not his concern. They traveled, for safety, in each other's company. Nothing more.

"How far?" she asked.

"Ten miles. Eleven perhaps. Less than four hours."

He had not mentioned to her yet that he did not intend to return to Cashel and the court there. Her heart was so set on seeing the place. Mostly, he didn't know quite how to go about it. Since she seemed eager to visit Cashel, he could just let her continue that way south from Bangor, and he himself would sail north to Iona.

After all, she was responsible for the fact that he walked today along a track far from Knag Burn and Larkin and the ruined experiment of Desmond's monastery. Had she not pressed the issue, leaping right into it as it were, he very possibly would have hesitated and reconsidered. Had he thought about this journey a little longer, he most likely would have made some other decision altogether. So it was all her fault.

In retrospect, he decided he really should have remained with Larkin's project. Had he persevered, he might eventually have possessed a monastery all his own, like Columcille on Iona and Enda in the Aran Isles and Brendan at Clonfert and . . .

Too late. Anne and he were fast approaching the Isle of Whithorn. No turning back now.

They followed the familiar west shore of a blue stroke of water the locals called Wigtown Bay. Dark hills rose ajumble north of this peninsula. Iona actually lay to the north and west, on an island beyond an island beyond those hills, or so Ibar understood.

But in and around those hills lurked slow-witted, suspicious Britons and fiery Picts in a political stew assiduously to be avoided.

At land's end, the Isle of Whithorn, they could find a wide range of smacks and curraghs—doughty, seaworthy vessels all—that could take them by water to whatever destination they required and thereby skirt political turmoil. He looked forward to getting away from the politics of the Piccardach, alliances as tangled as the hills, and to speaking good Gaelic again as it ought be spoken.

Anne Green Head rolled the foul Pictish r's and gutturals as smoothly as Desmond sang his Latin. How would she fare when she settled herself in the nest of the southern Gaels? Ibar hoped she was smart enough to be able to adapt to the new speech. He certainly wasn't going to accompany her and tutor her. She'd better not entertain that fond notion.

Whithorn to Iona, or Whithorn to Bangor to Iona. In the fine weather of this spring day (albeit very early spring), a sea voyage appealed to Ibar. He watched unfettered sunshine dance without a care upon the ripples out in the bay. He listened to the rhythmic wash of water against the land, a constant, pulsing swish reduced to a whisper by the distance to the shore.

Except for the frightening voyage across open water from Bangor to Whithorn, Ibar enjoyed travel by boat. He looked forward to this.

They arrived at Whithorn in midafternoon. Ibar pointed out a small stone church in the distance. "The first such in this country and the beginning of Ninian's work," he explained proudly. "Almost two hundred years ago, it was."

Anne acted more impressed than he would have anticipated.

Ibar was leading this journey. It was he who had come this way before. So why did Anne instantly and boldly march herself down among a half dozen beached boats, discuss the tides with the men seated on the shore beside them, and begin to talk about traveling to Munster? Surely she knew that none of these fellows would sail so far. These were fisherfolk who plied the coast, never leaving sight of local landmarks. But then, so far as Ibar knew, the lass had never before beheld an ocean until this moment. She probably pictured the great Irish Sea as nothing more than a rather hazy lake.

She held the men's attention right enough, but that was no

wonder. A pretty girl with warm, smoky eyes and copper hair is bound to. The freckles merely added to it all.

"The south of Erin," she explained again. "Cashel."

No, no, no! Ibar wanted to cry. *To the north, to Iona.* How was he going to work this? "Actually, to Bangor would be fine," he suggested.

An old fellow hunkering on the sandy beach grunted. His chin hooked upward, and his nose hooked downward, and they nearly met in the middle. He probably didn't have a tooth in his head. "Nae. Nae Bangor. Y'd have to walk the full length of the land, and robberff aplenty, effpeffally down around the Mourne."

"You've been to Erin?" Anne asked.

"Born dere." He stared at a companion. "The veffel coming up from Man."

"The very thing." His companion, a fellow equally old and crotchety, bobbed his ancient head. "They'll be stopping here for pilchards and salt cod, probably on the morrow. Yourself shall board that vessel, lass. They'll not take you where you need to go, but they'll take you close enough you'll find another coaster. Or you can join a party walking overland. Yes. Yes, the very thing." His voice drizzled off into a raspy whisper.

"Are they from this area, then?" Anne asked.

"Nae." The first fellow, the one with the eagle-beak nose, shook his gray mane. "From Iona dey are."

And for the first time in a year, Ibar began to think that quite possibly God did indeed involve Himself in the affairs of men. For a long time he had doubted that. When Desmond was swept away, he waved his doubts like flags to convince himself that his heresy was indeed truth. But now . . .

Now the thing he wanted most, passage to Iona, was laid before him, and not of his own doing.

Three thick, aged, waddling women with weathered baskets arrived, their bare feet gritting on the loose shingle. They settled to sitting beside a mounded pile of wet fishing nets near the boats. As old women so constantly do, they examined Ibar and Anne minutely without once looking directly toward either of them. From their baskets they brought forth coils of cord and large wooden bodkins and laid them out on the shingle.

Never before had Ibar ever seen a trace of timidity in the red-haired girl. In fact, toward Ibar she acted brassy. But not now.

Smiling shyly, she stepped up to the women. "I am Anne Green Head from west of Knag Burn. The young man is . . . er . . . Ibar of Munster. We're . . . uh . . . seeking a way to Erin." Just listen to the shy hesitation in her voice!

"Join us." One of the women dragged netting into her lap from the top of the pile as another threaded a bodkin. The woman nodded pleasantly. "Your head doesn't look a bit green, child."

Anne giggled. "Green Head is a copse not far from our rath. There were three other Annes in our clan."

"Ah. I know that sort of sticky problem. There were four Mellas in mine. Until the other three died, folks were constantly confusing us." And the women instantly included Anne in their conversation as they commenced to mend nets.

Anne watched the process a short time, picked up a bodkin, and began to help with the mending. Within minutes she was showing the women her drop spindle.

No doubt she would sell that also. Then she'd have a fistful of coins. What if there were enough silver to buy passage for one but not two? The purse was Anne's. Would Ibar be left behind?

He didn't want to think about it.

In fact, he disliked altogether the practice of trading useless coins for necessary things. Anne could make her way with a spindle, a knife, a cloak, a pot. What can you do with coins? Hold them in your hand. Look at them. That won't feed or clothe you. And yet these people, the ones who spoke of Rome especially, treated coin like something holy.

No more did the afternoon sun limit itself to golden twinkles dancing delicately on the ripples of the bay. Now it filled the southern sky with light and flung its full brilliance off the water into Ibar's face. His eyes hurt when he looked directly south.

But directly south lay the only interesting thing to look at. A large, square, gray sail approached, spread firm against the southerly wind. No mere fishing boat, this.

The hooked-nose fellow pointed. "Dey're back a day early."

The youngest of them stood and stretched. "I'll fetch Mull." Away he went, striding through the shingle on his mysterious mission.

Ibar glanced at the crones. Anne and they still babbled. They sat facing each other, bodkins flying. The net lay across their laps. The apparently completed portion was folded into a pile on one side, the as-yet-unmended pile dwindled on the other.

Presently, the fellow who had gone off returned, and no doubt that lad Ibar's age who walked beside him would be Mull. The young man led three donkeys. The donkeys' panniers, stacked full to overflowing with parcels, flopped against their sides and legs. The donkeys slogged lackadaisically to water's edge and stopped.

The curragh's broad hull took full form beneath its sail as she came in. So favorable were wind and tide that the crew didn't bother to put out oars at all. The fishermen waded down into the shallow water to greet the boat. The old women stood up, Anne among them, chattering.

Ibar felt rather generally ignored. It had never occurred to him when he traveled in Desmond's shadow that were he not in Desmond's shadow he would still be invisible.

This must be the boat from Iona. He watched from dry shore as a great, hulking monk greeted his greeters and leaped out into the gentle surf.

Ibar knew that fellow! Boyd Blond Hair. And Boyd belonged to the monastery at Clonfert.

Boyd came wading ashore.

The old woman named Mella stepped forward and took his hands in greeting. "Boyd, and a thousand welcomes! This is Anne Green Head. She wishes to travel to Cashel and needs sail with you."

So do I, Ibar thought. *But not with a crew from Clonfert. They'll ask about Desmond immediately, and . . . no.* And yet, the man distinctly said this boat hailed from Iona. Confused, Ibar watched, afraid he would be noticed and afraid he would not.

"Surely so!" The jovial monk addressed his words more to the man with the donkey than to Anne. "Mull, we'd like to leave with the tide. Can we be loaded that quickly?"

The young man grinned. "Tell your crew to spread their hands, and I'll start throwing fish."

The hooked-nosed man cackled. "Led diff monk-in-draining

help. He wan' do go wiff you aff well." He dipped his toothless head toward Ibar.

"Good. Good." The monk scarce tossed a glance in Ibar's direction. Immediately he turned to the women and strode up onto the dry beach as everyone gathered around him. Anne's red head bobbed in the midst.

Ibar felt left out again, and that just might be good. "Yes, let me help." He waded into the surf beside the donkeys. Instantly his toes turned so cold they ached. The water was nothing less than flexible ice.

The bulky packages stuffed in the panniers seemed to be dried fish, wrapped in oilskin. Pounds and pounds of fish. This must be the daily fare on Iona, they were shipping so much of it aboard. Mull passed packages from one pannier up into waiting hands aboard ship, and Ibar did likewise on the other side.

Ibar noticed that the seamen aboard this curragh, about half of them monks, spoke the Irish Gaelic. Boyd possessed the only familiar face. Desmond claimed that Iona was established to serve the Irish living in that area and to extend the Word of God to the Picts on the mainland. Columba himself was Irish, both sides. Ibar smiled to himself, suddenly feeling happily at home among these Gaelic sailors despite the threat of Boyd.

One donkey was unburdened. Mull brought up the next. In minutes all the panniers hung empty. Mull led the donkeys ashore.

Ibar would have followed, but here came another fellow, a new man dragging still another laden donkey. He sloshed out to the boat and paused at Ibar's side. He smelled like a fisherman, but he carried himself with a power and dignity that suggested a king. "A love gift for the voyage," the man announced.

Ibar was obviously expected to help. Without invitation or question, he began emptying the pannier nearest him. Perhaps if he made himself sufficiently useful he could sail for free.

These smaller oilskin parcels were closely sealed in bees-wax. Love gift for a voyage? Ibar would not have guessed Iona was so far away that going there would be called a voyage. No matter. He helped lade, handing the cargo up piece by piece, and then followed the donkey to the beach.

The clatter of conversation ashore had ceased.

Boyd was kneeling in the shingle now, and old Mella knelt facing him. He had laid both hands on her gray and kerchiefed head. In Greek he asked healing for her infirmity. Another old woman knelt close to Mella, and Boyd turned his ministrations to her next. Mella stood up and stepped back so that the kingly fisherman could take her place in the shingle. The ham-sized hands rested on his brow as Boyd muttered.

Then, eyes closed and face tipped high, Boyd raised his arms to invoke God's blessing on all present.

Instantly conversation resumed, as cheery as ever.

Ibar weighed the situation only briefly before he splashed back out, whistled to the nearest fellow aboard the curragh, and raised his arms. "I'm shipping aboard as well, apparently," he said.

The fellow took his word for it. Grinning, he reached down and gripped Ibar's wrists. "Welcome, friend."

A wiggle, a squirm, a lot of kicking, intense pain as Ibar scraped his armpits, chest, and thighs across the oaken gunwale, and he tumbled in over the side. He counted ten men aboard, including Boyd. Desmond and Brendan both claimed that twelve are barely enough when a large vessel battles storms or currents.

His chest and thighs burned.

Still on shore, Boyd knelt again as the men and women gathered around him. All laid hands upon him in a cacophony of quiet individual prayers.

Properly blessed himself, the monk rose to his feet, embraced his friends, and sloshed back to the curragh.

Ibar wondered how the huge fellow was going to climb aboard this vessel without careening her. Here came Anne behind him, her cloak drawn close around. Boyd scooped her up and slung her bodily over the side and in, as if she were the weight of a dog or chicken. Then he shoved the curragh away from the shore.

A bit shaky, Anne swayed, then crossed to the mast and stood there.

All Ibar saw of Boyd were two brawny hands gripping the gunwale. Three strong men ran not to help the monk but to fling themselves against the opposite gunwale, trimming the craft. Getting the hulking monk in and out of the boat obviously was a skill long practiced. Boyd hauled himself up over the side and twisted around to his feet, apparently without scraping his chest and legs raw.

The boat jerked backward foot by foot as the men and women shoved her free of the grasping shingled shore. Here in the craft, four men at each side set their oars in the water to draw her seaward.

Beyond the beach, a good two hundred feet up the track, a scrawny little fellow in a hooded cloak was talking to Mull the donkey driver. Now the fellow came running across the shingle, crying, "Wait!" He waved his arms.

The curragh floated free.

"Iona?" the little fellow called. That voice was familiar.

"Aye!" Boyd called back.

"Take me!" The fellow came flailing and wading, his spindly arms flying in all directions. He scrambled out into the surf.

Boyd reached over the side one-handed. He stood erect, and the skinny man popped up over the gunwale and onto the deck. For a moment he flopped about like fresh-caught fish, until he could reassemble his poise and get his legs under him. The hood fell back off his head.

"The traitor!" Anne pointed a long, graceful finger at him. "Willis!"

The little man looked from face to face, wild-eyed. "No!" he squeaked. "I swear." He pointed at Ibar. "You! You're supposed to be with Larkin. Deserter!"

The oarsmen stroked in rhythm. The curragh dipped aside, swayed crosswise of the surface waves a moment, and began to surge forward. They were on their way.

Boyd looked at Anne, at Ibar, at this latecomer. He studied Ibar. "Desmond's assistant, aye?"

"Aye." He was found out. But then he would have been anyway, the moment Anne opened her mouth.

"Interesting." The big monk crossed his arms, appearing more bemused than anything else. "Well, well. I've no idea what we have here, but we've plenty of time asea to sort it all out. I'm sure" —he glanced at Anne— "that it will all be absolutely fascinating."

15

Emerald Sea

In the deepest chambers of the night, after the nearly full moon had gone its way but the eastern sky as yet showed no pink, shadows took solid form and began to stir. If the gentry from the Other World chose to roam abroad at all, now was when they wandered.

Willis would much have preferred sleeping soundly during these latter hours of the darkness—and therefore safely, for everyone knows that the Other Worlders cannot disturb a sleeping person. But the whole crew of the curragh were gathered round the fire, wide awake.

Willis pressed as close to the firebox amidships as he could. His mantle was not nearly adequate against the raw spring cold of deep night.

"Like honeycomb they were, exactly. Black, spindle-shaped rocks marching in thick stacks and clusters out across the sea. Very black, and hardly a rounded dome in the lot of it. Every boulder's edge and corner was squared up straight and true." Freckle-faced, red-haired Anne sat by the fire hard beside Willis, as wide awake as everyone else, listening.

"When we passed close by a broken bundle of these rocks all fallen jumbly in the water, I could see the flat tops. Each column was perfectly six-sided. Just like honeycomb! I've never seen the like, that's sure!"

Massive Boyd did not sit near the firebox, for he would have taken half the space. He sat directly behind Anne, and therefore behind Willis as well, a welcome, looming wall against the night. "The folks who know will tell you how Finn MacCool himself laid those rocks down as a causeway to reach Staffa Isle," Boyd rumbled. "Stepping-stones."

Willis looked at the pleasant, cow-eyed face of Malo, the story-teller, sitting directly across from them. He could never quite tell when these brethren were serious, and that bothered him. Uncertainty puts you at an instant disadvantage. Willis worked against enough disadvantages under the best of circumstances.

Malo smiled slyly. "So they say."

"Then your Finn MacCool is an artist as well as a builder," Anne said. "Against the green sea and the white foam, they were beautiful. Jewels!"

"Emerald and onyx," purred Boyd.

One man on watch and one on the tiller left a dozen people still to crowd around the firebox. This vessel did not often sail in the dark, but the captain seemed comfortably certain they were far enough asea to clear any hazards, and the wind was right. Land-bound and raised, Willis had never paid much attention to wind. It made sense, though, that sailors would read and heed the most casual breeze. With this his first taste of the sea, he discovered he definitely did not like sailing.

Apart from the endless attention paid the vagaries of wind, and the ceaseless motion, what bothered him most was the con-stant creaking of the wood-and-leather vessel. The lashed joints murmured, muffled by their skin of oak-tanned hide. The hide it-self whispered as it massaged the oaken framing and ashen ribs. Drum tight, the great linen sail held its own hushed conversation with the breeze. Beneath the prow, the sea swished a constant, pulsing complaint about being disturbed.

And darkness surrounded. Total darkness.

Willis drew his trailworn mantle tighter.

"Fire to leeward," called the lookout.

Malo scowled. "Leeward? That's to sea."

"Another curragh," Boyd interpreted.

Instantly everyone but Willis had leaped to his feet. Willis scooted in closer to the fire. The low deck tilted violently as the entire herd moved toward the lee rail. The captain bellowed, and a few stepped back to return the boat closer to trim.

With a smith's tongs, Boyd picked up a thick coal and waved it aloft. Gifted with such a sudden breath of fresh air, it flared bright.

Ibar's voice warned him not to ignite the sail. Ibar seemed to thrive on late hours and palpable shadows.

Legs bumped Willis and toes poked him. He could continue sitting here and risk being trampled in the darkness by careless seamen, or he could stand up. Standing would expose more of him to the cold. With a heavy sigh, he pushed himself to his feet. Chill dampness instantly washed up and under his mantle.

"A lost fisherman?" someone suggested.

"Brendan," Boyd answered. "His firebox. Who else would be sailing directly south in the dark of night, so far from shore?"

South?

Willis wasn't the only one confused, for Ibar pushed in beside Boyd at the rail. "Wait! South?"

"For a week now we've been hugging the coast with land to port. Nor did you fail to notice we've been sailing into the sun?"

"I thought you were just working your way through the islands between Erin and Caledonia, and then we'd proceed north to Iona."

"Eh, lad, we did that the first day out. The rock formation Anne described a few minutes ago? Then."

Willis pressed in against Boyd's other elbow. "But you said yourself you were bound for Iona! I asked you before ever I came aboard."

The captain planted himself at Willis's back and roughly seized his arm, a rather obvious hint that Willis could sail with the ship or swim where else he wished. "We're from Iona. When we deliver these goods to Brandon Bay we'll return to Iona."

"Brandon Bay." Ibar's voice sounded weak, riddled with disappointment. "How far is that?"

"With favorable winds like these, another day." Boyd seemed to pay scant attention to the passengers. He was watching the orange dot on the horizon.

Ibar stared out into the darkness. "Then where are we now?"

"If you could see—" the captain pointed off the windward gunwale "—you'd be looking at the Aran Isles about there."

"Aran." Ibar's voice regained a bit of its normal excitement. "Enda's monastery! I'd be fine to go there. Drop me off there, pray thee."

"Can't. We must hurry on to Brandon Bay to deliver these supplies before they leave."

"Before who leaves?"

"Brendan." Boyd stepped back away from the rail, altering the boat's trim. He dropped the spent coal back into the firebox. "Some time ago, coming off a test voyage, we stopped at Iona to see Columcille. Brendan decided to call at a couple sites among the islands. So he sent me in this vessel around to the Pictish coast and Man to request supplies of the believers along there."

"Supplies? That salt cod we loaded."

"For a journey. No better salt cod or dried salmon than that from Whithorn."

"Dried salmon. That was the love gift the kingly fellow sent aboard." A few dim pieces of orange light from the firebox played on Ibar's face. A woman would no doubt say he wasn't a bad looking fellow. In fact, Anne was looking at him in that way right now. "Brendan sails all around the coasts, edifying the brethren here and there. He's done it for years. Why does he need special supplies now?"

Boyd pointed to the orange dot. "I'd likely win any wager that that's Brendan. And the vessel you see away out there is the very one that will sail to the Land of Ever Young."

Willis gaped. Now he knew these monks couldn't be serious.

Ibar obviously took him quite seriously, though. "No wonder he's gathering supplies from the four corners of the earth. Mm. That far. Indeed."

* * *

The winds turned against them early the next day, which put the seamen to the oars.

About midmorning, the captain explained to Willis in no uncertain terms that it was his turn to row. Everyone rowed. Even Anne took her turn. Willis plopped onto the stowage box directly behind her and, after a few false starts, got the rhythm right. Draw, raise, return, pause. Draw, raise, return, pause.

Presently Willis grumbled, "The passengers doing the crew's work. We might as well have stayed home, where there's work aplenty. There's no justice."

Anne said, "The exercise feels good. Sitting about on a sailing vessel for days on end soon grows wearisome."

You should try lying in wait for travelers for days on end, if you like wearisome. But he didn't say that out loud. He frowned and nearly lost the rhythm.

Up in the bow, Boyd and Ibar were engaged in an intense exchange. And now Boyd laid both his hands upon Ibar's head. The monk gazed heavenward as he mumbled unintelligibly. Ibar stood silent beneath those massive hands. Tears streamed down his face.

The matter apparently ended. Boyd smiled down at the lad. Smiling feebly in return, Ibar wiped his cheeks.

What was all that? These Irish monks never ceased to perplex Willis.

Boyd came wandering back. He tapped the shoulder of the fellow at the oar ahead of Anne and changed places with him. Ah, well. It didn't concern Willis. He had work enough keeping track of his own problems. Mindlessly plying his oar, he pondered nothing at all.

Apparently Anne was pondering her life, for presently she spoke to the broad back before her. "Have you ever been to Cashel, Boyd?"

"No. And you're English, so I'll hazard the guess you never have either. What's the attraction of Cashel, may I ask?"

"I don't know. It just sounds . . ." Her voice trailed a moment and took on an airy, distant quality, floating on dreams. "Prospects, I suppose. Peace."

"Peace? In the den of one of the two greatest warlords in Erin? The ard ri of the south?"

"Aye, peace. Perhaps even marriage."

Boyd chuckled. "I wouldn't guess peace and marriage could dwell together."

She giggled. Her soft voice sobered. "I can't tell you how much constant fighting has torn my life. It reduces our little clan faster than it can grow. We lose so many. Most of my older female cousins have stayed single. They can't make a good marriage, and they aren't willing to make a poor one."

"Ah. So your prospects didn't look good there, you're saying."

116

"They'll look no worse in Erin. Desmond's new monastery at Knag Burn seemed the perfect solution, the moment I first heard about it. It was drawing men in from all over. If I found a good marriage prospect there, I needn't worry about whether my clan was dwindling too fast to support a good marriage."

"I see." Boyd didn't have to lift that deep voice to be heard behind him. It rumbled clearly all the way back to where Willis was. "And that hope went up in flames, literally."

"Aye. It's so sad. Surely the constant skirmishing can be no worse elsewhere than it is back home."

"Did Desmond explain about those who possess the Spirit of Jesus Christ?"

"You mean that we're children of a common Father?"

"And co-heirs with Jesus. Commit yourself to Jesus Christ, and you enter into the greatest of clans, God's own. You then can join any community of the saved. Many are they who leave blood clans behind to make a new life with the saved."

"That would be so beautiful. What I want most, Boyd, is a peaceful community, reasonably free of strife. Strife destroyed my childhood, and it dogs me today."

"But Cashel, lass?"

"Desmond's Cashel surely enjoys the peace that comes to them who possess great strength. Exactly the opposite is my clan, don't you see? You never know when the next foray will come crashing down upon you. Friend and foe alike prey upon you when you have no strength of arm to pose a threat or a clear defense. Believe that."

Jovial Mochta stopped beside her. "My turn."

She shipped her oar, lest it tangle with Willis's behind her, and stood up. Willis watched her stretch her back mightily. Rowing might feel good, but you could tell from her actions that ceasing rowing felt better.

Mochta took her place, watched the rhythm a moment, absorbing it, and dipped his oar into the emerald sea. Willis had never seen an emerald, though he'd heard about them. And garnets and rubies and sapphires and topaz . . .

Willis and Ibar, he thought, could be excused for not realizing they were southbound. A thick, dull overcast, as usual, obscured the precise location of the sun. Anne retrieved her cloak from its folded little pile beside the stowage box, flung it around her shoulders, and wandered aft toward the tiller.

Hours—nay, days!—later, Ibar took over his oar, and Willis could stand up himself and stretch. He wobbled forward. A week at sea, and he still had not gained his sea legs. Now, thanks to a simple misunderstanding at the outset, he'd have to sail all the way north again to Iona, backtracking.

But wait. Clonfert. Desmond had talked of Clonfert. Ibar used to be there. Apparently Clonfert wasn't far from the landing place called Brandon Bay. Forget distant islands. Maybe Willis would just go to Clonfert or to some other monastic group near their landing. That might even be better. Boyd knew him, and Boyd knew the abbot of Clonfert. He could petition Boyd for a good word.

Maybe. What was it Boyd said that first day, as he and Anne and Ibar told their stories? "I hear your version well enough, thief, but that's not to say I believe it. I don't trust you."

Not exactly a ringing recommendation.

Willis glanced down toward the far end of the curragh. Boyd was handling the tiller now, supporting it with one bulky arm draped over it. He grinned like a teenager in the throes of first love. Across from him, grinning with equal inanity, Anne leaned back against the rough, laced gunwale. They were chatting about farming or some such. Willis couldn't make out the conversation clearly.

Farming. Bah. You can be a farmer and get wealth, or you can lie in wait and take the farmer's wealth after it's been gotten. Farming requires sweat, but robbery asked not much more than boldness and occasionally speed. Why sweat?

And then a chilling thought struck Willis. In Erin, wealth was measured in slaves and cattle. They didn't use money. It was hard enough to call a farmer to stand and deliver coins. But a cow or a slave?

He was going to have to either travel by sea to some other place, or join a monastery that would take care of him, or change his trade.

Any of those options made him sick.

118

16

Brandon Bay

How long would this go on? Ronan wasn't about to take much more. He watched Angelica and Fanchea—sweet and gentle, the both of them—stroll out the gate and down the hill toward him. On her head, Angelica balanced a big ash basket with easy grace. Fanchea carried a coil of cord and a stubby javelin, and that surprised him. The women did not normally walk about armed. At Ronan's left elbow, Crosan the Laughing Monk, not laughing at the moment, quickened his step.

Troll came barreling out the gate, romped a wide, happy circle around his mistress, and galumphed off to the gorse bushes beside the track. Ronan watched the dog a moment with a certain paternal interest. Puppy exuberance still overflowed onto everything the dog did, generously coating youthful energy with youthful enthusiasm, but there was a grown-up presence as well. Troll would be a fairly large animal by the time he quit growing, probably in another few months.

And now the irritating tug-of-war, the relationship Ronan had come to hate, began. Crosan hastened forward and kissed Angelica's hand in unctuous greeting. Ronan had to walk faster to catch up. Crosan cheerfully snatched her ash basket and balanced it on his own head, clowning, joking, making her giggle. Ronan hated having to chaperon Crosan every moment. And yet he relished being near Angelica in any capacity whatever. If that capacity be chaperon, then so be it.

Ronan moved in beside the women as they walked briskly along, matching his stride to theirs. "What are the chores of the day?"

"Gather fern sprouts and cattail roots, and lay snares for ducks. They're starting to come through now." Fanchea seemed much less wearied by life these days than she had appeared a month ago. Ronan wondered how much of the change was due to the easing of her grief and how much to the rejuvenating value of fresh spring air and warming sun.

At her other side, Crosan grunted. "Sounds like fairly wet work to me. Cattail roots?"

"They keep well, stored back in the souterrain. I cook them with pork joints. We'll eat a few of the fiddlenecks, but mostly they're pig food. The sow seems to farrow easier if she gets lots of vegetables."

Crosan proceeded to expound at length upon the joys of groveling in wet ground for pig food when pigs are so good at rooting for themselves. Ronan wanted him to shut up.

And Angelica—didn't she realize that with her smiling she was encouraging his nonsense?

They marched with purpose, like Roman soldiers, down to the creek with its winter-worn marshes.

Brown, soggy skeletons of last year's growth, sticks and duff and long lanceolate leaves, matted the ground and propped against each other, half reclining. The first green sprouts of the year's new growth thrust themselves up, struggling, through yesterday's dead vegetation. Most of the cattail heads had broken open over the winter, spewing their harsh lumps of fiber. As Troll bounded down into the soggy mat, a flock of little brown dunnocks left off worrying the seed heads and flew away deeper into the marsh.

On the edge of the lowest land, where the ground first gets soggy, Angelica set down her basket. Fanchea loosed her half dozen coils of strong cord. "Duck snares."

"Allow me." Crosan took her cordage, tucked most of it under his armpit, and opened out one of the hanks. "Ducks, geese, or swans?"

"What have you been seeing?"

"All three. I'll run the line over there." He gestured vaguely and slogged off across the marsh, his feet sinking into holes with every third step.

Fanchea watched his back a few moments, then waded out to a nearby thicket of cattails. Angelica followed with the basket, and they commenced prizing at cattail roots with the javelin.

Ronan slopped out into the fen. His shoes, soaked instantly, grabbed his feet in cold clutches. He bent double and dug his fingers into the icy mud to pull the roots. "Just as a point óf curiosity, why are we doing the pig's groveling for her?"

"Because she makes too much a muss and tears everything up. When I dig, I'm careful, and we maintain an abundant supply all summer. She can ruin the marsh in a week." Fanchea prized up a wad of roots, green-black and stinking with bog slime.

"I see. So your javelin there is for digging, then, and not for protection."

"Protection. The fishwife down on—" Fanchea stopped and stood erect. "Protection from Crosan? Sure and that's why you're constantly at our side, isn't it? To protect us from Crosan."

Ronan stood erect too. "Because I think you need protection."

"The question is, do we want protection?"

The import of that took awhile to sink in. Ronan stared at her. She met his eye fairly, steadily. He watched her a moment, trying to read the words she did not speak, and decided he couldn't. Did Angelica share her sentiments? That thought wrenched his gut.

And so, in essence, he lied about his reasons. "You're new and inexperienced in the faith, Boyd said. The Christian walk differs in many regards from the old ways. Not just in theological matters. Daily matters. Chastity, and the fidelity of husbands and wives, for instance. I consider it my Christian duty to lead as well as protect."

"Crosan can instruct me."

Ronan snorted. "A man with such a blatant disregard for the vows he made? If he can't be trusted before God, sure and he can't be trusted in matters of human morals."

She shrugged, and that shrug was also a lie, because it suggested she was relaxed and casual. She obviously was not. "Not all monastic societies renounce marriage."

"His does. I asked. Besides, you know and I know it's not marriage he's suggesting."

"And you know and I know I'm an adult who will make decisions for myself."

What decisions? Ronan didn't want to know.

Angelica stepped between them, her eyes darting from face

to face. "There's the fishwife too, Ronan. She told Fanchea about a foreigner with heavy eyebrows, looking for a runaway wife. He's apparently down around Currane, talking to fishermen."

Ronan grimaced. "So. Mac Larkin remembered me mentioning the Skelligs. It's logical he'd snoop in that area first. You should have told me immediately you found out."

"And what would you do?" Fanchea dipped her head. "Nobody around here knows about Angelica. I mean, where she's really from. They know her as a sister from Kildare, helping out here along with some brothers from Clonfert. It's nothing remarkable. Brothers from Clonmacnois are helping the ri tuathe at the mouth of the Shannon. It's going on all over."

Still, he wished he had more here than just one javelin—and that likely to be snapped in two, the way she was digging with it. He grimaced again, pretended it was a nod, and returned to the work at hand.

They dug in silence, he and Angelica together in the chill water and muck, Fanchea wielding a javelin that had no potential for adequate protection. When they had dug enough roots to fill the basket to a hand's depth, they turned to the hillside beneath the alders and began breaking off emergent fern sprouts, the first furled growth of spring. They had nearly filled the basket by the time Crosan returned from laying Fanchea's line of snares.

Fanchea excused herself then, promised to return shortly, and drawing her cloak close around her, walked off across the hill with the basket on her head.

Angelica watched the woman a moment and hastened after her.

Crosan returned and watched their departure. "So when are you going back to Skellig, brother?"

"I'm not. I don't even know if the brothers are still there. Even before I left, their resources were being sorely depleted, and I can't see the picture improving."

Crosan turned to face him. "I can't imagine a stodgy, world-weary fellow like you getting kicked out. You mope about like a wet rag, singing the offices with your eyes glassed over like potsherds and not a flicker of life about you. But then, I suppose anything can happen. You never did say why you left."

"And I'm not going to, especially not to you."

Crosan chuckled coarsely. "Love rivalry. We brothers are supposed to be above all that, right?"

"Some of us are."

The Laughing Monk's voice was not smiling. His words, brittle as flint, mocked with a cutting edge. "You sound so pious, brother. Leave you alone in the company of a woman, and she need fear no excitement in her life. Not even a suggestion. You seem to consider that a virtue. I'd call it a major defect in a man."

Fire flared up and roared to life. Not until that moment did Ronan realize how hard he had been working to keep it banked—and how good it felt to let it at last burn freely. "She is chaste, and she will remain chaste."

"Haven't you noticed, wet rag? I make them feel good, both of them. I make them smile. But Angelica especially. I want to give her life and beauty because she deserves it, and right now her life's pretty bleak with some Pictish ogre breathing down her neck. I have pleasing gifts for her. Exciting gifts. All you can offer her is that stupid brindled dog. And gloom."

Ronan's voice was rising without his trying. "Gifts! Your gifts are unholy. You made vows before God!"

"And what did you promise before God? Why did you leave your pious little aerie out on Skellig?"

It was the smirk on Crosan's face, more than his words, that precipitated Ronan's lunge. He was not a fighter by nature. But then he was not a cattail digger either, and he did that well enough. He slammed forward with both fists flying, one aimed to take out Crosan's wind and the other to flatten his face.

Both missed as Crosan shied backward and aside. Ronan continued pressing, angled toward him. He had to get a telling punch in fast, or Crosan, bigger, stronger, and faster, would take him. He probably should never have started this. No matter. He would win—he enjoyed the unbeatable advantage of being fully enraged.

This hound was demeaning his manliness! This hound was threatening Angelica's chastity, her very well-being!

Ronan connected on his second try, enough to knock Crosan backward. The clown lost his balance and fell heavily into the marsh. Ronan swung his free leg in a hard, fast kick. If he couldn't knock out Crosan's wind one way, he'd do it another.

The Laughing Monk managed to grab Ronan's ankle. He tipped Ronan's leg high, wrenched it, and yanked. Pulled off balance, Ronan fell on his side in the mud. He sucked in air as chill water pierced instantly to his skin. He flung a fist at Crosan to keep the monk from attacking, but it didn't work. Instantly, Crosan was on him, grappling, rolling, pinning his arms, slugging him in the face with his hard, flailing head. They rolled deeper into the mire. Crosan was trying to drown him! The Laughing Monk was leaning, shoving, pressing against him, pushing him deeper into the rank vegetation of the bog, trying to ram his head into a puddle of standing water.

Ronan kicked his legs free and, curling his spine, swung them up. He tried desperately to grab Crosan's head with his heels, to pull him away, to loosen the grip, to get room to swing. He managed to throw his weight enough to roll them both to their side.

Ronan was on top. Just as quickly he was on the bottom again, and they were practically floating in slime.

Angelica was screaming. Fanchea was whooping. Troll was barking—not helping by any means, just barking. The miserable cur!

Frustration joined with rage to give Ronan fresh strength. He could not forever keep this perverted lunatic from leading Angelica astray, and that frustrated him intensely. He could not guide those lovely ladies in the way they should go for they resisted him, and that frustrated him immensely. He managed by spreading his arms to break Crosan's grip around them finally, but the Laughing Monk scored an incredibly lucky blow with his head, slamming it into Ronan's face.

And then, curiously, Ronan and Crosan both began to rise until Ronan, on the bottom, hung a foot above the bog. A woman's voice cackled. Crosan let go, and Ronan fell back into the mud. He snapped around and rolled half a turn to his knees, ready to meet the next attack.

But Crosan did not attack. Crosan hung suspended, and behind him, suspending him, stood an irate Boyd Blond Hair. Then

Boyd's massive hands let go of the man's tunic and flung the Laughing Monk into the marsh.

Behind Boyd, Conn the handsome poet and a red-haired wisp of a girl stood watching, looking bemused. She had the most amazing, outrageous freckles.

Boyd pointed a gigantic hand and finger at Ronan. "Don't!"

Much as he wanted to, Ronan didn't. He would join the battle some other day, for his frustration and his fury suddenly drained away into the cold, wet swamp. What were Conn and Boyd doing here? Conn was supposed to be planting broadbeans. Boyd was supposed to be at sea, trying out the new boat with Brendan. And who was that strange young woman with the twinkling eyes and flame-red hair?

He struggled erect and very nearly fell again when his foot slipped in the slime. He was soaked with mud and water. His bloody nose was splashing the vivid red stain of defeat down the whole front of his tunic. And Crosan, that natterjack, looked as bad.

Ronan glanced at Angelica and instantly felt guilty for having distressed her. She stood wide-eyed with hands pressed against her cheeks. Fanchea stood beside her looking utterly entertained. The basket lay on its side at their feet, its cheery green fern fronds strewed in the mud.

Boyd scowled. "Is this over?"

"It's over." His feet making slurping noises in the muck, Crosan plodded up to firm ground. "And it's between the two of us. Understand, Boyd?"

"It's between the two of you and Brendan, because Brendan's your abbot. I came to get you. We're loading now to leave."

Crosan looked at Ronan, at Angelica. "I've decided to stay."

"Oh?" Boyd didn't seem to notice he was standing ankle deep in putrid water. He folded his arms. "You were among the original group of us who prayed together about this voyage and fasted together. You were chosen by God to go."

"I was chosen by God to pray and fast. That I did."

Boyd studied Angelica for a long time.

Ronan wanted to cry out, *It's not her fault! She didn't encourage him. Don't let him stay, giant!* He stood mute.

Angelica licked her lips. Why didn't *she* speak up and tell Crosan to go, as he had been destined? And then, in a flustered wave of shock and sadness, Ronan realized why.

Ronan's esteem for Boyd rose dramatically as the giant growled, "Protecting the lady from this fellow, is it? Don't bother. Conn here can do that if it needs be done."

Crosan simply glared.

Boyd grunted. "Very well. If that's your decision, you can go tell Brendan yourself. I'll not do it." He turned to Fanchea. "I wish to present to you Anne Green Head, a Pict from England. She's bound south, and I thought you might wish to help her. Some supplies, perhaps. Maybe you know someone in the area who's traveling to Cashel."

"We'll ask about." Fanchea nodded. "Welcome, Anne. I'm glad you came."

The red-haired Anne muttered something. Her Gaelic sounded like another language.

Ronan suddenly felt vividly, incredibly foolish standing there in the swamp. Mud and water dripped off him. He was starting to shiver. His nose hadn't really quit bleeding yet, and he could feel one eye beginning to swell shut. Everyone else, even Crosan now, looked much tidier and in control.

Ronan waded up onto firm ground, tilting and staggering across the soggy little hillocks of vegetation. He paused and looked at Angelica, but any words he might have spoken fled before he could find and use them. He wanted her to tell him to stay. He wanted her to tell Crosan to go. He wanted the world to be fair and just and beautiful.

He brushed past the sniggering Conn, past that frail red-haired girl, on out the track southward and up the hill. He felt like screaming and kicking and bodily dragging Angelica away.

Mostly, though, he felt like weeping.

He glanced back not by turning his head but by shifting his eyes as the track arched around the side of the hill. The group had dispersed. There lay the marsh abandoned, and the cattail thicket. And then the trail wound on around the crest of the hill, and he lost sight of the place completely.

He walked without knowing or caring where. He would eventually come to the sea. Then he'd have to quit walking. He still shivered, but his nosebleed seemed to have almost ceased.

He walked on.

The track joined the main way from the east. Ronan recognized this main track. This was the way he first entered the region, long, long ago when he never knew any honey-blonde beauty. Back when Troll was younger and followed him. If he continued along this path it would open out onto a hill above the creek where Brendan built his boat.

Ronan sat down. He stared at the miniature ocean of tangled green mosses in front of him. Each tiny frond, but an inch or so high, laced its leaflets into the fellow beside it to form a solid, undulant mat out across the glade. A spongy mass it all was, inviting him to simply lie down and rest and let the world go its way without him.

Brendan's voyage. The Land of Ever Young. Hi Brasil.

Of course!

As Fanchea pointed out, the women were adults in command of their own fates. Let Fanchea follow whatever stars she wished for herself. But Angelica . . .

Mac Larkin knew Ronan on sight. He was seeking the two of them together, under the mistaken impression that they were a pair. The last thing Angelica needed was Ronan hovering nearby. For her safety he must stay as far away from her as possible.

He would voyage to Hi Brasil. With Crosan remaining behind, Brendan would need another arm for the oars. Ronan would spread the word where he was going and intimate that Angelica was going also. That should lure Mac Larkin away from her trail.

And that was why she had not begged him to stay. She knew that the two of them together were conspicuous, and that spelled danger.

Yes. Yes.

Ronan lurched to his feet. He had sat there an hour or less, and see how painfully stiff he was already. And cold. He commenced shivering again. He hurried off along the track.

The sun had been hiding behind a pearlescent overcast. Now the haze was burning off. By the time Ronan crested the final hill, it gave a brilliant sheen to the distant sea.

Here was where he had left the trail the other time. He jogged straight down the hill, stepping in soggy cow tracks and puddles, working his way around the really wet spots.

Then he stopped abruptly. Below, he could see exactly where Brendan had built his boat. He saw where scores of busy feet had beaten the grass and mud to a dull brown flatness. The fire pit and steam box, cold and abandoned, sat forlorn. He could tell precisely where the boat had launched. He could see where Brendan had touched shore upon his return, somewhat down-stream in the creek. Brendan had come back for Crosan. Crosan decided to remain. May the rest of Brendan's plans go better.

There lay a second beaten place where Brendan, obviously, had just now finished provisioning his boat for his journey of journeys.

And there above the sparkling water a mile off shore, bearing north northwest beyond the point, Brendan's bright new sail was disappearing in the distance.

17

Larkin

"Tavish, you harebrain, that's not the way you do it!"

Tavish roared a whirlwind through his mustache. "Larkin, you lurking adder, you've been doing it wrong all your life! Accept instruction!"

In the dim light of a few smoky grease lamps, Tavish's extravagant mustache looked almost as dark as burly Larkin's beetling brows. How either man could see the gaming board well enough to play escaped Desmond. He sat cross-legged on the third side of the board, as close as either of them, and he could not see clearly.

As one they turned to him.

"Do you play?" Tavish asked, with a tone of voice that suggested you had to be an utter fool if you did not.

Desmond smiled. "Brandub and fidchell, of course. Nearly everyone in Erin knows brandub and fidchell. And senet. Interesting game, senet. Out of Egypt. Ancient, ancient game. But not what you're playing there. No."

Tavish bobbed his head. His mustache swayed. "The correct answer, because this game is local. Invented by Larkin's paternal grandfather, as I recall. Isn't that right?" He looked at his burly nemesis.

Larkin grinned proudly. "He did indeed, though it probably hasn't spread much beyond the local clans." He sobered, darkened. "So of any man here, I ought to know the rules, aye?"

"Hardly!" Tavish picked up the ale flagon and paused for a swig. "You've changed everything else your clan holds dear—no doubt you've changed the rules to this as well. I play by the pure rules, the original rules."

"Wait." Desmond raised his hands. "Your two clans are related? The Tavish and the Larkin?"

Larkin waved a hand. "Only through a couple of peripheral cousins with the bad taste to marry across the line."

"And a couple women," Tavish added, "who happened to get abducted by the wrong people."

"My immediate bloodline had nothing to do with that, Tavish. We didn't even know about the kidnappings until two of the babies were born and toddling."

"A Larkin is a Larkin." Tavish scowled at Desmond. "You're sure you're not familiar with this game, eh?" He studied the board a few moments. "Larkin, how about: the man who first lands in the back table has the choice of either ceding a man or moving forward?"

"That's how the rules were originally. It doesn't work at all well." He scowled just as darkly as Tavish as he scrutinized their game.

Desmond felt the strongest urge to end this petty dispute by simply tipping the board. He quelled the urge and held his peace.

Larkin grunted. "Oh, all right, if it will get the game moving again. We'll change it later."

A serving wench, looking droopy, came in with three freshly charged lamps.

"Is the moon down yet?" Tavish asked her.

"Been down for an hour, lord." She did obeisance and left.

Desmond stood and stretched. "No wonder I feel like an undercooked pudding. I thought it was my stupidity that prevented me from grasping your game. It's lack of sleep. Good night, gentlemen."

As one they bade him a quiet rest. And as he stepped out of the hall into the moonless night, they commenced another minor argument about the positioning of the side piece.

Whatever the side piece was.

This was a dangerous time to leave those two. Very late at night, politeness and inhibitions lay comatose anyway, and the ale didn't help matters. Besides, both kings tended to take that silly game far too seriously. They need only erupt into an unquelled argument, and two hundred people would come to blows.

How tenuous is peace.

"Desmond?"

He twisted around and peered into the darkness, but those lamps had ruined his night vision. A woman approached within three feet of his face before he could make out who she was. His neck felt stiff. "Larkin's wife. Good evening, Eva."

"Good evening. Do you suppose those two children in there will play through to dawn?"

"Quite likely." He smiled.

"What are the odds they'll draw swords?"

"I'd put them at four to five."

Eva cackled. "A practical man! I'll walk with you to your door."

Desmond would guess her age at about forty. She moved with the agility of a twenty-year-old and spoke with the authority of a high king. Larkin ruled an extensive clan. The moment he met Eva, Desmond realized who ruled Larkin.

"Certainly." Desmond commenced a casual stroll. His back felt stiff as well as his neck. Sitting hunched over a gaming board did nothing good for his body. "Are you settling in comfortably?"

"Very. Tavish's wife is a charming woman. A bit bawdy, but she's an excellent hostess. She made us guests feel quite at home. What I wanted to tell you—a traveler arrived a couple hours ago, the wife of the abbot at Ninian's church on Whithorn. She says she knows you. She'd like to join you tomorrow, when she's rested."

"Of course! Isle of Whithorn, Ninian's first church here. I conducted a few offices there when first I arrived from Erin. I remember her."

"She brought the news up from that direction. Much of it pertains to Britons and politics. But several items—"

"About your son?"

"He's abroad. He sailed to Erin in pursuit of that woman." Eva wagged her head. "Once he gets his mind upon something, he's like a weasel. He'll not stop until he sees it to the end. Just like his father."

Desmond nodded and took a wild guess. "And you don't think that the young woman named—what was her name?"

"Angelica."

"That Angelica is worth all the effort. How many men did he take with him?"

131

"Larkin only let him take five. That worries me, father. Six men isn't nearly enough protection to journey in a land of unpredictable fools as wild as those Irish." She gasped. "Not the brethren, of course! Not the monks. I mean the ordinary warriors! The trashy element."

"Of course. No offense taken."

"And you're quite right. Angelica is low-born in a weak and lazy clan. Not good material at all."

"A mother suffers most of all God's saints, I've heard."

"Ah, and could I ever dispute that? True and true again! And spiritual fathers also, for another of the items the abbot's wife's mentioned concerns your young Ibar. Apparently he shipped to Iona with a freckle-faced girl, Anne." She paused a moment. "And Willis East Bogg."

"Indeed!" Iona. The poor lad wouldn't last a week at Iona. Columcille's rules were stricter by far than Brendan's, and Ibar chafed at Clonfert. They'd throw him off the island and make him swim, particularly if the girl Anne tried to debark there. And Willis in any order at all? Unthinkable. His cynicism left him nowhere near embracing the faith. Interesting news, but Desmond didn't know what to think of it. "Iona."

"The lad's loss. He could have been a part of something magnificent." Eva cleared her throat. "You're a stranger, an Irishman. I doubt you realize the significance of what you've just done."

"The monasteries? They're coming very well, aren't they? Understand it is exclusively the work of God."

"Not the monasteries. Any goose can build an oratory and dig a wall around it. The reconciliation. The peacemaking between those two in there, bringing the two factions together."

"They did that themselves."

"No. Tavish's wife described the scene that first night of your arrival, after the feast, when my Larkin leaped out of your door. The surprise took ten years off her life, she says. And then you stepped directly between the two of them and told them exactly what to do and how to do it, and neither one of them dared gainsay you. It was a bold move on your part, Desmond Perfect. Only by God's intervention did their swords not clang together inside your chest."

Desmond stopped. "Desmond *who?*"

"The Perfect One. You surely know the epithet they've laid upon you."

He crossed himself rapidly. *O dear God, I pray You not listen to them!* "Whatever made anyone think I'm perfect?!"

"You haven't been guilty of a misstep yet. People have been watching. I suppose that weighed in their decision."

"Far, far short of perfect."

"Dead to sin. That's for sure. Good organizational abilities. And remember the Matthew passage you discussed this morning at primes?—'Blessed are the peacemakers.' You called Tavish and my Larkin the peacemakers. It's you. Everything you touch turns to success."

"I have my failures."

"Name one."

"You named him already. Ibar. My assistant. Former assistant."

"Oh, come, Desmond!" The woman sounded more and more like a queen. "When a half-grown youth decides to leave behind the scene of battle and run off with some girl, there's nothing you're going to do about it. You know where a young man's fancy drifts, even the most devout lad. You can't really fault him."

"I know, I know. Larkin says the same. Youth. It's sin, for all that. He had such promise. Then that girl . . ." Why was he telling Eva all this? He was the spiritual leader, the stalwart one who knew the will of God.

"Believe me, that girl isn't worth thinking about. Her family's the dregs of her clan. From over around Green Head they are. Not a decent farmer in the lot of them. Even that Angelica is a better catch than she, and I loathe the thought of my son pursuing her."

"All the same, I wonder what will come of them—of Ibar. Iona notwithstanding, I'm certain he's left the brotherhood. He'd have to. And such a waste."

Eva sniggered. "You see? You're so sure that everyone has to be perfect. No mistakes. No stumbles. You haven't been around Larkin long enough, or you'd know better than that. A mistake a minute with that oaf. With his eldest son too. I should know. I raised the lad."

They arrived at Desmond's door. "You speak ill of your husband, Eva?"

"Not ill. Truth. No one knows the man better than I. He's proud and clever and probably the strongest man alive, pound for pound. He's an incurable womanizer and braggart. In love or war, it's all or nothing. To the death."

"He plays games that way too, I see."

"Indeed." She smiled. "He does everything that way. He achieves triumphs and makes mistakes with equal enthusiasm. It's the one endearing quality that has kept me at his side all these years." She stepped back. "Rest, Desmond Perfect. You look like forty miles of abandoned siege works. Late hours take their toll on you."

"They seem to. Thank you for bringing me the news. I look forward to meeting with the lady tomorrow. Good night."

"Good night." She turned and walked away. Her form dissolved into the blackness long before her footfalls did.

He shoved his door open, entered, and pulled it closed behind him, stepping from utter darkness into utter darkness. The latch dropped in place with a clunk. It smelled musty in here, with no windows and a heavy door. Tomorrow he would air it well.

Tonight he didn't bother with formal prayers on bended knee, and that was not like him. He groped his way across the hovel and crawled between the linen liners of his pallet.

This ostentation immersed him in guilt. His brothers at Cashel and Clonfert slept in raw sheepskins, as devoted men ought to do. He on the other hand avoided direct contact with the itchy harshness of wool fleece by lining it with lengths of fine linen, as did kings, filidh, and druids. It was Larkin's idea, and Tavish went along with it. Desmond should not have.

His bed was very cold. It sucked his body warmth away, no matter how tightly he curled up. He shivered.

He ate too well. He suffered no privation. One cannot hone the soul and build the faith by living at ease. He commenced his prayers, not reverently kneeling but shivering between his covers.

And Ibar. *You were hewing well to the way, lad. I was proud of you. How could you have deviated so?*

Wait. Ibar. Ibar and that silly Willis on the same boat? Larkin seemed convinced that Willis betrayed him, though Tavish claimed not. What if Ibar and the robber were in cahoots in some way? He tried to picture Ibar being led astray by a robber. Especially that particular robber. Probably stranger things happened, but he still couldn't envision it.

He really shouldn't go to sleep. If the moon set an hour ago, that meant he would have to rise and celebrate matins in another hour. He should not have remained up so late.

He dozed. He forced his mind back to prayer. Pray for the souls of Anne, Ibar, and Willis. Pray for a comely end to Mac Larkin's strange pursuit of the woman named Angelica. Pray for the growth in faith of Larkin and Tavish. He dozed again before accomplishing any consistent supplication.

* * *

He could tell they were the gates of hell because they smoldered, black and smoky. He chopped at them with an old bronze battle-ax, but the blade curled under, rendering the ax useless. He pounded upon them with Willis's oaken club, to no avail. He thumped in vain at them with the side piece from Larkin's gaming board. With a crash the gaming piece, now four feet long, split asunder.

Larkin himself was roaring as he shook Desmond's shoulder. "Father! Arise!" In shifting, sallow lamplight, Larkin's dark round face and beetling brows loomed grotesque. "Father! Do you hear me?"

"I hear you." Desmond ached all over. He hated crawling out of bed for matins on cold mornings like these.

"We pounded on your door five minutes at least. Father?"

"You know, Larkin, brother, sometimes I hate getting up for matins."

"Matins?! It's tierce, Father. Midmorning. Six hours past matins."

Desmond pulled his linen-lined sheepskin in tighter. "Ah, Ibar. If only Ibar were here he could handle the offices. Pray thee, awaken me for matins, if you would."

"Father . . ." The hulking Larkin pressed his hands here and there against Desmond's head and shoulders.

Apparently this child-man was going to give Desmond no peace. Desmond so desperately wanted a few hours' peace, a few sweet hours without responsibility. Now Tavish's extravagant mustache loomed above him also. In fact, Tavish, it seemed, was holding the lamp. It flickered.

Desmond realized what else tugged at him too. "I so yearn for Erin, Larkin. I ache for her so much sometimes, I can't stand it. I didn't think white martyrdom would be this hard. Columcille does it. He swears he'll never return to her. He made it seem so easy to cross the emerald sea forever. I think about Brendan and the way he sails to Man and Wales and all over. Short trips. A few weeks. A summer. And yet he always returns to Clonfert. He doesn't rip out his roots."

"Yes, father. Help me here." Apparently Larkin was not asking help from Desmond. He was scooping Desmond into his arms as a father gathers up a small child who has fallen asleep in the donkey cart.

From up in Larkin's burly arms, Desmond frowned down at his floor and at the shattered timbers lying there. "You broke my door down, Larkin. Look."

"Yes, I did indeed, father. You wouldn't open."

"The oratory," Tavish said. The mustached warlord darted off ahead, calling to people, shouting orders.

"What do you need of me, Larkin? I want to sleep."

"Nothing, father. You may rest."

Nothing? Then what was all this? Ducking low and twisting sideways, Larkin squeezed through the oratory door, still clutching Desmond. Maybe Tavish had been right when he advocated a bigger oratory.

Tavish's wife was arranging linens and sheepskins into a bed at the front of the oratory beside the lectern. Other women were setting lampstands at the bed's head and foot.

Larkin laid Desmond down there on the pallet in full view of everyone. Say the offices from bed? It was all insane, and yet it all made sense somehow, as a bad dream seems right just after you awaken from it.

"Kieran of Saighir, one of twelve consecrated by Patrick himself when first he arrived in Ireland," Tavish's voice intoned. "Conleth, a hermit and expert metal craftsman, and a good friend of Brigid. Fanchea of Clogher, founding abbess of Rossory."

Desmond curled up on his side, comfortable on this fine pallet. He closed his eyes. "Larkin? What's Tavish talking about?"

"He's reading the roll call of saints who have died during the plagues. One of the new scrolls, which you yourself added to the scriptorium."

Tavish droned on, his words uniquely and characteristically sifted through the bounteous mustache. "Mochta, an immediate disciple of Patrick, at Louth. And now, as for the living—Maelor, a hermit, still alive on Sark. Noted for having ministered in Jersey during the plague there."

"Why is he reading that, Larkin?"

"It's the devotional for tierce. We'll repeat it during the other offices today. It's to edify and comfort the brethren."

"Obituaries are a comfort?"

"A reminder, then. Some of God's brightest and best have died of the plagues, and others, equally meritorious, live on. Whether you live or die, you live and die in the Lord. Praise His name."

"Larkin . . ."

"We fear you may be ill, so we've commenced a prayer vigil. It's far easier to pray over you here in the oratory than for people to be constantly squeezing in and out your cell."

"Not to mention the door broken down."

"That too."

So Larkin and Tavish thought he had fallen ill, was it? Desmond would tend to agree. He shifted onto his back because a very tender lump in his armpit made lying on his side painful. He didn't want to roll over to his other side, for then he would face the wall.

He saw people, dozens of people, looking at him. They knelt on the oratory floor, hands clasped. Some prayed with eyes closed. Others watched him. Now and again a few came over and laid hands upon him. As often as he himself had laid hands upon the sick, never had he felt it done to him. He was amazed at how much comfort the simple yet profound gesture provided.

Oblivious to the praying congregation, Tavish's druid came in, examined Desmond briefly, and left.

Desmond dozed. Someone was singing noonsong. Awfully early for that, wasn't it? Apparently not, for he awakened to hear nones, and the sun seemed poised about right for 3:00 P.M.

By nightfall, a dozen sore knots had erupted at random spots on his body. No position felt comfortable anymore, yet he was too wearied to toss and turn much.

The lay brother who served as abbot down at the Knag Burn monastery arrived sometime during the night. Larkin and Tavish came and went.

It was Larkin who sat beside his pallet when he awoke some time after primes the next morning.

Desmond forced himself to some sort of alertness. "Ah, Larkin, friend. I was delighted to see our brother from Knag Burn last night—and dismayed. I know how he abhors travel, so my condition must be grave indeed."

Larkin smiled beneath those heavy black brows. The smile looked strained. "You're a smart man even when you're asleep. I always suspected as much."

"How's the rebuilding coming down there?"

"Nearly complete! Tavish sent down a crew to help our people with the heavy work—resetting beams and posts. In fact, several of Tavish's workmen building her presently are the very people who burned her in the past. I'll have my monastery there as fine as Tavish's here, and this one here as fine as mine down there. A great awakening is happening there and here as well, Desmond father!"

Desmond's eyes burned, so he let them drop shut. "I'm sorry Ibar isn't here to take part in it. It's an exciting time. Ninian planted, I watered, God gathers the harvest. Praise to God!"

"Praise to God!"

Desmond watched the man a few minutes. This was the hostile, huffy warlord who, at their first encounter, had his man toss a couple of dead hares at Desmond's feet as a sop. This was the raider who pillaged his own lands and challenged his own kin. Look at him glow with his renewed spirit! And Tavish as well—what a magnificent beginning.

But it was only a beginning. Desmond saw that well enough.

"Larkin? What's the word about? That I am dying?"

"Yes, father." Larkin's voice croaked.

"I can't. Not yet. I can't leave this work, and you know that. It would fall apart. You and Tavish are wandering on new ground.

You're warriors, the finest of warriors. Putting up with each other rubs you both the wrong way. This present moment of cooperation between you is all very nice. But I'm afraid that neither of you is mature enough in the spirit to keep peace long enough to help both monasteries prosper."

"Yes, father. We've learned a lot from you, though. We've learned that some words are best left unsaid, and some deeds are best left undone."

"Good. But the real trick is knowing when."

Larkin chuckled.

"You need both monasteries, Larkin. For the two clans, and to serve the two areas. One central community would be too far from both clans to serve either of them well. We can't let one fade. I can't die. So let's just pray my deliverance until this work is farther along." Desmond was amazed at how much that one bit of speaking wore him down.

"Yes, father."

"If only Ibar were still in the brotherhood. If only Ibar were here."

18
Landfall

Whatever Boyd envisioned as a journey in search of Tir na n'Og, this wasn't it. In the first place, their craft seemed such an ordinary vessel for such an extraordinary voyage. Certainly this frame-and-leather curragh was bigger than most and was stepped with a large sail. But a curragh is a curragh for all that.

Boyd leaned against the forward half-decking, trying to stay near the middle so as not to dip the boat too badly out of trim. Leeson, the navigator, tended to yell at him when he leaned.

The weather was starting out fine. Except for a thin, even veil of high overcast painted across the blue sky, the spring sun shone. Boyd knew better than to think that would last. Indeed, he had rather anticipated that the weather would in fact be gloomier than this.

From the tiller aft, Leeson bellowed at him. He shifted.

And the crew. Ah, the crew.

When old Barrind first came to Brendan and told his story, describing his son's journeys to the Land of Ever Young, a group of brothers within Brendan's larger colony of brethren had gathered in prayer and fasting.

They were a unit, this small group. Fourteen common brothers and Brendan. They worked together; they sang the offices together; they built the boat together. Together they devoted themselves to social service in their Lord's holy name each Sunday. But then, after all that, they did not sail together, and it had been intended all along that they should.

What was God's will? God's intentions seemed far more clouded in Boyd's mind than did the sky above his head. Was Crosan in His will when he remained behind during the shakedown voyage? It seemed a small thing. But when it comes to God's desires, no detail is too small. Now here they were, well at sea, with three men not of the original group.

It just didn't seem quite right.

"It just doesn't seem quite right." Boyd gave his thoughts a voice since Brendan was walking up to him.

"What doesn't?" Brendan studied Boyd's position a moment, then leaned against the half-decking carefully. The deck evened up, back in trim.

"The crew. We don't seem as tightly knit as we used to."

"Perhaps I should not have voiced my reservations aloud. But the premonition was so strong . . ." Wiry little Brendan let his thought lapse and simply watched the horizon awhile. "My prophecy certainly didn't help matters any."

His premonition. Prophecy. Call it more an accusation. "One of you has done something meritorious," he told the three newcomers, "but for you other two, God is preparing a severe judgment."

He did not say which one merited grace and which two did not, and Boyd was reluctant to ask. Quite possibly Brendan himself did not know. Frequently he received direction from God without knowing what he was being directed about. He attributed it to his own obtuseness, his personal failure to comprehend the whole of God's intent. Boyd couldn't accept that. He never ceased to be amazed at how much Brendan received clearly by divine direction.

Three newcomers: the handsome Conn, the callow Ibar, the devious little Willis.

Boyd could understand that Conn would come. Although not one of the original group, Conn had been helping Brendan greatly all along by garnering supplies. Forty-nine oak-tanned oxhides were not an easy thing to come by. But he'd not only found them, he'd provided an additional fifty, which they stowed aboard for repairs and boat-building. Matched hides too. And although sheepskins were plentiful, Conn had hand-picked these, choosing especially curly, dense fleeces. You could toss a bucket of water on these, and they'd still keep you warm and dry as you slept.

Ibar had been attached not so much to the brotherhood of Clonfert as to Desmond, who had prepared for ministry abroad at Clonfert. Still, the lad was one of them. Boyd did not understand yet just what exactly went wrong on Desmond's mission to England. The lad was extremely reticent about discussing it. Nice enough young fellow, Ibar, but he needed less of theological learning and a lot more training in practical life. All in all, though, he'd make a good journeymate.

But Willis.

"Brendan, you are abbot of one of the most magnificent monasteries in Christendom."

"Thank you, Boyd. That is strictly God's doing."

"Fine. Still, you are abbot. You know all the brethren. You've examined them. How did you let that little Willis join us when we both know he's never been near Clonfert, as he claims?"

"It's possible. I'm away more than I'm there. I travel widely for a year at a time. Men I never meet have come and gone more than once. Should I accuse him of lying?"

"I think this time it would be justified, yes."

"If he is not lying . . ."

"Surely you don't believe that. He's a Pict! When's the last time a Pict entered our gate at Clonfert?"

"If he is not lying, I've offended a brother by falsely accusing him. If the man is lying, God will judge him. I don't have to. So when he said, 'I served at Clonfert a couple of years ago,' I took his claim at face value."

"Young Ibar told me where he probably got that. From Desmond. Willis had attached himself to Desmond. When he knew you were sailing with a crew of Clonfert brethren, he connected the 'Clonfert' Desmond spoke of and made his false claim."

"You're probably right."

And that seemed to be that. Apparently Brendan did not realize how powerfully and adversely one self-centered unbeliever could affect the whole crew. They were a close community, a group of common purpose. Except for Willis.

Ah, well. Brendan had said when these three newcomers came aboard that two of them would suffer judgment. Boyd prayed that Willis would do so quickly and thereby end the disruption he was causing.

Brendan depended utterly upon God with a cheerful vigor Boyd could probably learn by emulating his abbot. He must work on that.

The stiff breeze served them perfectly just now. With her sail set square and taut, and the wind quartering behind her, the curragh surged forward, her blunt prow plowing a solid wake. How Boyd loved riding down the sea like this! It didn't happen often. Usually Leeson was calling to brothers to man the twelve-foot oars, so many on this side and so many on that as Leeson himself held the tiller. Leeson seemed never quite satisfied with the direction the wind blew. Today even Leeson couldn't complain.

For a few minutes Boyd watched the play of wind on wave. The way the breeze stirred its different patterns on these swooping hills of water intrigued him. On the windward surface it drew one sort of design and on the lee slopes another. He twisted around and upward to listen to the thrumming, whispering sail with eye as well as ear.

They had cleared the islands to the east. Empty sea stretched to infinity all around them.

"Leeson!" Brendan broke Boyd's spell with a mighty bellow. "Ship the tiller and let her run!"

The navigator looked puzzled for only a moment. Obediently he raised their steering oar clear of the water. Obviously, navigators are not comfortable about turning the helm over to God, even when it is He who controls the vagaries of wind and tide.

Free of her leash, the curragh seemed to ride higher and lighter. Instead of plowing, she skated. Even with the wind nearly abaft, she sideslipped a little on her round, greasy bottom.

A grin the width of the sail behind them spread across Brendan's face. Pure joy. Boyd recognized that joy because he felt it too.

This feeling of intense pleasure seemed to radiate like the sun back through the vessel from Brendan and Boyd to Leeson and all the others—even Willis. The brothers hung off the gunwales or propped against the half-decking or draped their relaxed bodies against the drum-tight rigging. They let the wind blow their hair forward in their eyes and run its cold fingers up their backs. Eighteen men hurtled across the face of the sea as one man. Eighteen hearts rejoiced in this ultimate, racing freedom with one heart.

Over on the starboard gunwale, Conn commenced a five-tone Gloria in his strong, clear tenor. Yes! Glory to God! Boyd immediately picked up the baritone counterpoint. Malo took the deep bass, and three other voices filled in, then six. "Glory to God in the highest!" soared heavenward, swallowed by vastness above and all around.

Before the last notes could drift away entirely, Conn shifted to an eight-tone Gloria. Young Ibar, clearly, had been taught that one. He sang hesitantly at first, then stronger, until his thin, high voice climbed above the others in a beautiful descant. Boyd didn't have to look to know it was he—there was only one boy soprano aboard this vessel.

Boyd looked aft. Leeson had lashed the tiller high—God alone directed their course now. And then Boyd's singing faltered, for Willis had captured his full attention. The little cutthroat usually responded to prayer and teaching and song with a cynical smirk. Now an expression of intense wonder—call it amazement—had driven the smirk clean away.

The day passed, from matins through tierce through compline, and the sky still glowed orange at the midnight change of watch. How do you measure hours when the night never fully rolls itself out?

* * *

Days passed. Boyd lost track, in part because he found himself at odd watches and couldn't get a good daily rhythm going. Brendan kept an exact record, though, with his usual patient thoroughness. As a result, they never missed a Saturday of bathing and shaving their tonsures and never missed an office. Patterns and behaviors emerged. In the beginning they were a crew shipping out on a voyage of discovery. And then one day—and the clarity of the revelation surprised Boyd when he first noticed it—they were a tightly woven monastic brotherhood practicing the daily routine of faith just like any other brotherhood, except that they were using a boat for an oratory. A floating monastery.

Boyd wore with pleasure the comforting cloak of sameness that the daily routine provided. The jumble of watches together with the midnight sun might be disturbing his sense of time, but routine and liturgy kept his life on a straight and measured track.

Then came the day he began to serve his rotation as cook.

144

He examined their stores and instantly drew Brendan aside, back by the unused tiller. "Brendan, father, we've been eating well."

"Very."

"For how many days now?"

"Forty."

Boyd kept his voice low. "We've no food for the forty-first."

"Mm. Interesting."

Interesting! Boyd readjusted his voice to low. "Brendan, do you see land anywhere in sight? Anywhere at all? Do any seabirds swoop about our heads that we might snare one? Any fish below?"

"No more meat stores?"

"No smoked pork or beef, no salt pork."

"No cheese or oats?"

"Not even any hazelnuts." Boyd sighed. "I don't think 'interesting' is an appropriate word here."

"Of course it is. Forty is the Scripture's number for testing. Forty days and forty nights? How often have you heard that? Noah. Forty days in the wilderness—Jesus, in Saint Matthew. It's an honor, you see. We're being tested, not unlike Jesus Himself. God is trying us, brother."

Boyd welcomed attention from God, of course. But he'd welcome His divine favor better in the form of a full stomach. Boyd was known for his ability to handle generous portions.

"God will provide." Brendan paused and smiled. "However, to ease your doubts, inform the watch that we'll make directly for the first land raised."

"Thank you." There wasn't a whole lot more Boyd could ask for under the circumstances. The horizon offered nothing except a small pile of clouds to the north northeast.

How he wished he could enjoy Brendan's casual acceptance of adversity, Brendan's consummate faith in God, Brendan's easy way of sauntering through life virtually carefree. Most of all he yearned to be able to hear God's voice the way Brendan did.

One of you is destined for reward, and the other two are doomed. If Boyd did not have that kind of gift now, he almost surely wasn't going to be able to develop it in the future. It was given or it was withheld. It was not constructed. Now if Boyd were Ibar's age, perhaps . . .

On impulse he dropped the tiller and turned the boat toward that small blob of clouds hanging afar off. She arched gracefully aside in one of her sweeping, sliding curves. Boyd admired the artistry of her movement.

They approached the cloud bank quickly. Curiously, the curragh sailed better with the wind off her aft quarter than when it blew from directly astern. Boyd ordered four oars out to keep her from sideslipping away from the quartering wind.

Crosan the Laughing Monk ended up as one of the oarsmen, and he was not laughing. Aftmost of the four, he scowled at Boyd. "If we were going somewhere, I'd labor with eagerness. But heading for a cloud, Boyd, does not encourage my enthusiasm."

"Where else would we go?"

"Right, right. What do you see, lads? Naught but the horizon. Then head for the horizon, lads. It's better than nothing."

And then the watch called, "Land ho! Beneath those clouds."

It rose out of the horizon, out of the sea as they approached, as all islands do. But this one rose abruptly, jutting straight up as one continuous cliff. No beach, no shingle, no slope softened the line between sea and land. The island sat atop a dark, gloomy wall, impenetrable.

The island's coastline, highly irregular, bulged out in little peninsulas and dipped back in pinched embayments. Nor was the cliff wall smooth. It was creased by a number of narrow indentations, some very shallow and some deep canyons. A silver ribbon of water plunged down the furthermost, narrowest part of each defile. Were one of these niches and canyons found ashore in Erin it would be a waterfall of the most gorgeous sort, called unique and spectacular. Admirers would journey to the place from all over Erin, just to gaze upon its beauty. Here, waterfall upon cascade upon waterfall tumbled down a dozen defiles, and no admirer, so far as Boyd could tell, lived within a thousand leagues.

They sailed around the circumference of this strange bit of land. They found no landing place, no wall or defile safe enough to scale.

With one hand, Conn pointed to one of the shallowest of the waterfall defiles. In his other hand he held his leather watercup.

"You see how the ocean laps against the cliffside. No breakers, no waves. That means the water is deep right up to land's edge. We can sail in against the cliff wall and catch fresh water into our cups. We may have run out of food, but at least we can drink."

Boyd grabbed his cup.

"No." Brendan wagged his tousled head. "We'll explore this place another three days."

"We already did that." Boyd didn't want to stay here, but he had no better suggestion for traveling elsewhere. And he was outrageously thirsty.

"Three is a number of waiting. Jonah three days in the great fish. Jesus three days in the grave. This is more of God's hand. We will not plunder His bounty prematurely."

"I'd hardly call getting a drink of water 'plunder,'" Crosan muttered.

Boyd would agree, but Brendan was abbot.

And so because Brendan was abbot, they spent the next three days getting thirstier and thirstier and hungrier and hungrier, as water trickled recklessly in silver ribbons, tantalizing, beckoning. At night they tied up to the lee side on fifty feet of hawse line, for the tide coursed fifteen feet up and down the cliff wall.

The perpetually wet cliffs between tide lines fascinated Boyd. At low tide, sea mosses, kelps, starfish, mussels, limpets, periwinkles, knobby little spongy things, and a dozen kinds of slime clung tightly to the vertical black rocks, silently awaiting the returning sea. At high tide, the frothy waves splashed against essentially dry rock, without a sign of any living thing. Boyd found himself wondering which of the things he saw stuck to the cliff were edible and how much it would take to make them palatable.

Six oars out on each side still left six men to watch for the opportunity to land, which Brendan seemed sure existed. Boyd was not sure.

Crosan bellied up to the rail beside him. "I'm so hungry the hull is in danger."

Boyd nodded. "I wouldn't even bother to cook it."

"I don't know how it happened."

"How what happened?"

"How I ended up here. I was so certain I was going to stay

ashore. So certain, Boyd. I walk up to Brendan, tell him—I didn't tell him. I didn't get a chance. He just said, 'Get in the boat,' and I got in the boat. I didn't mean to. I didn't want to. Here I am." Crosan grimaced. "And I still don't want to. I confess I've been petitioning Brendan privately to turn back. He'll have none of that, of course, but I tried."

Boyd watched his brother's troubled face a moment. "Tell me something, if you would. You were so eager for this journey. What changed your mind?"

"I couldn't stand the thought of leaving the field to Ronan."

"The field—you mean Angelica and Fanchea. You'd abandon your calling and your brethren for a woman?"

"For Angelica."

"Eh." Much as he found women—Fanchea, Angelica, and especially that slight little Anne—interesting, Boyd had never become enamored of a woman enough to think of leaving his calling. The land, yes. Women, no. "This voyage will take the summer, perhaps. Not much longer. She'll be there for you when you return." *And I will seek a farm and quit the sea.*

"If Ronan doesn't wed her first."

Boyd had no answer for that. He desperately wanted Crosan to ask why he himself still served aboard this boat, he who loved the land too much to sail literally to Forever. He wanted to be able to explain to Crosan how he ended up coming aboard, and he wasn't certain he could.

And then Crosan asked, very quietly, "What do we do if nothing turns up in three days?"

Boyd tried not to stare. "With no food or water, we don't have any other options, such as sailing somewhere else. We'll be too weak."

"Water aplenty, tumbling into our laps. You can live without food for weeks. Miserably, perhaps, but you'll live. Without water we'll be dead in a couple more days. You know that."

"Brendan forbade . . ." And Boyd let his voice die, buried in conflicting thoughts.

The evening of the third day slipped away beneath the singing of vespers. They were poking along the wall of a dark cove when Ibar noticed what amounted to a crack in the rocks, a passage inches wider than the boat's width, cutting through vertical walls. Leeson guided the prow into the passage and shipped the rudder. They pulled the boat along the cut literally by strength of arm, reaching out to port and starboard and hand-over-handing along the rock wall.

Boyd craned his neck to look straight upward. The defile narrowed above them, the sky was a thin gray slit. He raised his hand to Brendan. Cold slime covered his fingers and palm. "Mid tide. We won't be able to come back this way at high tide. The pass will be too narrow."

The passage widened out like the pages of a book unfolding, and the very air brightened. At the water's edge, a steep shore of shingle and rocks offered their first chance to step out on land. Boyd leaped out into two feet of water and waded ashore to steady the boat.

Brothers came tumbling out, laughing. They dragged the boat above tide line. It took all of them to do it. Mochta tied her fast to a clochan-sized boulder.

Three days of searching brought them to this. It had to be the only means of access onto dry land. Boyd looked about in vain for a footprint, a mooring peg, a scuff above tide line to suggest that a boat, any boat, had been hauled up. The sparse grass tufts scattered above tide line grew lank. The long grass stems leaned upon each other, fell over, bent in two. Most of the stalks still sported the seed heads of last autumn. Nothing had nibbled them. The sharp hooves of sheep and cattle never failed to cut trails and little parallel ridges along hills. This hill arching up behind the narrow embayment looked pristine, untouched by cloven feet. Dried cow flops or sheep droppings serve well as fuel for heating. Boyd saw none such, and he looked carefully.

Almost gleefully, Brendan rubbed his hands. "Let's go exploring." He looked at Boyd, and a bit of the glee fled his face. "Well?"

Boyd pointed to a seedy grass tuft and had no confidence at all that it meant anything to this man of the sea. "You read the sea expertly, but I can read the land. Eggs? We can't go egging off the cliffs. It's too early for seabirds to lay eggs. We didn't see many seabirds to start with, and I doubt we can get out there to snare them. There are no small land birds, and no animals, not even rodents. We've spent three days without food and water. That's bound to weaken any man. We finally get ashore, and there's nothing here, Brendan."

"Yes, but . . ."

"Mussels, perhaps, though how we'll smoke or cook them I don't know. Fish possibly, but I'm not sanguine about that. Fish thrive in shoals and shallows, and the land drops away too quickly. There are no shallows."

Brendan opened his mouth, but Boyd pressed on. "No sign of seals or otters. Certainly no sign of human presence."

"Yes, praise God, but . . ."

"Praise God indeed. But nothing, Brendan. Nothing at all. Praise God we are unable to continue, and we are starving on an island with no food."

19

Island

Ibar was becoming accustomed to denuded hills. In his own clan territory in the south of Erin, logging and clearing for pasturage was fast making the once-wooded hills bald. The same was happening around Clonfert along the great River Shannon. He rather liked the open land better than dark and brooding forest, actually. He enjoyed being able to stroll out across the hills and see farther than the next tree.

But this was ridiculous.

The crew of Brendan's curragh had left behind the loose shingle of their landing place. They climbed a stony draw out of the barren cove and topped out onto an equally barren, stony island.

Denuded is one thing; practically devoid of softening vegetation is another. The land wasn't flat exactly—it undulated lazily. Tufts of grass and small, ragged bushes huddled in the lee of rock outcrops. Only a damp, salty breeze blew now, but the wind must really whip through here. Ibar noticed that the bushes were sheared off flat wherever they peeked above the rocks. That cloud bank still hung directly overhead, casting the whole place into muted, colorless gray.

But in the far distance, peeking out in a narrow line below the clouds, limitless hazy sea stretched out behind the voyagers easterly on three sides.

Nothing moved. Not a thing. There was not a breath of life.

"Surely there must be seabirds." Ibar looked around even as he wondered about the tingle at the nape of his neck.

Boyd stepped in beside him, and that massive, comforting presence allowed some of the tingle to subside. "We saw a few earlier. They're likely out fishing. They'll be back." He didn't sound confident.

Conn pointed inland. "If that doesn't look like Ronan's brindled cur!"

Whoever Ronan's brindled cur was, it must be scrawny indeed, for this ugly dog looked too emaciated to lift a paw off the ground.

Crosan smirked. "So much for your theory, Boyd, that the island is uninhabited."

The dog trotted in that loose manner dogs have of going, straight up to Brendan. The monk stooped to rub its head and its erose back. The mutt's very spine showed as a string of knobs beneath the ragged hide. The dog turned away almost immediately and took off at a casual jog.

"There is the way we are to go," Brendan announced, and he hastened off after the dog at double-step.

Ibar was far too hungry to double-step anywhere, but he certainly did not dare be left. Quite a sight they must be, eighteen monks trotting out westward across this windswept island-top, following a mangy dog.

The surface here above the sea cliffs was actually much more interesting than he first gave it credit for. Gullies and washes and massive cutbanks engraved their various lines through the rounded leas. Ibar would guess the island at about three quarters of a mile across, not counting a few points that stuck out farther and a few canyon creases that brought the sea inward. When they topped the rounded hill, he could see water stretching out ahead of them to the northwest. Golden evening sunlight poured out from beneath the cloud line. It was late; they'd be singing complines in another hour or two.

Then Brendan stopped so abruptly that Boyd almost ran into him. They both crossed themselves and gaped.

In a gentle vale beyond the hill nestled a stone building. Apparently it wasn't abandoned, for its slab roof was still intact. Moss, some dead black and some living green, overgrew the roof and the top bulge of every rock in the walls, creating remarkable patterns.

Brendan never hesitated. He marched directly down and across a draw to the building. It was big, and it grew more and more immense as they approached it. Most remarkable, no ringwall surrounded it, even though rock aplenty lay strewn about. The structure, of undressed stone, was longer than wide, with cunningly stacked sharp corners, and the only door Ibar saw was set in the narrow east wall.

Ibar tried to decide if it was a church—it had no cross to mark it so—or a banqueting hall. If a hall, whom did it serve?

Obviously Brendan held every confidence that it existed to serve himself and his crew. He led the way boldly inside. Vertical slit windows let in enough light that Ibar could see comfortably after a few moments' adjustment. Heavy, open rafters supported the peaked roof, and posts two feet in diameter supported the rafters. Where trees that size would have come from Ibar could not guess.

This was a storehouse, for pegs were stuck between the rocks all over the walls. From these pegs hung every manner of small goods. Without really studying, Ibar noticed bridles, spindles suspended on cords, rakes and shovels, and a number of iron and copper pots.

It was also a bunkhouse, for along the long south wall, a sort of continuous hay-filled manger, wide enough that grown men could lie with their heads toward the wall and their feet still in hay, provided sleeping arrangements for a score of people.

It was a refectory, for a long table ran close to the north wall. A score of persons could eat together here.

What it was not was warm. Ibar saw no fire pit anywhere in the cavernous room. He knew about stone buildings. The cold stone walls sucked up any heat a man's body produced. One could never stay warm in a stone building.

Brendan waved a hand. "Brothers, be seated."

Stranger and stranger. Here one did not sit at table on cushions and wolfskins with one's legs folded, as Ibar had been accustomed to his whole life. Here the diners sat on low benches, each of sufficient length to accommodate four or five men. Rather cautiously, for he was not accustomed to perching like a bird on a branch, Ibar sat down at the end of a bench near the foot of the table.

Brendan took a place at the head, appropriately, and stood there a moment looking from face to face. "Before we bless the food . . ."

What food?

". . . I must tell you of a premonition. I see Satan persuading one of you to commit a great theft. Let us pray for that man's soul, for his body is already given over to the power of Satan. And now let us bless the bread." He raised his hands, closed his eyes, and did so.

Satan? Theft? Ibar couldn't concentrate on the blessing for all the confusion stirring his thoughts about like porridge.

Brendan sat down. "Bring the meal God has sent us."

Abruptly, Boyd hopped to his feet. "Ibar? Come, help serve."

Did Ibar think he was confused before? He leaped to his feet, almost tipping the bench and dumping the three sitting there with him.

Boyd walked directly to the blank west wall. Ibar had not noticed that the west wall was actually a false wall, a stone screen. Boyd stepped around behind it and was almost too wide to fit through the narrow passage.

Ibar moved in behind him and gasped. "How did you know this was here?"

They stood in a cramped pantry lined with shelves. And on the shelves were stacked loaves of bread, a charger of what looked like cooked fish, and crude pottery jugs.

Boyd shrugged. "He said bring food, and this was the only place it could possibly be hidden." His lips moved, and his finger wiggled as he silently counted loaves. "One for each man. We'll serve the bread first and then the fish." He pinched off a flake of meat from the fish and tasted. "Mm. Cod."

Ibar's stomach howled a protest at having to wait. He gathered up a great armload of loaves and backed out into the main room. The bread smelled so rich, so sweet, as he trotted over to the table and passed the delectable loaves around. "One for each of us."

He finished the task of distributing bread as Boyd served the fish, holding the broad, round dish while each man took a portion. They set the jugs out on the table. Ibar flopped onto his seat and nearly dumped his seatmates again.

Brendan stood and raised his arms high. "Render praise to the God of heaven who gives food to all flesh!"

Ibar could say amen to that! Famished, he tore open his loaf.

For the moment he put away any question about where this might have come from. Right now, he didn't care. Never had he seen such marvelously white wheaten bread. Freed from its prison, the aroma lifted up and swirled in a great, invisible cloud, screening all his senses from the world. Reality tiptoed away, leaving only Ibar and this bread.

Wonderful bread.

He ate bread. He ate fish. He placed morsels of both in his mouth at once and let the flavors dance with each other. He drank sweet water from a jug.

They sang the compline right there at the table at the close of supper. They added a special service of thanksgiving, and upon Conn's urging they used the Greek liturgy rather than the Latin. Conn claimed that *artos* was a far more lilting and elegant word for this soft, white bread than was the explosive *panis.* He had a point. But then, he was the poet of the group. He probably should have been a fileh. There were many Christian filidh in Erin these days, men who recorded the deeds and sang the praises not just of kings and heroes but of Jesus Christ as well.

Jesus. King of kings and Hero of heroes. Ibar wondered if Jesus were bigger than most men, like Boyd, or lithe and quick like Brendan. Did Jesus let His hair grow long and fly about, the way Brendan did? Surely He was handsome, like Conn. He probably had a poetic streak too. Ibar's chin kept sinking onto his chest.

They spread out their sheepskins in the hay-filled sleeping trough along the south wall and lay down in repose. Ibar didn't even hear his head touch wool.

Late next morning the seabirds came. Brendan had ordered everything out of the boat, even the spare oxhides. Duffle and stowage lay scattered across the shingled beach, airing out and drying. Ibar, Boyd, and Crosan were patching a couple of seams where the linen stitching had come loose. And here came the gulls, sea raiders.

They circled above the narrow cove with their whining complaints. In good time, the bolder among them spiraled down to perch on the rocks round about.

Conn paused from his line-coiling to chortle. "Boyd, they have their eye on your extra bread."

"What extra bread?" Boyd pushed his awl through a stitch hole and stood erect beside the careened boat.

"Why, the bread you tucked down into your cassock last night—from the loaf I was too full to finish. Look at these poor starving birds, eager for any crumb."

The awl tip withdrew. Inside the hull, Ibar quickly poked his needle out the freshly opened hole. Boyd grabbed it on the other side and pulled it on through. Its length of linen cord whispered through the oxhide.

Everyone laughed except Brendan. He was taking the jest altogether too seriously. "I beseech all of you, take care that you carry away nothing belonging to this island when we leave. Not even crumbs."

Ibar shoved his awl through the next hole and withdrew it. Here came the needle.

Beside Ibar, Crosan muttered, "Heaven forbid that we steal any leftover bread that the gulls would otherwise get."

Ibar mumbled, "I want to know where it comes from."

"It's a miracle. Brendan was quick enough to explain that."

"I know. I'm as ready to accept a miracle as the next person. But . . ."

"But." Crosan nodded. "But."

Singing vespers that evening, they climbed the cliff track and returned to the hall. They didn't need a dog to lead them tonight, and no dog appeared.

These strange events both frightened Ibar and excited him. He was obviously taking part in something very unusual and surely very spiritual. The frightening part was that he couldn't tell exactly what. He wanted some hint of certainty. You didn't get that by depending upon miracles for your daily bread.

Most of all, he didn't like spooky premonitions. And Brendan seemed constantly to be getting them. Ibar wanted to sail great distances and see great things. He wanted to get far, far away from Desmond's relatives in Cashel. Perhaps, however, this was not the best choice of voyages to achieve those goals.

The brothers seated themselves as before at the long table. Ibar leaped up unbidden when Boyd stood, and hurried with him to that miraculous pantry. Eighteen loaves of fresh bread sat waiting and a platter of fish piled as high as yesterday's. Boyd announced that today's fish was plaice and carried the platter out to serve.

The bread was just as white, just as soft and aromatic. Tonight, though, with famine no longer gnawing at him and dinner therefore less intense, Ibar paid more attention to the hall itself.

Just about everything hanging on the walls was of metal or adorned with metal. The magnificent bridle near his head was well studded with silver ornament. In fact, he braved the notice of others by walking over to it and scratching one of the brads with his fingernail, for the silver had tarnished somewhat. The tarnish rubbed away; it was indeed good silver.

The copper kettle suspended above it looked freshly made and as yet unused. The rivets in a used pot not only turn greenish white, they weep black lines down the copper below them. These did not. Another new kettle hung above Boyd's head, and down there behind Crosan, Ibar saw an even more elaborately decorated bridle. High above the bridle was a pretty little iron cowbell, quite delicately hammered. And look at that sword and sheath by Conn, all inlaid with silver wire!

Bridles. Cowbells. Even a pair of wool shears. Farming tools. But where the farm? Ibar had yet to see a cow, a sheep, or a horse, or any sign of them. And no human beings. Only a friendly dog who now diligently hid itself. This mystery was even spookier than Brendan's somber premonitions.

After complines, he lay wide-eyed on his bed. Where did the hay come from, for that matter? Nothing here was real.

Something rustled by his ear. He froze. A mouse froze too, not six inches from his head. After a few moments the mouse resumed its business. He rolled his eyes to watch it without moving a muscle. The mouse clambered from stalk to stalk through the hay, searching out the heads among it that had not yet shed all their hayseed. Tiny fingers and toes gripped flimsy strands as it bobbed its way about. Ibar's eyes had adjusted so well to the hall's dim light that he could watch the long silky vibrissae twitch.

Mice, so legend claims, know everything, for they get about everywhere and listen without being heard, see without being seen. *You know who brings bread, and I bet it's not a divine fin-*

157

ger out of heaven. You know who fills the jugs with sweet water, and you know if there are other animals here. Who owns that magnificent bridle? Who rides the horse, and where? Who would make a beautiful copper kettle and never use it? Why a cowbell on an island so small that cattle cannot wander off, so deforested that you can spot a cow a mile away?

Here was one a mouse could not answer: Why did Brendan react so strongly about taking nothing from the island? Was that another of his premonitions? It would seem so. Ibar occasionally received premonitions also, but that didn't mean they always turned out true.

The mouse had long gone when Ibar finally drifted off to sleep.

20

Decoy

Braving wind and tide, the tiny curragh heaves up a wave and down as its stalwart oarsman struggles to make way. Gulls cry encouragement round about its blunt prow. Petrels skim the waves beside it, and the sea ducks bob nearby.

In his mind's eye, Ronan watched the wee craft. But he saw no such heartening vision on the actual sea before him. He sat in wet weeds on the brow of the sea cliff. Sandy cliffside fell away before him and spread out into shingle a hundred feet below. The pulsing waves sloshed white across the ragged line where sea met shore. Against the cloudy, dull orange sky of evening lay the Skelligs, two pointy pyramids of rock and shattered dreams, looking sorrowful and, oh, so far away.

Ronan was too distant from the sea to make out the petrels or the dark sea ducks, but away out there glided the white gulls. No encouragement there. Only mocking.

They were mocking him.

From where he sat, he could just make out the little seaside cot where one of the Skelligs' suppliers used to live. Its roof and part of its ringwall peeked around from behind the hill to the north. This was the fellow who brought out salt cod and about half the barley meal the brothers used. Ronan saw no activity whatever around the cottage and no smoke.

He should have visited the rath of the ri tuathe by now. It was customary to do so. Since the death of the former ri, Ronan had no idea who the successor might be. He ought inquire.

He couldn't.

He really did want to climb down to the fishing cot and learn if any still lived in this area. He couldn't. And most of all, he could not bring himself to inquire as to the health and viability of the colony on Skellig Michael.

His paralysis confused him. Why could he not do so simple a thing as walk a mile down the hill to a farmer's rath? Perhaps he was too afraid of what he'd hear. And then there was shame.

A powerful force, shame. He should have died with the brothers on the Skellig, if dead they be. And if they be not, he should go back there, take up again where he had left. Technically he remained under the abbot of Skellig Michael; he had never been released from that obligation. It was a thing left undone, and it bothered him immensely.

Another powerful force entered the scene, and Ronan's spine tingled. Six riders down by surf appeared from the south around the base of the hill, clattering along the shingle far below. Six armed men in brown tartan. They couldn't see him, wouldn't bother to look up this way, but he ducked down to prone anyway.

Why wouldn't Mac Larkin give up? Angelica had made her wishes abundantly clear. Surely no man would want a woman who resisted him so thoroughly as to flee the country. The Pict and his cohorts rode directly to the fisherman's cottage. The brow of the hill hid details, but Ronan could make out a couple of heads and a horse's rump as the riders milled outside the ringwall gate.

The spot where Ronan huddled lay perhaps ten miles from Fanchea's rath. Were ten miles enough to protect Angelica? He doubted it. Possibly the hulking Boyd could stop the Picts and their ponies both, but Brendan's crew were long gone. Only Crosan remained, Ronan assumed. Crosan. The Laughing Monk would not stand up long against six armed Picts, if he chose to stand at all. Ronan could not picture Crosan in a hero's role.

The mounting wind was bringing dark clouds up from the southeast, blotting out the evening light untimely. If Mac Larkin were smart, he'd take refuge at this rath or some other before rain and early darkness caught him.

But Mac Larkin, one would presume, was not smart. The Pict and his band reappeared and headed up the trail inland. He seemed to be traveling in a determined manner rather than randomly. What had he learned, if anything, at that fisherman's cot?

Ronan scrambled to his feet. A quarter mile of logged-over brushland separated him from the track Mac Larkin was taking.

He would follow them. He might even figure out their intentions. If they picked up wind of Fanchea's rath he would—he had no idea what he would do. One bit of luck and one only rode with him now. Mac Larkin had not brought dogs to Erin. Without dogs, the Pict was hardly likely to detect that he was being followed.

Would the displaced warrior leave the major trails of this area? Probably not. He had no idea where the raths of this region lay in regard to each other, or who represented the power figures in local society. At best he would probably conduct a hit-and-miss search. That, though, could well suffice, for Fanchea's rath sat prominently on the brow of an open hill, easy to see.

Ronan knew where the track went. He knew too that this cow-path along the ridge-top roughly paralleled it. He could stay close to the Picts simply by hewing to this muddy, informal trail. A fast walk and an occasional spate of jogging kept him abreast his quarry.

Behind them, black-bottom clouds became a densely packed charcoal-gray mass. *Mac Larkin, you fool, why didn't you take shelter when you could?*

Wait. Jesus Himself warned against calling anybody a fool. Ronan ought to pay less attention to his own will and thoughts and more to his Lord's. But then, what could you call the man but a fool? A dangerous fool for all that.

Two miles later, the Picts quartered out through the sheep meadow that spread across the hill below the abandoned Kellen place. Ronan could not hear their speech, but they were twisting on their horses' backs to look at the approaching storm behind them. They stopped now and milled about. Mac Larkin himself pointed uphill toward the old rath. As one they turned aside off the track and splashed up the waterlogged hill to the broken-down farm.

The palisade had fallen just about all the way around the ringwall. Only the earthen wall remained, and it had been breached here and there by digging dogs and badgers. Inside the ringwall, the conical farmhouse roof, once tall and sturdy, had partially collapsed. The front two-thirds of it appeared fairly firm, but the back third had caved in.

Thick rainclouds and gathering dusk had reduced visibility to nearly nothing. Ronan could barely make out the deserted farm in the distance.

Now scattered raindrops, hard as pebbles, began to slam in, rattling the leaves above his head. From a copse a hundred yards away, he watched Mac Larkin and his crew clatter up to the gate just as the rain turned from huge, clumsy drops into a drumming downpour. Hastily they drove the ponies inside the wall and hastily dragged fallen palisade timbers across the gateway to keep them in.

Ronan waited, partly to let the riders get settled and partly because he so hated stepping out into the cold, driving rain. A wisp of smoke lifted away from the ruined part of the caved-in roof and drifted low across the wall.

Now.

Hunched and hurried, Ronan left the concealment of his little copse and ran to the back side of the abandoned rath. He paused by the earth wall, waiting and listening, half expecting to have been discovered. Then he clambered up over the wall into the compound within. Mac Larkin's ponies had drifted to the back of the enclosure, alee of the rain. Ronan shouldered among them to the wall of the ruined house.

He could hear voices inside, and he now clearly smelled smoke. They would start cooking fairly soon from the smell of it. Ronan judged that their fire was just beginning to burn down to coals.

Darkness had closed in so completely now that he could probably climb up onto the house wall without being noticed. But how? In the gloom beside him, a pony, squealing, flung a mouthful of teeth at a companion. The companion reared and dipped away, presenting its rump to the aggressor. As quickly as it began, the equine tiff ended, with the second pony pressed against Ronan in the dark.

He would accept this as from God and use it. He swung up onto the surprised pony's back. As the pony pushed forward, squeezing against its mates, Ronan stood up on the slippery, wet back. The bony little horse started to move away from the wall, but Ronan had found his purchase. He gripped the end of a collapsed timber and the slimy mud of the house wall and pulled himself upward.

The timber creaked.

He dragged himself up to where he could throw a leg over the wall and waited. No one inside seemed to notice. He perched atop the wall. Now what?

Cautiously, blindly, he worked his way among the ruined and

tumbled roof timbers. The rain made them slick. With every shift of his weight he could picture himself sliding down a peeled pole into the midst of the Picts.

This was insane. And he had called Mac Larkin a fool?

With extreme caution he worked his way down through the fallen roof poles into the back of the house—the house where the Picts were taking refuge from the storm. *Ah, Ronan, ye blarsted donkey!*

His foot touched solid ground. Tangled timbers still lay all about, but he no longer needed to trust his weight to them. He found a spot and settled himself on the slimy, stinking thatch among the rubbish. By twisting his head and peering through the jumbled poles, he could even see shadowy figures out in the open part of the house that was still protected by an intact roof.

But could he hear? With difficulty, yes, particularly the fellows facing his way. Even beyond the sea, speaking slowly and carefully with people face-to-face, Ronan had trouble understanding the hurly-burly Pictish. Under these conditions, with the rain whispering its own tales all around him, they might as well be speaking Anglo-Saxon for all of him.

Mac Larkin said something about a whetstone. A protégé stood up and went outside. A minute later the fellow returned and handed a bundle to Mac Larkin.

They left their pot bubbling on the coals and built themselves a second fire, presumably for warmth and light. As they added wet wood, the smoke roiled up and filled the wrecked room from waist high on up, pouring out the gray haze faster than the collapsed roof hole could let it out. Even Ronan's eyes watered, and he crouched quite apart in the shadows.

With measured, guttural whispers, Mac Larkin's sword stroked across the stone. Was he describing quartering Angelica? It sounded so. Sure and his blade ought to be sharp enough to do that. Ronan strained to hear.

In a raucous voice dripping venom, Mac Larkin cursed his lady fair. God's servants had much work cut out for them, if they were to bring these Picts to a saving knowledge of Christ. The voice sounded slightly blurred and apparently for good reason. Others among them were discussing the merits of the ale obtained at this latest rath.

They proceeded then to make plans for spreading out and searching the Dingle. This was exactly what Ronan needed to learn. He curtailed his own breathing in order to catch their words.

Mac Larkin, fool or no, was an astute strategist. He knew no place names, but he had obviously read the land well and described landmarks tersely. And as he laid out their plan of action, Ronan's heart sank. If these Pictish fools and wise men did not come upon Angelica tomorrow, they would find her the next day for certain.

Their merry fire waxed brighter. Ronan could make out more now than just forms and faces. He could see into the dark corners of the ruined house. The place had either been abandoned abruptly, its occupants moving on, or the farmer had summarily died. Butchering knives, caldrons, blankets, and piles of tow sacks still lined the walls. In fact, back here where the roof had caved in, a downed clothesline still held the goodwife's wash.

What now? Come dawn, the Picts would explore this fallen house to scavenge any goods they might want. They could not help but find Ronan if he still cowered in this maze of timbers. He would have to make his way back out during darkness. He ventured a glance up into the wrecked and fallen rafters. Not that way surely. One misstep, one loose timber . . .

He must think. And plan. Carefully.

The Picts ate their gruel and let their cooking fire die. Darkness nestled into all the shadowed corners as they banked their greater fire. The black shadows expanded out into the room until only the barest hint remained of the Picts. They became dark blobs on the floor. A few scattered bursts of conversation, and they fell to rest.

Reluctant to move and possibly make noise, Ronan gave them an extra hour.

From the fallen clothesline at the back of the house he lifted a woman's garments, including the turban. He rolled them tightly and slipped the bundle beneath his blue cloak. And then, one slow, measured tread at a time, he began working his way toward the only door, out of his hiding place into the midst of the snuffling, snoring Picts.

He paused near the dark hulk he assumed to be Mac Larkin

164

himself and toyed with the idea of running a blade through the fellow as he slept. He knew it was wrong. Conscience and the Word of God struggled valiantly before overcoming common sense. *End the chase right here,* cried Reason. *It is morally wrong to kill a sleeping man,* retorted Ethic. Ronan hated having to be honest.

He stopped cold. One of the boorish Picts stood up in the dense gloom, scratched himself mightily, and headed for the door. He tripped over a companion; the fellow cursed him. He passed within two feet of Ronan before he noticed he was standing there, a black form in the blackness.

He grunted. "So. I'm not alone in my need to rise. Ale makes a night long, aye?" Chuckling, he walked on by and out the door from darkness into darkness.

Ronan gave him a moment, then followed him out. He stepped aside and leaned against the house wall. Presently the Pict staggered back inside.

Ronan wanted to hurry, but he could not in this darkness. He had to put each foot before the other carefully, lest he wander off the track. Come first light, he had traveled barely three miles toward Fanchea's rath.

The women, like all good Erse women, could defend themselves as well as any man. This time, that was not defense enough. Not against six. Not even with Crosan. Ronan came painfully close to calling a curse down upon the men of Erin who thought it godly to leave their farms for the call of foreign shores, the sea, the monasteries. Thousands of men, taking up the green martyrdom of devotion to a monastic life, or the blue martyrdom of sailing out across the water, or the white martyrdom of leaving Erin behind—and not a man of them thinking about the work and protection their women and children needed at home. And a forever curse upon the plague, which robbed Erin of thousands more.

No matter where the ri tuatha now dwelt, it was too far. Ronan knew all the raths near Fanchea's, and none of them could field a defensive force adequate to meet the Picts.

Fanchea and Angelica's own resources were inadequate for any sort of defense at all. Even if Ronan rushed ahead to help them, their combined strength was no match for Mac Larkin.

He stopped and turned then and waited among the gnarled

oaks of a hillcrest grove overlooking the track. Where strength could not prevail, cleverness must win the day. From here he could see a good half mile of the trail he had just come up as it wound down open leas and a creekbed. To his right the oak grove became a dense forest that blanketed the hillside, all the way down to a close, marshy tanglewood of heath and alder.

It was high noon. He felt outrageously hungry. He had not eaten for twenty-four hours at least. He sat in the thick, dirty duff of crumpled oak leaves and last year's acorns and tried to keep the flies and ants from taking up residence on his person. On its scores of legs, a millipede sauntered casually across a thumb-thick dead branch beside his knee. Under other circumstances, Ronan would find the creature fascinating, the way its many legs moved in perfectly synchronized waves. Today he could not generate the least interest. Indeed, he considered himself a patient man, but this waiting irritated him immensely.

It was late afternoon before a gentle haze of dust warned him of Mac Larkin's approach. He must time this just right—there would be no second chance. He stood, tucked the women's clothes firmly beneath his arm, and adjusted his blue cloak. He watched the track. There they came, just heaving into view as the creek bent toward the southwest.

He waited.

Now.

He stepped from the oaks out onto the trail and walked smartly down the path toward Mac Larkin.

Mac Larkin saw him. He shouted and pointed.

Ronan stopped dead, "noticing" Mac Larkin. So far, so good. Loudly he yelled, "Angelica! Turn back! Run, Angelica!" as he waved an arm off to his right, a warning. He broke into a run as he left the track, heading down into the thickest of the forest.

He leaped over fallen logs and jumped down off rocky outcrops. He slipped on moss and nearly broke a leg. As he ran he pulled off his blue cloak and struggled into the woman's striped tunic and rust-red cloak. He paused to catch his second wind and listen. He could hear the crashing of branches uphill.

Mac Larkin was still trying to penetrate the woodland on horseback. He'd abandon that notion soon enough, surely.

Ronan continued on, wrapping the woman's turban around his head as he struggled and staggered through the undergrowth. He rolled his blue cloak into a tight ball as he entered the soggy tanglewood of alder and marsh brush. If the forest didn't stop the horses, this mess would. He clamped the bundled cloak tightly under his arm.

The hillside sloping upward beyond the alder thickets was partially denuded of trees. Good. Mac Larkin must see him, but not for long and not clearly.

Again he yelled, not toward the hillside but rather back over his shoulder toward Mac Larkin. "Angelica! That way! Go that way!"

He slogged at a half-run up the hill, now in the open and now among trees, trying to take small and graceful steps the way Angelica would. His legs tangled briefly in the reddish cloak, and it nearly threw him.

By ear, plus an occasional glance, Ronan kept track of the Picts. Mac Larkin followed eagerly. They were afoot now, their ponies left behind, who knew where. All six came pouring up the hillside, staggering, stumbling.

Ronan heard Mac Larkin's bellow. "There she is! Forget him! Get her!"

The turban was slipping. He held it with one hand as he ran over the crest and down the hillside toward the distant sea. Running downhill, he could imitate Angelica's female way of going better. He was sweating profusely now.

Gulping air, his head giddy, he ran out across a seaside meadow, scrambled over a stone wall, raced toward the sea. He covered a quarter mile in a matter of a few minutes.

Two curraghs lay on the shingle just above the tide line. A hundred yards upshore, several old women sat in the gray half-light of the overcast, mending nets. He ignored them.

He seized the larger curragh by its gunwales, grabbed its oars, dragged it down into the surf. He must get well out on the water before Mac Larkin got close enough to see his face.

The final two feet of the miserable turban came loose. He'd lose the whole thing in a moment, and Mac Larkin would know the truth. Struggling with the curragh, he . . .

Of course! He paused long enough to wrap the loose turban end around his mouth and cheeks. Not only did it hide his two-day stubble, it thwarted recognition by covering half his face. He clambered into the boat and began fiercely rowing.

Ashore, Mac Larkin called to him using Angelica's name, begged him return, threatened him.

Mac Larkin tried to follow. He even sent one of his underlings out into the surf to attempt swimming to the curragh. Fool. What did Mac Larkin expect the doughty lad do, should he actually reach the boat?

But he did not, powerful swimmer though he was.

Ronan pulled away, beyond the breakers, beyond shallows a man can wade.

An inch of water was accumulating in the bottom of the little leather boat.

The owner of this curragh had carelessly tossed in a small linen sail furled around a modest mast. Its weight slowed him, and he considering jettisoning it. Then the tide off Brandon Head caught him and added considerably to his speed and progress.

Three inches of water sloshed in the boat, slowing him even more than the weight of the sail.

In the far distance from whence he'd come, he could just see men in brown tartans running along the shore. Did Mac Larkin intend to follow east along the shore, over the Shannon, and west along the river's other shore? It almost appeared so, but evening was quickly robbing Ronan of light to see by. He could almost turn around now and head back, or reach the north shore well ahead of Mac Larkin, but the tidal surge wouldn't let him.

With considerable difficulty, he stepped the little mast and raised the sail. He might as well use it, since he had it. Four inches of cold seawater filled the bottom of the boat. He refolded his blue wool cloak into a scoop to bail with.

Angelica was safe for the moment. And if she exercised normal caution, she would remain relatively safe.

Ronan, it appeared, was bound to drown.

21
Time

A mixed bag, death. Never there when you need it, but lurking nearby at the most inopportune of moments.

Desmond pulled a sleeve back to study the dark blotches growing on his arm. They would do nothing but spread until they daubed his body with the piebald stamp of death. They were tender, these ugly black blotches, but they didn't protrude as did the boils they replaced. At least he could shift positions a little now. He would die in better comfort.

He lay awhile exploring this unique and most curious condition of knowing in advance the precise hour of his death. That knowledge had its advantages, but that was not to say he liked it. At least he could put some affairs in order.

He had very few affairs out of order. He possessed no worldly goods to speak of. No family here in England. The undone work would remain undone. Indeed, the work he had so far accomplished would most likely be undone as well.

He sighed and shifted from his back to his left side. As decadent as linen might be, he welcomed it. He was horribly uncomfortable as it was. Without the linen, his misery would have multiplied.

Too, the linen protected him somewhat from the army of fleas to be found in every sheepskin. Desmond despised fleas. So often their bites raised red welts all out of proportion to the size of the creature biting. He didn't remember nearly this many fleas in his native Erin.

Here came Larkin, swinging an iron pot on a bail. If it contained much at all, that pot must weigh more than a large dog. Larkin handled it as if it were a dainty clay lamp.

The burly Prince of Picts dropped down beside Desmond's pallet and ignored the goodwife praying near Desmond's feet. "I brought you a wee mite of soup."

Desmond watched the pot thunk heavily on the dirt floor. "Just a wee mite, eh? Two gallons at least."

"I thought I might have some as well, while we're about it. You will eat some, won't you?"

"I'll try." Even with the protection of linen, Desmond's body itched dreadfully. Was it the blotches or the fleas or the wool itself? No matter. He prickled all over.

"Tavish and I spent quite a long time talking with the wife of the abbot of Whithorn this morning."

"She's still here? I thought she went home."

"She was going to, but she decided to wait . . ." Larkin's voice trailed off as he busied himself scooping soup into a small hard-leather bowl.

"Decided to wait until I die so she can report the news to Whithorn and beyond to Erin."

Larkin looked absolutely crushed. "You're taking this much better than I, Desmond father, and you have so much more at stake. Yes. She's waiting to report your death abroad. The word will spread fast. A lot of traffic from Erin passes by Whithorn or through there."

"As did Ibar and I when we came over. And your son in the other direction."

"My son. Would that I could stand on the shore and call him home." Larkin raised his voice and hardened it. "She says that at Whithorn she talked to a disciple of Brendan, Boyd Blond Hair. You know him?"

"A mountainous man with the heart of a loving puppy."

"She mentioned extreme size, come to think of it. Comparing him to me."

"He's bigger than you but not as strong."

Larkin almost smiled, however slightly. "After his evening spent at the church with the abbot and his wife, this Boyd made arrangements locally at Whithorn for supplies and then sailed with an Ionan boat down to Man to pick up more. Boyd told the abbot that Brendan is bound for Tir Na n'Og."

Desmond closed his burning eyes. "A shame. What a wicked shame. I've never met a man so wholly dependent upon God as he. The church needs more like him. And see? The few we have are swept away."

"Oh. Actually, he's not dying to get there, so to speak. He plans to sail there and return."

Desmond had to ponder this a moment, making certain that what he heard was what he heard and not some strange effect of his illness. He smiled. "And why not? He's sailed everywhere else."

Desmond had long envied Brendan his journeying, but only academically. Desmond did enjoy travel, though not at sea with the constant specter of extreme seasickness before him. He did not sail well at all. And Ibar fared nearly as badly. Ibar sailing to Iona? Desmond had heard about the tidal rips in those island channels and the howling storms on the sea side. He wondered how Ibar would ever choose to sail to Iona, of all places.

Larkin was trying to spoon soup into Desmond's mouth. It spilled on the sheepskin, probably drowning a few fleas. "Can you sit up?"

"Yes, he can." Down at Desmond's feet, the woman who had been kneeling silently in prayer stood up. In a mighty handful she dragged Desmond to sitting and then squatted on her knees and heels solidly behind him, propping him against her. He didn't have to flex a muscle.

"Tir Na n'Og," Desmond mused. "What would it be to fly there? No travel weariness, no seasickness. To break free of the land and sea altogether and fly?"

"We fly only once."

"Larkin? Do you suppose I might survive this?"

The burly nurse scraped some dribbled soup off Desmond's chin. "We've been talking about that, Tavish and I and the abbot's wife. It's a possibility. People do, you know, though it's rare. So far you've lived days longer than do most. And the black blotches were slow to come. I'd say the disease is having a—" he stopped, paused in thought, and continued "—a terribly hard time killing you."

"A man's language is the man. I commend you heartily, Larkin friend. You've mastered blasphemy almost totally, and even the minced oaths and casual curses are minimal these days. You're obviously working at it, and you've become a splendid example before the Picts."

"The Lord's work, not mine." Larkin never actually glowed, even when praised, but just now he seemed to bask a bit. He resumed the feeding in cheerful earnest. "Anyway, we figure that if you last until Easter, you'll live for forty years more."

"Which Easter?"

Larkin cackled. "You Irish never are going to accept the Roman reckoning, are you? The abbot's wife must have gone on for half an hour about the thick-headed Irishmen and the way they insist on following their own canonical years while Rome and the rest of Christendom practice a different calendar."

"Scripture's on our side. We'll be vindicated. You watch."

"Watch? Not I. I don't care which calendar you choose." Larkin sobered. "Tell me something, father, for you know all the Scripture. Whatever happened to Lazarus?"

"The beggar or the brother of Martha whom Jesus raised?"

"We know the fate of the beggar. The man Jesus raised."

"Good question."

"He dies. He lies abed in his grave for four days. Jesus calls him, and here he comes walking out. He eats supper with his Lord that night. And yet, you yourself preached just last month from the letter to the Hebrews that it's given to man once to die and then to receive judgment. Once. Lazarus had his once. Where is he now?"

"You're a splendid student of Scripture, Larkin! You try to see the whole by matching the parts. Excellent!"

Larkin chuckled morosely. "I had forgotten for a moment how you always manage to avoid actually saying that you don't have the barest notion of an answer to a sticky question."

"Understand, the Scripture talks about ordinary men. God and Jesus, being extraordinary, get to change the rules whenever They feel like it. If Jesus wanted to provide Lazarus with one death more than the usual allotment, He of all beings on earth had the right and power to do so. That's all I can say about it."

Lazarus. Dead and returned from death.

If anyone in Christendom could make it to the Land of Ever Young and return, it would be Brendan, the consummate sailor and navigator. More than one person testified that you could see paradise from the Aran Isles, when conditions were just right. Enda himself claimed to have seen it. So it must be reachable.

Desmond pondered intriguing possibilities were he to precede Brendan by the normal means, that is, death. Desmond would be waiting there on the other side for Brendan's arrival. The tricky question: could he perhaps return with Brendan? Could he come back on the boat and complete his work here, or at least see it further along before returning permanently to the abode of the blessed?

Too, how was Brendan so sure that, once he got there, *he* would be allowed to return? Other than human minds determine such things. He might be sailing into quite a surprise.

It wouldn't be a nasty surprise, though. Just not the outcome Brendan intended.

Larkin slurped a spoonful of soup. "According to that Boyd, a fellow named Barrind first put the idea into their heads. He seemed to think there was no time in the Land of Ever Young. You spend weeks exploring the place, and when you return it's as if you were gone but a moment." Larkin shook his shaggy head. "It boggles the mind."

"Our affairs are ordered by a hand we barely ken, friend."

The ramifications behind this conversation intrigued Desmond. They thrilled him. What if? What if? And with the capable navigator Brendan bound yon, had Desmond a chance unique among Christian men: a possible boat home?

"A place of no time." Larkin absently slurped soup. "That's too hard to imagine for an old warlord like me. I can't. Land of Ever Young. Time but no time. I wonder, what would it be like to step out away from the bonds of time?"

"I'll let you know."

22

Anne

Truth, and Anne hated Angelica.

Angelica was so abominably clever. She could do anything, working out in the fields or beside the hearth. With a flick of her knife she earmarked Fanchea's calves perfectly every time. That particular earmark wasn't easy, either. The top half of the left ear remained intact, and the bottom half flopped down like a hound dog's. You had to slash the ear just so below the outside point in order to get the bottom half to drop as it ought.

Angelica's honeyed hair and beautiful skin made freckly, fair-complexioned Anne with her red hair look pasty. No wonder Angelica had men buzzing around her like flies at the treacle jar. When Boyd first brought Anne to this rath, two monks were fighting down at the marsh. No one ever said anything about it, but Anne knew they were fighting over Angelica. Brothers, yet!

She had no idea where either of them went. With Brendan probably. The whole world seemed to want to go with Brendan to Hi Brasil.

Anne didn't want to voyage off to the unknown. She wanted to consort with kings. She should have traveled down to Cashel months ago. Instead, here she stayed at this horrid rath, working harder than she ever worked back home. She should never have let Ibar talk her into leaving home in the first place. This was all Tavish's fault. And Ibar's.

"Well now, Maura!" Black-haired, down-to-earth Fanchea swaggered in the gate under a load of kitchen wood. She dropped the great bundle of sticks beside the door and arched her back. "How is the mead coming?"

With an ungodly howl, Angelica's miserable cat popped out of the woodpile and leaped upon the wall. It scrambled up the palisade and perched on a pale, all four tiny feet bunched together.

Behind Fanchea, Angelica entered with another load of sticks, laughing at the cat. "Whatever makes her like the woodpile so much?"

Angelica and Fanchea. Quite a pair. Anne would turn'Angelica over to her Pictish husband in a minute if he would just show up again. After prowling the area on the coast awhile he had disappeared. He'd be back. What he was seeking lived here, and he'd find out sooner or later. Anne prayed it would be sooner. The silly brindled dog jogged in the gate with its tongue flopping out the side of its mouth.

She watched from beyond the quern in the shadow of the house. Now there was someone else Anne disliked—Maura. She didn't hate the old woman exactly. Typical of old women, though, Maura complained constantly, did next to no work, and kept regaling them with stories they didn't want to hear of the old days about which they did not care. She was an irritant of the first water.

So was Hilla, the other crone on the farmstead. Hilla, however, did not complain. She just stared gloomily at nothing at all for hours on end. Hilla made Anne feel uncomfortable any time, and when Hilla stared at Anne, her skin crawled.

Maura leaned forward on her stool beside the door. When she spoke, her s's and sh's whistled. She had maybe six teeth left in her head, none of them where they could do much good. She wagged a haggard hand. "Still tastes too much like honey. It's coming, though. It's coming. That Anne was up to no good again. I warned you when she came, there's no Pict worth dirt."

"Now what?"

"Sassing back to me and refusing to milk the black cow. I told her my hands are too arthritic these days, and you should have heard her. Disrespectful and disobedient."

"She's not a slave, Maura, to blindly obey."

"I should say she isn't. Slaves have brains." And the ugly old woman sat back against the house wall with a huff and a snort.

Anne stepped back farther, lest Fanchea realize she was listening. Anne really did have to get out of here.

She could understand that Boyd would go off with Brendan. After all, he was more or less Brendan's chief assistant. Much as

Boyd talked about settling onto a farm and living a quiet life, she knew he wouldn't get to it. He was too much Brendan's pet to break free.

But Ibar! Ibar was supposed to go to Cashel and take her along. All of a sudden he's talking about shipping aboard Brendan's boat to who knows where, petitioning Brendan on bended knee, and here's old Anne in the lurch. Ibar was supposed to go home to Cashel—to a king's palace.

Anne tried to fancy a king's palace. She'd heard tales of emperors' palaces in Rome. Sure and they wouldn't be hovels like these Irish houses, built of coppiced hazel and mud.

"Charity, Maura. Has the black cow been milked?"

"Anne didn't bring her in yet."

"I'll go get her. Where is she?"

"You know I can't leave out the gate. My arthritis is kicking up terrible, especially in this hip right here, you see?"

Angelica interrupted. "I'll go get her."

"No." Fanchea shook her black mane. "You start dinner. I will."

And Maura the crone babbled on about her arthritis to no one at all.

Anne walked on around between the house and the ringwall. She hated the way livestock hooves churned up the mud back here, so that it pressed up cold and slimy between her toes. Acrid cow smell permeated everything.

She moved around, squeezing past the lye barrels and butter bucket until she could see the gate. Maura stood up and doddered into the house. Fanchea disappeared out the gate, calling to Troll. The brindled dog trotted after her lackadaisically. Anne followed. When she arrived at the gate, Fanchea angled over the hill northward.

Anne distinctly remembered seeing the black cow wander off toward the southwest this afternoon. She would go west, find the cow, and put herself in Fanchea's good graces, as if she had not overheard Maura's invectives and accusations, as if she wished to please Fanchea.

It was nice to get out of the mud and into the open meadow. The close-cropped grass caressed her feet. She strode along comfortably, but then, going downhill was always easier than slogging up. Why did they always build farms on hilltops?

Actually, they didn't. There in the distance lay the farm of Fanchea's closest neighbor, abandoned now. It nestled in a gentle fold of the hills, with a craggy tor behind it to the south and this gentle, grassy slope rising away from its north side. The posts forming the palisade along the top of its ringwall had nearly all been pulled down. Fanchea's monastic help last summer built a split-rail caterpillar fence along a bean field. Anne would guess they used the posts from here, splitting them and hauling them off to Fanchea's. That's what Anne would have done.

Perhaps the black cow had come down here. The grass, largely uncropped, looked lush and green and inviting, were one a cow.

The prior inhabitants had planted rape in the drainage uphill of the ringwall. The patch sported rank new spring growth. From the mat of dead cover from last year, Anne would guess that no one had harvested it. She walked down into the drainage and in the little rill washed the last of the drying mud from between her toes.

She stood erect and sniffed. She was definitely upwind of a fire. Not a large fire, but a fire. By eye she traced downwind. A thin wisp of smoke, the most meager of fire ghosts, drifted from the cottage inside the ringwall. Most of the smoke settled into the compound.

She had been almost certain no one was living there. The place looked thoroughly abandoned—no tools or implements visible, no animals, no wash hanging on a line. A noisy crowd of rooks argued among themselves as they perched on the ragged thatched roofs of the sheds and biers or flew in tight circles around them.

Anne gathered up her skirt and hurried across the hill, giving the supposedly abandoned ringwall a wide berth. She jogged on down the drainage and around the curving hillside. On the slopes to either side, the pasture turned to brush thickets, which turned to woodland. Wildwood tended to make her nervous.

She stopped and let out a yelp. There lay the black cow, steaming in the grass. And there were two young ruffians with knives, skinning her!

"Stop! No! Stop!" She yelled loudly, and even as she shouted she realized it was a silly thing to say. Too late now, too late by far. The cow was half flayed. She ran toward them. "You geese! You've butchered the wrong cow! You made a mistake!"

One of the two lads stood erect from his nasty work and watched her approach. He looked puny and ill-fed. A pile of greasy blond hair hung in his eyes. He grinned wickedly. "No, lady, no mistake. This cow's abandoned. Available for the taking."

Of all the insolence! Anne let her voice remain pitched high in anger. "Apparently you have not observed, scoundrel, that her udder is leaking milk. Would an abandoned cow be milked regularly?"

"This whole miserable rath is abandoned." The lad seemed not in the least contrite for his grievous error.

"Then why does smoke issue from the hearth? I tell you lads, the cow strayed from a rath up the way to the east. You've destroyed the butter and cheese on which a whole household depends, and there you two stand, grinning like the rooks on the cowshed. Now what will we do?!"

Moments ago she did not care a whit for the black cow. Now here it lay, a victim of stupidity, and that stupidity enraged her. Nobody in this awful country had a brain in his head!

"What smoke?" The other lad, a melancholy sort of fellow with remarkably huge hands and feet, looked about nervously. Of course he would notice nothing—they were downwind now. What donkeys!

She sighed and stared at the cow. Its lost milk was trickling out all four teats. And these buffoons didn't bother to notice a full udder. "Well, you can just traipse up to Fanchea's and tell her about it. I certainly don't care to. She and her brood think ill enough of me already. Now we'll have to find another milch cow. Maybe even a heifer just coming fresh. It'll be months before we drink milk again. Months and months."

The only thing left to drink was mead, and that wasn't ready yet. For all her superior skills, the perfect Fanchea seemed to lack any understanding or desire for brewing ale. Imagine a household without an ale bucket.

"Where are you from?" The fellow with the shaggy hair stepped in much too close. "Your speech is odd. And charming!"

"Green Head." Anne moved back a bit. "I prefer you keep

your distance. Climb yon hill, and you'll see the cow's rath the next hill over. You'd best get there before dark." Wait, these fellows would need some extra incentive to walk that far to bare their deed. "The mistress of the rath bakes excellent bread and sets a full table."

The shaggy-haired one closed the distance between them again. He still held his knife in hand. "I much prefer to tarry."

And it occurred to Anne that she was alone. Why had she confronted these two when she really didn't care about Fanchea's old black cow? She ought to have turned around instantly and run back to the rath instead of yelling at these oafs. She looked over at the sullen fool beyond the cow. He too carried his knife. "Well, I do not. I'm going home to supper." She turned to make a hasty departure, but the shaggy-haired one seized her arm.

"Don't leave yet. I want to find out where Green Head is. I venture it's not in Erin. I'm a prince of Erin, you know, the son of a ri ruirech. We both are."

"Then act like one."

"Oh, we do, we do. I perceive you're a stranger to this area. So we really ought to explain to you what duties are expected of a ri, and when. It's quite interesting, really." And he was grinning wickedly again, wearing the same haughty expression she saw on his face when first she arrived.

Behind Anne, from the direction of the abandoned rath, a man's voice laughed. She twisted to look. A monk stood there, albeit a wildly disheveled monk. He hadn't shaved his Irish-style tonsure in weeks, for inch-long hair stood up all over the front of his head. He hadn't shaved his face either, and he boasted an excellent start on a lush, full beard.

"Sons of a ri." He wagged that unkempt head. "I am constantly amazed at how many sons of ris pop out of the woods right after a devastating wave of plague. Particularly when some lass is in the area. Always a ri ruirech too. Never a mere ri tuatha. Go home to your own, princes, and do penance appropriate to the cleansing of your evil thoughts."

The grin had fled. The shaggy-haired lad studied the monk for a long time. Anne watched his hand loosen and tighten on the haft of his knife.

And then his companion crossed himself rapidly. "Father, forgive us for we have sinned. Come on, Conan."

Conan did not seem convinced.

"We'll tell the widow about her cow," the monk offered, "a loss she can ill afford just now. You two thoughtless fools did her great harm. I will assume you intended no deliberate harm, or your penance would be far more than just contemplation and fasting."

Conan looked at the monk, at the cow, at the monk. "We're hungry, father."

"In more ways than one, I aver. Go. Assuage your hungers among your own people. After your penance, of course."

Anne's breastbone tickled.

For the longest moment it appeared that the two ruffians might care so little for God that they would challenge His monk. But then they backed away and with one last fond, loving glance toward the cow, hastened off down the valley.

His arms folded casually across his breast, the monk stepped in at Anne's side and watched them go.

She studied the face behind that so-recent growth of hair. Such a handsome face, and sad. "You look familiar, father."

"A bulky brother named Boyd brought you to Fanchea some weeks ago. I recall when you arrived with him."

"I remember! You were one of the two monks locked in combat down at the marsh." Fighting over the lovely Angelica.

He smiled sadly. "Ronan, from Skellig Michael. Boyd said your name when he presented you to Fanchea. I remember well your charming swarm of freckles, but I don't remember the name."

"Anne Green Head."

"That's it. A hare and two rooks are roasting on a spit in the house there. If you've not eaten, I invite you to join me. We'd have beef—" he nodded toward the cow "—but it's not well-aged."

Anne laughed and in the laughter realized that this was the first man besides Boyd that she had ever taken a liking to in this awful place. And Boyd had the good sense to leave it. "I've not eaten, and I would love to share rooks with you."

The two cattle killers disappeared down around the hill to the west.

Ronan turned and strolled off toward the ringwall. "No, you wouldn't. Rooks taste terrible. I'll eat them. You take the hare."

Anne fell in easily beside him. "Oh, really, I don't mind at all ea—"

"Take it as gospel from a man of God. You don't want the rooks. I've snared and eaten perhaps a dozen of them lately, and I know whereof I speak."

She laughed again, and when she said something—she forgot later what it was—he laughed. And so they chatted, light and airy, all the walk up to the rath. "I heard you go by and shout to those two," he explained, "though I must have been sleeping earlier when they did their dirty deed."

His fire had almost gone out, an obvious victim of inattention. A few stray coals flickered on the hearth. They settled beside the fire cross-legged, as if camping in the wildwood. He revitalized his fire. Then he blessed and broke the bread, a rather stale barley cake, and gave her the hare. He gave her a taste of rook because she asked, and she let him have them.

"Have you ever been to Cashel?" she asked.

He nodded.

"What's it like, pray thee?"

He dipped his head casually. "It's your average ringwall with palisade, and halls inside. It's perched on a hill that's steep on one side and very steep—a rocky precipice—on the other. Easily defended. The heads of enemies and executed criminals hang on the outside of the wall, drying out and moldering. Some hang by the hair and others are thrust onto pikes. Cattle and horses are pastured in the valley round about, and they keep the chariots in a low barn outside the gate."

"But what's the palace like inside?"

"I don't know. I've never been inside."

Anne wondered if Ibar ever had.

She looked around the hovel here. She saw no furnishings and none of the tools and implements one would expect of a farmer or boaire. This man did not live here.

He wiped his fingers on the last of his stale barley cake and popped it into his mouth. His speech came out a bit dry and crumbly as he said, "Those two are probably long gone, but let me see you safely back, just to be certain. There's a log dolly out in one of the sheds. With a bit of repair, I think I can use it tomorrow to haul the cow back to Fanchea's rath. If anyone is going to profit from the kill, it should be she."

Anne nodded. She was slow to get to her feet. She liked it here in this quiet, pleasant place. It smelled of dampness and age and abandonment, but that added to the peace. It was clammy cold in here despite his fire, yet most places were clammy cold, including that boat she spent so long in. And this Ronan was so polite, so relaxed. He looked and sounded sad too, and she could certainly relate to that. Best of all, he accepted her uncritically, with no expectations for her to fail to meet.

They arrived at Fanchea's gate late in the afternoon. He stopped fifty feet short of it. "Tell her I'll bring the carcass in tomorrow. Good night, Anne." He turned and headed back down the track.

Anne scooped up her skirts and ran after him. "Wait! You promised you'd tell Fanchea about the cow."

He stopped. "I did?"

"You told those two rapscallions, 'We'll tell the widow about her cow.' 'We.' Not 'Anne.' Not exactly a promise, but it was your word."

"An unfortunate word, if Angelica be living here still."

"She is." Anne frowned. Now what?

He studied the ground grimly. "Tell Fanchea if you would, pray thee, that I shall speak to her tomorrow when I come." He glanced almost guiltily at Anne. "I'm sorry, but I don't think I can talk to her today. Good night." And he continued off across the darkening lea.

Anne stood a few minutes trying to make sense of this. Somehow, it would seem, either Fanchea or the perfect Angelica had refused this disheveled monk.

And if these women, so adept at every skill, did that, they were utter fools.

23
Sheep

They were leaving now, with no intention ever of returning. His sheepskins rolled up tight and balanced on his shoulder, Boyd Blond Hair stepped aside out of the path and turned for one last look.

There it sat, exactly as it looked when they arrived—a giant hall with no builders, no inhabitants, no past, no future. Question: Was this stone building actual, or was it altogether a construct of the imagination, placed in the collective mind of Brendan's crew for this occasion because it was what Brendan and his crew needed? God could do that. He transported Stephen instantly from one place to another when the need arose. Overnight He grew a bush to shade Jonah's head and then produced an instant worm to attack it. Speaking of bushes, there was the burning one Moses talked to. God could do anything He wanted.

The wind had picked up so severely that Boyd wondered if they would be able to leave the island at all. The clouds today did not limit themselves to gathering above the island but, apparently, were spread generally across the area. They scudded low along the water, ugly and gray, and let the wind drag their raw dampness right through the warmest wool.

Boyd wished fervently for a climate someday where warmth pervaded instead of cold, cheeriness instead of clouds. None such existed of course, but he could dream.

The brothers filed past him up the path to the cove and the boat. He let Ibar, the last one, pass. And then Boyd acted impulsively, which was most unlike Boyd, who abhorred impulse. He laid his sheepskin down beside the way and hurried back to the stone building. He rapped on its door with his knuckles and thought he heard scurrying inside. He pushed open the oaken door and stepped into the dim hall.

He checked through it. No one in the pantry. He pounded on the shelves. Solid. No one in the main room. He stomped the beaten earth beneath his foot. He reached up and shook one of those silver-mounted bridles. It rattled with a good, clanging, metal sound as its bit rings hit the stone. He left, closing the great door behind him with a satisfying thud.

If the building were artificial, constructed temporarily by God in response to human need or prayer, it would surely evaporate when those who prayed left the area for good and the need no longer existed. Yet it stood. As he hastened after the others, Boyd decided the place was real.

That raised question number two: Who would build that particular structure, in that particular style, here? No Celt, that was certain.

From whence did they bring the massive timbers?

Question three—namely, how the bread and fish got there—only complicated matters.

Just before he took the bend in the trail that would hide the stone hall forever from his sight, he stopped to look at it again. It was not fading, though the brothers were getting farther away with every step.

He caught up to the party a quarter mile before they reached the cove. He fell in at the back of the line.

"Hold a moment." Crosan stepped aside and waited until Boyd came abreast. Boyd stepped aside also and watched the others hasten onward. "You're a sensible man, Boyd. Do you think what we're doing is sensible?"

"You mean leaving? Better we go while still liked than to wear out our welcome."

"I mean taking nothing with us."

"You mean no food left over? We each received a daily portion but not extra. Rather like the Israelites gathering manna."

"Water, Boyd. Water. When have you ever heard of a ship's crew leaving shore with empty water casks? Especially when there's so much? Look at it. Waterfalls all over. Creeks and rills. So we get a little hungry. I've gone hungry before. Call a fast. But water? You die without water."

"You're saying, slip some water aboard when he's not looking?"

"All right, I'll go along with Brendan's pronouncement—
let's not take anything from this island. But water doesn't count."

Boyd had to agree that Crosan made sense. He listened to
gulls mewing in their weightless circling, and he listened to the
trickle of fresh water running free down to the sea. Ample water.
Water used by no one. Water for no purpose.

Ahead, on the very rim of the cliff where land yielded abruptly to sea, just before the track disappeared over the side and led
down to the shingled shore of the cove, Brendan stopped. He
waved impatiently to Boyd. "Come! Come."

Now what? Had Brendan read their mutinous minds? Boyd
wouldn't put it past him. He heard Crosan crunching in the loose
gravel behind him as they made their way to the cliff edge.

His tousled hair whipping in the stiff breeze, Brendan looked
from face to face at the brothers gathered close around him. A
profound sadness darkened his eyes. "I warned that none of you
take anything from this island."

Truth, and he does indeed read minds!

Brendan closed those dark, sad eyes. "Look. Our brother has
hidden a silver bridle on his person."

Boyd looked instantly at Ibar. Ibar was the one who had tested the silver on the bridle in the great hall.

On the other hand, Willis was the known thief. How could an
inveterate robber resist the splendid silverwork hanging free on
the walls? And a bridle, by all that's holy. What would any of these
monks want with a bridle aboard a ship, and the nearest pony a
thousand miles away? It had to be Willis. Only he would steal
purely for the sake of stealing. No doubt this was what Brendan
talked about when he said, "One of you three has done something
meritorious, but the other two will face hideous judgment."

And then Boyd noticed that every other pair of eyes was focused on him.

He opened his mouth to protest and closed it again. The
wind whipped his words away unspoken. Of course. After all the
others left, he had gone back. If Boyd didn't know better, Boyd
would suspect Boyd.

He need only take off his cassock and unroll his sheepskins
to demonstrate his innocence. But what if he would find a bridle

there? Were someone to steal a bridle, what better way to get it aboard the vessel than to stash it in another's belongings? He had left his sheepskins unattended on the trail. And Ibar was the last in the line going back. Ibar, young and tender, not yet sturdy in the resolve that only time can strengthen . . . Willis, slick and practiced in his thievery . . .

The wind howled past, driving the cold through his woolen robe. In spite of himself, Boyd felt sweat break out on his forehead.

He sent his own urgent prayer to heaven. *I pray Thee, God, let the truth be known.*

Then Conn the Poet, Conn the Handsome made a strange noise, half a croak and half a cry. He dug down into the front of his cassock and pulled out a bridle. "Look at this piece! Poetry in metal! Craftsmanship as fine as anything out of Armagh or Tara." He held it out to Brendan. "I think it was the dragons on it that made it irresistible. Do you see them? Engraved in the cheek mountings here. Twined in themselves. Look at the intricacy!" He shuddered and tossed the work of art down on the cold, rocky lip. "I didn't . . . I couldn't . . . forgive me, father. I've sinned."

Brendan's voice carried the weight of the world. "Your soul will depart from your body this hour. Your body is lost. We must all pray for your soul that it not perish and be lost as well."

Terror contorted Conn's beautiful face.

Like a hammer crushing rock, the reality of sin slammed down upon Boyd's heart. Sin brings death. Death! You talk about sin, you discuss it calmly in a quiet monastic setting, you memorize the tidy theological rules of sin, forgiveness, and restitution. But you keep it at arm's length even as you embrace the theory of it.

Boyd fell upon his face on the ground, for he had just seen the reality of sin and it horrified him. He prayed prostrate for Conn the Handsome. He prayed for himself. *No, Crosan, we will not steal water. If a man of God calls that sin, sin it will be.* At length he climbed to his feet.

The contortion in Conn's face had not eased. He was having trouble breathing, it appeared. He clutched at his breast where the bridle had so recently lain. His skin was taking on a peculiar bluish shade that seemed more than a mere reaction to the piercing wind and cold. Another sucking breath or two, and he dropped.

Boyd gaped.

Conn's dying body relaxed, melting down closer, ever closer, against the cold, hard ground.

Boyd pointed to Ibar, to Crosan, to Malo. "Choose teams for yourselves and start gathering stones. We can't dig in this bare rock, so we'll bury him under a barrow, the way our ancestors did."

He watched his brothers, his fellow travelers, disperse silently.

Brendan picked up the bridle. "I must take this back and hang it up where it belongs. I'll return shortly." Tears streamed down his cheeks.

Boyd knew of at least one dog on the island, though they had seen him only once. So he directed the construction of a particularly massive barrow. The pile of cold rocks that covered Conn's cooling body stood almost head high when they were done.

The job took six hours and the service of interment another two, as each man eulogized the brother who could have been a professional poet. None of their words came close to poesy.

All we like sheep have gone astray. All we like Conn deserve his fate. Many times Boyd recited that Scripture, and never before had he so grasped the significance of Jesus Christ's gift for the taking.

Because of this tragic turn, they missed the first midtide, but by the time they finished singing vespers, the second was close enough that they could sail with it shortly.

Brendan led the way down the steep incline to the beach. Still shaken, Boyd boosted his brothers into the boat and passed their sleeping rolls up to them.

He and Malo, the last ones left ashore, put their shoulders to the prow and shoved. The curragh, only partially grounded, scraped backward into deeper water.

"Wait!" Up on the bow, Brendan pointed excitedly toward the cliffside trail.

Boyd twisted around to look. A lad with hair even whiter than Boyd's was descending. Stones rattled down the path ahead of

him and tumbled over the steep side. He was carrying a huge basket on a tumpline.

So there were people here. If this boy was typical, they were a
very fair-complexioned folk, strong and well proportioned, tall,
with clear blue eyes and pallid skin. The boy stopped in front of
Boyd and turned his back.

Almost without thinking, Boyd grabbed the basket.

The lad ducked out from under the tumpline and spoke in
stilted, halting Gaelic, not to Boyd or Malo but to Brendan. "Receive a blessing from your servants. Bread and water will not fail
you from now until Easter." He licked his lips as his eyes darted
from face to face. He wheeled and raced up the trail to the cliff-
top. In moments he had disappeared beyond the rock rim. Malo
looked at Boyd. Boyd looked at Malo.

"Bread and water, aye?" Brendan called down.

"That it is. Loaves and jars, and heavy as a pony." Malo gave
Boyd a hand, and they passed it up. It took four brothers to haul it
in over the gunwale.

Malo climbed up on Boyd's shoulders and into the boat.
Boyd gave the prow a final push and dragged himself kicking over
the rail, as he had so often done.

They drew the boat by hand through the narrow cleft out into
the wide ocean. They raised sail cautiously against the stiff
breeze. The curragh heeled and surged forward. They were on
their way again.

Boyd and Crosan had spent hours exploring the area around
that stone building. They had seen nothing. Whoever delivered
food and water (exactly enough food at each meal for eighteen
men) left behind no trace.

And then that lad.

Boyd draped himself across the tiller and watched the island
disappear in a hazy combination of dusk and distance. With it, the
body of Conn the Handsome faded into obscurity.

Brendan settled in beside him. "What do you make of it? The
lad, I mean."

Boyd rubbed the stubble on his chin. "You will say divine
providence and leave it at that, and that it is. I would say, divine
providence through the hand of men. In our three circumnaviga-

tions of that island, before ever we found the cleft, we saw no other nearby islands. Therefore our benefactors live there. We would have seen them from afar if they sailed in from elsewhere each day to deliver fresh food. At no time did we detect smoke or fire on the island, yet the bread was baked, the fish cooked. The best guess for that would be that they live in caves in the side of the sea cliffs, not noticeable to the casual eye, probably on that west side. The smoke dissipated before it could drift up and over. Since nothing grows on the island now, they receive supplies periodically from elsewhere."

"How would they know how many of us there are, except by divine instruction?"

"If they live up in caves in the cliff, they could easily count noses as we sailed by. Three times, in fact. They would not show themselves, and the lad appeared frightened, cautious. They offered hospitality, yet they feared us. Perhaps it was more than hospitality—a peace offering. That suggests that we outnumber them, that there are fewer than eighteen of them. I'd guess they're a remnant of a much greater population some years ago. The tarnish on the bridles suggests age, the magnificence of that stone hall suggests plenty of manpower. The lad was what?—twelve? Thirteen? So there were women in the group at least up to twelve years ago or so."

Brendan nodded. "If that fair young man is not an angel of God, who is he?"

"A people in contact with the Irish but not Irish. Gaelic is his second language, and not a good one."

Brendan pondered the vast space where the island used to be. "We could probably say that of angels."

Boyd would not disagree.

The bread gave out on a Wednesday evening, the water on the following Thursday morning. In between those two marks, the watch spied land.

"Here we go again," was the comment first to come to Boyd's mind. This seemed not much more hospitable an island than was that first one. It jutted abruptly out of the sea, black rock battered by restless breakers. Those breakers began to build a hundred feet or less off shore. They rolled crashing in, one after the other, a constant sweeping stroke of sea against land, wave after wave. The shores sloped precipitously down to meet the sea, uninviting but for a few rocky beaches.

But at least there were beaches.

The watch reported snow. It turned out to be a vast flock of sheep grazing on a cliff-top, and not a pied or black one in the bunch that Boyd could see.

Brendan ordered all hands to oars, and Leeson summoned Boyd to help with the tiller. Even so, a murderous tidal rip threatened with every yard of progress to flip the boat over and fling it against the rocks.

They managed barely to beach in a sheltered bay on the lee side. Wearied from the sudden, violent struggle against the sea, Boyd climbed out onto solid ground. Usually the reticent one, young Ibar led an exploration of the steep and wind-beaten island. They came upon fresh streams and fish aplenty. And sheep. More sheep. More and more sheep.

All white they were, and huge. Boyd admired them immensely. The young of the year, newborn, bounded and flitted like white butterflies across the craggy meadows. Yearlings looked the size of Irish rams.

The climate here must be mild all year. Even in the creases of the high mountains in the distance, no snow lingered.

And then, pointing to a flock, Brendan made a pronouncement that surprised Boyd, considering the abbot's prior take-nothing-from-the-island warnings. "Our pascal lamb. This is Maundy Thursday. Choose the sheep we'll sacrifice."

All we like sheep have gone astray.

Always in the past, Boyd enjoyed Easter as a bright and breezy spring observance. This year the death of Conn cast it in a new light. This year he was painfully and fully aware of the dark, dark shadow of the cross.

24

Other Sheep

Anne finally figured out why she didn't just strike out on her own to Cashel. She had not the slightest notion which way to go.

And besides, there was Ronan.

Ronan fascinated her. He walked around all melancholy. He kept a certain cool distance from Angelica, and yet he seemed so attentive toward her. Anything she mentioned that needed doing, he did. The brindled dog bounded about excitedly whenever he ventured to Fanchea's rath, obviously overjoyed to see him, though it would not come near.

He had quite a nice head of hair when he let it grow, but he didn't. He kept the beard, but he shaved the tonsure. He was as strong as he was handsome. He muscled that black cow in alone, using only the one-axle cart he found at that farm. All in all, the man was almost as superb a monk as Desmond had been.

Desmond. Ah, Tavish, you scoundrel.

Anne crested the last hill. There lay the little rath, Ronan's home for the moment. The rooks had gone off elsewhere, which suggested that Ronan was probably out in one of the sheds. She wondered how he managed to snare rooks so successfully. They seemed too wily to be trapped.

Having tasted one, she wondered why he would want to.

She paused by the rape patch and whistled.

Smiling, he stepped out of the bier with a manure fork in his hand. He propped it beside the doorway and crossed to her. "Anne, and the top of the morning."

She fluttered in a hasty little obeisance. It seemed the thing to do before a monk. "Peace to yourself, father. Fanchea would like you to choose a lamb from her flock and celebrate Easter for her household."

"My pleasure. I'll get my cloak." He disappeared inside his hovel.

Anne looked around seeking improvements, some indication he planned to stay. If he was mucking out the abandoned bier, perhaps he expected to obtain a cow. Were he to ask Fanchea for one, sure and the woman would give it to him. She had a good twenty head out on spring pasture.

Alas, everything remained in as great a state of disrepair as ever.

He came out with his thick wool wrap and a knife sheathed at his waist. He pinned the cloak as he came. "Any idea where the flock might be?"

"Aye. I'll take you." She headed up the hill along the familiar track.

He walked in one wheel rut, she walked beside him in the other, and she enjoyed his presence. He claimed to come from Skellig Michael, but *from* was the key. He didn't seem attached to the brotherhood just now. According to Fanchea, he worked comfortably with the brothers from Clonfert, that interesting little tussle notwithstanding, but he was not attached to them. He seemed an ambassador without portfolio, and that was practically unheard of. You couldn't be a monk without being attached to a monastery, just as you could not be a person without being attached to a clan.

So tell me, Ronan. Are you available to women or not? Might I consider you a marriage prospect? Fanchea and Angelica don't seem to, but that's their shortcoming. I'm asking you.

But Anne said nothing of the sort, of course. She was too embarrassed. The question would be presumptuous, yet it cried out for an answer.

"Ronan? This is a hard question, and you may not wish to respond. Many are the tales I've heard of impropriety among monks. Is there any problem of . . . uh . . . unseemly behavior in your brotherhood?"

He looked at her oddly. "Not those of Skellig Michael, nor of Clonfert that I know of. No."

He walked on awhile, immersed in distance, and she assumed he'd dropped the subject. She dared not take it up again.

Then he spoke. "Many the tale, yes. An abbot named Mel, for example, was a nephew of Patrick himself. His sister's boy, as I recall. Mel went along with Patrick for a while in his travels through Erin and then settled down as bishop of Armagh. Unfortunately, he settled down with his Aunt Lupait, another relative on, I believe, the father's side."

"Quite a scandal, I should think. Incest it would be, in our clan."

"Indeed. Patrick told them to live apart. The official position of the church Fathers is that they instantly obeyed, but the neighbors claimed they didn't. Since then, monastics and church leaders have been caught in impropriety every now and then. But by and large they're reliable, well-principled folk."

Desmond certainly was.

She would try another approach. "While Brendan's people were building that boat, did you get to know Boyd much? The big one?"

"We worked together on the rath frequently. Farming is his first love."

She nodded. "Even on the boat coming over from Whithorn, he talked about finding a small place. Farming, starting a little cell of studying believers. From what I gather, he wasn't thinking of a big formal monastery. Just a band of happy Christians."

"That would suit his manner. It wouldn't be too hard to find a good rath. Women considerably outnumber men these days, what with so many lads taking up martyrdom of some stripe or other. A man might marry into a very good situation."

"He should do as you do, Ronan. Move into an abandoned place and claim it."

He shook his head, a firm negative. "Land laws. I don't presume to claim it. I'm just staying there until a legitimate boaire takes it. I don't know how it is where you come from, but in Erin the land belongs not to the farmer but to the clan. You can marry into it and marry out of it, but the clan keeps it. To make a rath his own, Boyd would have to marry its clanswoman."

"Oh." Actually, that was the way it was at Green Head too. She was hoping things would be different here.

He glanced at her, smiling. "Boyd will be back in a few months, surely. Bring the subject up with him."

"Surely."

She enjoyed the hulking Boyd's simple, open honesty. Sometimes his gentle humor showed through. More often, he blinked, confused, as the humor of others swept past him like a north wind through alders. His sweet naïveté charmed her.

But she enjoyed this dark, sad man as well. She liked the way his face curled up in a smile, literally putting a good face on a thing, while his eyes screamed, *The heart feels much differently! Don't believe the mouth.*

Ronan seemed a decent sort. On the other hand, Boyd might come back soon. He was bigger and stronger. He'd be an even better husband. Ronan didn't seem in a mood to really work at farming. He apparently just drifted, except for the labor he performed on Fanchea's rath, and that labor seemed more a diversion than a calling. On second thought, Boyd definitely appeared the better provider.

She fancied trying to interest the ponderous Boyd. He didn't catch innuendo at all well. She'd have to be blatant in her suggestion, much more so than with the cynical Ronan. After a lifetime of absolutely pitiful marriage candidates (what dunces those Green Head lads were!), her prospects were definitely improving.

They found the sheep half a mile beyond the shepherd. Dotty old Hilla had been dispatched to tend them. She sat under a wych elm singing softly to herself as her charges browsed a hillside to the west.

Ronan left both the flock and the shepherdess in the hands of God, chose a yearling ram, and hoisted it onto his shoulders. The ram struggled mightily, but Ronan kept a firm grip on all four of its plump little ankles.

Anne led the way back across the open lea. By the time they reached the track, the ram seemed to have resigned itself.

Anne looked over her shoulder past Ronan toward the old lady. "We're just going to have to come back and get Hilla and the sheep, you know. While you were finding the ram, I must have told her three times that Good Friday is tomorrow, and she didn't even look at me. Those old women have made it clear they can't stand me. They absolutely hate me."

"If that be so, it's jealousy."

Anne felt her ears flush at the subtle compliment. He walked behind her, so she permitted herself a smile. Every now and then a lad pursued her with amorous intent, but never was it a fellow she would dream of encouraging. Wouldn't it be nice to be pursued by a man of her choice once—even this one!

She would pay better notice from now on to what Ronan said. She must take care with her response—be coy yet grateful, chaste without appearing cool. With attention and a little luck, she could put Ronan exactly where she wanted him—a sheep led to the shearing.

* * *

Eva, the wife of Larkin, had never before seen Larkin Round Face's round face wet with tears. That just goes to show what the Holy Spirit does in a man, even a warlord. She could always tell when her husband felt shame or embarrassment. So she perceived easily that he took no shame in his tears today, and that pleased her. He might shape up into a fairly worthy human being, with actual feelings, if he held with the faith long enough.

At Larkin's right hand stood Tavish Grand Mustache. Tavish and his dumpy little wife, Rhea, looked just as gloomy as Larkin.

The Abbot of Whithorn mumbled something in Greek—Eva hadn't the slightest grasp of Greek—and sprinkled water on the casket of Desmond Perfect.

It was a pity. Desmond had come so close to recovering. He lived through the worst of his illness. He survived Larkin and Tavish's clumsy ministrations. He started looking fairly good—good skin color, bright eyes. And then without warning he plunged into fever, delirium, and death.

The body wasn't cold before Tavish and Larkin, the dolts, began arguing over whom Desmond had preferred. Each trotted out his most specious arguments for status as the favored one. It didn't come as any surprise to Eva. Eva was rearing seven children, so she knew how small boys act. Men are nothing more than children with deadly intent.

She knew, though, the identity of Desmond's actual favorite, the soul who had weighed most heavily upon him, for she was present at his death. He died with the name of Ibar on his lips.

And possibly, if her own Larkin should die untimely, he'd be whispering the name of his son, for Eva did not anticipate that Mac Larkin would return any time soon. The lad shared his father's obdurate single-mindedness, particularly regarding a quest of magnitude.

Eva and Rhea took the nonsense between Tavish and Larkin just so long and stepped in to mediate. Both clans would carry the body, not to one monastery or the other but to a hallowed memorial on the border between the two clan territories. They would draw straws to see who took the right side first, and would switch off every mile. It was so easy when you thought about it sensibly. Above all else, that's what Desmond used to preach. Be sensible.

Larkin and his two sons stepped forward with Tavish and his two oldest. Together the six hoisted the coffin to their shoulders and began the long, lugubrious walk to Desmond's final resting place. Eva and Rhea fell in behind, leading the mourning followers.

A mile down the track, the pallbearers laid the coffin in green moss, rested, and switched sides.

Eva muttered to Rhea, "So far, so good."

Rhea grimaced. "Tavish was a bear this morning. Black as a thunderstorm."

"Eh, my goodfellow as well. Best to keep a close eye on them both."

On they went.

Eva was proud of the crew from Larkin's monastery. The moment the funeral party arrived at the grave site, the monks and nuns of Larkin's brotherhood laid out a repast fit for royalty. And a good thing. Between the ranking men and women of Tavish's clan in their green, and the ranking men and women of Larkin's in their brown, most of the mourners were wearing five colors or more. Status and royalty aplenty! The board groaned beneath beer and ale, wine brought in from Spain, venison and beef, pottage and greens, great piles of aromatic bread loaves. Desmond had constantly railed against ostentation. He'd roll over in his grave if he saw all this, except that he wasn't in his grave yet.

For the balance of the day, while Desmond lay virtually forgotten in the spring moss beside the hole in which he would lie once his followers got around to putting him there, the people of both clans regaled each other with tales of miracles and blessings. Eva told her share. And she alone among them related the intense disappointment in his protégé Ibar that Desmond carried to his grave.

She knew the feeling. She would never express it out loud before a rival clan, or even in private within her own, but of her seven children, six were disappointments. In a pitched battle, she'd back any two daughters against the boys any day—even the ten-year-old, who was in some ways the feistiest of them all. Except for Mac Larkin. He alone of the sons carried his father's warrior spirit undiluted. And he romped across foreign leas a-questing for a woman hardly worth the bother.

The Abbot of Whithorn, solemn and stodgy and white-haired and nearsighted, stood up as Eva sat down. He raised his leather cup. "I salute the man who brought together enemies and cemented them in the bond of Jesus Christ's Spirit. It is fitting that he be laid to rest on this Good Friday, the very day the Lord he loved was laid to rest. Jesus is risen!"

An uncertain cheer went up. Does one cheer at buryings?

"And because He lives, Desmond will rise again, as shall we all who are in Him!"

More noisy appreciation.

The abbot cleared his throat. "I trust your enthusiasm will carry you all to services of worship throughout this holy weekend, particularly Holy Saturday and Easter Sunday."

Enthusiasm as measured by noise waned a bit.

The abbot droned on. "And now, as I listen to Eva here relating Desmond's great sadness in regard to his fickle assistant, I understand the heartache."

You cannot understand, old man. But Eva kept her thoughts to herself.

"A tragic heartache! I propose for that callous and immoral deserter the most severe punishment the church can bring to bear." On and on he went.

Eva found herself gaping, then becoming angry. And then she leaped to her feet. "Wait! Punish the lad for what? For being young? For not wanting to get involved in a clan war in a foreign country? Desmond preached mediation and common sense. Where's the common sense in that?"

Tavish snarled, "You're speaking out of turn!"

Eva barked at him. "This esteemed churchman knew Desmond and Ibar a total of maybe two days. And he presumes to judge? Where was he when our monastery was just getting started and Ibar worked like a slave? The lad acquitted himself well, building and studying and serving Desmond. Suddenly he watched it all burn up, and Desmond snatched away. Are you faulting him for not being able to see the future? For not acting wise and mature? If that's not wisdom and maturity, there's not a man here who acts wise or mature, let alone can see tomorrow clearly."

Tavish roared, "Sit down and shut up!"

Larkin leaped to his feet with his hand on his sword hilt. "Enough, Tavish!"

Eva pressed her point home. "The lad deserves mercy, not this stranger's invective."

And then Rhea, the soul of common sense, turned on her. "How dare you speak to my man in that tone of voice!"

Eva snapped, "How dare he speak to me thusly?"

The bleary abbot looked from face to face. His dumbfounded gape told that world that he hadn't the slightest wisp of an idea what was going on.

A dozen warriors rose. Another score.

Eva realized too late what her bit of temper was turning into. She raised both arms and cried out, "Peace! Peace! It's what Desmond would want!"

No one listened to her, of course. Hardly ever did anyone listen to her.

She tried once more. "It's Easter week! I pray you, sit down and restrain yourselves!"

Restraint? Larkin was defending her honor, which she could do very well herself if she cared to, and Rhea was screaming at her, and Tavish was defending Rhea's honor, and Tavish and Larkin were berating each other for all the slights they had mutually committed, and the Abbot of Whithorn was muttering, "Oh dear." The abbot seemed to be the only one who didn't want to see blood drawn. Besides Eva, that is.

For some reason a lull occurred—perhaps all the plaintiffs

drew a breath at once—and Eva seized it. "Hear me! You're like sheep. One leaps, and they all leap. One panics, and they all panic, without knowing why. One draws his sword, and instantly everyone is up in arms! Stop! Don't undo his w—"

But the lull ceased before her remarks did.

Tavish and Larkin fell to blows, and instantly both sides raised swords to guard this battle of the titans from interference. The most ancient of Celtic custom decreed that the outcome of two champions meeting on the field of honor was just as binding as the outcome of a battle. Eva always strongly suspected that was because fights were so much more fun to watch than to wage, but Larkin denied that to be so.

Rhea seized Eva's arm and yanked her out of the way. "It's a heroes' fight! Get back!"

No pasty-faced Tavish was going to maul Eva like that. She wheeled and struck Rhea squarely in the jaw. The dumpy little woman dropped like a sack of stones.

Larkin's cloak hung in shreds, but 'twas he who first struck well. A feint and a jab, and he took a chunk out of Tavish's left arm with his sword tip.

The Larkin monastics cheered. *The sheep! The stupid sheep!*

The injury seemed not to slow the Mustache down any. Tavish pressed forward, still wielding his sword two-handed with as much agility as ever and no apparent weakening to the left. He engaged Larkin's sword to the hilt, gave a twist, then pivoted a full circle in place. Wildly, he flung his weight against his burlier foe.

The Tavish monastics cheered.

Thrown off balance, Larkin staggered sideways against Desmond's final home. He fell across it and just barely freed his sword in time to defend himself. Tavish slashed at him and missed. Larkin slashed back and drew blood again, though Eva could not see where or to what degree.

The Larkin monastics cheered.

Tavish fell upon him, howling. Both struggled like half-grown boys, fighting at too close quarters to use a sword effectively at all.

Larkin grunted as Tavish's elbow dug into his belly.

The Tavish monastics cheered.

The coffin scooted across the wet green moss, plowing a

broad, ugly, black streak. It scooted again as Larkin got a foot on solid ground and tried to push away.

The Tavish and Larkin monastics all cheered.

The coffin slid atilt, partway into the grave.

And then the heroes, oblivious to all save each other, wriggled and struggled and sent the coffin sliding. It tipped aslant and wedged tight across the open grave, the head jammed down inside and the bottom end angled high. The heroes slid gracelessly, their feet flailing, off the coffin cover and into the hole. They too wedged, stuffed like bungs into the cramped space left to them.

The monastics fell silent.

25

Jasconius

Willis Gray Mantle did not believe in Easter. He did not believe in celebrating equinox and solstice, and he did not believe in keeping time by singing offices every three hours. But, oh, how he loved the music!

He had never heard the plaintive song in minor key that Brendan's crew was singing just now. So he simply stood in place, mouthed the words, and listened to the harmonies all around him. This was the best place to hear the glory of a choir—in the middle of it.

Often, if Malo, the choirmaster, chose a song Willis knew, Willis could now join in and sing a part clearly. He considered that a triumph.

Brendan's crew had arrived on the harsh, rocky Island of Sheep on Maundy Thursday. Here it was Saturday, and they were still there, exploring, relaxing, and singing.

Like no other, this island invited singing. It rose steeply behind the concave beach where Brendan landed his boat, forming a natural amphitheater. When the brothers arranged themselves among the rocks in two close tiers, their voices flowed together into a single, glorious, magnified sound. Without actually echoing, that sound tumbled off the rock walls and poured out across a steep pasture to the beach, to the breakers, to the wide, wide sea.

More than three-score sheepherding Celts lived in this area, and more and more kept appearing. Unlike the strange inhabitants of that other island—assuming there were any—these people seemed open and friendly and eager to serve the brothers. Willis didn't mind being attended to. They gathered around now in clumps and pairs, wearing smiles as they listened to the voice of God filtered through the mouths of men.

201

Malo signaled the Gloria Patri, eight tones. They always finished their impromptu concerts with the Gloria Patri. Willis loved it because it began rather quietly and ended in a six-part crescendo over two octaves. Boyd's vibrant baritone rumbled behind his ear. Ibar's ultrasoprano rang to his left. World without end! Amen! Amen!

The whole ragged hillside reverberated with the silence that followed. After a long, hushed moment, all the sheepherders as one began loudly praising God. No one asked these people to do that. No one told them how.

The choir broke up and moved down the slope in among the locals. People Willis had never met and would never see again pumped his arm enthusiastically and called God's blessing down upon him. Not just one or two. A dozen. At one time Willis had hated being blessed. It happened so often now, he was becoming comfortably accustomed to it.

That old fellow was down by the boat talking to Brendan again. A patriarch he was, no doubt. He seemed to have taken Brendan under his wing. He constantly offered advice, wisdom, and prophecies. Some of them Brendan passed along to the other brothers. Some seemed to be his alone. Whatever they were, Brendan constantly accepted them at face value.

This troubled Willis. He had learned from childhood never to take anyone's word at face value. Count every man your enemy until he proves himself otherwise. Listen for the hidden agenda; everyone has one. Brendan, the father on this voyage, was supposed to provide all the answers. He was supposed to advise, not receive advice.

But then, Willis had long since given up trying to figure out what Brendan of Clonfert would do next. He didn't even feel as uneasy as he used to when Brendan made some inscrutable pronouncement.

Willis walked out through the sand toward the boat and stopped cold, utterly shocked by the revelation that hit him: he was actually glad he had come along on this journey instead of traveling to Iona or remaining behind in Erin! Glad. There was no other word for it.

And why not? The work was easy, the company wasn't bad,

the food was very good, and for once someone besides Willis turned out to be the thief.

"Willis?" Boyd gave him a friendly jab that punched a dent in his arm. "Help load."

Willis fell in behind the moving mountain and sauntered over to the boat. A pair of women nodded reverently to him and smiled as he passed. To him. To Willis.

The old man beside Brendan was pointing vaguely to the horizon. "Tonight—the close of Holy Saturday—and tomorrow morning, Easter, you will be on that island out there. Easter afternoon, you will sail to another island to the west, called the Paradise of Birds. Stay there to Pentecost."

Brendan blandly accepted that, it appeared. Then he asked, "The stone church on an island by itself. It stands stark and deserted, yet people live there."

Willis froze. He wanted to hear about that mysterious place with naught to boast of save magnificent bakers. Ah, but the bread had been good.

The old fellow nodded. "The great hall. Yes. Have you ever been to Aran?"

"Enda is my mentor."

Enda, Aran meant nothing to Willis. He listened anyway.

"You know how barren the island is. Bare rock, few trees, almost no soil."

"Aye."

"It was once a much richer land," the old man said. "Thick grass, trees, wildflowers. But too many people and too many sheep on too little land, and they overworked it. Killed the soil. The wind stripped it. Now they're using seaweed and sand, trying to rebuild soil. The made soil is not nearly so good as what God first put there."

"And the same thing happened to that other island? But the settlers there weren't Celts."

"Half. Danes from the north married into Celts who were already there. They speak Norse primarily. It was a thriving island once. Now the only food comes by the charitable hands of relatives from other islands down in the Hebrides. They keep thinking they'll rebuild it to its former glory one day." The old man wagged his head. "It'll never come back. None of these ruined islands will."

Brendan asked more questions, but Willis didn't listen. He was trying to spot an island anywhere near the direction the old fellow had pointed. He couldn't see anything. Was this one of those test-of-faith matters?

He scrambled up into the boat, and Boyd handed him bundles of bread and smoked fish—cod, probably. That was the common sort. However, the place abounded in salmon. Might these good folk possibly have packaged some smoked salmon for the brothers? He sniffed carefully. They had, and it smelled as delectable as the salmon from Whithorn.

Boyd passed up the last of the oilskin-wrapped packets and hung on the gunwale to stare at Willis. "Why are you grinning?"

"Grinning?" Why was he grinning? "The prospect of smoked salmon would make anyone smile."

Boyd chuckled. "True enough." He sobered. "Willis, I owe you an apology. When Brendan first declared his revelation about that bridle, I was certain either Ibar or you was guilty. I apologized to Ibar, and I apologize to you."

Now this was the first time ever in Willis's life that anyone had apologized to him. He had trouble finding his tongue. "Your apology is accepted."

"One more thing. I don't know which one of us has changed, but someone or something has. You fit into the crew well now. You're one of us. It didn't use to be that way." The great shoulders heaved in a helpless shrug. "No meaning there. I just wanted you to know. I'm glad you shipped aboard."

Glad. There was that word again, in a whole new context. Amazement robbed Willis of speech completely. No matter. The conversation had ended, for Boyd wandered off to join Brendan and the old man. They were talking about the island's sheep now and why they grew so well here.

Willis didn't care about sheep, except when they were roasted and perhaps served with a bit of mint and parsley.

The brothers took to their boat, the tide (with a shove from Boyd) lifted them free of land, and they were at sea again, spirits of a different realm. A land breeze rose behind them.

204

Willis was given the watch, and he still didn't see any island out there. Was Leeson on the right heading?

Maybe someone else ought take this watch. If this was some test of faith, Willis was failing it. He didn't believe in the God of these Erse, though there were moments he was thinking he had no choice but to trust the Great Unseen.

Ah, wait. There it was. A smooth, low hummock of land rose out of the sea afar off. Unlike their prior landfalls, it didn't look rocky or precipitous. It seemed more a reef than an island. No matter. It was about where that fellow said it ought to be. This must be the place.

Willis called the sighting back, and Leeson altered course. The boat heeled gently and plowed over to it quicker than Willis would have predicted.

They grounded well short of the shore. Boyd leaped out and dragged the boat up. This was a strange place indeed to celebrate a feast. The island was less than a hundred feet long and not much more than a dozen feet wide. Not a stick of vegetation grew upon it, and it provided no opportunity to moor the boat. Brendan must have been concerned about that, for he stayed aboard.

Debarked, the brothers just about filled the place. It felt spongy beneath Willis's feet, soft and giving, like a peat bog. When he walked about it seemed to ripple beneath his weight. That wasn't totally unexpected. The Island of Sheep contained widespread peat bogs on its wet, windy plateau.

They gathered in the middle, where it was flattest, formed a tight circle facing each other, and sang the compline. There were no reverberations now; every note flew sweet and clear into the wind and zipped away. The difference between this sound and the music in the island's amphitheater fascinated him.

The smooth curve of the land promised to send anyone who threw a sheepskin out upon it sliding into the sea. The brothers slept in the boat that night.

Dawn burst pink and clear.

Willis had never sung an Easter matins. It would take him half of forever to learn the litany if he heard it only once a year. They completed the office as Willis tried to mouth Latin he did not know.

He is risen!

We've acknowledged that.

Let the feasting commence!

Brendan, still aboard, passed joints of meat over the side into eager hands.

Willis would let others do that work. He arranged their lint and tinder on the flattest part of this odd, unsettling island and laid the sticks. From their chiseled stone case he lifted the coals from ashore that would bring the fire to life. If he wet his hands and worked rapidly, he could pick them up with his fingers.

Willis, with his quick touch, was very good at that. He had considered becoming a pickpocket and cutpurse once. He probably would have succeeded well at that calling, but for that one must work in towns, and he disliked towns. Too many people lived there who loved to hate you.

He paused. It was strange. He felt no call anymore to return to his chosen trade of just a few months ago. Economic redistribution no longer appealed—not robbery, not theft, not light-fingering, not even a wee bit of harmless pinching from farmers' clotheslines.

He blew gently on his fledgling fire. The grass crackled, the lint smoked, the wood shavings caught, and dinner was as good as cooked. Carefully he rearranged the sticks, that they might ignite more quickly.

Boyd hovered nearby. "You're an artist, Willis. From cold wood to strong fire in moments."

And then the earthquake struck.

A massive, rolling wave heaved up under Willis, flinging him. He heard others shrieking as he shrieked. The island rose higher and tipped. Willis slid into the sea. Icy water pierced instantly through his woolen cassock, his hair, his ears, his nose, his eyes. The shock robbed him of breath, and a good thing, for he struggled completely underwater now.

Never before had he been called upon to swim.

Never had he learned how.

He flailed the way children flop about when they play in puddles. He windmilled his arms and kicked. How his nose and lungs burned!

He careth for you.

It was like a voice pressing itself upon Willis's harried mind.
Trust in the Lord with all your heart.

What could he do but trust? He fought helplessly in this frigid waste, no more able to save himself than was a babe in arms. A powerful grip pulled him through the water as he struggled valiantly to hold his breath.

He popped to the surface. Strong hands slammed him against the boat's greased side, scraped him along the rough stitched seams, dragged him up over the gunwales. He tumbled onto the deck, safe.

Cold as a mackerel, but safe. His teeth chattered so hard he could not hear the calls being shouted back and forth, though he recognized them as the orders to sail.

The deck tipped gently, heeling away. They would have to raise sail without him. Loathe to move, he curled in a tight ball, shivering violently.

A black shadow blotted out the morning sky. Boyd, the giant, laughing, hauled Willis to his feet. "Here, friend. I want you to see what manner of island you brought us to last night."

The brothers were nearly all crowded against the stern half-decking. Pointing and murmuring they were, all amazed. No one bothered to help Leeson, who snarled at the world as he struggled to bring the tiller into play.

Out in the middle distance beyond the stern, the island was moving away. The boat was moving away from the island, true, but the island was moving also. Willis could see the water rippling along its leading edge, could make out the wake behind it. Their fire still smoked on it, and there lay all their supplies—the food, the fire-making tools, a water pot, their roasting spit.

The middle of the island humped up. The supplies and the coals remaining from Willis's fine fire rolled down the side in a flaming display. The island's leading edge disappeared beneath the waves as its trailing edge rose. And rose. And rose. Giant tail flukes, huge flat fins broad enough to cover a house, burst up out of the water, snapped high in the air, and slammed down upon the sea. In a noisy cloud of spray, the great fish dived.

The smooth back surfaced again a quarter mile from the boat and spouted a steamy geyser. Its fire and their food were gone.

Crosan the Laughing Monk roared. He slapped Willis's wet back. "Brothers, I warn you—the next time our beloved Willis here reports a landfall, don't you dare believe him!"

The awkward tension exploded in laughter.

Crosan and Mochta set about stripping off Willis's soaking-wet clothes.

Willis's jaw trembled so badly he couldn't speak well. "M-m-m-my thanks. I can't m-m-move my f-f-fingers."

Brendan watched the process with a certain gentle bemusement. "Let's not be too hard on Willis here, lads. Our mentor on the island told me about the beast. It's known to them. It even has a name. Jasconius."

"Wonderful," Boyd rumbled. "We know the name of the fish that has swept away our fire and food. Now what?"

"We shall do as our mentor on the Isle of Sheep described," Brendan replied. "Sail to the Paradise of Birds. Don't mourn our lost goods. We will be well supplied."

Willis watched helplessly as his brothers cinched a dry cassock on him. They threw a sheepskin around his shoulders and wrapped him close.

His brothers. He had been thinking about these men as brothers. Willis had no brother. In fact, he had never known his father. And yet, these were indeed his brothers. See how freely they ministered to him when he needed them! And when he sang the beautiful music, he was indeed singing to his Father. *Gloria Patri. Glory be to the Father.*

What witchcraft was Brendan the Navigator practicing that he could turn Willis around so thoroughly? Willis had hated the religious spouting of the Irish monks. His whole adulthood he had hated it. And now look at him. He was one of them, in spirit if not yet in fact.

And he knew it wasn't witchcraft.

Malo commenced a recitation that he referred to as "The book of prophecy of Jonah." He rattled off a constant narrative in Latin for some minutes. Then he returned to Gaelic for what was apparently a summary. In stilted, archaic language he told of a fellow who tried to escape God. The man's folly was rewarded by a dreadful storm at sea. He begged his crewmates to throw him overboard, and the storm ceased. A great fish swallowed him alive and spit him out ashore three days later.

Willis would have dismissed the tale as fantasy, except that he had just seen a fish big enough to handle the task.

Other lessons and cautionaries followed from the story, but Willis didn't pay attention to them. He was struck by the power of God in heaven to do anything with men's fate that He cared to.

Boyd grinned at him. "Feeling warmer?"

"No. But I will."

"At least now you're not stuttering."

"True." On impulse Willis followed Boyd forward. The giant leaned against the halfdecking, watching the sea ahead.

From aft, Leeson yelled impatiently.

Boyd shifted his position closer to the middle and resumed leaning.

Crosan joined them and shot a sly grin Willis's way. "'The lad's cold,' they said. And I say, 'No, not so. He's not cold; he's made out of blue glass.' So how are you doing? Softening, or shattering?"

"Shivering." Willis grimaced. And as he thought about it, he knew it wasn't a grimace. It was a smile. Bantering equaled acceptance.

Crosan pointed to the distance. "There's the Island of Sheep. And I'll bet that's the Paradise of Birds right near there. See it?"

"Brilliant deduction," Boyd mocked.

A white cloud of birds rose off the far bit of land, thousands of them. The cloud dispersed, shimmering, out across the water.

Willis watched in awe. Never had he seen such a great mass of birds. Then puzzlement took over. "Boyd, friend. Was it you who dragged me to the boat?"

Boyd looked at him. "I shoved you up the side, and Brendan and Crosan hauled you aboard."

Crosan chuckled. "You were so wet you weighed double. I've seen drier fish."

"I mean before that. After I fell in and before you pulled me aboard."

Boyd frowned and shook his head. "When the beast started moving, everyone panicked. There was a great crush to get off and into the boat. Brendan was still aboard, so he hauled people in. You went in maybe fifty feet from the boat, as I recall. I don't know who swam back and got you."

Crosan looked at Willis oddly, as if he were foolish to ask such a thing. "I was one of the first aboard, and I saw it all clearly from up at the gunwale. Nobody had to go get you. You came swimming over on your own."

"But . . ." Willis stopped. But what?

Crosan chuckled again. "You were as panicked as we were, Willis friend. I've never seen anyone move more swiftly through the water. You came so fast you didn't even surface."

26
Birds

Birds. Clouds of birds. Thousands of birds. Circling, settling, squawking, flapping, soaring. Scores of them lit on the churning water. They bobbed on the surface and dived out of sight. Scores more coasted on stiffly set wings around about the boat's rigging.

If one were a bird who loved to roost on a vertical surface, the Paradise of Birds could not be more aptly named. Birds swarmed on the jagged cliffsides that erupted out of the water. They perched on the narrowest of ledges to argue with one other. As Willis mindlessly plied an oar, he gawked at the wonderful, exotic birds.

So abruptly did the island rise out of the churning sea, he assumed this would be another case where they would have to sail around three times before they found a landing. But no. On the south side, the land sloped gently enough that a river could run out across a broad floodplain.

Like home that floodplain was. The first goodly trees he had seen in ever so long graced the rivershore and snugged in against the crags. Grass and wildflowers rippled in the breeze.

River? The stream was scarcely wider than the boat. Yet Brendan told them to head upstream. Willis and the other rowers shipped their oars. A dozen stout brothers hopped ashore and drew the boat upriver with ropes. Even with Leeson at the tiller, the boat's leather sides kept scraping protruding rocks. What was Brendan up to?

A big island, this. They hauled the boat nearly a mile, dragging it across a few riffling shallows until it wedged between the banks and stopped. Even a narrower boat would not go much farther, for the river tumbled down steep cascades ahead. Above, the dancing staircase disappeared into a narrow cleft. For whatever it was worth, they had reached the headwaters.

Mountains craggier than any Willis had ever seen before punched skyward. The entire archipelago was nothing but mountaintops sticking out of the sea. He wondered idly what the mountain bottoms were like and how far below the water they extended.

And once you put the mountains behind, what manner of sea bottom lay beneath you?

Brendan remained aboard as the brothers pitched camp. Willis watched in amazement as a white bird with long pointed wings settled onto the prow near the abbot. Man and bird seemed to engage in conversation, which was ridiculous to contemplate.

Boyd didn't seem to notice the bird, or if he did he tactfully ignored it. He jumped out of the boat with an armload of sheepskins. He handed them to Willis, grinning. "Beautiful place, isn't it?"

"A pleasant change from stony ground. Trees actually grow here. I miss trees." Willis didn't often bare his feelings. It surprised him that he felt comfortable saying that to the hulking seaman.

The hulking seaman nodded. "And I. And the soil. Those stony islands—I miss the soil, deep soil. I wish we'd be staying here long enough to plant a crop." He rubbed his foot across the ground beneath their feet. "I'd love to plant a crop in this delta soil. We'd have barley six feet high, I'll wager."

"How long will we be here? Do you know?"

"Brendan's mentor said till Pentecost. He'll be bringing us supplies, apparently. So it's good that we have such a pleasant situation here. I'd hate to be stuck on that first island that long."

"Pentecost." Willis had heard the word. "How long until that?"

"Fifty days." Boyd's voice softened. "If we're going to sail to the Land of Ever Young, I wish we'd just go do it. Two months here and two months there. We'll never get anywhere."

Willis understood. "More important, friend, we'll never get back."

"Amen." Boyd smiled grimly. "One great advantage here, though." He looked at Willis. "No plague. The plague—the death—was getting too heavy for me." And he headed back to the boat, probably for another load of sheepskins.

212

"Willis. Let's go egging."

Willis looked behind him. It was Crosan.

The Laughing Monk was coiling ropes across his arm. "Didn't you ever go egging? I spent much of my otherwise misspent youth gathering eggs off the crags of Mutton Island. Fetch the greens basket."

Willis paused a moment to watch Brendan and that bird (was it a large tern?) at the prow, looking at each other, their mouths moving. Shaking his head, he dug out the ash-handled gathering basket and hurried after Crosan.

They walked out to the sea-cliffs through waving grass and dainty flowers. The pleasant day reminded Willis greatly of his childhood. Even the gathering basket conjured up thoughts of youth and home, for many were the days he spent with his mother digging roots and seeking berries.

They climbed. They climbed and climbed. They worked their way up black and jagged rocks made wet from seaspray. Willis discovered quickly that he was not a mountain person, and he thanked God he was not born among the Picts of the far north, where mountains were a constant and necessary part of life.

And the fact that he caught himself thinking *Thank God* added to his confusion. He recognized no God to thank. He was a law unto himself—always had been. At least, that was his past. His present confused him, his future worried him. What would this God whom he refused to recognize decide to do to him next?

A whale, by all that's holy! And he thought it was land. And Brendan let him do it!

They topped out at about midday. Somewhere behind them, far below, the brothers were probably singing noonsong about now.

Crosan sat down on the very rim of the world. "If we go over the side now, a million birds will peck our eyes out. If we wait a few minutes for the tide to turn, they'll all go out to sea fishing, and we'll have the crags to ourselves."

Good. Not only did Willis value his eyes, he was more than ready to sit. Sucking in air like a sweaty old plowhorse, he dropped down near Crosan and even ventured to dangle his legs over a crumbly ledge. There in the mists, not far off, lay what was probably Sheep Island. Willis made out a few other islands in the area. Beyond them the hazy gray sea stretched forever.

Birds in a constant cacophony circled around the cliffs below. White birds, gray birds, brown birds. Little black and white birds with huge, comical, multicolored beaks and a rapid, choppy wingbeat.

A year ago, when Willis sat behind trees waiting with his oaken club for strangers to chance by, trying to keep the ants away, could he have imagined sitting here in this wind and bright sunshine amid all these birds? Truth, he had never even seen the sea. What an amazing road he traveled this last year.

Crosan gazed out across nothing. "On the Island of Sheep, it was so good to see women. Talk to them. I didn't realize, when we left, how much I'd miss seeing women. Just seeing them, you know?" And then his voice trailed away.

Willis said nothing. He hadn't thought about that until Crosan brought it up. Except for his mother, who loved her ale, women were never a significant part of his life. There was, though, one woman . . .

Crosan asked idly, "Did you ever marry?"

"No. I almost did once, but she found something better." What would his life had been like had she not decided to marry a farmer instead? Why try to fool himself? He almost certainly would have abandoned her. Thieves do not good marriage prospects make.

Crosan wasn't laughing now. "I was going to marry. Quit the brotherhood and take up farming. She's beautiful. Honey-blonde hair, warm skin. But I tried to explain my decision to Brendan, he ordered me into the boat, and that was that. I don't know why I didn't just . . ."

"She'll wait, surely."

"I doubt it. Why should she?"

"Didn't Brendan even offer any argument?"

"Said we weren't to oppose God's will. He was so certain it was God's will that I come. And I couldn't tell you what God's will was one way or another. I never have been good at that sort of thing."

Neither was Willis—obviously, for he had lied about being a brother. He didn't expect himself to discern the will of God, but he certainly expected an actual monk to know that sort of thing. If Crosan described his situation accurately, one could reasonably say that everyone aboard this boat was here because of God's will. And that would include Willis. It had certainly never been Willis's intent to do this. Sailing to Forever made no dream of his come true.

He could not imagine God's being concerned enough about the infidel Willis to care whether he sailed anywhere. And yet, beneath the water, that voice that was not a voice, as Willis struggled between life and death—*He careth for you.*

Realization was piling upon realization in Willis's life lately.

Crosan continued, "I was confused. Angry." He shrugged.

As if stirred by the shrug, a swarm of squawking birds lifted away from the cliffside.

Crosan straightened. "There they go."

In an enormous, mind-boggling burst, the birds flew out to sea. Thousands more came whistling overhead from elsewhere on the island. They flowed out in a brilliant, living stream across the water. Stragglers called. And then a peculiar silence descended, intensified by the noise that had been before.

Crosan hopped to his feet, tossed his cloak aside, and began uncoiling a rope. "The plan is, we lower ourselves over the side, using the rope for safety so we don't fall, and gather eggs off the ledges. Let me go down and show you what we're looking for."

Willis had absolutely no intention of dangling off a cliff above those roiling waters. He watched Crosan disappear over the side, the basket high up on his arm near his shoulder.

Presently the Laughing Monk crawled back up. He scrambled over the lip of the world and sat down beside Willis. "Here. You see, this egg is freshly laid. Note the feel of it when you shake it. Candle it by holding it to the sun. See? Compare it with this egg, which has a chick half-grown inside." He handed Willis the two small eggs. They were remarkably narrow and pointy. "And when you spin them thusly, the fresh egg does this and the other this. See?"

Willis hefted them, peered at them. "Interesting." He was going to say next, "I shall hold the ropes and support you while you go over the side. I shall take your filled basket from you, empty it, and send it back down to you."

215

But he wasn't fast enough. Crosan had unpinned Willis's cloak, tied a rope around his waist already, and was leading the way over the side.

Not the least certain he wanted to be anywhere near this cliff, Willis ventured a few feet over the brink into another world. He knew only a horizontal world; this world sat vertical. He knew a woodland world, not this domain of sea and stone. Sloshing foamy white against the rocks, the sea swirled back and forth, far, far below. Gusts and backdrafts and vagrant breezes tugged at him but not the persistent wind of the cliff top. A peculiar odor pervaded.

He plucked an egg from a narrow ledge, hefted it, and put it back. A few feet farther down he found two more, one of them fresh. He glanced toward Crosan. Crosan was ignoring him. Also, Crosan had the basket. Willis reached up and behind him and dropped the egg into his cowl hood.

A certain heady joy filled him. That's what one had to call it—joy. He was tackling an alien task in an alien universe and succeeding. The joy lasted not nearly as long as he would have hoped.

With extreme care he moved from foothold to foothold, from ledge to ledge, from clinging bush to welcome outcrop. He leaned in close and clung as a swirling wind whistled through, attempting to pluck him off. His fingers and arms ached. Sweat popped out on his brow, and it wasn't from heat.

And then a handhold he had trusted crumbled and fell away, nearly tossing him off his perch.

God, if I'm operating in Your will, what am I doing here? Take me out of here to safety!

Crosan now worked well below him. Willis was not about to go that far. He started up again by a somewhat different route, carefully choosing eggs at every step. There were thousands on this cliff. He accidentally knocked a couple off their perches and stepped on a couple of others.

His body threatened to quit. He looked briefly down—straight down—and warned his body, *Quit now and you'll regret it!* Another handhold crumbled and gave way. He nearly fell. He paused, terrified, and flexed that hand a few moments, trying to get feeling back. He proceeded more cautiously now, testing his purchase with every movement. Forget about picking eggs. Just get back to the top. *Help me, God, I pray Thee! Help me!*

A cluster of small, wind-formed bushes crowded in a crease just above his head. He reached up and grasped the stems of one. It seemed sturdy. He drew himself up. He pulled at another and used it. To his great joy he discovered that these bushes grew on the rim of the cliff. He was up! He was there.

With aching arms and cramped hands he crawled to grass and a few loosely panicled wildflowers and safety. Eggs filled his hood, more eggs than ever he remembered collecting.

"Thanks be to God! What can I do to repay Your kindness, Father?"

If we confess our sins . . .

The unspoken response startled him. He'd seen and heard much about confession. These monks seemed obsessed with it, when they had nothing, it seemed to Willis, to confess. Not as Willis did, certainly.

All right. Very well. If You insist, I shall. I owe You my life. I'll never be that foolish again, I promise, God.

But later. At a better opportunity. He watched Crosan's rope wiggle. Its end was firmly knotted to a rocky little outcrop.

The Laughing Monk appeared above the ledge, grinning. "So, Willis! Back up already?"

The remark didn't deserve an answer.

When they returned to camp around vespers, the basket and both their hoods were filled with fresh eggs.

217

27

Ailbe

Silent monastics irritated Willis. In the first place, he liked being able to speak when he had a purpose—and also now and then when he had no clear purpose. God gave men voice for a reason. In the second, you never quite knew what they were thinking. That always put Willis off somewhat. Even when a person is lying, you at least get his general drift. Third, you cannot banter and joke, and increasingly Willis enjoyed that sort of thing.

He was developing a strong bond of friendship with the Laughing Monk. For all the differences between them, they seemed to see life from much the same slant, egging adventures notwithstanding. Crosan considered rules a thing to be bent; Willis looked upon them as things to be circumvented altogether. Crosan practiced his sleight of hand on Willis, and Willis, with his pickpocket propensities, taught Crosan a few deft tricks for lifting small items.

But they now performed their mutual bits of activity in silence, for they were beached on an island in the middle of nowhere. And on that island, they slept and ate with a band of twenty-four silent monks.

It wasn't a bad monastery. Built of dry-laid stone, the refectory, oratory, and dormitory kept out the winter winds that howled across the barren isle. No one had bothered with a palisade on top of the ringwall, but that didn't surprise Willis. No wild animals or human raiders existed here to plunder the meager livestock. As a windbreak the wall served well; as protection, it served no useful need at all. Willis knew the place was called Ailbe only because Crosan read for him the word *Ailbe*, chiseled into the stone above the monastery gate.

Fortunately, these monks still sang the hours, masses, and feasts. Willis would have tried swimming home had they maintained utter silence. They knew several litanies Malo had never heard, and vice versa. Willis enjoyed immensely the practice sessions as each learned the other's songs of praise and worship. Malo even assigned Willis a monk whom he was to teach his part of the Gloria Patri. This too was a first for Willis. Never before had others wished to know what he knew.

One major problem with the silence remained. Willis felt himself under increasing pressure, he knew not from where, to confess his sins to someone. He must speak aloud in order to do that, for he could neither read nor write.

A solid fortnight of driving rain and gale-force winds penned them all in so constantly that Willis and Crosan were reduced to amusing each other with cat's cradle. Ibar joined them, but he had no new patterns to offer.

During a break in the weather (and that was more a manner of speaking than a pleasant reality), Crosan appeared after complines one night with fishing line and poles.

Silently, eagerly, Willis followed him out the gate.

A full moon sailed high, skipping from broken cloud to broken cloud. In its uncommon brightness, the two brothers walked down to the shore and clambered out across slippery rocks to the water's edge. High tide crashed against the boulders around them.

Crosan perched himself on a wet and craggy seat and handed a pole to Willis. He gave Willis a dead herring. And then, as a boisterous wave came smashing in, Crosan screamed at the top of his lungs.

Above Willis's laughter he shouted, "Glory, that felt good!"

Willis threaded the herring on his hook. "I am a fisherman of ponds and streams, what little fishing I've done. You lived on the seacoast. You cast my line."

Crosan took the pole from his hands. "If you live with us for long, you're going to have to learn this for yourself." With a practiced arm he whipped the pole tip forward. The weighted herring sailed away into the night. "Darkness at noon. No daylight at all. Only night light." He glanced up as the moon skated behind another cloud. "And that none too good."

Willis accepted his pole. "I couldn't agree more. I'm accustomed to the short, short days of home, but this is horrible!" He pondered all that had happened in his life this last year. "Do you remember back on the Paradise of Birds, when we first arrived at our campsite? Brendan stayed in the boat, and there was a white bird there."

"On the forward half-decking."

"They appeared to be in conversation. It's bothered me for months. What was that, do you know?"

Crosan chuckled. "It could be one of his former monks, for all that. Have you not heard the tales about him?"

"Tales?"

"Aye, tales. 'Tis said he was fishing in a lough one day much as we're doing here. A stranger came up to him, claimed the lough as his own, and forbade the holy father to fish in it. 'Very well,' says Brendan and hauled in his line. Then he proceeded to curse the lough, and from that day hence, nothing with fins has ever swum in it. Sure and I'd vow that unfortunate stranger is getting tired of crayfish every meal."

Willis knew better than to believe what he heard. Still . . .

Crosan rolled on, no doubt as eager as Willis to speak awhile. "Then there was the boaire with a patch over one eye—his left, I believe it was. One of the oxen from Clonfert—"

"Boaire—farmer?"

"Cattleman, aye. One of the oxen from Clonfert wandered into the fellow's field, so he purloined it and slaughtered it. Now, they claim, there's a one-eyed stoat running about in that field. The left eye lost, of course."

"Of course."

"So that bird could be an unfortunate monk and shape-shifted, for all we know." Crosan grinned in the filtered moonlight. "By and large, though, I'd say 'twas just a happenstance it sat there."

"Probably so." But they had looked as if they were steeped in discussion.

What to talk about. Willis yearned to talk. "Christ's nativity is fast approaching, am I correct?"

"Aye."

"I perceive that from the songs we sing during special collects."

"You know what else that means? It means that somewhere in a more hospitable clime, druids are this moment celebrating winter solstice. Pouring out children's blood to wheedle Crom Cruiach back with the sun again. The Otherworldlings roam abroad. Dagda couples with the River Boyne after eating a ton of porridge in a hole."

"Dagda?"

"Eons before Jesus. It is said Dagda built the hill palaces for the Tuatha da Danaan, and he sings up the seasons with a golden harp."

The richness of the imagery delighted Willis. So many worlds flourished out there, and he knew nothing of them. That included the world of Jesus Christ. He had wasted so much of his life cowering behind trees.

Crosan caught a fish and rebaited his hook. Discussion of what kind of fish it might be (they finally decided on rock bass) took up a few minutes. Then, but for the rushing sea, silence.

"Crosan? Do you hear confession?"

Crosan opened his mouth and closed it again. He looked at Willis in the sallow moonlight. "Strangers'. Not the brothers'. Only the abbot hears the brothers."

"Mm. I'm not a brother, exactly."

Crosan lurched to his feet and began drawing in his line. "Close enough. Let's go sit you down with Brendan."

"No!" It exploded out of him. "I'll think about this."

They fished a bit longer and talked without substance awhile, but a curtain had descended between them. Willis regretted mentioning anything. It had spoiled this happy fishing trip.

Crosan caught what they decided was a sculpin not worth keeping. Something robbed Willis's bait, so they wound the lines and retired from the sea. They stopped by the boat to put the fishing gear away, then climbed the hill to the monastery's drab and drafty dormitory.

Crosan retired.

Willis turned around abruptly and walked back outside. He strolled back down the hill in the light of the waning moon, knowing not quite where. He paused awhile by the boat, lying black and bulging on the beach.

A stabbing, giddying wave of homesickness suddenly engulfed him. It took him by surprise. He wanted trees and daylight, the old places and old times. This blunt craft careened on the beach had carried him nine months' voyaging away from everything he knew and cared about. He would not see home again unless this ugly vessel took him there, and it looked increasingly as if that would never happen.

He didn't want these new decisions he had to make. He wanted peace and stability after a lifetime of uncertainty. He wanted to get rid of this need to confess.

But he didn't want to confess before Brendan. No. Anyone but Brendan. Why couldn't Crosan do it, as a favor to a friend?

Was God really up there beyond the drifting clouds and gliding moon? He settled himself back on his fishing rock and let the churning sea croon platitudes at his feet. He believed no man, and he didn't believe the sea either.

He spoke his confession to the restless sky and restless sea and also, possibly, to God. He pronounced the words aloud. Hearing them in his own ears gave them weight somehow.

"I confess what You already know, God, that I am a sinner and a sham. You know I belong to no brotherhood. I lied. You know I sinned daily all my life and do so yet, living under that lie. You know my carnal appetites and impatience, my angers and fears. All sins. I confess it all. I pray You forgive me all that, God, knowing how hard it must be for You to do. After all, there's so much of it. Now Your servant Desmond, God, there is a sinless man. Not like me. No. I beg You, beg You, forgive as much of it as You can."

Jesus' nativity marked His arrival and Easter marked His passion. From Brendan's many homilies, Willis had an idea about Jesus' paying for men's sins with His blood, but only in the most general terms. Brendan talked about "Your sins and mine." *Foof!* Brendan didn't have any worth mentioning. That left Willis wondering to just what degree Jesus' blood could cover the charges. All? The little ones only? Where was the line drawn on God's holy slate?

"Now about restitution, God. I'll tell Brendan I lied, though I don't know what he could do about it now. It's not going to reverse anything, but I'll do it anyway. I can't pay back the people I've robbed. I know not where they be. And truth, God, you know I didn't manage to rob all that many of them. Tried aplenty, but failed aplenty too. I'll be more diligent in my gifts to the poor to make up for the robberies in part—that is, if I ever get back to civilization so as to bump into some poor again."

He perhaps ought to ask God to get him back home, but somehow he didn't think he should be requesting favors after dumping all this confession on the holy ear. Brendan claimed God knew his every thought. He'd let God make the move on that, granting him his desire if it pleased the holy Father.

"Now on regard to that blood payment, holy Father. I don't understand it, but I do understand I better minimize further sin, aye? It would help immensely if You'd let Your Spirit enter into me. The Spirit of Jesus Boyd talks about. This is hard, I know. But I don't want to offend You further, and Your Spirit in me would help mightily. 'Tis Yourself I'm thinking of mostly, but also me." He pondered a moment. "I guess that's all for now. Thank you, holy Father, for hearing me."

He did think of one other thing however, while he was there and speaking aloud, before he returned to the brooding, silent monastery. "Thank You, thank You, God, for the music."

28

Eva

"The finest monastery in Christendom!" Larkin Round Face paced the length of his brand new oratory. He wheeled to face Eva and spread his hands. "Don't you think so?"

Eva watched her husband's bombast with a certain disdain. After nearly thirty years of marriage, she was not only accustomed to it, she was getting a little bored with it. "Do you want my opinion now, or shall I wait awhile?"

He deflated somewhat. "I'm going to get it sooner or later, I'm sure."

"I'm sure." She stood casually by the door. He was right. It was a wonderful monastery, and this oratory was its crowning piece. Shaved panels on all the walls, lamp sconces end to end, and even a puncheon floor, that worshipers need not kneel in dirt.

"Now." His mouth tightened.

"I can't remember the passage word for word. I'm not good enough yet with Greek. This learning to read is difficult for me, and the language . . . It says, no matter what I do, if I don't have love it's worthless. I can give away everything I own, but if I don't have love, it means nothing. And that particular passage ends, 'Faith, hope, and love, these three, but the greatest of them is love.'"

"So? I don't love you enough?"

"Toward me you've done splendidly, considering." The acoustics in here were very good too. She didn't have to raise her voice to be heard clearly at the other end.

"Then I don't love whom enough?"

"Tavish."

He roared a profanity Eva hadn't heard in more than a year. Bombast took the floor again, and he ranted about that miserable beast Tavish, that slime, that profaner, that ingrate.

She waited.

He fumed. "The Bible isn't foolish enough to insist you love enemies and strangers! He's outside the faith."

"Desmond called him a brother, as he called you a brother. And besides, the Bible does too say you have to love your enemies. Your own abbot tells you that much. And you surely still remember the dressing-down the Abbot of Whithorn gave you."

"He was talking to the wrong man. He should have been talking to Tavish. He's a fool."

"As you wish. I will be making a pilgrimage to Desmond's memorial at Christmastide. Come or not as you care to."

He blustered some more, but she walked out the door anyway.

Now what? The ox could not be driven, but he could be led. How best to lead him became the puzzle. In her years of living with Larkin, she could point to as many failures as successes in bringing him to her way of thinking. Her own temper waxed too hot too often.

She drew the hood of her woolen mantle up over her head against the cold drizzle. Somewhere behind this dense overcast the sun was setting, two hours before vespers. It would not return until two hours after primes. That was five hours after matins, when all industrious folk began to stir. And yet, in summer the sun preceded matins and set well after compline. She liked summer better by far. Too, in summer the rain was warmer.

She heard Larkin close the oratory door and come down the path behind her. She turned to wait for him. He scowled, and she didn't really blame him. She was definitely clouding up his sunshine. But she was right, and she knew she was right!

She fell in beside him. "I've read all the material we have on hand. I shall travel to the coast this week to seek more books."

"And talk to that fool at Whithorn about me."

"Possibly. I need wiser counsel than our abbot can provide."

"You going to be back for solstice?"

"I'll try. Travel is chancy in winter, but I'll try." He knew her convictions, and she knew how he felt. No need to rehearse that particular battle again.

"I just bet you'll try." His gift for sarcasm matched his penchant for bombast.

She stopped instantly and grabbed his arm to stop him too. "If I say I'll try, I will. You know that. Don't you ever call me a liar, Larkin Round Face."

He could melt, or he could explode. He'd done both many a time, and on less provocation.

Rather to her surprise, he melted. "Yes. I know that." He offered no apology, but the softness in his voice was a fair substitute.

They continued on beneath black and dripping trees.

"I have heard," Eva offered, "that there are places without trees. Not a tree as far as the eye can see."

"Hard to imagine. I wouldn't want to be there."

"Nor I." And whatever would the druids do, without trees around which to build their lore? She kept those thoughts to herself. She could be sarcastic too. She just didn't air it.

She left early next morning. She brought along a retinue of only about half a dozen, for she wanted to travel light and fast. A monk to say the daily offices, one handmaid to handle the details of her garments and toilette, a hostler to care for the ponies, a couple of retainers for safety, and a seneschal to manage gifts, trade goods if any, and supplies—what more does one need? She never could see the wisdom of taking twenty people, as so many women did.

They followed the old wall to the coast, pressing hard, and camped on the salt shore that night. Another two days and she arrived at the little stone church on the Isle of Whithorn.

But what was this? Hundreds of people were gathered here, with camping space at a premium. She picked a narrow spot hard beside an itinerant trader and his family, greeted him with her burly retainers at her elbow, and suggested he might feel more comfortable elsewhere. He decided he would rather stay nearer some relatives and packed up. She instructed her people to set up in the widened site and rode with her monk down to the church.

The Isle of Whithorn, not an isle at all from low to mid-tide, was crowded with scores of morose people sitting or standing about.

"Any notion what's going on, Artor?"

Her monk spurred his pony up beside hers. "A death. From the numbers, I'd guess the abbot, his wife, or a brother."

"Pity if you be right." She left her pony in his hands outside the church and pushed inside. She'd never been in an actual church before. It was nothing more than a large, elaborate oratory, with an altar and baptismal built in.

Artor, unfortunately, was right. The abbot lay in state on a slab in front of the altar. A little fence of split rails separated him from the kneeling worshipers pressed together on the floor. Sadly, the fence seemed appropriate. The dear old man never did have the slightest idea what really went on in the lives of his flock.

Eva worked her way through the kneeling crowd without actually treading on anyone and stepped over the rail fence. She crossed herself and gazed upon the ancient face. From the man's skin color and degree of deterioration, plus the temperature inside this unheated church, she would guess he died two days before, probably of natural causes. His skin wouldn't be that blue if he had bled heavily. She gently lifted a hand, testing for degree of rigor mortis and decided her first estimate was accurate. She crossed herself again, stepped back over the rail, and threaded her way to the door.

She moved aside quickly. Here came a quintet of somber monks, their hands folded in prayerful attitude, headed for the altar. The church ought to have a door in back, so that the clergy could come and go without stumbling over the faithful. As she walked outside, the monks within began the office of nones.

Artor handed her the pony's reins. "I've been talking to people here and there. No one takes written material out of the scriptorium, not even the abbot. If—"

"Certainly not now, he won't."

Artor smirked. "If you want to read or copy something, you have to do it in the scriptorium. However, they don't guard the building, and it will be dark in an hour. If you want to borrow anything, I'll tell our people to break camp. Leave after dark, and we can be back at the river by complines. There's full moon. Even with the overcast, we should be able to follow so wide a track."

"A fine plan, but I see a better one. A guilt-ridden thief would make haste to quit the place, to hide as far from Whithorn as possible. We'll do better than that. We will remain encamped as ex-

227

pected until tomorrow and leave after first light. No need to hurry with a load of firewood, aye?"

He grinned. "Aye."

"Know why I like you best of all the brothers? You think like I do."

They walked, leading the ponies through the crowd, and kept their voices low.

Eva waved a hand. "Ninian came as apostle to the Picts. Look at all these gathered at his church here—more Britons than Picts by far."

"True. And the Irish swarming into the Argyll. The whole world is going to the dogs, lady. Will you be paying respects to the abbot's wife?"

"I was going to, but with this latest plan in the offing, no. I want as few people as possible to know who we are." She sidestepped a knee-high tad toddling out unattended across the gravel bar. "I'm sorry the abbot is not available. I need his wisdom. He had no common sense regarding practical matters, but he knew the Scripture end to end."

She glanced at her monk's face. In contrast to the many sorrowful mourners round about, he looked expectant, almost cheerful. She muttered, "Set it up. I leave the details to you."

"Then if you would, lady, go to the scriptorium and choose what you wish to read in greater detail. I suggest about the amount of material that would fit in a firewood pannier."

"Certainly." She handed Artor her pony's reins. She too felt expectant, even cheerful as she wended her way back out to the stacked-stone church.

In contrast to the splendid church, the post-and-wattle scriptorium seemed almost an afterthought, a shed for books instead of cattle. She stepped inside. Despite three windows, thick, damp darkness crowded together in the corners, lay beneath a couple of wooden tables, and lurked in the rafters.

No one challenged her. No one asked her business. A few monks and at least one prince—five colors in his attire—stood at tables poring over scrolls or browsed the shelves.

She lifted down a great book and instantly realized it would not fit in a firewood pannier. She thumbed through it out of curiosity and returned it to its place.

228

Scrolls. Scrolls were the thing. She chose three quickly at random, carried them to a table and opened the first. *Haec sunt nomina filiorum Israel qui ingressi . . .* She'd never read that before; this one was new. She unrolled the second, something about the first kings. *Fuit vir unus de Ramathaimsophim, de monte Ephraim . . .* She'd not seen that one before either. The third, in Greek, began with words of Moses to Israel. That would be Deuteronomy. Desmond had talked about that. She looked forward to Deuteronomy.

The other scriptorium patrons left. She chose two more scrolls for good measure, though it was getting too dark to read them in here. When did Artor plan to get here, anyway?

Torches flared at the doors of the church, whipping and smoking in the stiff breeze. The drizzle had commenced again. It would be an altogether dismal night. Mourners packed the broad, open shingle in front of the church. Eva could imagine the close crowding inside. From within the church, a full choir sent vespers out into the wet night.

Out of the thickening dusk came a monk riding one pony and leading two others. Artor. One of the ponies on lead carried coarsely woven panniers slung on each side, great, bulky sacks stuffed with firewood. Of all shapes and sizes, limbs and branches poked bulges in the pannier sides and stuck out the top.

Directly to the door of the scriptorium he rode. He slid off his pony and began emptying the panniers into a stack.

Eva stood in the doorway watching him. From a pannier he pulled several heavy branches, chopped to about two feet in length. Eva handed him a scroll. It slipped out of sight in the space the wood so conveniently left behind. Another. Artor stacked quite a nice pile of wood beside the door. The remainder of the wood they took along with them—and five books of Scripture.

As she swung aboard her pony, Eva realized she had underestimated the size of the panniers. She probably could have brought that great book after all.

They were well settled with the rest of their party in camp in time for Artor to sing compline. Even at this late hour, pilgrims still filed south through the intense gloom, spiritual and actual, headed for the stone church. With camps spread all along the stream, where did they think they would find space to pass the night?

But a heavier question plagued her. Larkin was a major prince. Why did messengers not tell Larkin immediately that the abbot had died? It would appear that the message had reached all the rest of Christendom quickly enough. The whole world was parading down to Whithorn.

Artor looked smug as he sang matins before cockcrow the next morning, as well he should. They kept the scrolls concealed. The less the rest of this entourage knew, the better. But, oh my, wasn't it difficult, having to wait until they arrived home before beginning these new reading projects!

How smoothly their little dance had gone.

They broke camp and headed home.

Eva had not gone but a quarter mile when she dragged her pony to a halt. Blocking the track before her, there sat Tavish astride that big dark dun of his. Nothing about his mustache or his mousy little Rhea had changed in the months since Easter and Desmond's interment.

Rhea, on a pony just behind him, looked frightened. Did she fear Eva? More probably she feared what could erupt.

Eva's retainers spurred their horses forward beside hers and drew swords.

"Tavish."

"Eva."

The dark forest shouldered in close to the trail on both sides. Someone was going to have to disperse among the trees before the other could pass through. Tavish's party contained four retainers. The rest of the dozen riders seemed to be unarmed attendants.

If only she had been able to draw some guidance from the unfortunate abbot. "So, Tavish, they sent you word of the abbot."

"They did indeed. We're bound down to Whithorn to pay respects. Are you yourself not headed the wrong direction?"

"I've done so, and now I'm returning. How goes your growth in the faith?"

He studied her suspiciously, not an unreasonable response to such a question. "We do what we can. Yourself and Larkin?"

"The same. Out of love and service for our Savior Jesus Christ—though not because of my station, for my station is the equal of yours—I am proud to be able to stand aside so that you might pass, Tavish of God."

She motioned her retainers aside and kneed her own pony between two dark yews. She rotated the pony end to end the moment it cleared the trees. Mildly, pleasantly, she watched Tavish. *I do not fear you in the least. I'm doing this as a Christian service.*

Whatever response Tavish planned at first to make, he apparently abandoned it. Carefully, slowly, he sent "Godspeed, Eva" through his mustache. Then he rode on, his extensive retinue clattering by on little pony feet.

Artor brought his pony up beside Eva's as she pushed back out onto the track. "If Larkin hears you gave way to Tavish, he'll burst. I realize they're stronger than we, but a little bluster would have looked appropriate."

"What I said to him I meant, Artor. I am working to conform my heart to Christ's."

Conforming Larkin's stony heart would be another matter altogether.

29

Christmastide

Five new scrolls to read! Eva could barely wait. She led her entourage northward at a faster pace, probably, than she ought to, hard along the long trail to home. They would head east at the ferry, and then . . . Her mind skipped from fantasy to fantasy, from plan to plan, like a small child's.

She would set five of their better pupils to copying the new material. In fact, she might work at it herself. The duplicates wouldn't be perfect—neither she nor the brotherhood at Knag Burn were skilled copyists yet—but as study material, the reproductions would do just fine.

Behind her, her handmaid gasped. "Milord, lady!"

Here he came along the track southbound, the man himself. Larkin grinned broadly at Eva and pulled up beside her. Besides his usual retainers, he was leading a coterie of at least a dozen monks and nuns. Eva could not see clearly for the dust cloud toward the back of his retinue. His pony was sweating, which told her very little, because Larkin's overburdened mounts always broke out in a sweat almost instantly.

He sobered. "You've heard, I trust, that the abbot of Whithorn died."

"I was there and paid my respects. So they sent a messenger to you after all."

"Messenger?" His beetle brows knitted together. "I got it from an Anglish merchant traveling eastbound."

"Indeed."

And Tavish had received the news directly.

The great man waved an arm toward the river. "We're stopped, and here's a pleasant glade. Let's pause for a meal before we continue on."

"As you wish." Eva could afford a mild delay now. In a few

weeks her people would complete the copies, the library at Knag Burn would have grown by five, and she would send Artor back to return the originals to Whithorn. Perfect. She yearned to describe her escapade to Larkin, but that was best left for when they conversed in private.

She handed her pony off to her hostler and walked through the wood to the opening. She pondered what she ought to tell Larkin and how much she ought keep to herself. She remembered Desmond's frequent admonishment: "Some words are best left unsaid, and some deeds are best left undone. The trick is knowing when."

Were Larkin to learn that the bereft brothers of Whithorn had favored Tavish with attention Larkin did not receive, it would do naught but further inflame his odium. On the other hand, her own anger burned hot. The nerve of those people! She was glad she had defied their silly rules. The power-mad monks in charge of the Whithorn scriptorium obviously felt duty-bound to keep written materials out of the hands of readers.

She would talk about it later, when they were retired together. Time enough then.

She settled herself on a stump near the meat safe, delighted to be able to sit for a few lovely moments upon something that didn't move. Her handmaid brought her a leather cup of water and hustled off.

Artor came crashing through the trees. For such a swift scroll thief, he was very clumsy of step. A stranger in an Irish tonsure trotted at his heels.

Artor stopped before Eva. "A brother from Iona, lady. Darran of Armagh."

"Armagh. Patrick's seat. Welcome, Darran. Sit and sup with us, I pray thee."

"Thank you, lady, and all God's blessings upon you." His Irish accent was so thick you could walk upon it without falling through. The chirring bur reminded her so much of Desmond, and her heart ached.

Then she happened to think, *What if the crew uses the firewood in those panniers for dinner?* "Artor, you'll go see to the firewood."

"Of course, lady."

He hurried off as Larkin joined Eva. Darran settled himself before them.

Here was an opportunity, perhaps, to win one battle. Eva asked, "Darran from Armagh, give me your opinion. Patrick confronted druidry throughout his long pilgrimage in Erin, is that not true?"

"That is true."

"Then, being from Armagh, perhaps you know the heart of Patrick in the matter of how far one should condone druidry."

"That was a hundred years ago, lady."

"But there must be a tradition to it. You see, my Larkin here observes the old druidic customs as well as the Christian feasts, and it is my opinion that he ought to dispense with druidic observances altogether."

"Eh, Eva, tell him the reason," Larkin interrupted. "Many of my Picts, you see, still have not embraced the Christian faith. I'm a leader to them as well as to my Christians."

"Then be an example for Christ." Eva repeated by rote the familiar argument.

"I am, I am," thundered the Prince of Picts.

She had to admit, though she'd not do it here, that he'd cleaned up several areas of his erstwhile sorry state. Still, he had a long way to go. With Desmond dead, he quite likely would grow disenchanted with improvement and become the old Larkin again. Desmond himself must have worried about that; he had talked about it more than once.

"Let's see if I can give you an historical perspective on that," Darran began. He proceeded to carefully explain the politics surrounding Columcille and his mission to the Picts, involving expatriation to Iona and Tiree.

Artor had rejoined them. Eva noticed him sitting down beyond Larkin.

Darran then described the political background whereby a branch of an Irish tribe, the northern Ui Neill, emigrated to Pictish lands across the North Channel from their Erse territory and established the Dalriada of which—Eva lost track and lost interest. She could not anticipate how all this reflected on her question. Such things did not concern her.

Scrolls did.

"What?" Her startled mind skipped back to Darran's conversation.

Larkin was laughing heartily. "I can just see him, the hothead!"

"I'm sorry. I missed that. What?" Surely she had not heard scrolls mentioned here.

Larkin was bobbing his head. "A fellow with a wondrous mustache, aye?"

"Tavish Mustache, they called him, aye. 'Tis a war brewing, I'd guess."

"What war? Start over. Explain. And I don't mean about the Dalriada." Eva was all ears now.

"This all came to a head as I was leaving Whithorn. The Tavish fellow, a Pict, set up quite a row because the brother in charge of the Whithorn scriptorium refused to allow him to take some materials back to his abbey for copying. The brother became suspicious and investigated. They discovered that, in a fit of pique, this Tavish stole several of their scrolls. As I understand it, when they confronted him he denied it and accused them of besmirching the Picts and his clan in particular." Brother Darran wagged his tonsured head. "He's awaiting his reinforcements. When they arrive, any moment now, there's really going to be a row, with honor at stake."

"I can well imagine." Eva looked at Artor, and Artor was looking at her.

Larkin cackled, absolutely elated. "Honor, is it? And more! The Old Mustache can't abide being told no. Never could."

"And a war in the offing." Eva stared at the sward at her feet. And what would Desmond Perfect say to this? She raised her eyes and her voice. "Artor, we leave at once. We're returning to Whithorn with our firewood."

"Milady!" The bedraggled monk looked crushed.

"My dear Eva!" Larkin babbled forth a protest, but she was already signaling to her hostler to fetch the bay. She was sorely tempted to ride her favorite mare, but the little dun was too trailworn for fast travel. Eva grabbed a wad of bread to eat on the track, watched Artor reluctantly pick up the pack pony's lead line, and they were off—of course, with her battle-ax.

It became clear within the hour that Artor was not accustomed to rapid horseback travel. Against her better judgment, she paused near the river mouth to rest her horses and her monk.

Artor flopped on his back on the grassy berm beside the track. He breathed deeply, eyes closed. "If I may say, lady, we err in not waiting for your husband."

"No, we don't. The time to quench trouble is before it erupts. Every minute counts. He'll come at his own pace, with his entourage. We can't afford to dally."

"You face an army alone, perhaps."

"Perhaps." Eva leaped to her feet. "Time to go."

Pouting like a six-year-old, Artor adjusted the panniers on the pack pony and mounted again upon his own horse. A horseman he was not. He picked up the pack pony's lead line.

Eva led off onto the track.

Here came a shepherd northbound, driving a flock of sheep before him. With clicking little hooves and many a *baa,* the flock scrambled along, further churning the churned-up mud and visibly unnerved by these strangers.

Impatient, angry, Eva pushed her mare in among them, swimming upstream as it were. She called back to Artor, "Hurry!" She scowled at the simpleton with the shepherd's rod. "Do help us pass! You see the forest is too close on either side."

His smile definitely gave the impression he had the brains of a toad. He continued to chirr to his charges, in no hurry whatever. They filled the track from forest edge on the left to forest edge on the right, an effective bung in a very narrow flask.

By the time she finally punched through the flock and out the south side, Eva was ready to slash every ovine throat, the shepherd's included. She glanced back. "Wait! No! Oh no!"

Her two ponies and Artor were nowhere to be seen. And the firewood panniers were gone as well.

"The man on the pony!" Eva shrieked. "Where is he?"

"Departed northward at a swift pace."

"Why didn't you tell me?"

"You didn't ask." With maddening smugness, the shepherd turned away and followed his flock on up the trail.

"I have to turn back! Make way!"

The shepherd twisted toward her, smirking. "Tell the sheep."

She could not afford the time or effort to work her way back through that dense flock, even if she were going in the same direction. And then catch Artor, and retrieve the panniers, and work her way through the flock yet a third time. Her pony was dangerously jaded now. To add all that . . .

Artor could hide anywhere in the woods round about, extract the scrolls, and abandon the panniers. By the time Larkin arrived, Artor would be long gone. Indeed, he could simply stay in place, hidden, while she and Larkin searched in vain within a yard of him.

And while they sought him, Tavish would receive his reinforcements. She must get there before the additional green kilts showed up.

"Never mind," she amended.

"I didn't intend to."

Absolutely maddening. The churl.

She should have seen this. She should have known Artor would take the coward's way rather than face the monks of Whithorn with his deed. Eva recalled their conversation during that rest on the berm. Then was when she should have weighed her monk's tone of voice (surprisingly intense) against the externals he conveyed (casual repose) and seen the contradiction.

She rode her pony as fast as she dared.

The crowds she passed as she approached the church at Whithorn seemed restless, agitated. Some were breaking camp. Others stood about like crows, chatting. A stream of them poured this way, leaving the church. That bothered her. People as a rule are smarter than to swarm toward a war in progress; they run the other way lest the battle engulf them.

Up ahead, the church roof floated upon a restless sea of people. Its outbuildings were buried to the neck in the crowd. The center of activity seemed to be the church gate. Eva applied the spur liberally and drove her pony like a wedge through the clustered onlookers. Not all took kindly to her progress, but she didn't care. She ignored the shouts of pain and protest in her wake. She ignored as well the spreading silence of the crowd as people began to notice her approach.

Awaiting more manpower, Tavish the Mustache stood at bay, holding the monks of Whithorn at bay. And an ugly stand-off it was, with swords and javelins bristling everywhere like hedgehog spines. Tavish and his retainers stood within a small open circle surrounded by a solid ring of hostile men, none of them in green.

Eva freed up her battle-ax as she recklessly pushed her lathered pony into that lonely circle. She balanced the ax on her shoulder and pointed with its handle to the only other familiar face in this crush of people, the sour, officious brother in charge of the scriptorium. He did not not look pleased.

People were now quiet enough that her voice probably carried fairly far. "Brother, you in charge of the books and manuscripts—I've forgotten your name. Sorry. Greetings." She turned to the man with drawn sword standing beside the monk. "Your tartan tells me you're a king." So did the smug and haughty look on his face.

"Liam, Lord of Dumfries and Man." His voice rang with authority and unwarranted egotism.

"That should come as quite a surprise to the Manx. Their warlord is an old family friend, and I doubt he's ready to bow to you. But that's to argue another day. I'm Eva, Queen of Picts, wife of Larkin Round Face, and a disciple in Christ Jesus of Desmond of Munster, surnamed Desmond Perfect. You"—she shifted her attention to the monk—"I understand from an itinerant Irish brother that you have a bone to pick with Tavish here, a matter of some scrolls."

Tavish and the monk agreed on one thing: "That's not your concern." They voiced that sentiment simultaneously.

"I differ. And you, Liam, Lord of Dumfries, being the protector of Whithorn, want to bring Tavish here to his knees quickly before—"

"You're interfering in—"

"I am a queen!" Eva roared. "And you will not interrupt again! You want to bring Tavish to his knees before more of his green kilts arrive. You owe this Tavish a massive apology and reparations for his stained honor. He had nothing to do with the removal of any scrolls."

"Eva, I'll defend myself!"

Eva pressed on. "An unknown benefactor left a pile of firewood by the scriptorium door. About two large armloads. When the wood appeared, brother, that was when your scrolls were taken. Tavish did not arrive until later. I know, because our parties passed on the track. Five scrolls are missing from your racks, Exodus and Deuteronomy among them."

"Five?" Tavish had swung around to face the men behind Eva. "How do you know so much of this affair?"

"I know who purloined them, and if he were not a cowardly cur unworthy to carry the name of Jesus Christ, I could lay them in your hands this minute."

Liam didn't look exactly nervous, but he gripped his sword more tightly. "Why are you lying to protect this fellow?"

And from behind Eva came a booming and most welcome voice. From the periphery of the circle, the man himself, Larkin Round Face, thundered, "Horrible error, friend! I made that same error once, and she was on my back like a wolf on a lamb. Never, ever call Eva a liar. For one thing, she'll skewer you, and for another, she never lies."

Tavish cackled delightedly, and a most remarkable transformation came over the man. A moment ago he was a beleaguered and angry warlord defending his honor. So far as Eva could see, that situation had not changed. And yet, he now bubbled with a certain élan, a light and airy enthusiasm for the fight. Eva did not share it.

Larkin rode into the circle and swung his exhausted horse around against Eva's. He sat knee to knee beside her, beaming. He was brandishing his lightweight damascened sword, the slim blade that was easily wielded one-handed. If her pony was weary, his looked near collapse.

Larkin addressed not just Liam but the circle in general. His voice rolled across the gravelly isle, across the great, wide sea. 'My people are making haste on their way here and spoiling for the fight. Tavish, my friend, Prince of the North, man of God, what do you demand of these false accusers?"

Without taking his eyes off the hostile crowd, Tavish replied in tones equally sonorous, "If I say 'their blood,' Larkin, Prince of Picts, man of God, do I have it?"

"You have it!" Larkin and Eva both said it.

Tavish nodded, and that massive mustache bobbed. "Very well." He walked over to Liam and stood before him nose to nose. "In that case, I demand nothing. You see, Lord of Part of Dumfries —for that's all you are—I was wroth until Eva reminded me that my service is not to men or to my pride but to Jesus Christ. I'm a disciple of Desmond also, as are she and Larkin here. Desmond taught us to forgive and let God take His own vengeance. Therefore I forgive your accusations. I forgive you. Not because of any merit on your part but because my Lord Jesus instructs me so."

On the inside, Eva gaped, flabbergasted. On the outside, she maintained a casual smile, pretending that she still relished the prospect of a fight.

"That's not the end of all," Larkin bellowed as he extended his sword toward the throat of the monk beside Liam. "You, simple brother. Why did your people send a messenger to Tavish here but not to me? We both rule our dominions with equal strength. We both serve God in the maintenance of monasteries established by no less than Desmond of Munster himself. Why one man and not the other?"

The monk looked flustered, worried, but it was Liam who answered. "They feared, Larkin. They were afraid to summon both of you Pictish chiefs here at the same time, lest fighting erupt. Your constant squabbling is well known."

"Do you hear that?" Larkin roared with gusto.

"How can I fail to hear it?" roared Tavish with just as much gusto. "That requires our forgiveness also. An extraordinary amount of forgiveness for so paltry a lord as the ruler of Dumfries. But given, all the same. And now, Liam, I bid you farewell. The abbot, rest his soul, would be proud of you for defending his holding here—and most put out that you'd falsely accuse a servant of God. But he's gone to join Desmond and all the saints in the Land of Ever Young, and we remain behind to fight the good fight. Be thankful my fight's not with you. God rest your soul." Tavish tucked his sword directly into his belt with such vigor that Eva wondered if he might slice the cinch in two.

Larkin reined his pony aside and spurred it forward against the crowd.

240

People learn quickly. Larkin had attempted to run them down coming into this circle, and they knew better than to stand in his way as he left it.

Tavish followed Larkin's pony, and Eva pressed her own mount in behind Tavish, lest the swath which her husband cut close up before she got through it. Tavish's people sauntered out behind Eva. They made a fine exit, and no one opposed them. And thus they continued up the northbound track.

Eva waited until they had marched at least a quarter mile from the church, and well beyond earshot of Liam and his monk. "I say, Larkin, that argument about observing winter solstice and Christ's nativity might as well be laid aside for a year. What with all this to-do, we've missed both of them." She twisted on her pony to look at Tavish squarely. "Bold words of forgiveness, Prince of the North."

"I've been studying the Scripture under my abbot's hand, and I've learned a thing or two lately. When we're at better leisure, I'll ask you both to forgive me and Rhea, and I'll expect your forgiveness in return."

From beyond Eva, Larkin rumbled, "That can be arranged. We make better yokefellows than adversaries anyway."

Eva grinned. "It's what Desmond wanted."

Tavish grunted. "He wanted fair play too. You didn't have to come to my side. Your bold action today spoke to me about friendship when words would not do."

"I'd have done it Christian or no." Eva straightened and twisted in the other direction. Her neck was getting stiff. "The Picts of Larkin are honorable, as are the Picts of Tavish. Infinitely improved by the sweet love of Jesus, but honorable."

"Honorable?" Tavish waved an accusing finger. "Your business about knowing the identity of the culprit didn't slip past me, Eva. So you stole five scrolls." He cackled, and that wonderful mustache floated on the joy of it. "Well, lady, I stole three."

30
Song

Willis Gray Mantle—Willis East Bogg to the rest of the world—leaned on the half-decking, closed his eyes, and drew in deep draughts of fresh, wet, sea air. Were you to ask him at Imbolc last year whether he would relish a sea voyage, he would have pummeled you with his oaken club. And now see him! Standing watch he was, just like an able seaman. He listened to the thrum of the wind in the rigging and the constant whisper of sea sprites in the bow wave.

Malo the musician knew much about the Greek and Roman divinities of eld. And half-divinities, the fruit of the gods' lusts toward humankind. As Malo pointed out, the Greek and Roman gods were nothing more than magnified human beings with magnified sins and foibles. Jesus Christ was no such thing. He alone claimed both immortality and purity.

That all said, Malo would then go on for hours about the quaint Roman and Greek Otherworld folk of former times. One kind were the Nare-ee-ids, sea nymphs who played in the bow waves and wakes of boats.

Brendan paid scant heed to the gods of a people in eclipse. "The Greeks and Romans are a dying race. Why dwell upon them when the Celts are lively and vibrant and will one day rule the world?" Rather, he regaled the lads with tales of mythic Celtic divinities. He seemed to know everything about them. Apparently his foster father, a Bishop Erc, was a druid as well as a Christian. Then Brendan would preach at length on the meaning of Celtic symbol and ceremony in the Christian faith.

Willis already knew all about Imbolc. Candlemas. As a lad, he floated lighted Imbolc candles out across the still waters of the loch hard by his mother's hovel. Many a time he watched in wonder at the hundreds of dancing points of light, the play of fire on

242

ripples. When did he lose the wonder? He couldn't remember, though he could recall the dark days when there was none. It was coming back now, that wonder, bringing renewed youth with it.

All this added interest to Willis's days (after all, what do seventeen men do all day aboard a curragh, except tell tales and preach and sing?), but he did not care excessively for learning something just to learn it. These new horizons, however, added meaning to the music, and in that he gloried.

One new thing he did learn: how to recognize a whale. He smiled even now at the incident concerning Jasconius and the fire they built upon the beast. He was a man of forests, a lurker behind trees. Little could he imagine a beast a hundred feet long, let alone anticipate one where an island ought to be.

He stood erect, scowling. "Land ho—or whale ho!" He extended his arm to show the way, a few points off starboard.

Leeson hurried forward. He squinted. "If it's land, it's low. Look!"

A tiny white poof, barely visible, shot upward on the horizon. The land disappeared.

"Whale!" announced Willis in triumph.

Leeson chuckled and moved aft.

Willis was about to chuckle too, but the chuckle died in his throat. "Leeson? Brendan, father? It's coming this way."

Bleary-eyed, Boyd sat up in his sheepskins. He didn't look fully repaired yet from his duty on night watch. "Land?"

"Whale." Brendan came forward to lean on the half-decking beside Willis.

Boyd grunted and snuggled back into his sheepskins.

In his youth, Willis had heard about the terrible Roman war machines—great, wooden, wheeled contrivances as heavy as a dozen houses, built to batter down the strongest wall. That's what came at them now, a Roman war machine.

When the whale's massive back broke the surface, the water foamed. A squirt of its white spout and it would dive with a splash. Then here it would rise again, much closer, roaring inexorably down upon the little curragh.

"Deliver us!" Willis squeaked. His imagination pictured a great maw clapping down on this insignificant boat, and nowhere to hide! "Help . . ."

A dozen more brothers clambered forward. And here came Boyd, awakened by the pandemonium.

The thing came. It came. It came. It was hard upon them! The leviathan surfaced not thirty feet from the bow and veered away in a great splash of seafoam.

Water sprayed across the half-decking, drenching Willis. He squeaked again, but his cry was buried among the terrified shouts of his brothers.

"We are undone!" he moaned, for here came another whale, smaller than the first, with unusual white marks. Wait—two. No, three, bounding in the water! And then he happened to glance at Brendan.

The abbot stood at the gunwale with a pleasant expression of interest and bemusement on his face. "Trust God, lads," was all he said.

Trust God, while four ferocious beasts, each bigger and fiercer than a hundred boars, swarmed down upon them? But then, there was not much else to be done. Even the small whales were each as big as the curragh.

Very well. I trust You. But Willis's frantic heart still leaped up and lodged in his throat.

Diving and surfacing willy-nilly, the small whales could be three, and they could be six. Then, like a pack of wolves, they fell upon the giant beast. The great whale arched high out of the water and dropped back down with a mighty splash. One of the small whales hung onto its jaw with a death grip. The huge wave from their dive caught the curragh and flung it high. The sail spilled and sagged. Just off to port, a red stain spread across the sea.

The brothers stood silent, listening to silence. The boat wagged, hung in silence. Waves lapped quietly against the hull, for the nereids were stunned to silence also. The bloodstain spread.

Willis drew a breath and realized it was his first for a while. He relaxed. He smiled. Look how God had just proved Himself trustworthy!

Then the sea exploded.

That great whale burst out of the water almost close enough to touch, and three whales clung to it. One long flipper had been chopped off.

The curragh heeled crazily on the churning sea, tumbling Willis to the deck. Boyd fell on top of him, and he no longer breathed at all. The curragh bucked and pitched like an angry pony. Boyd rolled aside, and Willis landed on Ibar. Icy water splashed in upon them, drenching everything.

And yet for all this, they remained afloat. Back and forth, back and forth the boat wallowed, gradually returning to an even keel. The silence returned.

Willis struggled to his feet and staggered to the rail, for he feared the excitement, plus Boyd's blow, plus the wild rocking, would make his nausea a sorry reality. Hard to port, a massive, pearly white blob bobbed to the surface. Shreds of gray-blue skin clung to it, and the sea ran red.

"They ripped it apart," Willis whispered.

They had torn a monstrous whale apart. He tried to picture the forces of evil that could tear asunder a beast the size of Jasconius.

Someone to starboard called out, pointing. The pod of smaller whales was moving off to the north, arching and gamboling.

They ripped it apart. Willis crossed himself. This curragh had just been delivered of far more than he could describe. Those vicious beasts did not have to eat the brothers alive to kill them— merely swamping the boat would have done the job quite as efficiently.

Ibar in his thin, sweet soprano began a five-tone gratulatio. Willis picked up the song of thanksgiving instantly, and Crosan right behind him. As all the brothers sang, Brendan and Leeson reset the sail, and the boat surged forward purposefully.

The gratulatio ended, and Willis instantly commenced the eight-tone gloria. The others joined him. It was the first time he had ever initiated a song. His heart filled as it had never filled before. He thought back for only a moment on his prior life, with its pinched existence, pinched attitudes, and pinched misery, and put it away forever. *Gloria in excelsis Deo!*

After the songs, Brendan motioned to Willis and walked aft.

Willis followed, frowning.

"Willis, son—" Brendan sounded very grave "—you were sore afraid."

"Truth, father." Understated, if anything.

"What if you had died then?"

"I'd be cold now."

Brendan nodded acceptance of that. "What about your soul? I'm concerned for your soul, though I don't know exactly why. Have you confessed your sins to almighty God?"

What was this—another of his famous premonitions? "Well, I did, father, but I'm not sure He was listening. It was getting late in the day."

"Did you confess Christ? Has His blood paid for those sins?"

"I asked Him to pay for as many as He was able, father."

For a moment Brendan looked bewildered. Then a bright smile burst forth. "Go in peace, son."

A day later and with Willis again on watch, they raised land. "Absolutely land this time," he called. "Not a whale."

Laughing, Leeson engaged the tiller and called for oars. Brendan took the watch, so Willis manned an oar with glee. Trees! He had seen trees, even from afar.

Two hours later, Leeson ordered the oars shipped. Willis stood up and watched over the gunwale as the curragh, under sail only, glided in close to a pleasant shore. Dark, dense forest pressed down hard against the shingle beach. Unlike any forest Willis had seen before, this one looked to be nearly all one sort of tree, a very tall, very straight evergreen, with an understory of thick scrub.

"A whale!" Willis pointed not to sea but to land. He corrected his observation. "The whale. The great whale that attacked us."

The back third of a whale it was, its massive flukes lying torn and limp across the shingle. Its skin had blackened, but the resemblance remained.

Brendan called to Leeson, "Beach it here."

Boyd stepped up beside Willis. "You've quite an affinity for whales, friend."

"A gift not particularly desired." Willis watched the sail luff slightly, then spill. The curragh bobbed to a halt as its belly announced the shingle beneath them in a stage whisper.

Willis scrambled ashore to help tie her, then stood a few minutes to simply bask in the unique song only a forest sings.

How long it had been since last he heard rustling boughs and waving branches.

The music lacked only one thing: no birds sang here to complete the melody. Logically, that suggested it was an island, separated from land by too many miles of water for a bird to cross. If so, it was a very large island.

Willis was not in the habit of asking permission. He rather assumed it was none of Brendan's business what he did. But he asked a favor now. "Father, I wish to go exploring in the forest."

"Not today. We must stow as much whale meat as we can aboard, for beasts are going to come in the night to devour whatever is left."

Another premonition? *I fear that with this one, though, Brendan, father, you fell away wide of the mark.* If there were no birds, surely there were no large beasts.

Willis could disobey, or he could help. He chose "help" when he saw Boyd thrusting a pike pole into the carcass to roll it. Already Mochta and Crosan and three others were wielding heavy knives, hacking at the overlayer of fat. Laying in the store of meat took them until vespers.

They camped on the shore that night in grass just above the shingle. Horror of horrors, Willis found it almost impossible to sleep on a solid, immobile surface. This voyage was ruining him.

An hour or two before matins he crawled out of his warm bed and walked up to the edge of the forest. Still air with no hint of breeze had rendered his beloved forest mute. Blurred by haze, the first quarter moon hung close to the western horizon. Boyd's snuffling snore sounded the same ashore as it did asea.

Willis took three steps into his forest and stopped when a branch lashed his cheek. Total darkness and total silence blotted out nearly all sensations. Why explore when you can neither see nor hear? He backed out and instead followed the narrow, grassy line between forest and beach.

Out on the shore lay the black hulk of whale tail. High tide lapped at the limp flukes. The hulk shivered.

Willis froze in his tracks. The hulk jerked. A huge white spume of seafoam rose above the far side of the remains. No, it was not foam, for here came another like it. A bear it was, a white

247

bear. A huge white bear. The carcass moved again as the bear tore another chunk out of it.

Willis had seen a bear only once in his life, a dead one hunters brought into the farm where his mother worked. These bears were twice that size. Maybe three times. Then the two white bears, each bigger than any other bear alive, were joined by a third.

The third thrust its narrow, pointy nose into the air toward Willis and wagged its head from side to side. It knew he was there.

Carefully, a step at a time, he backed up the way he had come.

The three bears paid him no more mind. They gathered around the whale carcass. From far down the shore, a fourth was ambling in this direction, barely discernible in the moonlight. Were it not the purest white, it would be a shadow, a phantasm, and altogether undetectable.

Willis ran. He stumbled and fell twice getting back to camp. "Father! Father Brendan!" The palms of his hands, all scuffed, burned like fire. He didn't care. His cassock was torn down around his knee. He didn't care. He gulped air. "Father! Up! Everyone up!"

Piles of sheepskin stirred. Heads rose out of them.

"Father, great bears have attacked the whale. Huge bears! Immense bears! We must put out to sea immediately before they fall upon us next!"

"Bears? Willis, what do you know about bears? Go to sleep." Crosan burrowed back into his sheepskins.

Brendan's voice, smooth as oil, purred, "We're safe, Willis. Good night."

Safe! With those meat-devouring beasts roaming near?

What could he do? The abbot had spoken. He wrapped a sheepskin around his shoulders. He wrapped two of them around. If a bear sneaked in and grabbed a mouthful, let it bite sheepskin. He sat on the shingle near Brendan, the safest place to be in a very unsafe world, until matins.

They laughed at Willis about his bears until they walked down the beach to fetch more meat. The only thing left was bones.

* * *

248

Three days of storm kept them beached. On the fourth, the boat laded to the gunwales with meat, roots, and fresh spring water, they departed.

Willis hung off the aft half-decking and watched his forest melt into distance. The song it sang with gusto as the storm moved through tantalized his memory.

Brendan settled in beside him, studied the set of their sail a few moments, and looked at Willis. "You're disappointed."

"I was hoping that was Tir Na n'Og, father. Because of the trees, I suppose. I'm certain Paradise is rich in trees."

"And bears?"

"No foul beasts, of course not. Just flowers forever, and trees. Plenty of leafy trees. We seem to be sailing about at random, without purpose. I was hoping we were set upon a destination. Someplace definite."

From behind him rumbled Boyd's massive voice. "I agree."

Now here was something else new in Willis's life. No one had ever heartily agreed with him spontaneously. In the past people more or less ignored him.

Boyd stood at Willis's shoulder. On the other side of the tiller, Leeson waved a hand at Boyd impatiently, motioning him to move in closer amidships.

Boyd shifted a step. "From the beginning, Brendan, before ever we built this boat, we had a dream. A goal. I thought we had a destination in mind when we started. Now I don't know."

Doubting Thomases didn't seem to put off Brendan at all. "Some of the brothers accept the gift of premonition God gave me. Others distrust it. That doesn't matter to me one way or the other. I have it. Until now I've been waiting for a clear direction. That direction has come at last, both by word from God and by the favor of the winds and sea. We're stocked with meat. We'll call at another island and lade vegetables. Then we're on our way. An exciting voyage lies ahead."

Willis wasn't certain whether he welcomed that bit of foresight or not. He'd had quite enough excitement. Ah, well. It was certainly better than the tedium of lurking behind trees, of robbery attempts on the highroads of home. Or was it? He yearned for peace.

Ibar stepped in close to Willis. Willis hadn't noticed him

near. Together they watched Brendan wander forward. Brendan settled against the forward half-decking, apparently one of his favorite places.

Ibar looked more than disappointed. He appeared pained. "I was going to sail to Iona. Here I am in the middle of who knows where." He looked at Boyd. "I don't want to go any farther."

"You said you did when first you came aboard with us in Brandon Bay."

The lad grimaced. "That was about a hundred storms and whales and weird places ago. If you people are pushing on, I want to go ashore and stay ashore until another boat comes along to take me home."

Boyd shook his fair head. "You'd be breaking a pledge before God."

"I don't care. I rescind it. He's not going to hold me to a pledge that's making me miserable. He's a loving God. Remember? Talk to Brendan, will you? About me quitting the voyage?"

Willis wanted to quit too, but he wouldn't. He had promised. And there was still another thing he could not have said or done a year ago. A year ago, he found it an easy thing to promise whatever was expedient and to break his promise the moment it became inexpedient. Somehow, he couldn't do that now.

His whole life was upside down.

His trees had disappeared.

* * *

Their next landfall, an island, lay so low and flat that Ibar, the watch, nearly missed it. He called it out belatedly, and Leeson veered the boat toward it.

Never had Willis seen such surf. The waves began afar out, building until as they rolled in against the island they had become mountains of blue-gray water. Just before they shattered themselves upon the beach, they would break over into massive, blue, roaring tubes almost tall enough for Peter to duck through, were that apostle close at hand to walk upon the water.

With extreme disappointment, Willis gazed across the island as they beached. No trees. Not a tree. Who would want to live here?

250

And then he heard the music.

A knot of boys in white tunics stood nearby in the soft sand, a sort of welcoming party. In pure soprano they sang a lovely melody. Farther up the beach, a group of men in blue cloaks picked up the melody and embellished it with two more parts. They appeared to be about Ibar's age, near adulthood.

Behind them, a choir of grown men in purple dalmatics walked toward Brendan. The older men broke the melody into two patterns and with close harmony wove the patterns together.

Never, ever . . .

This voyage had been one great "first" after another for Willis. But this was the biggest first of all. He listened to perfect, ethereal music from a fraternity of boys, youths, and men. Heaven it would be, if only there were a few trees here.

If Brendan or Boyd actually talked to anyone from the island, Willis didn't notice it. Certainly none of the choir members stepped forward to speak to any of the common brothers. As the brothers pitched camp ashore, the choirs sang the offices. Willis yearned to join in, but he didn't know this litany.

During a dinner of roots and whale meat, the brothers listened as the choir stood near at hand singing psalms.

"They are Anchorite monks," was the only explanation Boyd offered. Except for that sentence, the brothers ate without speaking.

Willis observed that although the robes were the same—white, blue, or purple—the faces sometimes changed. Choir members joined the group at apparently random times, and others left, except for the youngest. The boys in white sang the offices and a psalm now and then. But then they retired. Willis presumed that young singers were in short supply here. The blue-clad youths didn't have enough members for a constant concert either. They rested periodically.

But the men. Ah, the men. Men they had aplenty. Were all these men to sing at once, surely the music would ring loud enough to carry back to England!

The choirs didn't cease with compline. "Thanks be to God," normally the last words spoken at the close of day, didn't slow them down a bit. Willis and his brothers slept ashore, literally listening to the music of the night.

The next morning, Willis dreaded the order to launch. He had sailed away from a lovely forest. Now he would sail away from matchless music more enchanting and welcome than any number of forests. With a sigh he rolled the supply tent and handed Boyd the pegs. "Boyd? Where do they get the singers, do you know?"

Boyd shrugged. "I've heard it said that they take whom they want from passing boats. They're sort of chosen by God. But not many boats pass by here. So I don't know. Get the guy lines there."

Willis picked up the coils of rope and carried them to the curragh. Listlessly, he tossed them up over the side. Crosan, on deck, snarled something and picked them up.

Two boys Ibar's age came striding down the beach with a huge basket slung between them. They were the only two people Willis had seen here so far who weren't singing. They stepped in close and handed the great basket up to Crosan. Willis thought he smelled turnips in it. It was filled with something purple, anyway.

Immediately the boys turned and did obeisance to Brendan. "Accept fruit from the Island of Strong Men, father. Give us our brother and go in peace."

From the pile of sheepskins waiting to be loaded, Ibar came hurrying. The most wonderful look of anticipation crossed his face. He shouldered in beside Brendan.

Willis watched him a moment. It was to be expected they'd want Ibar, for he was young and soprano. And yet, the island would be wasted on him. Ibar wanted to go home. To get off Brendan's boat and get on someone else's. He didn't want to spend his life singing.

Foolish, callow Ibar.

"Embrace your brothers and go with those who summon you," Brendan said. "I perceive you are clean, having been washed in the blood of the Lamb. Don't worry that you cannot fully understand about salvation. God's ways and means are so profound, we all live in degrees of ignorance. You'll understand it better as you grow in the Lord. Go, and pray for us."

He was talking to Ibar, no doubt, but he looked at Willis as he spoke. They all were looking at Willis.

Boyd burst into a grin. "Brother, I thought certain Brendan made a mistake bringing you. How wrong I was! Go with God in peace!" Those great white bears could not have hugged Willis any more powerfully than Boyd did.

Squeezed breathless, Willis staggered back. With a great salmon leap, Crosan came flying off the gunwale to hug him as well. Malo. Mochta. Leeson. The others in turn. Lastly, Brendan.

"Wait . . ." Willis looked from face to face. "Father Brendan, I'm a sinner! You said yourself one of us would do something meritorious and be blessed. I've done nothing meritorious."

Brendan was grinning. "Ah, but you did." His voice dropped to a sweet, avuncular purr. "Willis, lad, what is the very greatest gift any man can offer God?"

"Uh, I suppose . . ." Willis grimaced. He couldn't even answer the simplest sort of catechistic question.

Brendan answered it for him. "Faith. To trust Him. That's what He wants, at the very bottom of it."

It seemed too simple. And then one of the lads in blue extended his arm and clasped Willis's hand. He allowed the youth to lead him up the shore, for he didn't quite know what else to do. A dozen men in purple dalmatics, singing an eight-note laudatum Willis had never heard before, came down to meet him. They surrounded him with smiles and warmth and glorious song.

At the top of the beach he stopped and turned. His brothers were pushing the boat out into the surf. And now they were all climbing into it, except for Boyd and Mochta. The burly monks leaned against the prow, shoving it back afloat, then scrambled aboard as the vessel lifted free of land. The doughty curragh heeled to port as the brothers raised sail.

It was the first time Willis had ever watched the curragh leave shore.

His heart wrenched with joy and sorrow as his brothers sailed away, and the music of his brothers filled his soul.

31

Crystal

Ibar seethed. He of all the brothers aboard this boat most wanted to quit these aimless peregrinations. Boyd talked about taking over a farm, perchance to marry. Crosan talked about returning to a honey-haired beauty. But he knew these men were here for the duration. They had given birth to the idea in the beginning, and they would see the voyage through to the end. Ibar was bound by no such conviction.

He was a year older now and wiser in every way. He was sure God would never hold him to a half-made promise from his youth. Well, all right, a whole-made promise—several in fact—but made in the foolishness of childhood all the same. He had watched Desmond carried away and saw his world burn up. A promise made or broken in the wake of such duress would not be taken seriously by any man, let alone God. God understood. Ibar had promised to serve under Brendan's aegis on this voyage. How was he to know how onerous it would be?

He wanted off this boat!

And then to see Willis walk away with men Ibar's age—and you could tell from the dumbfounded look on Willis's face that he had no idea he was going to stay ashore. That was the final folly.

Ibar paused at Crosan's side beside the starboard rail.

The Laughing Monk, hardly laughing at the moment, sat on deck pawing through that huge basket the singers had given them. He lifted a bunch of grapes. They were the size of apples, the stem bigger around than Ibar's thumb. "From the Island of Strong Men. They were in that basket, along with some turnips. Amazing, eh?"

"Eh." Ibar twisted the corners of his mouth up, pretending.

Crosan nodded. "You look as glum as I feel. I agree with your mood. I too miss the silly little pickpocket, crazy as he was. Funny. I didn't miss Conn in the same way at all."

Ibar did not miss either of them, Willis the imposter in parti-cular, but he let it go.

Crosan rattled on. "I'm happy for him, though. The only thing he really likes is singing, and there he is now in the world's great-est choir. I wager he'll teach them our litanies if they don't already know them. Aye, a blessing, his streak of fortune there."

And then Crosan's eyes grew as big around as one of those grapes. "The premonition!" He looked wildly, fearfully at Ibar. "Remember what Brendan said when you three first came aboard? You latecomers? Two of you would be doomed to destruction, and the third was bound for glory." He shook his head. "Nah."

Ibar leaned on the starboard gunwale beside him. "Is man a free agent to choose Jesus Christ or reject Him?"

"Of course he is, or there's no use in sending out missions to evangelize the lost."

"If I choose Jesus Christ, nothing in heaven or hell can keep me from Him."

Crosan grinned brightly. "Of course. I came to about the same conclusion, but it's nice to know other minds besides mine agree." He went back to fishing grapes out of the basket to serve the brothers at dinner.

Up at the bow, Brendan began the litany for St. Peter the apostle, a prelude, no doubt, to the office of nones. It was fast approaching 3:00 P.M.

Ibar draped himself loosely across the gunwale, too frustrated for words. A perfect opportunity lost. The Island of Strong Men. Willis's blessing was Ibar's curse.

He had spoken bold words to Crosan. Did he believe them? Absolutely. He need only declare his allegiance to Jesus Christ at any time, and God would be required by His own statutes to take care of him. He would do that sometime. Right now he was angry with God for denying him the chance to stay on the Island of Strong Men. It would have been perfect.

Behind him the sail luffed on one corner. Leeson called out to someone on the other gunwale. The sail flapped once and spilled, dropping limp.

Ibar twisted around and looked up. They had entered an ab-solute calm. Not the slightest breeze riffled the slack linen canvas.

And then he happened to look down.

A great fish to rival Jasconius himself lurked just below them. Ibar opened his mouth, horrified, but nothing came out. He stammered and pointed with a stabbing finger. All that monster need do was rise in place, and it would tip the boat over.

Crosan slumped against the rail at his side and peered over the gunwale. "Where's Willis when you need him? He's the one who calls in the great whales. Wouldn't he love this beast!"

"Father, please!" Ibar raised a palm to Brendan. "Don't sing so loud! The monster might hear and come at us!"

Brendan walked over to them singing the Dies Irae. He paused before launching into the Recordare and leaned over the side. "The creature is much bigger than you think, Ibar. Look how crystal clear the water is."

As Ibar watched, a long, slim fish, itself quite a long way down, swam by between the monster and the surface. If the monster was that far away, it was twice the size he had thought.

"Amazing clarity!" Brendan stepped back from the rail. "Our Lord has delivered us safe thus far. Trust Him." He returned to the bow, loudly singing the Recordare.

Yes, but why tempt Him?

Was Brendan mocking Ibar's fear? He seemed to increase the volume with every passage, until by the time he reached Hosanna in Excelsis his voice could have filled the sail.

Ibar watched in horror as the monster began slowly to rise from the depths where it had been hanging. It came, and came, and came. Still it lay deep below. Ibar could now see a pattern of marks on its back, just like a squared-off gameboard. Each square even had a gaming piece, a dot in the middle.

The moment Brendan completed the office, brothers leaped up and crowded the rail. The giant now hung suspended almost directly below them. With a casual, elegant snap of the tail, it glided away. The brothers oohed at its grace.

Malo commenced nones. Ibar barely murmured his part, but the music filled sky and sea anyway. A pod of whales surfaced and breached not a quarter mile off. They approached the curragh, sounding, sliding deep beneath it. Ibar could see every element of their fluid movement.

Hundreds of fish, great and small, gathered between the green depths and silver-blue surface. Was the song calling them in? Fish don't observe the offices of the day with no men nearby to sing them. Or do they? Ibar remembered back home in Erin, oh, so long ago, when he would go fishing with his foster father. The fish would bite at certain times of day but not others. No use to try at noon. Fish as hard as you might, you'd have no luck. Return at dusk to the very same spot and catch your supper easily.

"Psalm eight, all versicles." Malo hummed the key note.

"Domine, dominus noster. . ." Ibar had to concentrate. He didn't know the Eighth well, particularly in the five-tone configuration.

"Et constitutuisti eum super opera manuum tuarum." What came next? *"Omnia subjecisti sub pedibus ejus . . ."* You have given man dominion over all the works of Your hands and put all things under his feet. The birds of the air and the fish of the sea, who travel the paths of the sea.

They bobbed just now above a major path of the sea, and the fish passed literally under their feet. Ibar lost the words and melody and let less distracted brethren finish the Eighth. He was too caught up in the psalm-made-reality to be able to remember the song.

Crosan pointed. "Cuttlefish." Three slim, opalescent cylinders with undulant fins coursed beneath them. "This is amazing! You know, if it were any other time of year besides June, we wouldn't be able to see this deep. But with the sun so high in the sky, the light can penetrate."

"I've never seen water so clear." Boyd nudged his way to the rail and leaned over. Leeson bellowed at him as the boat dipped to starboard. He moved and took a new position off the stern.

With vespers, a fair breeze returned. The sun, though, had sunk low enough in the west that the greatest depths turned dark, fading from vivid green to black as compline approached. A dense school of shiny mirrored fishes swarmed by. They shifted directions suddenly, the whole school at once, flashing brilliant silver as they darted beyond view.

If Ibar would be an adult and make adult decisions, he must think like one. Were Desmond at this boat's rail, he would be asking Ibar questions to make him think about the meanings buried within the passage. The fur first, Desmond counseled, then the meat of the passage, and then the very bone. First the literal meaning, then the applied meanings, and then the depths of wisdom that come of long study.

The fur was the fish themselves, the work of God's hands bringing the psalm to perfect life.

And there Ibar's cogitations stalled out. He wanted to find deep meanings here, literally and figuratively, but the deepest things he could think about were simply more fish in deeper water.

* * *

For eight days they sailed through lucid waters rife with fish of every sort. About the time Ibar became bored with watching normal fishes, a languid, lazy jellyfish would pulse by. And whales. So many whales. They came in so close he could see details of their tiny eyes. Tiny? Huge. And yet compared to their bulk, the eyes seemed tiny. Ibar ceased feeling nervous about them eventually, though he never learned, as Boyd apparently did, to love them.

If Ibar could not come up with a deeper interpretation of the Eighth or the crystal sea, Brendan would. Brendan was the sage of sages on this voyage. Throughout the whole week, Brendan did not say a word about fishes, or the paths of the sea, or the wondrous visions around and beneath their boat.

The only time Brendan came close was one sunlit afternoon as he hung over the rail beside Ibar, gazing. "The dark ones there—do you know which ones? They're very difficult to see."

"Mackerel, I'd guess. Patterning on their backs."

"They are exceedingly numerous, but you don't notice them. There goes a little silver darting thing. Look there. We notice it, but it's only one. The myriads we do not notice, yet those are the strength of the sea. Rather like the church. A few people stand out, and we call them saints and leaders. But the strength of the church is the many, many workers going unnoticed in the shadows of the faith."

"Desmond is a leader." Not that it did him that much good— or did the church much good, for all that. He's gone to who-knows-where, his mission to the Larkin cut short. And where was the strength of the church in Knag Burn? Spent in ashes.

"Aye. He's the rarest of sort, a leader who also works in the shadows." Brendan stared a while longer into the depths. "Would that we could see into men's souls so clearly." He looked at Ibar. "What would we see?"

"I suppose we'd see depravity."

Brendan nodded. "When Jesus Christ cleanses sin, He cleanses the depths of our nature. Fascinating it is to think about: no man can see into another man's soul. Therefore no man can say whether another is saved or damned. But God sees the deepest parts. Just as I peer through the water here, He peers through man's soul to see depravity—" he paused "—or the fruit of Christ's cleansing. He can tell at a glance who is His and who is not."

Guesswork. Who can know what God sees? Ibar gave up on deep thinking after that. If Brendan couldn't come up with any profound ideas, no sane person could expect Ibar to. Besides, he was constantly cold, and being constantly cold put him constantly out of sorts.

They were supposedly sailing through midsummer now, but the air seemed colder than spring. The sun never really set—and hadn't for a month. Still, it offered no warmth. Cold sun on a cold sea.

The watch called, "Land ho, due south!" just about the time the morose Ibar was resigning himself to sailing into frigid oblivion. Leeson ordered oars out, and Ibar took his place to port. He would explore this latest landfall, but he wasn't sure he wanted to remain here—not if it was this cold in summer. Although they could clearly see the mountain in the distance, it took them three days to reach it.

And what a mountain! It towered in stately magnificence far above mere mortals, steep and jagged and pristine white. It possessed all the attributes of any proper mountain—cliffs, valleys, a ragged peak, broken rock and smooth meadows, and sleek, wind-sculpted lines where the land met the sea. It reached to the sky, as high as any mountain Ibar had ever seen. The marvel of this mountain was that it was built not of snow-clad rock but of crystal. Glass. As the curragh sailed in close, cold blue light glowed here and there from its depths.

Where the mountain met the water, a wonderful network of arches and pillars protruded from the sea. Some connected to the mainland of the island. Others, of the same crystalline nature as the mainland, stood like spires in the ocean.

Boyd pressed against the forward half-decking to port. Ibar, Brendan, and Crosan balanced him to starboard.

Brendan called back to Leeson, "Drop the sail and ship oars." He returned his attention to the wonder at hand. "What do you see?"

"No birds of any sort. No life. No intertidal stuff along the shore." Crosan pointed. "In fact, the water line hasn't changed in the last hour. I'd guess it doesn't even have a tide."

Boyd snorted. "Every shoreline has a tide."

"Every shoreline has seaweed," Crosan retorted. "This one doesn't."

Ibar peered over the side into the depths. "The water's not quite as clear as when we were watching the fish, but it's clear. The shore extends out under our boat here, see?"

White crystal, dim in the depths, lay below them. Ibar could just make out smooth curves and interesting features on its drowned surface. He could see where it swept upward gracefully into a spire that broke the surface nearby.

Brendan looked deep in thought. "No tide. And although we saw it clearly, it took us three days to reach it. I'd say it's afloat and drifting south, and we had to catch up to it."

Ridiculous!

"Nah." Boyd gazed upward. "A whole mountain? Too massive. And too steady. See? It doesn't bob. It would bob if it were floating."

Casually, the boat bumped into one of the arches. Ibar reached out to the arch and shoved the boat away. "It's terribly cold. Like ice."

"Really?" Brendan stared at the arch as they passed beneath it. "A mountain of ice. That would explain why it looks so smoothly sculptured at water line. Salt water melts ice."

"It sucks the warmth right out of you, like ice," Ibar complained. "You can feel its coldness on your face when you're turned toward it."

"And ice floats." Crosan studied its magnificence a few moments. He shook his head. "No way water could freeze into a chunk the size of this island. Lakes don't even freeze solid."

An impossible thing, this mountain of ice. Yet here it was. There had to be some other explanation. One thing was certain: Ibar was not going to ask to be put ashore. "It's midsummer, and there's not a blade of green here."

Incredibly cold. Incredibly barren.

Beside him the hulking Boyd grunted an affirmative. Then he muttered, "I hate cold."

A kindred soul.

To circumnavigate the mountain, they dropped the mast and stowed it lengthwise down the center deck, giving them the ability to glide beneath low arches and overhangs.

The play of light within the mountain intrigued Ibar. As the sun coursed across the sky overhead, the land appeared opaque, a dull white. In morning or evening, with the sun aslant, some of the mountain's canyons and gullies glowed in a gorgeous array of gentle greens and blues. He wondered if the mountain glowed in darkness, but there was no darkness. When the sun swam red on the western horizon, the mountain turned from white to gold to a brilliant pink. The pink faded rapidly through purple into gray, and day was done.

The frigid, eerie, lifeless mountain attracted him, he decided, in the same way snakes did—with a certain morbid fascination. Because Patrick had driven them all into the sea, no snakes remained in Ireland. Ibar did not meet his first snake until he crossed to England. He had been impressed with its dull color, its sinister face, and the way it glided, legless, with such slack, casual grace. This mountain of ice or whatever similarly attracted and repelled him.

They explored the island for four days. Boyd and Crosan went ashore for an hour, poking and prodding to assuage their curiosity, but Ibar remained aboard. He would save his curiosity for warmer climes.

Brendan finally ordered them back to sea, and they began working their way out from the mainland through the lacework of arches and spires to open water. They restepped the mast, set sail, and put the towering wonder behind them.

They weren't using the tiller, because Brendan wanted God to navigate unfettered by human misunderstanding, so Ibar climbed upon the tethered tiller bar. It made a fine perch from which to view the mountain.

Boyd came wandering back and leaned on the bar. It creaked. He nodded toward the mountain falling away behind them. "Don't tell Brendan, but I'd have to agree with him. That thing's floating south. Think how long it took us to get to it, and how rapidly we're leaving it. We're miles away, and we've been under sail less than two hours."

Ibar was getting rather good at judging directions from the sun through the day. "And we're being carried northwesterly."

"Look!" Boyd yelled, "Brendan! Brendan!"

The mountain was moving. It tilted casually to the south or southwest. Farther. Farther. Slowly, majestically, inexorably it leaned.

Its peak began to move faster as it lay over. The arches and spires of its north side heaved high into the sky in a curtain of water, still attached by a long, thick neck to the mainland. The peak, which had once towered so proudly, hit the sea. White spray splashed a hundred feet in the air.

Brendan arrived barely in time to see the mountain turn over. The arches and spires of the north side, now suspended high above the sea surface, began to break off and fall. The island gave a single massive bob and returned to stability.

He stood as if pole-axed, gaping. Then he leaped suddenly to life. "To the oars! Quickly! Quickly! All oars out! We must row for all we're worth!"

Yanking out his seaman's knife, Boyd let fly an expletive, and he rarely used expletives. Even as Ibar jumped off the tiller bar, Boyd cut the tether free and dropped the rudder. Ibar flopped onto a sea chest and ran an oar out the deer-antler lock. What was the hurry? Never mind. The panicked look on Boyd's face was enough to spur him to frantic action.

Boyd called cadence as the brothers bent their backs to the oars. He increased the tempo. The sail lost its tautness. They were now rowing faster than the breeze. Leeson dropped the sail almost single-handed. Boyd kept looking behind them, as if the mountain were going to take after them in hot pursuit. Ibar broke out in a sweat from the exertion.

Suddenly Boyd cried, "Drop the mast! Brendan, drop the mast! Malo! Help me!"

"Yes!" Leeson leaped to it also. "Yes!" As twelve oars plied, the four unstepped the mast. Four men are not strong enough to manage a mast as it's coming down. Fortunately, one of the four was Boyd. Even so, they nearly dropped it on the oarsmen.

Boyd cried, "Here it comes! Ship the oars, lads, and lie down! Flat on the deck! Lie down!" His voice, normally so melodious and gentle, shrieked.

As he dragged his twelve feet of oar inboard, Ibar saw a wall of water rising behind them. The wave of all waves, it mounted higher and higher, higher than the mast top would be were the mast still stepped. He flattened out on the deck, terrified. Bare feet kicked him.

The boat lunged upward beneath them, pressing Ibar tight against the deck, and tilted steeply. He began to slide down the deck toward the bow, and he couldn't catch himself. He slid into a soft mass of brothers and stopped. He could see that wall of water astern yet.

Still the boat rose higher, shoved upward, upward. Every joint and knot creaked. Suddenly the wall disappeared, and the stern dropped.

The bow now nosed high in the air. The mass of brothers came sliding against Ibar. He squirmed around and managed to get his feet pointed downhill as they all scudded to the stern. Then the boat more or less evened out, though it still wallowed.

"Another!" Boyd yelled.

The second wall of water did not rise quite so high behind them as did the first. They rode seven such waves, each a little less than that which went before it.

Was this the end? Ibar lay still, sweating now from fear rather than exertion. In a shaky voice, Malo commenced vespers. No new wave assailed them during the service. The office closed with a rather general sigh of peace.

"Psalm forty-six, all versicles, eight tones," Malo announced.

Deus noster refugium . . . et transferentur montes in cor maris

. . . God is our refuge . . . even though the mountains be transported into the heart of the sea . . . . Though its waters roar and be troubled . . .

Ibar tried to sing soprano descant to the versicle "Be still and know that I am God," as he so often did, but his voice broke out of the octave. He had to content himself with singing the descant part in tenor range.

They completed the psalm before they tried to untangle themselves from each other.

Seven of them restepped the mast. Leeson ordered the sail raised as he lashed down the tiller bar. They were on their way again.

At his first opportunity, Ibar sought the crystal mountain. Were it visible at all, it would be glowing its vivid, translucent pink now. But the horizon to the southeast lay flat and empty in the haze.

In the gloaming, draped over the stern half-decking, Ibar pondered the day and the featureless horizon. Either they swiftly left the mountain behind—not a bad assessment if, as Brendan first suggested, it indeed was floating south—or it had sunk into the sea. Was rolling onto its side a random event? Did floating crystal mountains do that often? If so, what if that event had occurred a day earlier than it did—or even a few hours earlier?

He remembered sailing through those great arches and past those spires. When they reared into the air, they looked tiny. As their weight broke them off and they crashed, what a mighty roar that must have been. Just the falling debris of the bits and chunks, not to mention the waves if they fell into water, would have been enough to destroy the curragh and anyone nearby.

In any case, the curragh would have been crushed, swamped, driven to the bottom of the sea however deep that lay. Were they any closer, the violent shock wave would surely have capsized them even if they escaped the mountain itself.

They had fled certain death by a matter of an hour or two.

Brendan was right. This voyage and everyone on it led a charmed existence, blessed by God. Ibar didn't have to worry about his safety. Security was assured; God had demonstrated that amply.

He just wished it were not so cold.

32

Fire

"A little taste of hell." Leeson drew the tiller in a bit closer to his waist. The boat heeled slightly to port.

"A rather large taste of hell, I'd say." And Crosan the carefree Laughing Monk nervously crossed himself.

Boyd moved over a few feet to bring the boat back into trim without Leeson's having to yell at him. "In some ways even more awesome than the crystal mountain."

He had been asleep when, in the half-light of midnight, the watch called, "Land ho!" The lookout had espied the landfall not by the sight of a mountain but by the fire on the horizon.

That in itself was not unusual. Occasionally in Erin they first spotted islands by the night fires of shepherds on the hills behind the shore. What was unusual was that this fire issued from the mountain itself.

A dense, ugly column of gray-black smoke boiled straight up into the sky, then spread out as a black roof above them. It churned wildly, tumbling within itself, and lightning flashed through it. The mountain roared and rumbled without ceasing. And it stank to high heaven with an acrid stench more penetrating even than the odor of smoldering wet manure.

Tongues of orange and red flashed at the base of the smoke column, though Boyd could tell the smoke obscured most of the fire. The dirty-gray cloud glowed where it emerged. At random, fireballs arched into the sky, leaving short-lived, curved, yellow tracks. Warm, powdery ash dropped onto the boat, turning every horizontal surface a dull gray.

Hell had broken forth from its nether confines and erupted out of the sea. And Brendan's saints were there to see it. Boyd did not find this the least reassuring.

Mochta left Boyd's side, headed off on some errand or per-

265

haps no job at all. Instantly, young Ibar squeezed into the open space.

Boyd looked at the lad by the uncertain orange light of yonder mountain. "You don't seem particularly frightened, son."

"I'm not." Ibar looked smug. "God takes care of us."

"He does indeed. You're growing, lad. Growing spiritually, I mean. A year ago—nay, a month ago—something like this would have terrified you." Boyd did not feel compelled to mention to a stripling that he was mightily discomfited himself, though he wasn't yet frightened to the point of crossing himself as frequently and as frantically as some of the brothers were doing.

Ibar beamed. "The crystal mountain taught me a thing or two. No matter how strange and ungodly it seemed, God was in it. He made certain we got away safely."

"Aye!" Boyd ought to be immensely pleased at the lad's growth. Somehow something seemed wrong, though. It couldn't be the hint of bravado in the boy's voice or his proud, confident demeanor. You want that in a fearless servant of Christ. A darkness nagged at Boyd as he listened.

Or perhaps the darkness was merely that cloud immediately overhead. They had not experienced true night for months. They had night now, for the smoke and ash turned midday to lightning-streaked blackness.

Boyd tried to find some rock on that island other than black rock. Even the narrow apron between the sheered black cliffs and the dark, dark sea was made of black sand or shingle. The strand between hill and water hardly existed. Steeply cone-shaped, the mountain rose directly out of the sea.

"I've been thinking," Crosan began, and everyone groaned. "No, no, this is serious. The contrast. The crystal mountain—we're presuming it was ice, if you can figure out how to freeze that much water into that shape. Frozen cold at any rate. And silent. Remember the silence?"

"Can I ever forget?" Actually, Boyd had not noticed the utter silence of the thing until Crosan mentioned it. But Crosan was right. The thing had sat in the water—rather, floated in it—with a hushed expectancy. "Except for the creaking now and then, from inside. And very occasional cracking sounds."

Crosan continued, "And the clarity. Pure white, clear water, brilliance. Know what I mean? Here we have blackness. Look at the rocks and cliffs rearing up out of the water there. Black. And the cloud overhead. Can you see into the water? Not a foot. The stink here too. There was no odor about the crystal mountain at all. It was absolutely serene. This thing is wild. Frantic. Enraged. Everything is in total contrast. All opposite, except one thing."

"What's that?" Boyd asked obediently.

"The crystal mountain was devoid of life. So is this place."

"So what does that tell you?" Leeson tipped his tiller sharply, arching the boat aport.

"It tells me that life is a balance of extremes. Moderation is not just desirable, it's necessary. You have to have the fire and the ice in combination. Water, for example. You have to have water, which is in the middle. It freezes as ice or evaporates before fire. All sorts of ramifications, when you meditate on it."

Ibar spoke up—another sign he was growing, Boyd thought. The boy never used to do that. "But the balance. This part of the world is too far tipped toward cold. The sea is so cold that if any of us falls in, we'll die before the others can help us. We would do much better were the balance more on the warm side. Life does best in warmth, not cold. Man is a creature of the warm. Warm friendships. 'Warm the cockles of your heart.' Warm memories. Who would cherish a cold friendship? Who would cool off the cockles of his heart?"

Crosan laughed aloud. "Excellent point, lad!"

"We've got trouble." Leeson stood erect. "Boyd, take the tiller. Everyone to the oars!" He scurried to the starboard sail sheet. "Ibar! Loose the port sheet. We're resetting her to make way due south."

"Due south." Boyd pulled the tiller against him. "She's not responding." They were sideslipping directly toward the fiery mountain.

"Drop the sail! Drop the sail!" Leeson looked up toward the mast-top. The spar came sliding down in a great cloud of fine gray ash. Leeson ducked his head away, snarling. The cloud settled, enveloping him.

Out from under the wind, the boat sideslipped less. Boyd

could no longer guess which direction south might be, for that black cloud obscured all the sky. He hauled the tiller tight, bringing the boat's prow directly away from the island. They would sail away from the mountain, regardless which direction that might be. Even with fourteen oars in the water, they weren't making significant headway.

Brendan left his watch post in the bow and jogged the distance to Boyd. "Like a lodestone it is, drawing us toward it."

With a dull boom, the mountain spewed a great belching cloud of fire and smoke. The fireball rolled toward them and dispersed upward and outward over their heads. A sulfurous stench descended.

Leaving an acrid trail of smoke, a glowing chunk from nowhere dropped into the water hard to starboard. Mochta yelled in terror. The water hissed and steamed where the mass entered. Its dark, smoky tail dissipated.

"Here." Boyd left the tiller in Brendan's capable hands and jabbed young Ibar. "Ship it!"

Confused, the lad shipped his oar and leaped up. Boyd plopped down on the chest. "Row on the other side." He paused to pick up the rhythm, dipped his oar, and pulled mightily. If the mountain sucked them into its fiery maw, it wouldn't be because Boyd Blond Hair stood about in idleness at the tiller.

Another fiery lump plunged into the water astern. Yet another fell not twenty feet away. The fiendish smiths on that accursed island were flinging burning brands with a vengeance. If one chanced to fall in the boat, it would burn right through and stave her before they could remove it.

They toiled for a solid hour. Sexte came and went, but no one had breath to sing the noonsong. They spelled off then, two-thirds rowing and a third resting. Nones came and went, but they did not sing that office either. From the tiller, Brendan said an abbreviated sort of version, punctuated by fervent prayer. They broke out from under the cloud into sunlight an hour before vespers.

Cautiously, Leeson raised sail. In a cloud of fine gray ash, the canvas flapped, luffed, and picked up the breeze. The boat heeled aport and plowed clean water northwesterly, away from the fragment of hell behind them.

Brendan ordered the oars in. Ibar unsealed a new water jug and passed it around.

"Saved." Seated on the deck and leaning against the sea chest, Boyd took a deep breath and grimaced. "I still smell like that island. My clothes." He sniffed his sleeve as he stood up and nearly choked on the ash he drew into his nostrils.

Brendan collapsed into a lax pile in the stern. "If only we could somehow convey to the unsaved the horrors we just experienced, people would flock to the shelter of Jesus Christ."

Crosan stood and stretched mightily. A silent cloud of ash drifted off him. "We're going to be a week cleaning this stuff up. It's everywhere. Look at this." He picked up the nearest sheepskin and shook it over the stern. A gray cloud floated above the water near their wake, then settled gently into the sea.

Ibar pulled off his cassock and shook it over the side. "But did you notice? The ash as it fell was warm."

"No, I didn't notice. And it's not warm now." Boyd sweated too easily. He loved warm, but not hot, weather.

That cloud still hung perilously close, a black blot across the whole northeast horizon. "You know," Boyd ventured, "I'd say it's following us."

Brendan twisted around to look. "I wouldn't doubt it. It's carried on the wind. We're being carried on the wind. And I doubt it's going to dissipate soon, as much smoke as the mountain was putting out."

They supped and sang the compline. With the final "Thanks be to God," Boyd shook out his sheepskins for the second time (disenfranchising just as much ash as from the first shaking) and collapsed for welcome rest.

But he could not rest. A foreboding prodded at him, a sense of gloom and doom. He felt the black weight of impending death, and he could think of no reason for such a feeling. He was still tossing and turning when Brendan commenced matins.

* * *

They bore west, ever west, and Boyd over the next few days began to think that possibly they would find Tir Na n'Og after all. More than once he had caught himself doubting. Now, praise God, the doubts had faded.

The black cloud disappeared, although another grayer cloud formed ahead. "Do all the mountains burn up here?" Crosan asked.

It was a good question, for here was another one that did. A column of gray-white smoke issued from a conical peak on an island to the north.

"Let's not pass so close this time," Boyd suggested.

But a strong wind carried them in before Leeson could drop his sail and order out the oars. None of the brothers seemed to feel the urgency that the other raging mountain had elicited. Boyd certainly didn't. The boat drifted in close to sheer onyx cliffs with a jumble of black rocks at their feet. She passed near to a black shingle beach. In bright contrast, white surf crashed across the shingle, wave upon wave. Much like the giant causeway that Finn McCool laid down in his haste to travel from Erin to the Dalriada of Scotland, black bundles of hexagonal columns rose out of the sea.

Leeson gave Boyd the helm and reset the sail to make way before the wind.

Ibar hung off the aft half-decking and gazed at the mountain. "Do you see the wildflowers?"

"I assume that's what they are. Daisies of some sort, I'd guess. And yellow flowers. Curious, isn't it? So few things asea are yellow. No yellow fish to speak of, no birds." Boyd looked at a thin dotting of white against the black shore. Beyond the gravel, tufts of tall grass marked the line where the tide could no longer reach.

"A very pleasant place, this."

"I wouldn't go that far. Habitable." Boyd glanced up at the smoking mountain. The pearlescent cloud seemed thicker than when they first approached. "Warm air. Interesting."

Suddenly the sail dropped flaccid, and Boyd's neck prickled. Ominous clouds were gathering overhead. He listened to a low-level bass rumbling, which he determined was probably coming from somewhere in the mountain. The grasses above tide line bowed suddenly, pressed by a land breeze. Moments later a breath of warm air washed across the vessel. The sail flapped.

Boyd felt uncomfortable, but Ibar seemed unduly agitated. The lad burst out with, "I want to remain here for a boat that will carry me home."

"Here, lad? Surely not!"

"Aye, here! Did you not feel that breeze? It's warm here! Marvelously pleasant. Here is where I will wait."

"But food and drink, lad . . ."

"God doesn't dare let me suffer. He will provide."

"I've every confidence He's able, but will He? You pledged for the voyage. That means you stay with us." Boyd shuddered as his vague premonition of last night became a powerful message. It welled up inside him and burst out as a cry. "Don't go, lad!" He turned and shouted forward, "Brendan! Help me!"

He heard a splash behind him and knew without looking what it was. "Brendan!" He turned back astern and leaned over the half-decking to shout to Ibar. "Ibar! No!"

Ibar waded chin-deep in water, his arms held high, eagerly plowing toward shore. He stopped and turned to Boyd. "It's warm, Boyd! The water's warm! You'll love it. Come with me." Ibar cackled delightedly.

"Return to us, lad!"

"Tell the next eastbound boat you see to pick me up!"

The grass bowed mightily, and another warm gush of air swept across the boat. It smelled vaguely sulfurous.

"Oars out! To the oars!" With another uncharacteristic epithet, Boyd shoved the tiller hard away. They would beach, drag the stupid lad back into the craft, and row directly out to sea before Ibar could put into practice any more impossible ideas.

"No!" Brendan was there beside him, pushing the tiller back to centerline. "No. We have to flee!"

"Ibar, the daft lad, went ashore. We have to—"

"We have to flee!"

"We can't leave him behind!"

"We've no choice."

And then Boyd saw the sorrow in Brendan's eyes. And tears.

Boyd had no idea what was happening. He knew who was in command, though. He had to obey. He shoved on the tiller. The boat heeled aport.

With a prolonged splash, the brothers dropped their oars into the water. Malo began counting cadence. Brendan shouted orders to Leeson about the sail.

Dripping water, Ibar sloshed across the black shingle, safely ashore. Boyd breathed a sigh of relief. Perhaps an eastbound boat would indeed pick him up. Perhaps this very boat would retrieve him on her return from the Land of Ever Young.

Ibar turned and waved. He shouted something, but already the curragh had moved beyond easy earshot.

A thin gray cloud skimmed down the mountainside beyond the shore. It swept past the waving grass, past Ibar, past the curragh. The sail snapped and filled as the boat lunged forward. Acrid smoke choked Boyd momentarily. Then a fresh breeze cleared the air and drove the curragh southward away from the island.

Brendan was staring off astern. "It's not my will, Boyd. Not mine. It's God's." He wheeled, his cheeks wet with tears, and called to Malo, "Increase the cadence. We must get away!" He began snapping his fingers rapidly, bringing the count up to twenty strokes per minute.

Another noxious cloud raced down from the mountain summit and whooshed past them. Boyd coughed uncontrollably. His eyes watered so that for a few moments he could not see. Fourteen other voices were hacking and coughing just as badly. Finally he managed to clear his eyes.

Young, foolish Ibar was standing knee deep in the surf, waving his arm in a gesture of good-bye. Then suddenly he doubled forward as though he too was coughing and choking.

No longer content to spew smoke, the roaring mountain now began spitting fire near the summit. A vapor cloud just above its flank burst into flame, flaring into brilliance, converting itself to a churning black billow.

The fresh breeze together with the oars bore them rapidly away. Boyd could just barely make out Ibar. The lad appeared now as a tiny mark in the surf, standing where the white foam drew its lines across the black shore.

Another thin cloud rushed down the mountainside. From out here Boyd could see its route and progress even more clearly. It almost totally obscured the tiny mark that was Ibar when it poured across the beach. As its leading edge spread down across the shingled shore and out across the water, its upper end ignited. The gray mist, all of it, turned instantly into a sheet of yellow flame from mountaintop to sea.

And then the flame became churning black smoke that hid from view the mountainside, the shore, the rushing surf, and everything.

33
Fog

Conn.

Willis.

Ibar.

They were back to their original fifteen, just as Brendan's premonition had promised so long ago and so far away beyond the emerald sea in Erin. Boyd stared out past the stern half-decking, past the tiller, past the wake, past the horizon. He tried to weigh the cost of this journey, and he could not. His heavy heart burned.

They had forty days' worth of food and water if they husbanded their supplies carefully. Brendan seemed to think that by then they would have arrived in the Land of Ever Young. Boyd's doubts, once beaten into silence, surfaced again and clamored at the back of his faith.

Wind and currents carried them fairly steadily to the southwest now. The curragh did not creak as much as it used to, and Boyd couldn't decide if that was good or bad. If it meant that the hundreds of knots and joints were finally adjusted to one another, it was good. If things were wearing and ready to break, on the other hand . . .

"Boyd, brother, tell me something." Crosan's voice startled him, snapping him back to the moment at hand.

"What's that, Laughing One?"

Crosan sprawled in the corner joining the port gunwale to the aft half-decking. "During that storm two days ago, we trailed a bag of oil at Brendan's behest and laid the waves down noticeably. We drag knotted ropes to slow ourselves while exploring various strands, and we bend linen to the bottom of the sail to increase our speed. We can do just about anything we have to, to manipulate this creaky old boat."

"And . . ." Boyd hated it when someone's tongue got rolling

274

all around a point without actually getting to it. The Irish, bless them, were notorious for that.

"Now myself. I grew up on the coast, with Mutton Island in sight from my front door. I've been a man of the sea my whole life, but I could hardly call myself an expert."

"So?"

"Well, Brendan claims Bishop Erc, his foster father, taught him all that sort of lore whilst he was yet a lad. Taught him the sea. And myself, I more or less picked it up. But you, Boyd, you grew up inland, near Kildare. How did you become so expert a seaman?"

"Not expert."

"Expert. When the crystal mountain rolled over, you and Brendan didn't have to say a word to each other. You both knew the giant wave was coming. How did you know what to do?"

Boyd studied the deck a moment. "I don't know. Observation, I suppose. If a mountain falls in the sea, it stands to reason it's going to make waves. Mountainous waves, literally. And—" he smiled, more to himself than to Crosan "—do you remember the blue martyr in the tiny curragh, when we were shaking down this vessel and sailing up to Iona?"

"No. Oh. Yes. Middle of the night."

"He rode out that storm—a violent storm—with no sail, no tiller, no oars. He just lay down in the bottom of the boat and let it bob. I remembered that."

"You remembered that." Crosan wagged his head and laughed suddenly. "Learn as you go. Remember everything and sooner or later you'll use it all."

"More or less."

"Ah, well. I did ask, didn't I?" Flopping around the other way, he leaned his elbows on the half-decking and watched the horizon behind them awhile. "I wish I were home in Erin."

"Me too."

"Solid land beneath your feet. The smell of fresh dirt under your plow. The feel of it all loose and cool between your toes. Cattle smells."

Boyd grunted agreement.

Crosan laughed. "And you know what? I'm not even a farmer." He sobered. "I'm not anything."

"You're a monk."

"Kicked out of one monastery for—shall we say, indiscretion. Asked to leave another. If I'd been around Clonfert long, I probably would've gotten kicked out of there too."

"I'm not the only one who learns as he goes, friend."

Crosan nodded. "But I tend to learn too late."

Out of the corner of his eye, Boyd noticed a heavy white cloud hard beside them to the south. He straightened and looked forward. They were entering a fog bank thick enough for crows to perch upon. One moment, the sun shone. The next moment, they drifted inside a cloud so dense that he could barely see from one end of the boat to the other. It parted silently ahead of them and closed silently behind.

The silence penetrated conversation. Voices dropped to hushed tones or ceased altogether. The moist air made their sail wilt, and a coating of little silver droplets beaded on their hair.

Drawing his cloak in close, Crosan muttered, "I wasn't ready to agree with Ibar that warm is wonderful . . ."

Ah, Ibar, rest your soul! Boyd's heart ached anew.

"But sure and the lad had a good point that sometimes these climates get a little too cool."

The sail flapped, slack.

From the bow, Leeson called for oars.

Boyd untethered the tiller bar. "It's been getting warmer, you'll notice. And we have actual night again. I welcome night. Stars. It's nice to have it back."

"Agreed." In no hurry to comply, Crosan wandered forward to man an oar.

They rowed until an hour past dark, lashed the tiller, and retired, letting God take them where He would.

When Boyd awoke, fog still surrounded them, and he had no idea what time it was. He often wondered in amazement that Brendan seemed always to know the hour, starting the offices right on time. No matter whether the sun provided a clue or not as to when to begin, he commenced the day in such time that sexte always and ever fell exactly at noon when the sun burned highest. Malo enjoyed that gift also.

All about them drifted a uniform pink haze. The sun was coming up, brushing the fog with morning color.

Their sail had filled. It stretched taut in the near darkness, driving them firmly through the mist, and at fair speed.

Until someone who knew the time began the offices, Boyd would rest. He burrowed back under his sheepskins.

The deck jolted violently. Boyd slid forward a foot as the boat bottom growled in angry protest. He rolled out of bed, dreading to find out what, exactly, the boat bottom was protesting. He peered over the side. They sat immobile and aslant on a gravel bar.

Crosan joined him, looked over the gunwale, and casually announced in a conversational tone, "Land ho."

Boyd jumped over the side into two feet of lapping water. Its depth retreated to six inches as his feet hit the shingle. He noted the seaweed line practically at the boat's bow. High tide. From warm sheepskins to cold water. His feet ached. And yet, the sea was not nearly as cold as it might be.

"I think we're taking on water," Malo called from on board.

Boyd groped around where gravel met oxhide. He stood erect. "Brendan? We're going to have to unload her and careen her. Some stitching ripped loose."

"Good. Good." Indefatigable, Brendan appeared at the gunwale. "About time we regreased her too. We'll rest and work. Another forty days should do it, I believe."

Forty days would put them into August.

Between matins and prime they worked, carrying ashore the tents, sheepskins, cooking pots, food stores (not many of those), cordage, spare hides, oars, mutton fat, firebox, water pots, spare cassocks—more duffle than Boyd could imagine would come from a boat that also had room for fifteen men.

August. On to the westward then, and by when? September? They'd still be six months at least away from home. It was not likely that they would sail through winter storms, so they'd wait for spring. But in spring the winds might be wrong. After all, they rode the wind in this direction. It might be a long, hard row. They weren't going to return to Erin until late next year at the earliest, if at all. His heart lay like a rock at the bottom of his soul.

Between prime and tierce the fog moved offshore, peeling away from an intriguing vista. As far as Boyd could see, this land was covered with mats of vines. Small islands featured small coves and a generally convex shoreline. This land did not. Whether it was an island—and, if so, how large an island—was anybody's guess. But vines it had aplenty.

They careened the boat above high-tide line and broke out the needles, awls, and cord. Seam by seam from stem to stern they checked the stitching. It was holding up well. They repaired the rip just made and a few other loose places. The job took three days and untold hours of tedium.

Boyd lost interest quickly. On the fourth day, after nones, he left the welfare of their boat to Brendan and went off a-tramping.

The vines were grapevines, growing wild and unchecked, with their first fruit just coming ripe. Grapes like apples hung pendulant beneath a thick canopy of leaves and gnarled stems. He chose a dark red grape, admired its frosty-white bloom, and tasted. Sweet, sweet fruit.

One does not easily go exploring when the terrain is covered with such an impenetrable tangle. Boyd found his way blocked everywhere—except for a path snaking through the vines. He could see it from the open strand as a dark hole through the undergrowth. It punched into the vine mat like a tunnel. The new growth of summer had arched over the path, screening it from the view of someone as tall as Boyd. He followed it by feel, kicking his legs forward beneath the overlying leaves. A quarter of a mile up from the beach he paused, armpit-deep in grapes and a mat of leaves as far as he could see, to simply stand in amazement at his situation. These vines had to end sometime. He kept walking.

The mat and the trail through it rose, climbing a low hill. Boyd groped his way to near the top and looked back. He tried to see the boat turned upside down on the beach, but he could not. The rise of the land and the grapevines hid the shore above tide line. A white wall hung a mile or so offshore. Between there and the gravel beach, sparkling bits of sunlight rode the smooth waves and foamy breakers. Cloudless sky. Blue water. Bright day. And this unique pebbled mat of green, stretching endlessly across the land.

Thanksgiving filled him. He stood among the vines and sang to God, not a formal gratia, which is certainly expression enough, but a Gaelic tune from Patrick's day. It seemed somehow more fitting.

Here grew enough grapes to feed the world. Boyd thought of the grapes, as large and juicy as these, in that basket of food from the Island of Strong Men, and he thought of Willis. Willis's redemption and subsequent calling seemed to surprise Willis as much as anyone. The little thief—ex-thief—was a splendid musician too. A wise calling, but of course God is wise in all things.

The mat broke up somewhat as Boyd topped out on the hill. The solid canopy became clumps of vines interlaced with grass and wildflowers. It occurred to him that unless he in some way marked this spot, he'd not likely find the trail again. And if he did not, he'd not be able to get back down to the beach. He removed his cincture from around his waist and tied it to the top twigs of a vine beside the trail.

This was not a solitary hill but rather, apparently, the end of a long, gentle ridge. He followed along the crest for a time, weaving among low bushes, and wondered if he would come across any trees. A white fog bank masked the ridge ahead. There'd be no use to explore further. He'd be able to see nothing anyway, and fog is an easy thing to get lost in. He stopped and turned around.

And froze.

A hundred feet behind him, a half-grown boy froze.

They stared at each other for a long, long moment.

Boyd smiled and signed the cross. "Good day and God bless you, lad." He waited.

The boy, an astonishing lad, was half Boyd's height, square-built and powerful-looking for one so small. The fellow wore nothing at all save a loincloth. On his belt hung a sheathed knife and a quiver of arrows. He carried a short bow. Was he out hunting and chanced to happen upon Boyd, or had he been stalking him?

Boyd noted the boy's skin—a warm golden color—the rich black hair, and the eyes, set at an odd angle above high, smooth cheekbones. He decided this was possibly not a boy. His whole appearance was so unusual that this might be a very youthful-looking man. And if so, they might already have arrived at the Land of Ever Young.

Boyd glanced over his shoulder. A second hunter, looking much like this first, stood fifty feet away. Boyd smiled and blessed that lad also. He turned back to address the first. He was gone. No sound. No whisper. And when he looked again over his shoulder, the second had disappeared as well.

Did leprechauns abide in Hi Brasil?

He walked back the way he had come, watching the ground, seeing no signs of human beings, knowing that if he did see such signs he probably wouldn't recognize them. He could read the land very well in Erin, where he knew the birds, the terrain, the people. This place was a different story. Those two hunters' feet left no mark. In fact, neither did Boyd's.

He paused on the brow of the hill. The clumps of vines coalesced into the now-familiar solid mat and spread away down the slope. He should be able to see his cincture somewhere along here. He paced up and down along the hillcrest, searching, assuring himself he didn't simply miss it.

They must have taken it, those two. Why would they take it? If their motive was to confound him, they had succeeded brilliantly. The hour was vespers or past. He didn't have the daylight to do much exploring for another way down the hill, even if he could find a passage this side of the fog.

Bold words did he speak to Crosan when they talked of remembering everything. Very well. He would follow God's instruction as described somewhere in Paul's letters to the Corinthians and proceed decently and in order.

First, give thanks. He had done that, but he did it again, and why not? So far, no calamity loomed.

Second, pray. He addressed God on behalf of Jesus to favor Brendan, the voyage, the pagans (presumably) he had just encountered, and himself. He asked specifically to be reunited with his shipmates.

Third, bless. He turned toward the ridge and in a loud voice called, "I forgive you freely. God render His blessings upon you without ceasing."

Fourth, think.

That was the hard part. He recalled coming up the hill. Did he look back to place his position at all? No. Did he do so when he emerged from the vine mat? Not right away. He wholly relied upon the cord he tied on a bush. A lesson there.

He worked his way down to where the mat became really thick and unbroken and explored carefully along the hillside, seeking details. Ah. Here a tuft of grass was mashed down, and, hard beside it, a leaf in the vine mat had been bruised. He recalled how loudly he crashed through the overlayer of leaves and branches. He surely bruised more than a few. This must be the place. Poking and probing, he found a trail, much less obvious than the hole he first spied down on the shore.

This would suffice. He pressed into the waist-high growth, his elbows held aloft, and began groping a path downhill toward the sea. While he worked his way along, he might as well complete vespers. He sang sometimes the bass and sometimes the melody pitched an octave low. He couldn't think of any psalms glorifying grapes, so he finished with an old Celtic hymn identifying Christ as the vine and His people as branches.

He arrived on the beach just in time to help his crewmates finish off the last of the whale meat.

34
Sun

Boyd sat cross-legged in the sand and watched the campfire cast orange light and odd black shadows across Brendan's face.

"Hi Brasil lies beyond a dense fog," Brendan began.

Dense fog.

"There the trees ever bear fruit . . ."

Grapevines.

". . . and people never lose their youth or potency."

Youthful. Those two alien boys or men.

"It is a land to which all those who die in the faith ultimately go. We must also presume that the dead of other lands go there also if they be redeemed."

The only other lands Boyd knew anything about were Spain to the southeast, the Holy Land far to the east, the Danes' lands beyond the Vik to the north, and, of course, England. None of the people in those lands, so far as he knew, resembled the two people he saw three days ago, but there must be a multitude of lands about which he knew nothing. Ethiopia, for example. He'd heard about Ethiopians, and that they had dark skin, but he'd never seen one. Maybe those two were Ethiopians.

It didn't matter. This country fit the qualifications in every other regard. In fact, alien people only added to the probability that Brendan and his crew had achieved their destination at last.

And then Brendan ended his remarks with, "We will sail south and west again. I'll know Hi Brasil when we get there."

Boyd opened his mouth, realized that if he said anything it would be an argument, and shut it again.

Brendan looked from face to face. "Our boat is ready, greased and mended, and in perfect condition. We can refill our water vessels from any of the streams nearby. Crosan and Boyd have been snaring fowl, which we are preserving in brine. Fishing is excellent. And of course there are the grapes."

Tons of grapes. Boyd never thought he'd ever grow weary of sweet grapes, but he was getting close.

"Mochta glimpsed a large wild beast half a mile up the beach and wants to go a-hunting. He claims it's bigger than a cow. I suggested he take a party out tomorrow after matins and be back by nones, when the tide turns. Boyd, I'd like you to join his hunting party, at his request. He thinks he'll need your muscle to bring all the meat back. Crosan, would you go along?"

"A bit of an optimist, isn't he? Sure, I'll go along."

"While the hunting party is ensuring our meat supply, the rest of us will lade and be ready to leave."

Boyd frowned. "I thought you said we'd be here forty days."

"We will travel this final leg a total of forty days, of which about a fortnight has already passed."

Boyd grunted. He liked that. It did not mean, however, that they'd return home to Erin any time soon.

* * *

Why by tradition must hunting parties go roaring off before dawn?

Tradition or whatever, Mochta and his band of meat-seekers, Boyd among them, left at matins the next morning through extremely heavy fog. They traveled northwesterly along the ocean shore, with those mats of vines to their left and the restless sea to their right. Boyd could not see across the water beyond the waves lapping immediately against the shore. He could not see more than a rod out over the grapevine mat.

Twenty minutes after they left camp, Mochta murmured, "Here."

"Here" was a swampy delta where a stream emptied into the bay. An extensive forest of cattails and rushes wedged apart the ubiquitous vine mat, marking a broad, soggy stream channel. Clammy wet, the fog hid all but this very end of the channel. Had Boyd been unable to find his trail back, he probably could have come down a streambed such as this. He must remember that. Crystalline waters came rushing out of the swamp, tumbling onto the shingle. They cut a dozen spreading fingers that laced in and out among themselves down the beach to the sea.

Mochta squatted on a muddy playa above high-tide line and pointed. The tracks of cloven feet bigger than any cow's cut into the mud.

Boyd stood up and looked around, half afraid that the beast that made those tracks was watching them—and licking its chops. "I wonder, do you suppose four men with only six javelins between them are enough?"

"It's rather like the elk of the northland." Mochta stood up. "Did you ever hear one of those described? An ugly, ugly face—incredibly ugly face—and huge shovel-shaped antlers. Huge! And broad."

Crosan smirked. "Fermenting some of the grapes, are we?"

"Wait till you see. It frequents this area."

"So the tracks would indicate." Boyd looked down at them again and gauged them against cow tracks. He didn't like this expedition. Their dried fish and pickled fowl were quite enough. He wished the fog would lift, so that they could see farther and better.

They moved up the beach. A bit farther on, the vines gave way to a flooded salt marsh. With low tide less than four hours hence, the fen was draining. Mochta led out across it, moving from hummock to hummock over the coarse saltgrass.

By tradition, Satan had cloven hooves. Boyd couldn't stop thinking about that.

And there he was!

Dark in the filtered light, a monster stood belly deep in a black, glossy pool, its head underwater. The fog dulled light and gave an ominous, haunting feel to the whole unworldly scene.

The thing raised its head then, a head with flopping ears and a great, bulbous nose. Water streamed off an extraordinary rack of immense antlers. From its tines on one side hung a few water-weeds, and the beast placidly chewed a great mouthful of plants.

The giant ears flapped forward, the bulging nose swung their way, and the beast exploded up out of the pool.

Mochta ran forward and flung his javelin. It sailed swiftly, with very little arc, into the creature's shoulder. Right behind it, Crosan's javelin lodged low in its belly.

On remarkably long, graceful legs, the beast trotted three strides across the hummocks and wheeled toward them. Its sudden change of direction spoiled Boyd's aim. His javelin pierced completely through the beast's neck at an angle. The fourth weapon missed completely, as did Mochta's second attempt.

Only Crosan was armed now. He did not raise their only remaining javelin to throw it. Rather, he gripped it tightly two-handed and braced with spread feet in the soggy ground.

Boyd did not even have the presence of mind to follow by eye the two stray javelins, that he might run and retrieve one. He yanked out his knife, but still he felt horribly helpless.

The monster rushed toward them, with nose down low, presenting to them nothing but its broad, spreading rack. Where did Crosan expect to thrust a javelin, when all the monster's vulnerable parts were hidden behind that wall of bone?

What we need is an arrow!

Silent and sure, a fletched arrow sank into the creature's ribs. Another lodged in its breast just below its neck. The moment hung suspended. Then the monster slowed to a walk, staggered, and stopped.

Boyd could see a new-moon crescent of white as it threw its head high and rolled its eyes. A great, pendulous wattle flicked back and forth beneath its jaw.

A third arrow found home between the beast's ribs. It dropped to its knees and struggled back to its feet. Then its hindquarters collapsed, and it flopped on its belly in the marsh grass.

Mochta started toward it and froze as a man's voice yelled loudly—an obvious warning, but not in Gaelic. Boyd wheeled. Three men, attired like the two he had seen before, converged from positions perhaps a hundred feet apart. Two of them held their bows at ready, arrows nocked and pointed at the beast. The third raised a hand toward Mochta, a universal gesture to stay back. He carried a shiny black knife.

The monster rolled heavily to its side, then forced itself back up to its belly. Its eyes showed their whites again.

The hunter stepped in behind it. Recklessly, it flung that rack toward him. With a loud cry, he fell upon the beast's back and drove his dagger into its neck behind the skull.

The ponderous head dropped into the grass. The legs twitched and jerked and melted limp. Either Brendan was right that this was not the Land of Ever Young, or God's gift of freedom from death did not extend to monsters.

Ah, but didn't that brave fellow with the dagger gloat, and rightly so! With a victorious grin he stood and raised both arms, the bloody knife still in his hand. His two hunting companions unnocked their arrows and hastened forward, laughing.

"Brothers, we have been delivered from death. Let us give great thanks." Boyd began an eight-tone gratia. The other three picked it up, and Mochta slipped into a tenor descant.

The three native hunters waited politely through the "Amen," then closed their eyes and sang a strange, haunting melody in their own language.

The Laughing Monk walked a half circle around the deceased monster. He gestured at it and raised his eyebrows. "Name?"

They conferred, probably trying to confirm the question.

"Moose," a fellow replied. The man bobbed his head. "Moose." He spoke a few other words also.

Crosan smiled. "Moose." He looked at his companions. "So, brothers. Whose moose is this? We struck first, aye, but we'd be mashed into stirabout now by those horrendous cloven hooves, not to mention the antlers, were it not for these doughty lads. I say give them it, or at least the most of it."

"I heartily agree." Cautiously, Boyd touched an antler. Its hardness amazed him. It was as dense and solid as deer antler, which is harder than oak. His fingernail made not the slightest mark or dent in it, no matter how strongly he pressed.

"Oh, look!" Crosan reached over to one fellow's ear. His hand came away with a smooth red pebble from the beach. Crosan and his magic tricks.

The fellow gaped. His companions stared, dumbstruck, then roared.

Crosan pointed to another. "And you, fine fellow! You harbor stones as well." He reached out and drew a pebble from that fellow's ear. He gave both stones to the third, rubbed his hands together, handed two stones to the second, rubbed his hands together again, and gave two stones to the first. Boyd wondered how long it had taken him to find six such closely matching stones.

Boyd wagged his head. "Crosan, are you sure this is the time and place for such foolery?"

"Look at them! Grins wide enough to fit the antlers in. We've made friends fast and easy."

"I've a better idea. Let's do it by working." Mochta whipped out his knife and slashed the huge, hairy throat to bleed it. He hooked the blade tip under the hide and began the work of skinning and butchering. A gentle cloud of steam lifted off the carcass as the skin peeled back, and the familiar smell of new hide.

The three hunters watched the process intently, discussing it in low tones.

"Mochta? Hold a moment." Boyd nodded toward the three. "They seem fascinated not by your prowess but by your knife."

"My knife?" Mochta stood erect and twisted it back and forth in his hand. "An ordinary general-purpose knife."

"None of them carries an iron knife." If this be Tir Na n'Og, or near there, one obviously left behind the iron implements of civilization when one died. The old Celts, who buried implements and jewelry with their corpses, did so in vain.

Boyd knew there was a day in the distant past when, folklore dictated, iron was rare or absent in Erin and people used bronze instead. But these folk fashioned their cutlery by chipping glossy black stone. That must be the only material available in these far lands.

He handed one of the fellows his own knife and waved a hand, an invitation to join in the butchering. The man did so with alacrity. He and his companions chattered away. Then they with their stone knives lent a hand as well.

"Crosan?" Boyd stood back. Only so many men can gather around a butchering job at once. "We must discuss this with our father Brendan. If this land lies near Tir Na n'Og, perhaps these are souls who died outside of Christ's blessing."

Crosan nodded. "Perhaps they never heard of the Christ."

"A probability. We speak His name, and they do not cross themselves or pay any heed." Boyd raised his voice. "Jesus Christ."

No response. By way of demonstration, he recited the first lines of the great prayer in both Greek and Latin. Not a glimmer of recognition did the three betray. "It's obvious to me, therefore, that either they are forever lost, or this is a magnificent mission field, even more important than that of Europe."

"Perhaps too this is simply a land of common men we've never heard about before. We are awfully far west, you know."

"Either way, a matchless opportunity to bring Christ to the unsaved."

"Now how do you plan to go about that, my powerful but simple friend? There seems to be a language barrier beyond ken. We know Latin and Greek, which gives us congress with anyone in Christendom. We can speak freely with anyone of Celtic origin. Enough Danes have come down from the north, particularly into the outer islands, that a missionary to the Scandinavians could get by. But these people speak gibberish altogether. Listen to it. We know one word now. Moose. Not a good start on discussing things theological."

"I'm confident God wouldn't want that to be a bar to their salvation."

A tremendous puzzle, this.

The fog parted—one moment the marsh lay gray and shadowless, the next moment bright. Awash in sunlight, they took all the meat and organs, the hide, the head and antlers, and two of the three hunting friends back to Brendan. The third ran off.

The third man joined them soon after they arrived back in camp. How he could manage through these vine mats amazed Boyd. He handed Boyd a rope.

His cincture. He bowed and thanked the fellow.

The man in elaborate gesture said, essentially, *You tied this to a vine. You left. You returned. You went away without it. I brought it to you.*

Did Boyd simply miss finding it on that hill? He'd never know.

Reticent at first, the hunters seemed to grow more comfortable as the smiles proliferated. In his own inimitable way, Crosan told the story of their adventure, holding aloft the victorious hunter's arm at the appropriate moment. The fellows may not have known the speech, but they grasped its content well enough and grinned broadly.

Brendan bestowed gifts: an iron knife for each, a honing stone—which Boyd demonstrated—the beast's hide, and the most of its flesh.

In return, the three with flamboyant fanfare presented Brendan with the moose's skinned-out nose. They gave him to understand that the cooked nose was a great delicacy and an honor to receive.

Boyd had doubts.

Malo ordered the brothers to gather around their three new friends and called an eight-note benedictus. That seemed appropriate to Boyd. He could not speak to them of Christ's salvation and glory, but he could bless them all the same.

The three seemed mightily impressed. They sang a response of some sort and departed with their burden of gifts.

Brendan bobbed his head. "We'll strip and dry the meat while we're under way. Except the nose." He looked grim a moment, then brightened. "Into the boat, all of us, while the tide is still right."

Benedictus.

God bless us all.

35

Leviathan

"The last time we did this, we took out the bottom of the boat." Crosan leaned on the port gunwale beside his stowed oar and stared glumly out across absolutely nothing. The heavy fog hung tight around them, obliterating every detail of the sea. And yet the sail thrummed, drum taut, before a brisk following breeze. Fog and breeze together? Unworldly. The fog was warm—even more unworldly.

Boyd agreed, but he wasn't going to encourage Crosan's misery by letting him think he had an ally. He peered over the side. "We're still on green water. If we run aground soon, it's going to have to come up under us in a hurry."

Leeson shouted at him from the stern. He stepped back closer amidships.

This was not a cold fog, even though it was as excessively damp as any other. Boyd felt remarkably like stripping off his cassock and simply wearing a loincloth, like those native hunters.

Malo dropped down on a sea chest by Boyd's knee. "We've raised land six times now, and every single time the father says, 'Not yet. This isn't it.' Six times. I'm beginning to wonder."

"What? Tired of our company already? I'm offended." Crosan sat down nearby. "Look on the bright side. Seven is the magical number. Joshua seven times around the walls of Jericho? The next time's the charm."

"Promises, promises." Malo looked very weary. Boyd watched the musician's face a few moments and realized that he was seeing a rapidly aging monk. They were every one aging, of course, as mortals do. Still, somehow it didn't seem that time passed at all as they explored these seas, even though they faithfully sang the daily offices, bathed and shaved on Saturdays, and celebrated Sunday mass and holy days. If it were not for the old monks such as Malo showing the effects of it, one would never think of time. The younger men—Crosan, Mochta, Boyd himself—showed no effects at all. And Ibar, the youngest . . .

Alas, Ibar.

Crosan stood up and pointed forward. "We're breaking out."

Ahead of them, the gray curtain glowed white. Boyd balanced carefully against the center of the forward half-decking and leaned in casual repose. It would be nice to see sun again, perchance to thoroughly dry the droplets off his hair.

So soundlessly that even the nereids in the bow wave whispered softly, she glided out of the fog into dazzling sun. Boyd sucked in air, astonished.

Before them from north to south as far as eye could see stretched a shimmering green coast. A rippling, vibrant haze hung above it. It was forested as Boyd had never seen before. Trees crowded each other, trees of dark green, trees of bright green, trees of curious fronds like ferns. Breakers washed rhythmically against endless beige beaches.

Immediately before them the sea danced, sparkling in the sun. Its color amazed him. Its base colors of emerald green and deep blue mingled among each other and yet remained separate. Amid them floated a mottling of irregular patches of soft, light green in several shades. He could not get over the intensity of its hues.

"It's warm!" Crosan waved a hand randomly. "Feel the air. So warm."

"And yet damp. Not dry heat, as if you're too close to a fire." Malo inhaled deeply. "A pure aroma. Nothing you can put your finger on, but there's a clean quality to it."

Warm. Yes. *Ah, Ibar, poor lad, how you would love this!*

The last Boyd had noticed Brendan, the father was puttering around at something in the back of the boat. The father appeared now at Boyd's elbow, paused, then moved up against the half-decking.

He gazed for long, long moments at the coastline and the wonderful, vivid colors. He spread his arms out wide and closed his eyes, and he began to sing.

Boyd had never heard the music before or anything remotely like it. Brendan sang not in Latin or Greek but in Gaelic, fitting gorgeous and profound poetry to a hauntingly beautiful melody. He sang of God's majesty and justice, His integrity and love. There was not a word in his song about humans or their frailty, but then, none was needed. He sang praise upon praise.

The song ended, echoing faintly off the shimmering shore.

What glories did the father see behind those closed eyelids? Boyd did not dare ask, and he knew why. No mere spoken description could suffice to convey the wonders.

Brendan had found his Tir Na n'Og.

They drove steadily toward shore on a pleasant breeze. Suddenly the boat lurched and growled and stopped so abruptly that Boyd cracked a shipped oar when he fell against it. The sail strained to move them. Leeson stumbled across fallen brothers to the port rail to loose the sail sheet.

Crosan stretched away over the side. Suddenly he undid his cincture and stripped off his cassock. He leaped up on the rail and jumped. Boyd could lean now without being yelled at. The ship lay immobile, thoroughly grounded. He peered over the side.

Crosan stood waist deep in emerald water. "It's warm! Would that a bath were so delightful!" He ducked beneath the surface. Boyd watched his white back hover by the boat hull as Crosan explored their problem. He stood up presently and, with water cascading down his face, reached up an arm.

Boyd hauled him aboard. "So, brother, what do you find?"

"If the tide is coming in, as I suspect, we'll lift off it. It's a massive chunk of very sharp, very crumbly, chalky rock. They're all over the place, these rocks. That's what all these pale emerald patches are. Starfishes galore. And hosts of other things. Wonderful things!"

Leeson knelt more or less upside down, groping beneath the deck. "We're not shipping water. To the oars. We must navigate with care."

"Row if you like." Crosan grinned. "I for one shall draw. Boyd, join me, and you'll probably lighten the vessel enough that she'll lift off without the tide's help."

Curiosity got the best of him. Boyd jumped over the side. Warm water! Warm, warm water! He'd never felt a sea so warm. Mochta jumped. Other brothers. The boat bobbed free.

Leeson yielded to the mood of the moment and threw out the beaching lines. With the happy work song one usually sings when dragging roofing beams, they pulled the boat ashore, guiding her among those amazing hillocks in the surf.

So this was the Land of Ever Young. They had arrived. Mindlessly, Boyd helped unload their goods and pitch the tent above tide line. Without thinking about it, he helped the cook prepare their evening meal of roots and salt fish. His hands did one thing, but his thoughts soared off elsewhere.

He was anxious to meet the dead and learn firsthand what daily living is like beyond the shade. He wanted to know more about this beautiful land itself. He searched his memory for Scripture passages describing paradise. There were none. Heaven was pure promise, with no well-founded conjecture possible.

Then why did God permit them this insight?

The sun hung low behind the forest, painting the hazy air at sea in shades of peach and gold. The whole scene soothed the senses.

"The place to try moose nose," Crosan suggested.

The delicacy their northern brothers proffered still lay stashed in the coolest part of the boat, under the decking. Leeson hauled it out. They roasted it according to the gestured suggestion of one of the hunters.

Brendan licked his fingers of its juice. "Enjoy, my brothers." He passed it on.

Boyd tasted it. "One bite's enough for me. You lads savor it."

Crosan cut off a piece, tasted, and passed the piece on along with the rest of the nose. "I dare not be so selfish and greedy as to deny my brothers this pleasure."

When the nose got back to Boyd again, fifteen tiny nibbles had been eaten. When he passed it around again, it came back unchanged.

Crosan summed it. "It tastes like the glue with which you assemble a book."

They all agreed, however, that it was food given by God. They would throw away the small piece and save the rest, should God ordain that they need it. Leeson stowed it back under the deck.

As the others cleaned up the campsite, Boyd carried the cut

bit of moose nose, along with the scraps and fish bones from dinner, out to a midden apart from camp.

He stood awhile where the forest met the shore. What peace! But then, that's what one would expect here. Half of the trees that he could distinguish individually bore either flowers or fruit. That was what one would expect also, when he thought about it.

A flock of noisy birds settled in a nearby tree with broad green leaves and reddish-purple fruit. Brilliant red! Brilliant yellow! Brilliant blue! On every one of them! With their wonderful, long, flowing tails, they were nearly the length of Boyd's arm. They clattered and squawked to each other, constantly aflutter, as they dined on the fruit.

With the final "Thanks be to God" that night, the brothers retired in sheepskins that were much too warm for the climate. But that, too, would be expected in a land where no happy citizen ever suffered cold or privation.

But Boyd couldn't sleep. So far as he knew, they were the only men among all mankind to ever make this journey. Would God let them return? Why should He? Quietly Boyd shoved his sheepskin aside and crawled out onto the silken sand. In light like day from a nearly full moon, he strolled down the silver beach.

A shadow moved in beside his. He stopped and looked back. Crosan couldn't sleep either. The Laughing Monk stepped up beside him, and they walked through the near silence together.

A very flat, gentle surf, hushed, lapped against the sand with more a sigh than a whisper. The trees rustled faintly beneath the barest of night breezes.

Crosan jabbed Boyd's arm and stopped. He pointed up the beach to their midden.

A cat was dining on the scraps. The way some people treated their pets, one would think that perhaps pets as well as people might travel from death to Tir Na n'Og. But this cat was never someone's pet. Its body alone had to be six feet long. Add to that a yard-long tail and a huge head.

Boyd could not distinguish its color in the moonlight, but he clearly saw the numerous black rosette markings all over. Leopard. That's all he could think of. He'd read of leopards. *Can a leopard change its spots . . ?* He never dreamed a leopard would be so big.

The cat turned its great head toward them, regarded them in silence a few moments, then glided soundlessly up the shore into the forest.

Crosan wagged his head and whispered, "Whoa."

Boyd hurried over to the midden and bent low to examine tracks in the sand. They were definitely cat tracks, broad and lacking claw marks. He laid his hand out flat across one and barely covered it.

Crosan laughed and pointed. "The bit of moose nose is still here." He sat down in the sand, cocked his knees up, and crossed his arms over them. He kept his voice low. Boyd doubted he realized he was doing that. "Boyd, brother, what do cats eat?"

"Not moose nose, obviously. Mice. They catch birds now and then." Boyd kept his low also. "Fish."

"As does this one. If this is the Land of Ever Young, where no one dies, what does a cat eat? Especially a cat that size?"

"What are you saying?"

"Either only the people live forever and animals follow the same laws of predation and death here that they do elsewhere, or we're not where we think we are."

"Brendan misguided?" Boyd shook his head. "I heard his song."

Crosan said nothing. They wandered back down the beach to camp.

The next day, Brendan organized work details, some to bring in wood, some to gather fruit, some to prepare cordage and supplies for the return trip.

Boyd, with Crosan and Malo, formed one of the fruit-gathering parties. They brought with them the huge basket they had been given on the Island of Strong Men. Boyd carried a coil of rope on his shoulder. He was not about to trust his own weight to a rope, but maybe Crosan or Malo would want to climb a tree. Crosan took a javelin along, the longest they had, to knock fruit out of lower limbs, because oars were too heavy to haul through the forest.

They fought their way inland through the dense thickets near the shore. The forest opened up then. Great looping vines hung down. A few spindly trees and bushes grew here and there, and lovely ferns, but the forest floor was surprisingly clear of vegetation. The vegetation all grew in the crowded canopy above their heads, a mat of fronds and leaves as opaque as any tent canvas. The party had only to weave among the tree trunks to go just about anywhere they wished.

A cacophony of birds twittered and called, but Boyd could see nothing moving. Nothing at all.

Malo asked, "We're supposed to be looking up, seeking fruit. What are you two constantly looking for on the ground?"

Boyd and Crosan glanced at each other. Crosan shrugged. "Wondering what kind of tracks are about."

Malo grunted. "The fruit is all a hundred feet above our heads. We'd do better to work along the shore."

"What's over that way?" And in the direction Crosan pointed, the vegetation did seem thicker on the ground.

The earth became spongy beneath their feet, and then soggy. The forest growth opened up overhead as it closed in here at ground level. They pushed through swamp to a stagnant pond.

A tree had fallen across the pool. Its branches, now dead and devoid of leaves, began at least seventy-five feet from the root mass. Crosan hopped up onto the fallen log and walked out on it. He stood there, the javelin lying loosely on his shoulder, and looked about. "Nothing here to eat. Not even cattails." He peered down. "I don't even see any fish."

"Then we'd best head back to the coast and work along the top of the beach." Malo started to turn away.

Crosan screamed. A huge monster came roaring straight up out of the pool hard beside the log. Silver water splashed up with it and fell all around it. Its maw was massive—long, narrow jaws opened wide enough to swallow a pig! It slammed against the log as it fell back into the water. The log shivered and tossed Crosan into the pond on the far side.

The monster churned the water dreadfully. Silt and froth boiled up. Boyd glimpsed a row of huge plates down the creature's back.

Almost instantly, Crosan scrambled back onto the log. Without taking time to regain his feet he came scurrying back along the log-top on his hands and toes, four-legged.

Boyd ran toward him, sloshing clumsily through the miry water.

The monster reared out of the water again. Its long snout gaped and slammed shut. Crosan screamed again, reaching out frantically. Boyd grabbed his hand and pulled. The monster fell away with a mouthful of Crosan's torn hem.

Boyd yanked Crosan off the log even as he turned away. Dragging the Laughing Monk through mud and swamp water, he began to run. He kept running over the spongy ground until they reached solid land again, with Malo at his heels.

"Up here!" Boyd led the way. A tree had tried to fall in the dense forest, but it didn't quite reach the ground. Its crown lodged among others. This log slanted upward at an angle, not fully prostrate among its vertical brethren. Boyd only then let go of Crosan as he scrambled up the tilted log and finally, straddling it as if it were a pony, paused to catch his breath.

Gulping air, Crosan lay along the log, his arms and legs adangle.

"Leviathan. The book of Job, the last portion." Boyd started with *extrahere poteris leviathan hamo* and recited to *omni sublime videt, ipse est rex super universos filios superbiae.*

"King over all the children of pride indeed." Malo sat on the log, hung both legs over one side, and rubbed his face. "'Any hope of overcoming him is vain.'"

Boyd shuddered, translating in part. "'Who can open the doors of his face with those terrible teeth all around? . . . Rows of scales . . . . When he rears himself up, the mighty are afraid.'"

"Amen and amen." Crosan seemed finally to be getting his breath back.

Boyd concluded, "'He makes the deep boil like a pot. On earth there is nothing like him.' I always assumed leviathan was some sort of sea monster. No. It's that beast right there."

Crosan sat up and swung a leg over, so that he perched like Malo. "The thing was—what?—twenty feet long?"

"At least. Long dragonlike tail. Great platelike scales."

"A fabulous monster described in Scripture turns out actually to exist in Tir Na n'Og." Crosan shook his head. "That thing wasn't out to greet me and inquire about my day. I looked right down its throat. And the teeth—brothers, I very nearly died just now by the mouth and force of a scriptural creature. I don't know where we are, or why we're here, or how we'll get back. But I know for certain—sure and we're not in the Land of Ever Young."

36

Home

"There's the midden, a quarter of a mile down the beach there." Boyd heaved a sigh of relief. He left the dense growth of the forest edge behind and stepped out onto smooth sand.

Malo staggered and kicked free of a vine around his ankle. "I was beginning to think we were going to spend the rest of our lives wandering lost in that forest."

"Rest of our lives? Remember," Crosan crooned, "if this be Tir Na n'Og, we'd have the rest of forever to wander around lost in."

"True." Malo looked back. In the dying sunlight of late day, the forest was turning black. Night calls were already replacing day chatter high in those mysterious leafy realms. Down the beach at least half a mile, the black hulk of their boat rested, and not far from it was the little orange dot of a fire.

Boyd began a five-tone gratia, and both men joined him in the prayer of thanksgiving. He took off walking, not in a hurry. "We lost the basket. We lost the javelin. We return empty-handed. So what and how much do we tell Brendan?"

"I hear what you're saying." Crosan fell in beside Boyd's right elbow. "He's confident we've reached Hi Brasil. We're certain we've not. Do we want to destroy his fond confidence?"

"Actually, he could be right." Malo seemed to be moving slower than usual. "Nothing in Scripture says paradise has to be a place with no danger and no ugliness. That's a notion on man's part, a tradition. Not a word from God."

"Come on, Malo!" Crosan exploded. "Land of Ever Young. No death. You didn't look down that maw, or you wouldn't say that!"

"Who died?"

"Nobody did, but—" Crosan hesitated, than burst out with a most uncharacteristic expletive "—I almost did."

"Almost. I repeat—who died?"

298

"Paradise, then," Boyd mused, "would offer men potentially fatal excitement and adventure, just as the world does. Is that it?"

Malo nodded. "I believe man thrives on excitement. Without an element of danger, of competition, perhaps of death itself, paradise would soon lose its appeal."

Crosan growled, "Teeth like skinning knives, a maw deep as a dry well. Not that much excitement!"

"Would you be happy with less?"

"I believe we have company." Boyd pointed into the distance toward camp.

Brothers in cassocks were moving about. But others moved about as well, two-legged forms with huge heads.

Boyd walked a bit livelier. The leviathan that rose up against Crosan was exactly the creature described in Scripture. Since Boyd had never heard of a living creature matching that description—and he had committed the book of Job to memory many years ago—Malo made sense. Was perhaps, like leviathan, the behemoth of Job a similar creature found in paradise to titillate man's fancy and make his forever more appealing? Speculation.

Brendan was entertaining guests. Four men and three women sat around the fire on the beach, regal in finery and smiling happily. They looked somewhat like those hunters on the northern shore. They had warm brown skin and uniquely set eyes made to look even larger by the use of black paint. Their noses protruded prominently, eagle-beaked. They all wore elaborate head ornaments braided into long black hair.

A man with a great spray of long green feathers in his hair appeared to be the leader. The dying light of day made the fellow appear all the more impressive, as shadows played across his commanding face and figure. He wore naught but a loincloth, woven sandals, and a spotted leopard skin. The skin was arranged as a cape, with the head at the bottom. The tail dropped down the back, and the hind legs draped over the shoulders to the front. Monstrous claws graced the four skinned feet.

Crosan poked Boyd and muttered, "Our cat."

"Indeed it is."

The lady beside him wore a wrap of softest white fabric, embroidered with a brilliant border. Great gold rings hung from her ears and nose. Her face was most artfully and carefully painted with red-and-white lines and figures. Over her shoulders lay a magnificent cape made of the feathers of brilliant birds. The others with them were dressed similarly, though not quite as ornately.

They obviously employed servants or slaves. A number of men dressed only in loincloths gathered around a separate fire farther down the beach.

Brendan boomed, "There you are! We were about to send out seekers. These people have men among them with a sense of smell so delicate they can track human beings."

"We could have used them." Boyd tossed the rope aside. "But we are here. Can we help you, father?"

"No. The day's tasks are completed. We'll be going with these people directly after matins tomorrow morning. By the grace of God, we'll sing prime in the city of the blessed." Boyd waved a hand toward a young man sitting somewhat apart from the dignitaries. "This fellow knows a rough and ready version of Gaelic. He claims his father was a sojourner from another land who spoke the language I am using now. Praise God! We have decided after discussing him that possibly the man was one of the first of Erin's blue martyrs, one of those who set out to sea to heed the will of God and subsequently died in God's service."

"Whoa." Crosan frowned. "Men and women have children in the Land of Ever Young?"

Brendan's expression looked as if Crosan should never have questioned such a thing.

"And he speaks both the native tongue here and ours?"

"In Tir Na n'Og are people of many nations. But always, God provides a means of congress between them."

Boyd looked at Crosan. Crosan appeared unconvinced. But then, Crosan was the one who had looked at death down the throat of leviathan.

They left camp directly after matins next morning, following the dignitaries. The dignitaries apparently were above walking. They rode in litters on the shoulders of their slaves. Boyd had heard tales of wealthy men and women doing that in the old Roman Empire. They all walked south down the beach and ducked into the forest along a well-used trail.

They passed clearings and extensive cultivated fields of strange, lanceolate-leaved plants with decorative tassels at the top. They passed water-filled ditches and canals. Numerous huts and tightly bunched groups of hovels lined the road. The natives, all people with large noses and warm skin like their dignitaries, bowed as the litters passed by, then stood gawking at the brothers of God who followed after.

Boyd saw no cattle, no horses or ponies, no sheep, no hogs. Interesting brown-and-black birds with fantails strutted here and there, birds larger than geese. Dogs barked.

The road broadened out into a marvelously elegant way. With an immense colony of houses clustered at its feet, a huge cubical building reared up ahead of them. It was more a mountain than a thing of man. It had a flat top and terraced sides.

Other such buildings, each made of cut-stone blocks, stood at the ends of radiating roads much like this one.

Crosan was gaping, and Boyd realized he gaped too. Crosan wagged his head. "I listened to brothers tell tales of their visit to Rome. It must be like this."

"Not as elegant as this." Beyond the great open park with its stupendous buildings, Boyd could see glimpses of an intricate tangle of hovels. He nodded toward one. "It appears that the common people and the gods live far apart in paradise, as in the world."

Crosan smiled. "Don't you remember, brother? 'In my Father's house are many mansions. I go to prepare a place for you.' If this indeed be Hi Brasil, and if you see people living in something other than mansions, those people did not die in Christ. But then why are they here?"

"You're beginning to believe we reached the Land after all."

"I'm reconsidering my position."

Boyd did not see a fleck of metal anywhere, but these residents of paradise worked stone as if it were clay. He himself had seen the ogham stones of Erin—he could read them, in fact. But these went ages beyond ogham. Elaborate symbols and representations graced a huge, carved, stone wheel in the center of the park. Others, such as heads of animals and demons, decorated the roof-timbers of the buildings all about the central park. Everywhere people wore that soft white fabric—as capes, as women's draped garments, or as loincloths.

Crosan stood behind Brendan as other dignitaries in leopard skins approached to greet them. He muttered, "I remember hearing from a former druid that there was a time in Erin before anyone worked metal. Stone implements and decoration only. Could these people have come from that time?"

"And still exist today, no longer touched by time? Here forever, but limited to stone? Possible."

Not just possible. Probable.

It was all adding up. And yet, none of this was the way Boyd envisioned paradise to be. Was that bad? He had nothing upon which to base suppositions. Of course the reality could differ strongly from the fantasy.

Crosan stepped forward to talk to the fellow in the leopard skin as the young man translated. Crosan did obeisance to him and stepped back. He muttered an aside to Boyd, "Just act delighted."

That wasn't hard. Boyd was indeed delighted. He was introduced, he did obeisance, he returned to his place.

The group was conducted to a speaking platform in the middle of the open parkland. The dais was built of beautifully dressed stone, flat-topped and broad enough that all fifteen brothers could stand or sit comfortably without wondering if someone would make a misstep and fall off. The grass all around the platform lay short and green and well trimmed, but where were the grazing animals who would keep this meadowland so neat?

Brendan commenced the office of nones. Boyd paid half the attention he ought to a service of worship, for the gathering crowd around them stole his eye and ear.

They sang a few extra psalms, since the people standing about seemed to like the music. A group of their own musicians climbed the stone staircase to the platform and played an interesting melody on flutes, drums, and seashell horns. They retired. Next an old man in leopard dress told a story. The translator put it into Gaelic.

"I was tending my nets near the Beach of Guavas when a magical boat appeared out of the mist offshore. It was bigger than any common craft, a boat of gods. It paused. It surveyed the scene. It shrank itself to man's size and moved forward with attendants preceding it and singing. These men came forth onto the beach. They sang and very humbly awaited the arrival of our prince. They did not presume upon the land or upon the people. They demonstrated their own royal blood in their song and robes. They declare they are from the supreme God. We welcome these people from God."

Brendan stood up presently. With the translator at his side, he carefully preached the gospel. All men commit evil and therefore are unworthy to enter paradise. Jesus came to save those people. Men will fall into evil and error again. And then, one day Jesus will return with glory to right any wrongs and fetch the blessed to the eternal city.

Crosan murmured, "Isn't he preaching to the converted?"

"Aye, but perhaps he's warning them about falling away during the Millennium. That's important, I should think, particularly if this really be the promised land."

"True. True. His coming again will be as momentous as His first coming."

"Besides," Boyd added, "if these people died before metal came into use, they wouldn't have heard about the Christ. This may all be news to them."

By then it was time for vespers, or close enough. They sang the vespers in five-tone and the final psalm in eight-tone. They finished up with a full-throated Gloria Patri that rattled the stones and put smiles on the faces of the gargoyles.

A feast followed, composed almost exclusively of vegetables and delicious flat cakes. They slept on soft white beds and with great ceremony were dismissed the next morning.

The young fellow acted as guide to return them to the coast. Crosan engaged the lad in conversation along the route, but Boyd was fascinated by the farms and the farming. In one patch, a woman was hoeing her crop with a tool just like that Boyd grew up using near Kildare. He stopped and looked at her crop more closely. Long, leathery leaves rose out of the central stalk and broke over gracefully. The tassel at the very top was really quite intricate. The fruit of the plant, ears wrapped closely in leaves, most unlike ears of grain, sprouted here and there along the stalk.

The party had stopped. The young man came over and spoke to the woman, apparently introducing her to the man of God. She hastily fell to her face in a deep obeisance. That bothered Boyd immensely. Only One deserves reverence of that sort.

The fellow pulled up a plant by the roots and handed it to Boyd. "The corn is not quite ripe yet. A bit early. It's not ready for seed yet, but it's tasty enough. See? The juice is in the head." He pulled off an ear, stripped the leathery leaves from it, and pressed his thumbnail on one of the grains. White milk spurted. The fellow trotted off to lead the party onward.

Boyd thanked the shy woman, blessed her, and ran after them, nibbling his corn. Delicious.

They readied the boat next morning. They shoved it out beyond tide line and laded their sheepskins, tenting, and duffle. A retinue from the prince appeared just before high tide. With baskets of corn and fruit, strange bundles, ducks and geese with bound legs, and a number of birds, they burdened the men of God with welcome gifts.

Boyd stood aside and watched the lading. Other shoulders than his carried the burdens for once. He liked that.

Beside him, Crosan asked the young man, "What is the meaning of the leopard skins your princes wear?"

"Leopard." The fellow frowned. He brightened. "The great cat. Jaguar. *Balam.* It represents kingly power."

Crosan nodded sagely. "Kingly power," he muttered in Latin, "munching fish bones at the midden."

"Kingly intelligence," Boyd reminded him. "He passed up the moose nose."

Crosan laughed aloud and switched back to Gaelic. "And a horrid monster the length of three men, and a mouth this wide." He arranged his arms in the shape of that open maw. "It lives in water."

"Crocodile. Or alligator. We have both. Be careful when walking near quiet streams and pools and certain places along the coast such as estuaries. They are dangerous. Extremely dangerous."

"I don't doubt it for a moment." Crosan pressed his lips together, grim.

The young man was beaming. "I rejoice in this opportunity few have ever enjoyed—to accompany and serve men of God. We look forward to the coming of the Son, the God-Made-Man, when He shall return on a boat as you have come."

Boyd looked at Crosan. "The Son of God will return in a boat?"

"And he will have pale skin and fair hair such as yours. We look forward to greeting Him as royalty."

Boyd shook his head. "No. He'll come again from the heavens in glory. Out of the clouds. The part about the boat isn't right."

Crosan held up a hand. "Does it matter? When Jesus returns, everyone will see Him and know Him. Boat, no boat, blond hair, dark hair, what's the difference?"

Boyd shrugged it off. Crosan had a point. And besides, Brendan was ready to go. The last of the gift bearers sloshed back to shore.

The young man had a better memory than Boyd could ever hope for. The fellow had heard their names only once, and yet he addressed each monk correctly by name, all fifteen of them, as he sent them off. "Happy are they that live in your house!" he told each of them. "They shall praise you from generation to generation."

For once, Boyd and Mochta didn't have to wade into the surf to push them off. They climbed into the boat with everyone else, and the prince's servants pushed them off.

They dipped two oars to swing her around, Leeson raised sail to catch the offshore breeze, and they were on their way out into the warm, wonderful emerald sea.

"On our way where?" Boyd asked Brendan.

"Another of my premonitions, but the prince confirmed it. They send trading canoes all up and down the coast here and over to islands to the east. He seems to think, and I believe I have also received it of God, that strong current with prevailing winds will take us directly to Erin in forty days. Well, actually, not directly. We'll make one stop at the prince's behest, an Island of Delights east of here. Then home."

"Straight through to Erin?"

"According to the prince, who apparently also receives premonitions, I shall die soon after my return." Brendan smiled. "I feel old already." He strolled aft to talk to Leeson.

Boyd looked at Crosan.

Crosan shook his head. "It can't be. It took us much too long to sail to this place. A current straight home?"

"I don't know. Remember Barrind claimed his son made it back from his journeys to Tir Na n'Og in no time at all." Home. A quiet farm. No more bobbing, or fighting the storms, or getting cold and wet as high winds whip the spindrift off the wave-tops and into your face. Cow smells, and gathering eggs, and sowing barley. The familiar, the commonplace, the quiet. Boyd was not sure he agreed with Malo's contention that a true paradise required danger and excitement. He'd had quite enough of excitement.

"Know what I didn't do?" Crosan leaned his elbows on the half-decking. "I should have done some magic tricks on that platform in the holy city."

"Born a jester." Boyd chuckled. "Your court is the emerald sea, your audience the people of forever."

"For a big fellow, you're fairly poetic."

"And the jester leaves the sea to return to the monastery."

"The Laughing Monk." Crosan snorted. "Who am I fooling? I like this sailing a lot better than monastic life. Not so many temptations."

"You mean women."

"Vows of chastity. God gave Paul his thorn in the flesh, and He gave me mine."

Boyd had made that vow—and kept it too. He had given his service to God and given it with purity and honor. Now it was time to move on. He wanted to go home.

37

Return

On Scattery Island a fierce monster dwelt, the Cata, preventing anyone from possessing the land. One day near the time of his departure, Senan was led by an angel to the summit of Mount Tese. The angel showed him Scattery, promising that he and his spiritual heirs would possess it. The only problem—and a small problem it be for so devout a man as Senan—was that monster. Senan defeated the monster and founded a monastery. But there are monsters, and there are monsters. Identifying the true root of all men's woes, Senan declared that no woman should ever set foot on the island.

Now Cannera, an equally devout and equally venerable nun, took it upon herself that she would die on Scattery so as to be availed of the holy offices there. An angel brought her across the water, but Senan on the shore met her with an upraised palm.

"You cannot proceed," he declared.

"If Christ will receive my soul, why should you reject my body?" she retorted.

"That is true, but for all that, I'll not allow you to come here. Turn back. Do not plague us."

"Plague you! I am pure in soul."

"You may be pure in soul, but you're a woman."

"I will die before I'll go back!" And Cannera made her point thoroughly and permanently by dropping over on the spot. She received extreme unction and was buried on the island, the only woman there. Some monsters are not so easily defeated.

Angelica smiled. She loved that story. Ronan the Sad Monk told it to her at Easter, and she must have related it a dozen times since then. "No man is a match for a good woman," he said, and she almost believed him.

She reached the top of the hill behind Fanchea's farm and

paused to catch her breath. From here she could just see the waters of Brandon Bay and in the far distance the mouth of the Shannon. Somewhere in the mouth of the Shannon—Ronan said about thirty miles from here by water—lay Scattery with its thriving all-male monastery and the grave of a determined woman.

Brandon Bay. *How are Boyd, and Crosan, and dear old Brendan himself getting on?* she wondered.

Troll the brindled dog yapped and bounded ahead. She paused to wait. Moments later, cows bawled impatiently in the woodland beyond the hillcrest. Here they came, their milk bags and dewlaps flapping wildly, and Troll nipping at their heels. She drew her cloak closer and flicked her hazel switch, making it sing. The cows jogged down the path toward home.

Well, well. Angelica saw that Anne had finally decided to get up. The first of the cows was jogging to the gate as Anne came out of it, her cloak wrapped close around her. That red hair glowed in the early morning sun.

Angelica wondered if Maura had a hand in rousting Anne out of bed today. Quite possibly. Anne complained that the old woman pestered her. So, in Anne's presence, Fanchea asked Maura not to, knowing full well the old woman would do so anyway. No doubt Fanchea didn't mind that a bit. Anne had a habit of shirking work while never missing meals.

"Top of the morning, Anne. Going out?"

"Top of the morning. Aye, I told Fanchea, and I'll tell you. I'm leaving." "For where? Cashel?" Angelica paused to rub Troll's bony head and give him a few words of praise. She stood erect.

"Aye. I should've done this months ago."

You were making a play for Ronan. What thwarted you? But Angelica didn't ask that. Rather, "May I ask? I know this was your plan when first you arrived. Why did you remain here so long?"

The girl looked at her a moment, apparently weighing possible answers. "I thought I'd wait for Ronan to return. But I doubt he's going to, or he would by now. Besides, the way he suddenly disappeared like that right after Easter, you wonder if maybe something's very wrong with him, you know? Here today and—*poof*—gone. And I was thinking Boyd might come back, but he won't. Winter storms—they won't sail any more this year."

"They're monks. You were waiting for monks?"

Anne smiled coldly. "Better than no one at all."

Angelica would not grace that with a reply. Shame on a girl with that kind of attitude. On the other hand, she ought to argue the Lord's position of chastity and attention to vows. She couldn't do that if the child wandered off. "You've inquired as to the way?"

"I'll find my way well enough."

"Anne, robbers abound."

"I'll take my chances."

Angelica pressed her lips together. Here was a grown woman—well, nearly grown—who knew her mind. Angelica would say no more. "If you're leaving, Godspeed and His blessings."

Anne looked at her curiously. She murmured, "Thank you," turned, and walked off southbound.

No embrace, no blessing in return.

Angelica walked in through the gate.

Perched on her stool, Maura was already milking the spotted cow, her head pressed into the cow's flank. She cackled victoriously. "Did she tell you?"

"She told me."

"Good riddance, I say."

"You would."

The spotted cow was the easy milker, the only cow they had who just stood there placidly and let her milk down. Too bad she yielded so little.

Fanchea was not inside the house and had not been visible during Angelica's foray out for the cows. Fanchea disappeared a lot lately. Her absences left the weight of responsibility on Angelica's shoulders. Angelica didn't mind working for her keep, but . . . She lifted the rope off the gate post and hung her cloak there.

She walked after the red cow. Maura wasn't up to milking the red cow. Hilla wasn't up to anything anymore. How Angelica hated milking the red cow. She would recommend it as the first to go if they had to butcher. Daily she vowed that—and daily rued the loss of the black cow. She still wasn't certain Anne didn't somehow have a hand in that.

The red cow saw her coming and trotted behind the house, knocking over the butter churn in her haste. Angelica cornered her against the spare split-rails and tossed the rope over her horns. She was able to move in close enough then to slip the other end of the rope through the ring in the cow's nose. Subdued, the fractious beast followed her out into the compound. Angelica didn't dare milk the creature back here in these close quarters— she was too likely to be stepped on or kicked.

She stopped at the door of the house for a scoop of barley and dumped it in the wooden box by the wall. As the cow busied herself lapping up the grain, Angelica set the bucket and stool, pressed her head into the beast's warm, smooth flank, and got started.

She had to coax a few minutes before the recalcitrant creature would let down her milk. Finally it came, first in a thin, pallid squirt, then in a full, rich stream. Angelica began a crooning song. If the cow would just remain still for a few—

The cow snapped her tail. Angelica grabbed up the bucket as the cow bolted forward. A cloven hoof tipped her and her stool and her bucket. Warm, sticky milk splashed in her face and down the front of her as she fell back into the mud.

"Maura, stop her!" But Angelica knew Maura wouldn't stop her. Maura didn't help catch the cow, didn't help with the barley scoop or the bucket or anything, didn't help by holding the cow for milking, and Maura wasn't going to reach out and grab the rope as it went by either. Maura wasn't going to do a thing except taste the mead to see if it was ready.

Sobbing, Angelica flung her empty bucket across the yard, suddenly enraged at life. Or maybe the rage wasn't so sudden. She didn't want the responsibility of these two old women. She wanted to forget this horrid place. She wanted to go to Cashel. Or sail away forever. Or just walk out. Anne had the right idea, after all.

Maura began scolding, explaining what Angelica did wrong to make the cow run like that.

"Oh, quiet!" It felt so good to scream that! "Just be quiet!" She lurched to her feet, muddy and milk-soaked and crying so hard she couldn't see.

Powerful arms grabbed her and pulled her in. She started to struggle until she realized Maura wasn't this strong.

It was Ronan. He was back.

His tonsure was grown in and already long enough that he could wear his hair Roman style. He had abandoned the monk's robe and cincture in favor of a plain tunic and cloak in one color. He asked no questions. He offered no advice and no comment. He smiled and drew her in tight.

She melted against him, buried her face against his shoulder, and let herself cry. Only after several minutes had passed and the first intense wave of weeping had subsided did she notice that he was holding the red cow's nose rope.

Maura told him in shocked dismay how disrespectfully Angelica had just addressed her. Maura openly and extensively questioned his integrity for having left so abruptly. And now Maura jabbered on, explaining how it was all his fault their farm was falling on hard times because he wasn't here to do his God-given duty of helping out, because heaven knew Anne didn't lift a finger, and Fanchea was certainly incompetent half the time, and the cattle were gone wild with that miserable brindled dog biting at them. If only Ronan had not—

"Maura!" Ronan's voice stopped her in mid-sentence. "Here." He handed her the rope. "You and Hilla figure out how to get her milked. We must go down to the shore. Good-day, grandam."

Maura hesitated, stunned, then started in again.

But by then Ronan was leading Angelica quickly out the gate. He grabbed her cloak off the post for her as they passed.

A few stray sobs kept catching her unawares. Trotting along at his side as he strode down the track, though, helped her bring herself back together.

She took a deep breath. "Why must we go down to the shore?"

"To get my things. I don't want to just leave them there."

Troll frolicked along the trail, then jogged off to test new smells and sights beneath bushes along the way.

"Your things." She ought to make light conversation and work her way carefully up to the important topics. "Why did you just disappear like that?!" She blurted it out. She didn't want to ask. But she had to know.

"Perhaps we'll discuss it sometime."

"No." She stopped in the muddy track and held his arm to stop him. "Let's talk about it now. You celebrated the Easter mass on Sunday, and Monday morning you disappeared. Not a word, not a hint, not anything. Half a year later, here you are, showing up as if nothing happened. Why? What's going on?"

"I was ashamed and embarrassed. And guilt-ridden."

"Ashamed?" She stared at him. Of any answer she might have expected, that was not one. "But . . . you did a very fine job. We have no father in this area. We needed your services, and you provided them. That's to be commended. Ashamed?"

"Not before you. Before God. It's a long story."

"Ronan . . ."

He took her hand and led off down the trail. "Indulge me, pray thee. This is very hard for me."

Her head filled to overflowing with questions. He had asked her indulgence. Very well. She walked beside him in silence.

The dog put up a hare, but he abandoned the chase after a few hundred yards.

They ambled in that way all the distance of the familiar path down to the shore of Brandon Bay. Here was the smooth, open strand where Brendan built his boat. Fanchea had described it all in detail one afternoon when they were crabbing. And then Fanchea had pointed to the crumbly old rock wall. That, she said, was the first place ever she spoke to Ronan, and he looked sad even then.

Deliberately Angelica crossed to the wall, sat down there, and leaned her back against it.

He hesitated, then sat beside her.

From here she could hear the gentle lap of water up into the drowned mouth of the creek. Brendan and Boyd and Crosan sailed from here. And that silly fight back in the marsh—Ronan and Crosan. Did he even remember it? It seemed ages ago. And she could hear from very far off, out on the rocks in the bay, seals barking.

Ronan must have heard them also. "The seals off the Skelligs sound like mourners keening. They say the seals there shape-shift—take human form. Because of the seal in them, they're never content ashore, and because of the human in them, they're never content at sea."

She looked at his profile. He seemed to love dismal, depressing things, the story of Cannera on Scattery notwithstanding. Perhaps to him that one was depressing too—a woman winning. She said nothing.

Ronan drew up his knees and draped those strong arms over them. "I grew up with scholarly parents. They loved books—Scripture. I knew more about Scripture when I was small than some bishops do. When plague took my mother, I decided to live on an island, where disease is rare. Skellig Michael was the most exciting place to be—where the most exciting things were happening. So I rowed out there and begged them into letting me stay, and I was happy."

She could not picture him happy, but she accepted his word. She said nothing.

He flapped a hand helplessly. "Then the plague hit there too. I was . . . I couldn't stand it. They sent me ashore to help the mainlanders, and I never went back. I wandered awhile and ended up here—and met you."

"And you're ashamed because you broke your vows and left the monastery."

"I'm ashamed because I never took vows in the first place. When they examined me on Skellig, I could answer the theological questions just fine. So I made up a fictitious monastery and claimed holy orders. Otherwise I would have had to come back to the mainland."

She pondered the ramifications. This cast a whole new light on things.

He continued. "Anyway, after I celebrated Easter here, providing Eucharist and everything, I felt so guilty I couldn't think straight. That's a profoundly serious thing, wrongly using the holy sacraments. I confessed my sins to God and begged His mercy. And then I knew I had to go home to Skellig. To go home and start over. It took me two weeks to return to the coast, another two weeks to just look at the islands, and finally then I got the strength and nerve to return."

"And you've been there ever since?"

"Not really. I confessed to the abbot there. It's not home anymore somehow. We talked a long time. He's not the same fellow who was there when I was. I've been doing penance, some there and some on the mainland. And now I'm back. It's autumn, harvest time. You need help."

"Am I part of your penance?"

"Yes." He smiled at her. "A most welcome part."

She smiled too. She was glad he said that. She would have hated to be forced labor, even to relieve someone's soul.

He gazed off at blue sky and broken clouds. "It was months before I learned Crosan sailed with Brendan. I thought he was here, with you. The last day before he left . . . ."

"That fight?"

"Then. Why didn't you speak up?"

"And say what?"

"Tell Crosan to go as fate dictated."

She mulled her memories, trying to find an answer—trying indeed to figure out what he was asking. "Tell Crosan to go?" She shook her head. "I had no idea whether Crosan was supposed to go or stay. I was afraid. I'm not privy to the voice of God as you people are. I was afraid I'd say the wrong thing."

"So you didn't declare a preference?"

"Preference for what?"

"Between Crosan and me."

Aha! So that was how the wind lay. "I thought you both were in holy orders. I wasn't about to suggest . . .no." She shook her head to clear it of the very thought. "No. And when you learned Crosan had left, you stayed here to protect me from Mac Larkin."

"I stayed here to be near you. Mac Larkin was the excuse."

She looked at him carefully, trying to read those sad, sad eyes. The thought intrigued her nonetheless. "Mac Larkin rode off to the east along the north shore of the Dingle and hasn't been seen since. He's not an excuse anymore."

"I inquired about. He's been warring up north. A mercenary. They were in the area, and some ri needed the muscle. He's still in Erin. You're not safe."

"In nearly a year? He'd be back looking if he hadn't found someone better." She pondered this latest development. "So

314

you're actually free to marry or do anything you want." *So if Anne only knew, she could really set her hooks in you—not that she let vows be a deterrent anyway.*

"Anything I want."

"What do you want?"

"I've been thinking a lot about that."

Troll came jogging in, his sloppy mouth lax, his tongue hanging out, and curled up beside Angelica.

And then the thing she least expected, the thing she least wanted, hove into view on the hillside track, headed this way.

Anne.

38

Truly Home

Boyd hung off the starboard gunwale up near the forward half-decking. He was pulling the boat out of trim a little, and he didn't care whether the boat was in trim or not. "Blasketts. Those are the Blasketts!"

Leeson wasn't yelling at him because the navigator was crowded up in the bow here with everyone else.

"See?" Crosan crowed. "I told you we were looking at the back side of the Skelligs! No mistaking those little pointy islands. Sure and it's Erin! We're home, lads!"

"And dead ahead there is Brandon Mountain!" Boyd chanced to glance down by his elbow at Brendan.

The following breeze, the breeze that so beautifully filled their sail, was blowing the venerable father's gray, unruly hair forward into his eyes, as it did so much of the time. An expression of totally serene, absolute contentment made his face virtually glow.

And tears streamed down his cheeks.

They angled past Brandon Mountain to hook around and head down into the bay. Boyd was certain Brendan or Leeson would call them to the oars any minute as they swung around the mountain and turned to the southeast against the wind.

But once they turned the point, they found a local sea breeze sweeping south down the bay and up the creek. By the grace of God, they would come home under full sail.

Pity, Boyd thought, *that they could not somehow send word ahead to Clonfert announcing their return, so that people could be waiting for them on the shore.* But then, he himself had not anticipated they would raise Erin this soon. Amazing! After all that long journey out, they returned on favorable winds and currents in less than five weeks.

No wonder they doubted Crosan, the watch, when he announced, "Land home!"

Brendan said, "Straight home." Straight home it was.

Boyd saw movement and glanced over his shoulder. Crosan had left the happy throng at the bow. The Laughing Monk sprawled casually against the aft half-decking all alone, staring at the mountain beside them.

Boyd wandered back and joined him. The boat heeled a little, so he gave the untended, tethered tiller a nudge with his foot.

Crosan looked at him. "Your stint is done. Going to leave the order and go farming, eh?"

"I suppose. Have to find a farm. Remember that one with the rooster and the dogs, out on that island?"

"Where you and the boat were both nearly eaten alive? Could I ever forget?"

Boyd was certainly never going to forget. "And you?"

"The old man needs someone to write up his adventure—someone who went along on it, I'd guess. He started talking to me about it a couple days ago. I think he wants me for the job."

"Oh?" Boyd grunted. "He didn't mention any amanuensis to me. He was talking to me about sailing to Wales. He wants to see Gilda again before he dies, I think. Gilda the Wise, you know?"

"Gilda! She has to be older than dirt. She was a chum of Brigid's—Brigid of Kildare—and Brigid is old enough to be a tree."

Boyd shrugged. "That's what he said."

They lapsed into silence, and Boyd welcomed it. He should be content now, as happy as Brendan. They dreamed, they achieved, they returned. Praise God for His mercies! So why did he feel so restless and uncertain?

Mochta called, "We've a greeting party."

Who would know they were coming? But then, Brendan was not the only person in the church to enjoy second sight. Possibly someone had a premonition about their arrival. Two women and a man stood on the shore watching them. A familiar brindled dog scurried about.

Boyd followed Crosan forward. "Can you see who?"

Crosan's stood silent a moment. "Angelica," he answered quietly.

"And that Anne. I can see the red hair." Boyd liked the girl well enough. She didn't seem particularly industrious, but he could say that about a lot of monks too. She certainly was open and pleasant.

Crosan spoke a fairly innocuous word of frustration and sighed. "I wanted to get back to Clonfert without talking to her.

What lay behind that? Boyd searched his face briefly and saw nothing. But then, Boyd was terrible at reading people well or understanding meanings and motivations. He knew such things existed, but he was one for hearing the words spoken and accepting them.

Boyd and Mochta poised, waiting. The boat rode a shallow, welcoming surf into brown water. Its bottom scudded, a naval sigh of relief.

They had come full circle.

Boyd and Mochta leaped over the side. Cold water pierced instantly through Boyd's woolen garment and chilled his toes. He thought briefly, happily, of the warm, warm water of that distant land. Crosan threw him a tow line, and he drew the vessel farther up onto the strand.

The observers ashore crossed themselves and clapped and cheered. They were only three, but they sounded like a crowd. Boyd just barely recognized the man in the middle. Ronan, no longer in a tonsure.

The brindled dog snarled and made a feinting dart at Boyd's leg. He kicked at it as Angelica, the fair-haired beauty, called the dog away.

Angelica was openly weeping, and her face suggested they were tears of happiness. Boyd would not guess that a homecoming of near strangers would be so emotionally vivid. He glanced at Crosan. The monk glared at Ronan, but it was not a glare of fury. It appeared more frustration.

The brothers came tumbling off the boat and gathered in the semicircular choir formation. Brendan commenced an office of thanksgiving. Boyd entered eagerly in. Thanks be to God. Yes!

The women and Ronan sat down a way apart and simply listened. The dog gave up worrying the people it didn't like and instead lay down near Brendan.

A few nasty details clouded Boyd's pleasure. Anne here had arrived in Erin with Ibar. Boyd would have to tell her about her erstwhile traveling companion. He dreaded that. Crosan had just been crushed, no doubt, with Ronan's sitting beside Angelica in definitely non-monastic attire. Boyd hated to see the Laughing Monk kicked so cruelly by fate.

They completed the service with the One Hundred Seventh. Boyd knew why Malo would choose that one. The words and music meshed especially well in the eight-tone version, and it said exactly what they felt. Those who go down to the sea in ships. Yes! They see the works of the Lord and His wonders of the deep. They did indeed.

The second and third couplets, in fact, fit perfectly as well. They found nowhere to dwell on that strange island, their first landfall. God provided. They sat in the shadow of death. God delivered.

It wasn't just temporal deliverance. Hear the last line of the third couplet: "He satisfies the longing soul and fills the hungry soul with goodness." If farming were what Boyd was made for, why would he feel dissatisfied by the thought of it?

As they completed the final *et intelliget misericordias Domini*, Ronan stood and joined them, placing himself at the tenor end. What was going on now? They launched into the Gloria Patri. Boyd listened for the additional voice among the voices he knew so well.

It wasn't hard. Ronan more or less faced him in the semicircle. There he was, a clear tenor, high but not reedy. As the music swelled to its magnificence, Ronan kicked his voice up an octave, nearly a falsetto. His perfect descant climbed right out over the top, a splendid finale.

The music was a paean of thanksgiving to God, and to God went the glory. But the majesty of it filled Boyd's heart too.

The group disassembled. Brothers gathered around Ronan, thanking him for his contribution and praising his voice. Boyd stayed close to Crosan. He wanted to know what was happening in his friend's life over this next hour, so as to figure out the best way to help him.

Anne, not the least shy, stepped up to Boyd. Here it came. Now he would have to explain about Ibar. And even as he braced himself, he realized he wasn't quite certain how he would go about it. They sailed away and left the lad behind to die. He knew it was what they had to do, under the hand of God, but how would it sound?

She was smiling brightly. "I headed out just this morning to go to Cashel. And I didn't but get over the hill when a fellow I passed on the track pointed out a ship upon the water and said, 'That's Brendan come home.' He explained how it's a big sail or linen bonnets or something. Anyway, he knew. And so I hurried here, and he was right. Was it a good trip?"

How should he answer that? It was a perfect trip, being fully and completely in God's will. But do you tell this girl it's perfect when her Ibar died on it? Boyd stammered something more or less positive, and she rattled on. Then the conversation between Ronan and Crosan grabbed his ear and his attention.

Crosan and Ronan were being decent toward each other, a nice touch considering that the last time Boyd was here he was shaking them apart from each other's throats. Crosan was acting as if Ronan were already married to the honey-haired beauty, and Ronan was asking detailed questions about whether Brendan conferred orders. They were talking in two separate conversations, neither of them really hearing a word of what the other said.

Boyd stepped up beside Crosan, smiling. "Angelica, lady. Delighted to see you. And Ronan of Skellig Michael. You were asking about orders at Clonfert, Ronan. Brendan does indeed confer orders at Clonfert, for brothers and for lay workers both. An excellent program of teaching and devotion. Crosan may not be able to answer all your concerns, though. He joined us not long before we decided to build the boat and undertake the voyage, so his experience isn't what you might call typical. You really want to talk to Brendan himself. Here. Let me arrange an audience for you. Come."

Crosan stood speechless, and Ronan babbled something about there being a hurry, an immediacy. Boyd shuffled Ronan over to Brendan, interrupted the venerable father, and with a swift, almost impertinent introduction, hurried back to Crosan.

Crosan was describing the crystal mountain to Angelica. Had Boyd not seen it himself, he would swear Crosan had been fermenting too many of those grapes. She clearly didn't believe him either.

Where did Anne go? There she was, insinuating herself with Brendan and Ronan, of all places. Perhaps Brendan would tell her about Ibar.

"Crosan? We would talk a moment." Boyd reached out, a beckoning.

Crosan frowned. In fact, so did Angelica. Reluctantly, he followed Boyd a hundred yards up the hill.

Boyd turned to him and sat down on a rock. "I've been thinking. More so, God, I think, has been sorting my thoughts out."

"Do we have to talk about this now?"

"Yes. Did she marry the fellow?"

"What? Who?" Crosan looked confused. "Angelica and Ronan? They didn't say. I didn't ask. Boyd . . ."

"What do you think? Are they?"

"What are you talking about?" Crosan looked ready to run. Then he settled a little. "No. They don't act like two people who are wed. Maybe not yet. Also, he didn't actually say it, but I got the impression he's been out of the area."

"Why did you become a monk?"

"What?" Crosan scowled at him. The scowl softened.

Boyd waited, held his eye.

Crosan wandered over to a mossy patch and sat down. "It was the thing to do. And my parents encouraged it. Insisted, you might say. They were right. I'm not born to any royal line. The closest I ever got to the royal court was jester. Not the biggest apple to bite into by far. Druidism is losing its privilege. The way to get somewhere is in the church."

"So that was your parents. What about God? When were you called to holy orders?"

Crosan shrugged. "I don't know." He idly plucked a pretty blue flower beside his elbow and studied its face.

"Then you weren't, friend. You'd know. Besides, you're not happy now. You're not cut out to be a monk."

And then Boyd voiced another insight about the same time it came to him—and when it came, it came like a light in his own heart. "It's the same with me. You know how I want to just settle down and be an ordinary person. A farmer. But that's not my call. Much as I want to, I wouldn't be happy at it. Always there'd be the tug. The pull."

Crosan looked up at him. "What are you going to do?"

"White martyrdom. I've been thinking about that. That's the call. Much as I love the old sod, leave her. Maybe find that Island of Grapes again, settle in there, and tell them about Jesus. Find out how to cook moose nose."

Crosan smiled. "Your mission field. We work well together. I ought to go along."

"No. It's not your mission. That's what I'm trying to tell you."

Crosan's eyes flicked up and down, as if trying to read Boyd's face. "What do you think I should do?"

Boyd grinned. "Pick another fight with Ronan. This time I won't interfere."

Crosan his Laughing Friend stared at him for long moments. He burst into an uproarious guffaw, then sobered. "I listened to her, and, more important, I watched her actions. She's not interested in me. Ronan, yes. Me, no."

"You're so sure? You might ask her, you know, before you jump to conclusions. You've been waiting to see her a long time." Boyd hated to see Crosan thwarted in love—not that Boyd knew much about love. He wanted to fix, to mend, to patch. Crosan and Angelica—so right together.

"You're a good friend, my burly brother, but not worth dirt at reading people."

Boyd grimaced. "I'll not deny that. How about Fanchea? We'll convince Ronan he's the man to write Brendan's chronicle for him, and you can help Fanchea out on her farm."

The Laughing Monk laughed heartily, and his laugh almost sounded sincere. "A matchmaker you're not, but you do know how to buoy a fellow's spirits."

Boyd stood up. "God's peace, friend."

Crosan leaped to his feet. "God's peace." He hung suspended upon the moment. Suddenly he moved forward and embraced Boyd in a bearhug. "And God's speed on your voyage, wherever He sends you."

He turned away, stopped, and looked at that mossy patch. With a wicked grin he plucked three more little blue flower heads. "Wee bit of magic never hurts." He tucked one in his cincture toward the back, very delicately positioned one inside his cheek, and, carefully folding a third, gripped it just so between the third and fourth fingers. It disappeared within his open hand.

With a final nod, he hurried off down the hill.

Boyd took his time returning to the beach. The more he thought about it, the more he was certain this was right. This was all right. Brendan would not likely want to sail west to the Island of Grapes and Moose. No matter. If Boyd was in God's will regarding white martyrdom, the plan would materialize. The people who ought to be joining him would come.

Anne had engaged Malo in spirited conversation. Crosan joined them, and even from here Boyd could see the surprise on her face as Crosan plucked a small blue flower from her ear, then spit out another. If courting was the game, Malo didn't stand a chance.

Brendan and Ronan were talking away like jackdaws, and Angelica hard at Ronan's side. The lady was smiling broadly. Her blue eyes sparkled.

Curiosity swiftly overcame propriety. Boyd joined them.

Brendan laid a hand on Ronan's head and invoked a blessing in Greek. He did the same to Angelica. Ronan smiled that sad smile of his, and somehow it didn't seem sad anymore. With thanks and good-byes, the two of them headed up the track toward Fanchea's rath.

Boyd watched them go, and the sprightly manner of their walk. "What's that all about?"

"He's going to take orders at Clonfert. And she—she'll make a splendid lay mother to the orphanage we're building. Clonfert needs all the strong young people like that it can get."

Boyd frowned. "I thought he was already in orders."

"I'll explain it all in good time. Also why he's in such a hurry to leave. About a Pict. Let's unload. From the stench below the deck, I suspect something is very dead under there."

Actually, Mochta and the others were already commencing the laborious chore of unloading the boat.

Boyd sloshed down into the cold, cold water and waded out to the curragh.

Just ahead of him, Mochta accepted an armload of sheepskins from the brother inside the starboard gunwale.

Boyd stepped in behind him and received the next load. He waddled ashore, trying not to drop anything. He dumped it on the beach.

What was this? Grinning, he stood erect. "Dog? Troll? Here, dog! Catch!" Distrustfully, reluctantly, the brindled mutt circled near. Boyd tossed the dog the chunk of moose nose.

Leeson paused to watch. "What a cruel thing to inflict on the poor dog! Whatever did he do to deserve it, besides bite you now and then?" He cackled as the dog dragged the bulbous lump off down the beach and began energetically to dig a hole.

39
Full Circle

"She's coming, lord!"

Mac Larkin looked up at his hostler, standing in the doorway, and smiled for the first time in weeks.

"She's just come into view, says Sell, on the track about half a mile away. Ten minutes." Smugly, the hostler stepped back outside the door and crossed to the ringwall gate.

As Irish farmhouses went, circular mud hovels surrounded by circular walls, this one seemed fairly spacious. The widow who owned it kept it neat, everything stored in its place. The palisade topping the ringwall needed work, and the outside sheds were getting somewhat ramshackle, but all in all the black-haired Fanchea didn't have a bad place here.

Mac Larkin popped another bit of roasted lamb into his mouth and licked his fingers. "Well, Maura. For a while there, I wasn't certain you were being truthful." He enjoyed another healthy swig of Fanchea's mead. Robust and well-aged, the brew hardly tasted like honey anymore at all.

"Doubting my truth, is it? Foreigner! 'Tis yourself whose word be shaky. She and that Anne. Ugly wenches, to treat an old lady so. A caution, the both of them. Y're taking the disrespectful hussies away, aye? Ye promised, and no harm to ourselves."

"Indeed I did." He remembered that freckle-faced redhead when she was working at his father's monastery. He'd return her to her rightful clan as well, should the opportunity present itself—mayhap even to elicit with a minimal show of force a reward for her return. Why she ran also, he had no idea. He didn't even know Anne and Angelica were friends. No matter. His search was ending at last. Angelica. And the monk named Ronan out on Skellig Michael. He glanced across the room at Fanchea.

She glared back at him with pure, malevolent hatred.

He smiled graciously. "We do appreciate your hospitality, lass. Good food, well-matured mead, a helpful informant. What more can a beleaguered warlord ask?"

"Beleaguered." She spat. "Making your fortune at Erin's expense."

He drained the last of the mead, wiped his greasy fingers on the cushion beneath him, and lurched to his feet. This lengthy sojourn abroad was taking its toll on him. Sitting in one position too long made him stiff. "You neglect to notice, Fanchea lass, that I lost two dear cohorts in this last year. We came six. Now we be but four."

"That's not to mention the four mercenaries you picked up here in Erin. Irish fighting for Picts against Irish. Despicable!" She knelt by his leg. "Eh, the mess you made!" Crossly, she straightened the cushion and began throwing the leavings from his meal into the fire.

Mac Larkin walked outside into the muddy dooryard. On impulse he scooped up the mead pot and tucked it under his arm on his way. The crone named Hilla sat on a Roman-style stool beside the door, staring intently at nothing and muttering to herself, her withered hands folded in her lap. This place gave Mac Larkin a chill.

He stood behind the wall between the gate and the woodpile and peeked out. If the lookouts spotted Angelica several minutes ago, she should be visible from the rath gate here any time now.

Although silence was not yet necessary, he murmured to his hostler, "Is Dumphy down in the alders?" He swilled a draught of mead.

Brannaugh nodded. "I saw him head that way about an hour ago. No doubt he's worked his way around behind your lady by now. She won't go running in that direction."

Mac Larkin nodded. "Then there be nothing left but to wait." His mouth smiled, and so did his heart and soul.

Fanchea was right. He was doing well. Still, he hungered to return home. Surely by now the newness would have worn off Desmond's monastery project, and Mac Larkin's mother and father would be more inclined to pay attention to their son again. He hated the way they so constantly and totally absorbed themselves in some new idea to the exclusion of all else. Maybe when he got back he could convince his father to strike at some of Ta-vish's holdings.

For years, Tavish of Cheviot had been encroaching on the Larkin territory, a bit here, a bit there. The Moustache ought be put in his place. Together, Mac Larkin and Larkin were the men to do it. After all, look at Mac Larkin's success here in Erin. Good train-ing, good results. He helped those clans north of the Shannon regain their lands—perhaps add to them somewhat. As soon as he completed this final bit of business regarding the odious An-gelica and that miserable Ronan . . .

Soon. Soon.

He enjoyed another generous taste of mead.

A large brindled dog appeared on the trail down by an oak copse. It ranged out to a hazel bush and returned to the trail. Mo-ments later she appeared. Yes! It was she. She had pulled off her turban, letting her honey hair float free. His stomach tightened.

How many false rumors did he trace down when first he ar-rived on this remote little peninsula? Scores. Then to see both Ronan and her, mere moments after he officially gave up search-ing and assumed she had fled elsewhere—what a stark piece of barren luck. Barren, too, had been his attempts to find her on the other side of the Shannon, even though with his own eyes he saw her heading there.

What if he had decided to return to his clan lands without coming here for one more try? You see? It pays to never give up. Never give up! The gods reward the diligent.

Another lesson: pursue every avenue, no matter how chancy. By chance he had stumbled upon rickety old Maura tending sheep. Had he not stopped to ask her, he would never have known she was ready and eager to point him directly to his Angel-ica. It was so simple, once you find the person who knows the right information.

Downhill on the track, Angelica paused and turned as if to wait for someone.

Brannaugh whispered, "The monk!"

From the oak grove emerged a male companion. No tonsure, no walking staff. But that blue cloak told the world that Mac Larkin's luck was suddenly soaring higher than a raven. His heart trilled behind his breastbone. At last! And both of them! The crone had not mentioned a monk even when asked. But there he was.

Still cross as a bear, Fanchea came stomping out the door with that cushion under her arm. She growled about messes, and Picts being no better than pigs. Angrily she shook the cushion, brushing fiercely at some fancied bit of dirt. Mac Larkin certainly wasn't that boorish, that she should go on so. He'd tend to her. If there was a thing he could not abide, it was scolds.

But later.

Scowling at her cushion and shaking it, she marched over to the woodpile, hard beside the gate.

Suddenly she whipped the big cushion up and swung it mightily. It caught Mac Larkin squarely in the face and knocked him back two steps.

He felt the pot go flying. It sloshed amber mead all over him. His legs tangled in the firewood. Caught off balance, he fell backward heavily into the woodpile. Half-dry limbs and branches snapped and cracked, poking him, stabbing him, tipping him further off kilter. A stick gouged the back of his neck.

He could follow by ear exactly where Fanchea was—running out the gate, she was—as her voice shrieked, "Get back! Run, Angelica!"

He struggled, flailing on his back amid those sticks. Every time he leaned on something to pull himself up, it gave beneath his weight or rolled aside. He couldn't free himself, couldn't reach his feet. Finally he simply tucked in his head and knees and flung himself. Across the wildly crackling sticks, he tumbled unceremoniously out onto solid ground, rolling.

That hussy! That witch! He scrambled to his feet, drawing his sword. Then the woodpile, alive with screaming banshees, exploded in his face. Stilettos stabbed his cheeks and eyelids and raked his bushy brows. He dropped his sword to bat at the demons with both hands. He grabbed two great handfuls of fur and flung it away from him.

Angelica's yowling cat!

Enraged, he snatched up his sword and ran out the gate. The gouge on the back of his neck and the slashes on his face burned with fire. He could feel where a hundred sticks had poked into him. Fanchea had just earned herself the same painful death that loomed in the faithless Angelica's immediate future.

Her black hair flying, the vixen was running full tilt down the track toward the oak copse, with Brannaugh on her heels. Angelica too was racing down the wind away from them, her hair streaming out behind her.

The monk—that foolish, stupid monk—stood in the track weaponless. Surely the oaf didn't think he was going to protect the women with his bare hands! Surely he didn't realize the might arrayed against him.

The women screamed as Dumphy and his partner came riding up out of the alders to cut them off. Delightful! He had not known Sell had concealed himself behind a massive haystack to the northwest. Now here he came, bursting forth from behind the hay on his big dun gelding, to block the women's way from that direction.

This side, that side, another side—the trap closed down around the perfidious Angelica, her miserable monk, that stupid Fanchea. Mac Larkin slowed to a walk, thence to a casual saunter. He sheathed his sword. The chase was ended. Now for the delicious revenge.

She seemed not the least contrite, watching him approach. Was that perspiration or tears or both besmearing her beautiful face? Fear certainly clouded it—but defiance too. She didn't huddle against the monk and Fanchea exactly, crowding against them in fear, but all three did stand very close together.

Dumphy and Sell dismounted. All seven of Mac Larkin's retainers stood close around the luckless three, a sturdy pen of warriors surrounding a flock of feckless sheep.

Angelica grimaced. "Obviously I should not have returned to the rath for my cat."

"Obviously." When he reached out toward her chin, she jerked her head back. "And to think that once upon a time, I loved you."

"No, Mac Larkin. You never did. I fled to save us both from the error of thinking that was love."

"A pity. Were it not for your foolishness, you could be suckling an infant prince now and living in the luxury of a warlord's aegis." He raised his voice. "But here you are, about to die on foreign soil. Ah, Angelica. Were it not for your foolishness, you would not be gone by sunset—and taking these two fine people with you."

Her voice rasped. "Why are you doing this to me?"

"Why did you do that to *me?*" He was startled that the expression on her face said, Did what? But then, she wouldn't know about the ragging from his brothers and their comments—that a woman would flee clear across the emerald sea to avoid him. And how would she know about the tittering among the clan—nay, all the clans!—that went on behind his back? The raw and bitter shame. The knife-twisting, gut-wrenching shame.

Angelica practically whispered, "I'll go with you. Leave these people alone."

The monk moved suddenly, stepping between her and Mac Larkin. "When you return to your clan, Mac Larkin, you can tell them anything you wish. Anything. That you hanged her—" he paused briefly "—that you drew and quartered her, as you discussed that night in that ruined farmhouse while you honed your sword. Anything you want."

Angelica gasped. "Ronan, don't!" but the monk stayed between them.

Mac Larkin caught himself gaping. His mind sped as he tried to think how the monk would be privy to such a thing. He glared at his lieutenant. "Dumphy! You told him. You were the only one with opportunity, and that not a good one."

"I told him nothing! I didn't know he was here."

"You harm her at your peril, Mac Larkin," the monk continued. "She's under the protection of Desmond's Holy One, as am I. How else but by God's intervention would I know that night you prepared a pot of gruel on a small fire on the south side of the house—that is, the two-thirds of the house with roof intact—and built a light fire to the north. Your horses remained clustered in the lee of the house, behind where the roof had caved. Were I not under God's protection, could I have entered your fortress in Pictland, evading dogs and sentries, to steal her away?

"If you're wise, you'll let us all go our way. In return, we vow never to reveal what's happening here. Whatever you tell the world, that's what the world will know."

"Fool. What a sorry, utter fool." Mac Larkin kept his voice hard, his face impassive, but his insides churned. It was uncanny what this monk knew. "If you didn't fear me, you wouldn't be disguising yourself with the hair and such. A monk doesn't grow in his tonsure for anything short of terror." But he knew as he said it what silliness that was. If the monk was consorting with Angelica, he'd not be active in his brotherhood.

Confusion began to tangle Mac Larkin's thoughts. Real and fancy held equal sway. How could he save face before his men if he let her go? After all this time, the searching, the chase, he did not dare show mercy. It would be perceived as weakness. Worse would be to release from his grip the man who entered his stronghold and stole her out from under his very nose.

And yet . . .

He looked at that Fanchea and saw defiance. He looked at Angelica and saw defiance. He looked into the eyes of this irritating monk and saw . . . not simply defiance, but certainty. Confidence.

The confusion multiplied. He forced a grin. "A man alone, surrounded by swords, offers to strike a bargain."

"Not alone. The fellow has lots of friends!" From beyond Mac Larkin's men came a strong, rollicking voice.

His eyes never left Mac Larkin's as Ronan the ex-monk called, "Crosan! Go back!"

So they *were* friends. They recognized each other by voice. Do monks fight well? Do monks fight at all? Mac Larkin stepped aside to see who was coming up the trail.

Two monks in Irish tonsure strode this way. The one, a fellow with a foolishly happy grin of anticipation, looked eager for a fight. The other—ah, that other. A mountain. The laughing monk's head came to this fellow's armpit. The man had to be twice as wide as any in Mac Larkin's retinue. But the two appeared to be armed with nothing more than the heavy walking sticks monks so often carried.

Even with the monster behind him, Ronan was well outmanned. These monkish types had no experience fighting, certainly not like Mac Larkin's well-honed warriors. Three men and two women against eight seasoned professionals. What a fool, this Ronan.

"So you must be Mac Larkin. Ronan told us all about you."
The smaller monk strolled directly up to Mac Larkin and pointed
at him. "Boyd, you remember the tale."

"Could I ever forget?" The burly fellow rumbled like a distant
thunderstorm. "Nor could I ever forget the fight between you and
Ronan—the blood spilt."

"A friendly tussle. I much prefer fighting for keeps." The
laughing monk stepped in front of Mac Larkin, so close he
brushed Mac Larkin's cloak, and grinned. But, curiously, he
wasn't really smiling.

Why did Mac Larkin feel so much like taking a hasty step
back? He suddenly wanted to be near his horses. He wanted the
security of walls. He pointed to the new arrivals. "Ignore those
two. They've no part in this. Bring the others to the rath." He
turned on his heel and marched up the track toward the farm gate.

Behind him he heard the laughing monk's voice roll along,
describing why he and that Boyd thought they'd come help out
Fanchea. Why weren't Mac Larkin's retainers turning those two
away? Crosan was saying how, nice as the girl named Anne might
be, she owned no kinship or land in the area. He was rather hoping to attach himself to . . .

Ronan's voice sounded totally relaxed. "I've yet to hear details about your voyaging to the Land of Ever Young. Brendan just
glowed with pleasure."

"And why not?" the voice of Crosan replied. "A voyage no
other man has ever made. The wonders, Ronan! From this voyage
I learned much about how God operates, much indeed! And do
you know, Ronan—death no longer holds any terror for me. I've
stared straight down the maw of death . . ."

"He certainly did," rumbled the giant. "I watched it try to eat
him."

"And I've seen the Land of the Blessed. Paradise! And warm!"

"Aye, warm!" echoed the giant. "And we've been standing
about in that boat for the last two months. More than time to
stretch a bit."

Mac Larkin would take their conversation for the nonsense it
certainly was. No one ever sailed to paradise and returned. He
thought about Desmond's description of the Isle of the Blessed,

soon after the Irish monk brought the Larkin under his sway. Tír na n'Og. Mac Larkin stepped inside the gate and felt better already.

And then the banshee that had possessed the stupid cat possessed the crone named Maura. The moment he entered the compound she came at him with an ax, shrieking. "You churl! The mead! You spilled it all!"

He flung up his arm to defend himself and parried the blow barely in time. He managed to grab the ax near its head. He wrenched it out of the hag's hands and swung the handle at her. It caught her in the neck, lifted her off her feet, flung her against the wall.

Angelica. She was the reason he came to this crude and hideous land. He would take care of Angelica first. He wheeled, seized her arm, and yanked.

She screamed as he pulled her off her feet and dragged her through the mud of the dooryard into Fanchea's house. He would let his retainers take care of the others. He must get her apart to kill her, in privacy as it were, so he could watch the terror in her face, see the horror in her eyes, hear the pleading from her lips. Sure and he had waited long enough for this.

Her clothes were gray and slippery with mud. It spattered her face and streaked through her hair. He hauled her to her feet, her arm locked in his grip.

He heard outside the shriek of a dying man—it sounded like Brannaugh. He must hurry. He reached for the dirk in his belt. Gone!

The honey-haired witch smirked. "Crosan specializes in sleight of hand." Where was the terror? He must see the fear in her face as he—

Another banshee! A gray wad of fury flew at his face, snarling. Great iron dog teeth ripped his arm. His hand lost its grip. Angelica twisted free. The dog's weight threw Mac Larkin back, but not down, and fell away. He pulled his sword and flailed with it. On the second swipe he caught the dog with its tip and slashed it end to end.

Angelica screamed, "Troll!" as if it were a man Mac Larkin had just skewered.

He swung his weapon around to catch her before she could

flee. If he couldn't slit her pretty throat with his dagger he would eviscerate her with his sword.

He could feel his mouth drop open as his arms melted. He stared down in surprise at his tunic. The blade of his own dagger was buried in it. He recognized the haft.

Quietly, ominously, Ronan the erstwhile monk stepped between him and the woman. With a rapid yank he pulled the dagger and raised it at ready. "You have two choices, Mac Larkin. Go back to your ancestral Pictland or die. We can't trust you in Erin."

Mac Larkin felt no pain to speak of and saw little bleeding. No real problem, this injury. With a wee bit of luck, his sword would easily take care of that dagger. Why would the silly monk think that he could . . .

Then it all happened so quickly. Dumphy burst through the door with the massive monk right behind him. He wheeled, swinging his sword two-handed, but the monk's great walking staff parried the stroke. Bent nearly in two, the iron sword went sailing. The monk lunged forward, knocking Dumphy off his feet.

With a shriek, Dumphy landed on the fire. He howled, arms and legs flying, flinging fire in all directions. A powerful thrust of that walking stick lifted the Pict off the hearth. The fellow's clothing smoldered and broke out into open flame.

And then Mac Larkin had his wee bit of luck. Dumphy's problem had seized Ronan's attention. The man was yelling something about rolling. Mac Larkin stroked, putting all his weight behind his sword to deliver a killing blow. Enough of this toying about!

Ronan swung up the dagger to parry, hilt to hilt, and the strength of his response surprised Mac Larkin. It stopped the main force of his blow. Mac Larkin's blade caught Angelica and sent her reeling.

Mac Larkin spun a full circle on his heel, whipping his weapon around to cut Ronan in half. He had once killed two men in less than a moment that way. But Ronan was not there. The monk was slamming into him even as he turned. They crashed to the floor with Ronan falling upon him.

He could not breathe. He could not get his arms up to handle his sword. He had lost his grip. Ronan wrenched his sword away.

And suddenly he lost his nerve. Pummeling the monk with

his fists, he squirmed out from under, scrambled to his feet and ran out the door . . . into a war!

Monks do fight, and they fight well. And noisily. More monks than just those two waged the war, monks Mac Larkin had never seen before. Behind him, Ronan yelled, "Mochta! Grab him!"

An aged brother, gray of hair and ruddy-cheeked, made a feinting lunge for Mac Larkin. The Pict ducked aside just barely. Weaponless, he ran through the mud out the gate. Wide-eyed, their ponies milled about. He chose Dumphy's. Not only did the gelding run well, but Dumphy was half Mac Larkin's weight. This pony would be far less jaded than his own horse.

The little bay gelding, its reins dragging, sidestepped. Mac Larkin scooped up the looped reins and flung them over the pony's ears. He had to kick and struggle to swing himself aboard— possibly this wound was more severe than first he thought.

That monk Ronan was right in a way. Anything Mac Larkin told the world was what the world would know—at least the Pictish world back home. By sheer strength of arm he twisted the pony's head aside. He dug in his heels and shouted. The pony leaped forward, slipped in the mud, recovered, and swapped ends, frozen in place.

Ronan was hanging onto the reins, gripping them in one hand, Mac Larkin's sword in the other. Mac Larkin kicked out at him wildly, The monk dropped the sword and grabbed the bay's ear. And then, with a jerk and a yank that Mac Larkin could not clearly discern, Ronan threw the pony down onto its side.

His leg firmly and forever pinned beneath the fallen pony, Mac Larkin flung up his arms to protect himself. And he knew that would be no protection at all. And he knew from the fury on Ronan's face that whatever resources the man had engaged, those resources were far superior to his own. And he knew that he was doomed.

Monks surrounded him, familiar faces and strange ones. The struggling pony lurched to its belly, clambered to standing. Mac Larkin ought to get up. He wanted to die on his feet, not groveling before a flock of Irishmen. The best he could do was prop himself up on one elbow.

Behind them on the hill, dense gray smoke boiled up out of the ringwall. Dumphy's scrambling foray in the fire must have spread brands to something combustible. The whole rath was going to go. Mac Larkin could see above the wall that already the thatch smoldered. Bits of the dry surface thatching caught and flared up here and there.

And then Angelica, the cause of it all, appeared at Ronan's side. Her arm dripped blood. She gripped the arm, and she was sobbing. Not even tears and mud and blood and fury, though, could dim the beauty of her face.

In that moment he realized how much he had just lost, how much his mindless desire for revenge had cost him. Not just life, as it appeared, but love. And that, almost, was the bitterest of losses. He tried to take a deep breath.

Ronan snatched up the sword. It was over now. He raised it two-handed above his head. Smoke filled the sky behind him.

"Ronan!" Beside Mac Larkin, a frail old monk with an unruly tangle of hair, barked, "You are always and ever a man of God, orders or no."

"Father Brendan . . . you don't realize the misery . . ." Ronan looked at the feeble little fellow. Ronan was physically far the superior. He could cut the little old man in two with but one hand on the blade. Why did he hesitate? Why did he lower the sword?

"I made the full journey," the frail man purred. "Now you must. Full circle, well made."

"Father . . . I can't . . ."

"The full journey. Full pardon."

These monks, all of them, some bloodied and some not, gathered about silently watching Mac Larkin as if he were a slave on an auction block. There on the periphery stood the giant. Beside him was the aging monk Ronan had called Mochta.

Ronan stared hard at Mac Larkin. The monk suddenly jammed the sword tip into the dirt and stomped on the blade. It bent neatly in the middle, practically back upon itself.

Ronan tossed the sword aside. "Mac Larkin, son of the Prince of Picts, I forgive you your sins and trespasses against me and mine. May our Lord do the same. In the name of the Father, the Son, and the Holy Spirit." Ronan signed the cross between himself and Mac Larkin. "And it's far and away the most difficult thing I have ever done."

He turned his back on Mac Larkin then, an insult in itself, gathered Angelica against him by wrapping an arm about her, and walked away, up toward the burning rath.

Mac Larkin collapsed onto his back, suddenly totally wearied. He was dying. He felt pretty well certain of that. Let death come.

Brendan glanced at the sky. "Vespers, brethren. We will end with a psalm for the dying."

The venerable father named Brendan knelt by Mac Larkin's head, tenderly took Mac Larkin's hand in his own frail, cool one, and began a quiet litany in Erse. Mac Larkin had heard of the death rites Christians performed. He never expected such to be done for him. He appreciated, in a vague way, that the monk would use a tongue he understood.

Mac Larkin could not say if his eyes were open or closed. He saw darkness only. He still heard clearly, though. If anything, his sense of hearing sharpened.

The monk called Crosan began a strange song in some language unfit for Pictish ears. Several other monks picked up the words and tune one at a time, adding point upon counterpoint. Mac Larkin was struck by the beauty of the song as Brendan's soft voice purred in prayer.

The fellow called Mochta muttered, "It's over, is it? I'm surprised we lost no one."

The giant kept his rumbling voice low. "Not even the dog. But for the first time in his life, he let me touch him without snarling at me as I carried him out of the house."

"I'm tired of land-living already," Mochta said, "and more than ready to serve asea again. So, Boyd, where shall we sail to next?"